Her dreams are WILD!

Her imagination is MAGICAL!

And her whiskers are always a MESS!

Welcome to . . .

THE BIG ADVENTURES OF
BABYMOUSE

HEY! THAT'S ME!

OOOH! THIS BOOK LOOKS GOOD. I CAN'T WAIT TO READ IT!

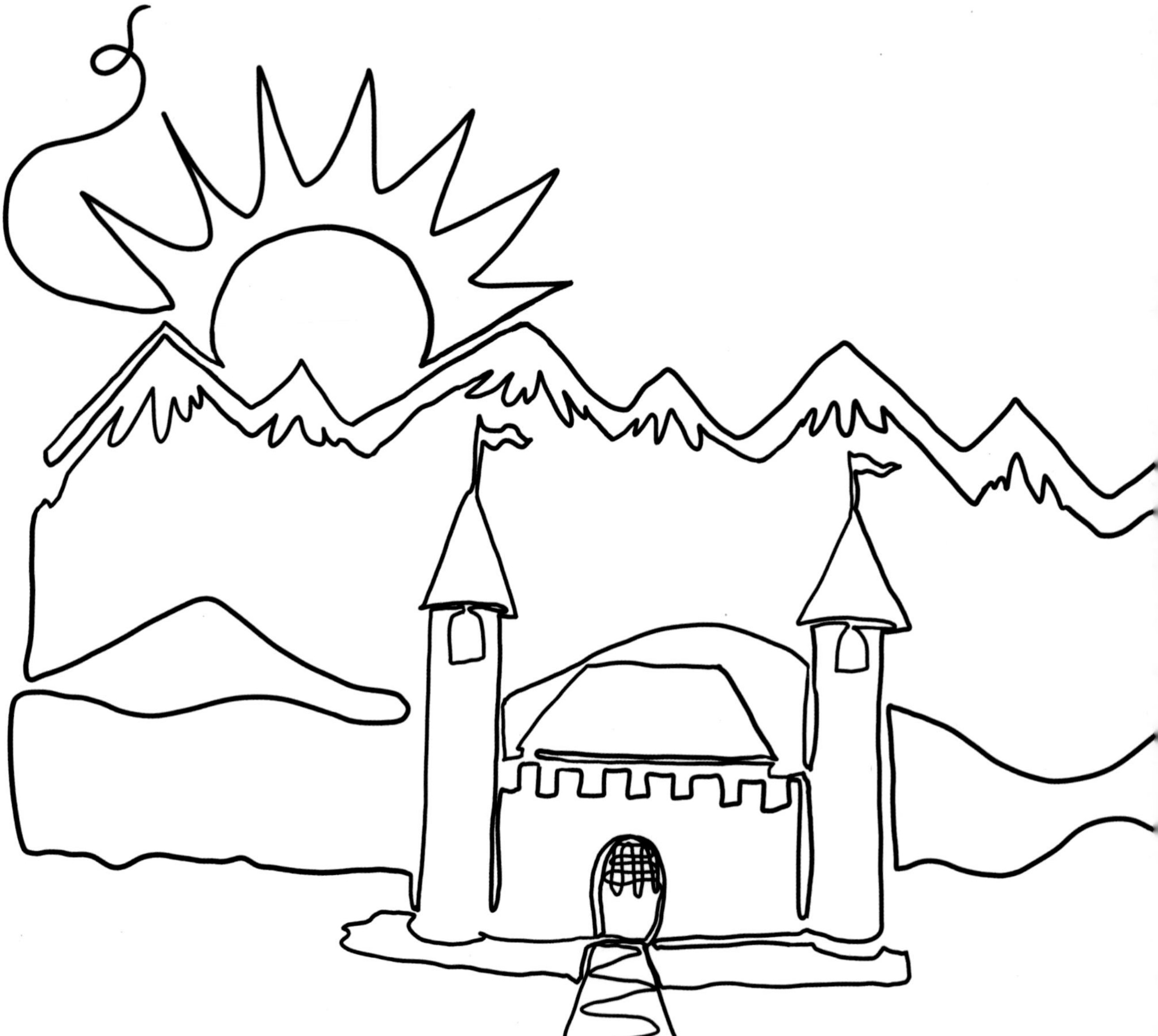

THE BIG ADVENTURES OF BABYMOUSE

ONCE UPON A MESSY WHISKER

JENNIFER L. HOLM & MATTHEW HOLM

Random House 🏠 New York

Copyright © 2022 by Jennifer L. Holm and Matthew Holm

All rights reserved. Published in the United States by Random House Children's Books, a division of Penguin Random House LLC, New York.

Random House and the colophon are registered trademarks of Penguin Random House LLC.

Visit us on the Web! **rhcbooks.com**

Educators and librarians, for a variety of teaching tools, visit us at **RHTeachersLibrarians.com**

Library of Congress Cataloging-in-Publication Data is available upon request.
ISBN 978-0-593-43090-3 (trade) — ISBN 978-0-593-43091-0 (lib. bdg.)
ISBN 978-0-593-43093-4 (trade pbk.) — ISBN 978-0-593-43092-7 (ebook)

MANUFACTURED IN CHINA

10 9 8 7 6 5 4 3 2 1

First Edition

For Teri Lesesne

PART ONE

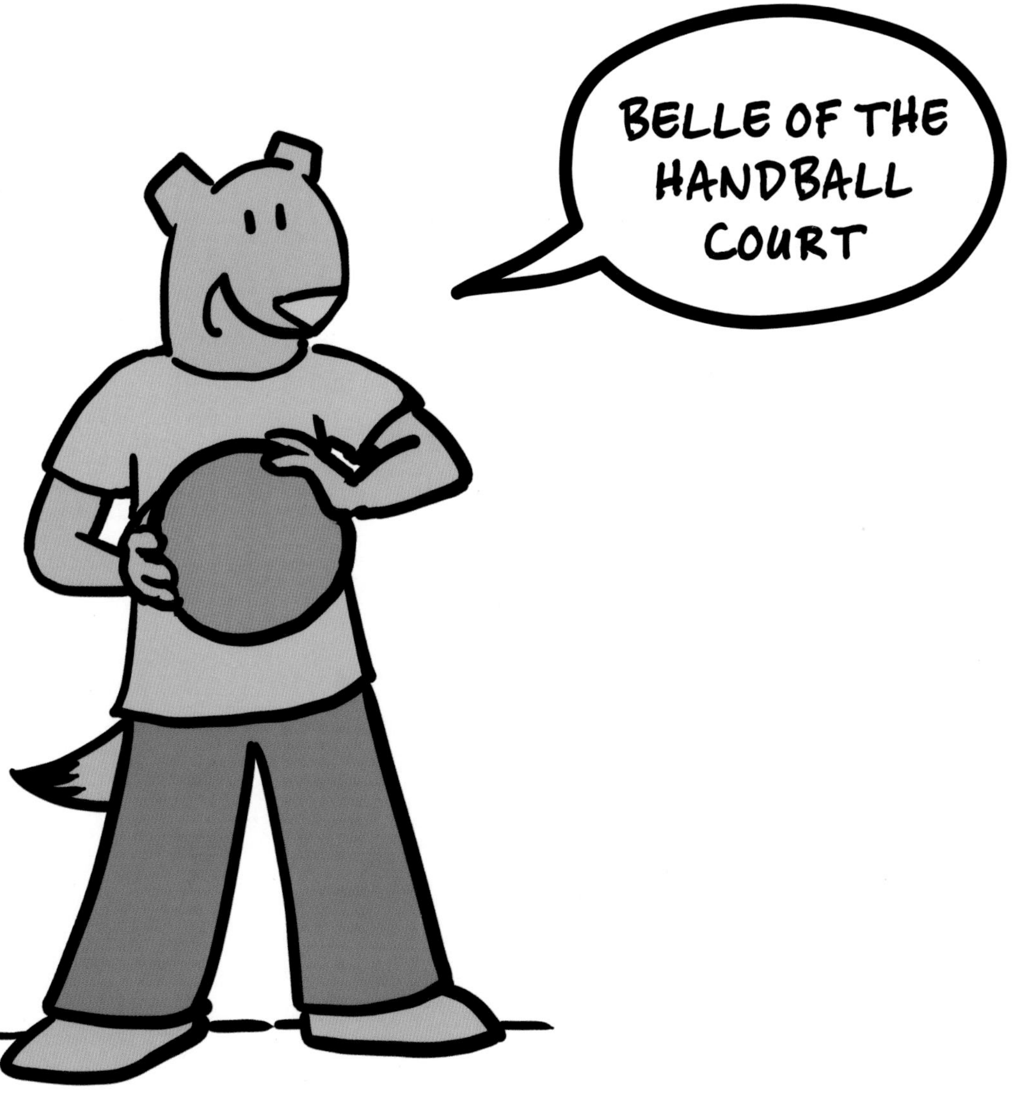
BELLE OF THE HANDBALL COURT

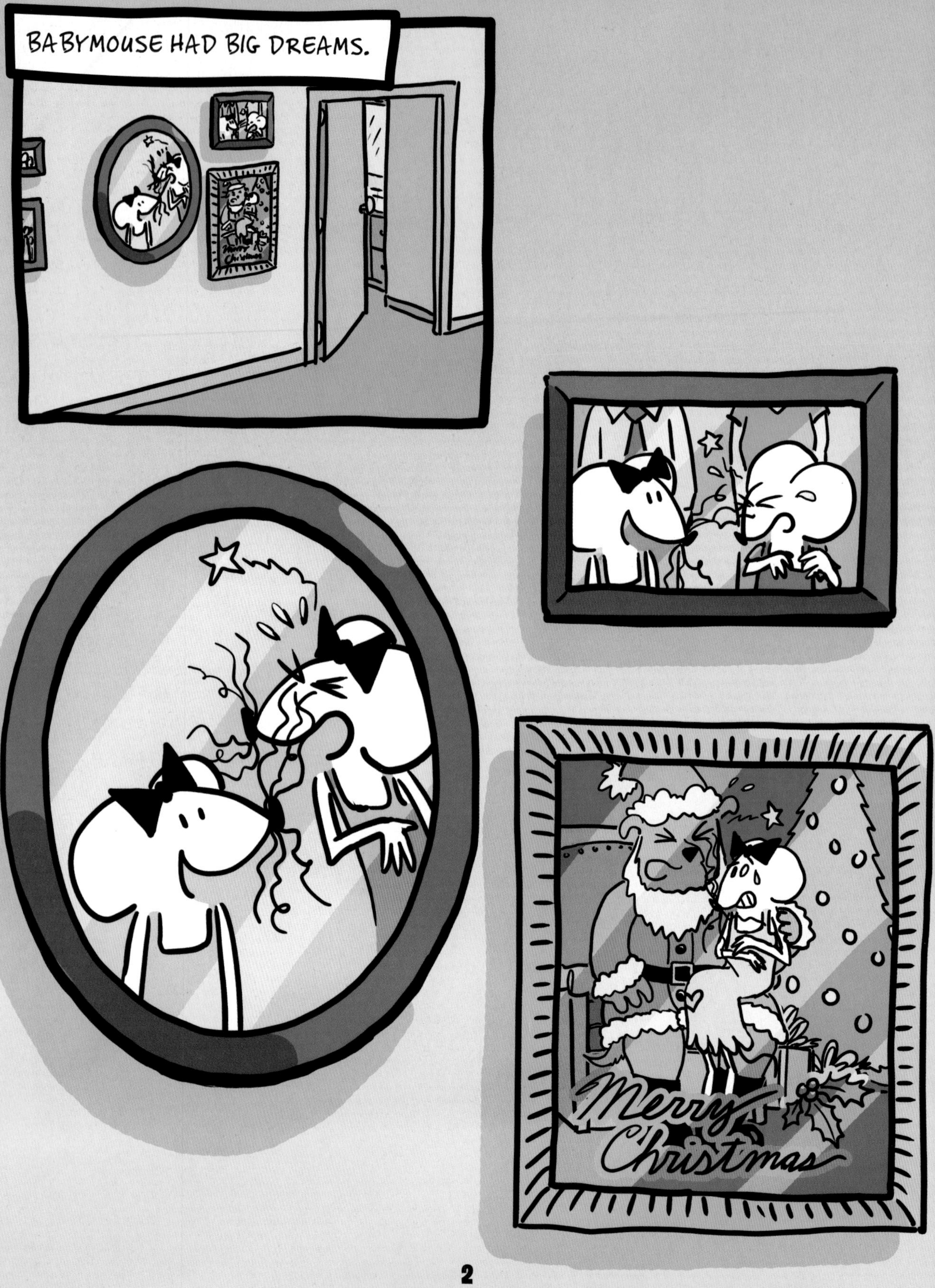
BABYMOUSE HAD BIG DREAMS.
Merry Christmas

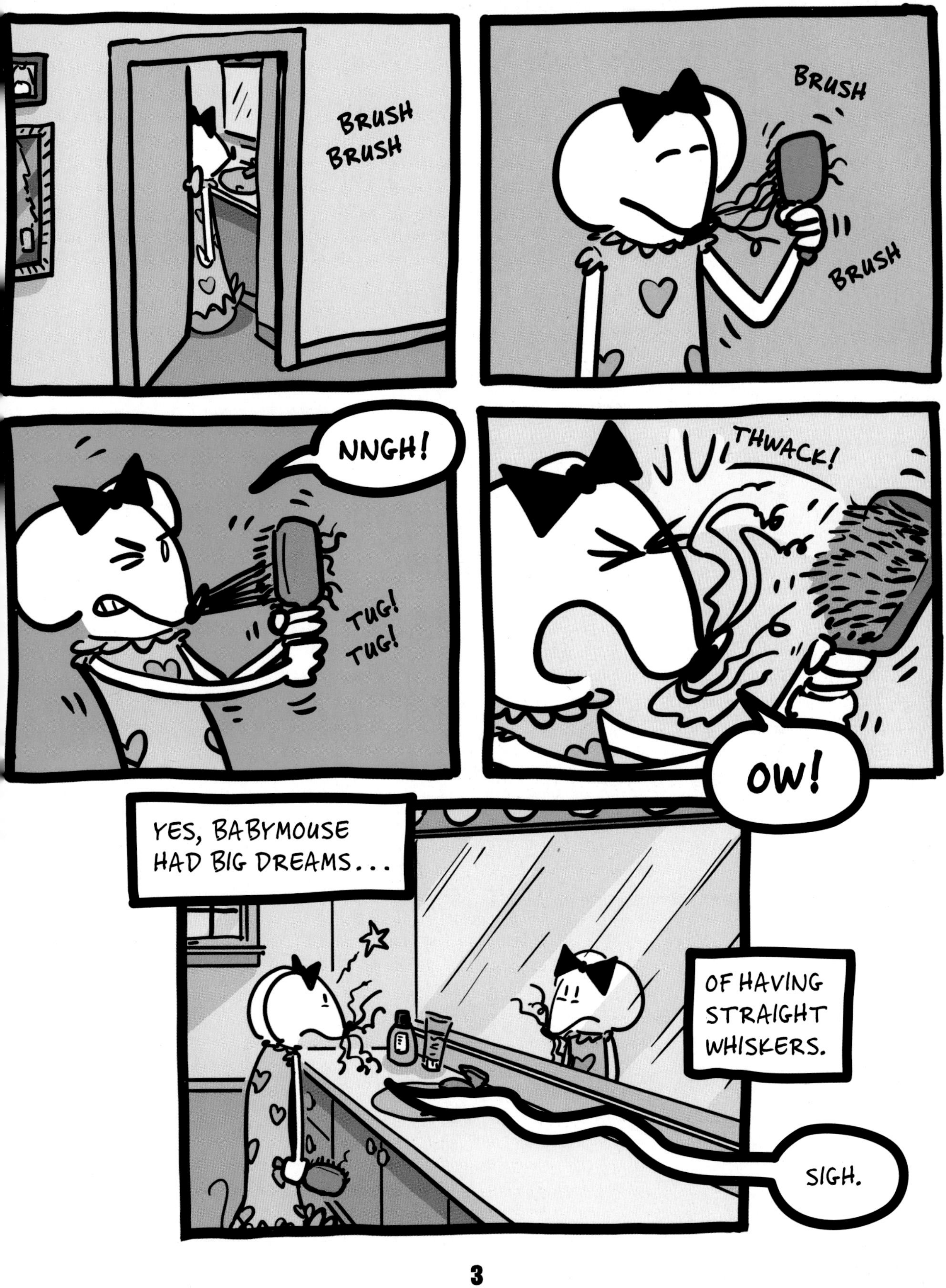
BRUSH
BRUSH
BRUSH
BRUSH
NNGH!
TUG!
TUG!
THWACK!
OW!
YES, BABYMOUSE HAD BIG DREAMS...
OF HAVING STRAIGHT WHISKERS.
SIGH.

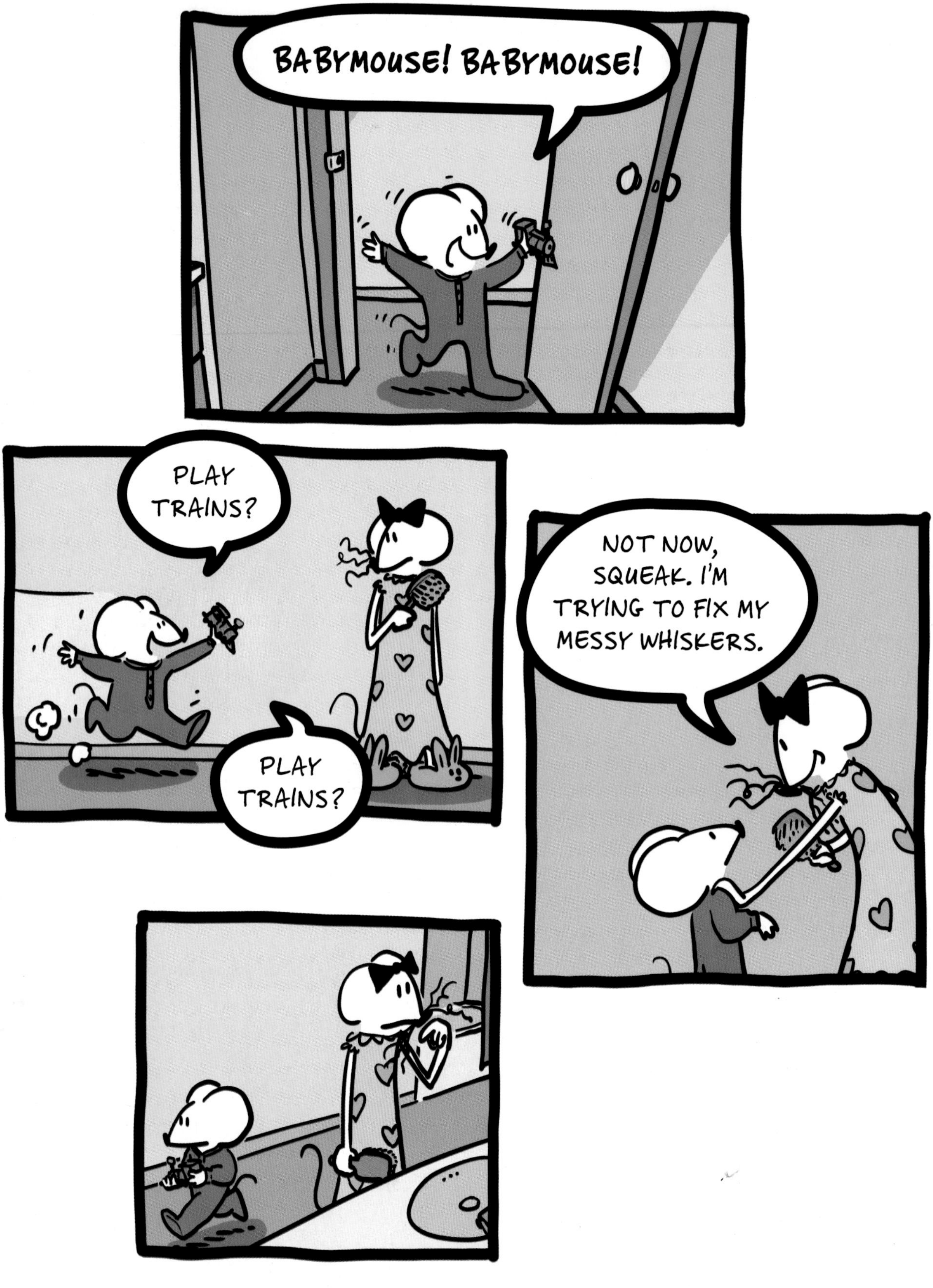
BABYMOUSE! BABYMOUSE!
PLAY TRAINS?
PLAY TRAINS?
NOT NOW, SQUEAK. I'M TRYING TO FIX MY MESSY WHISKERS.

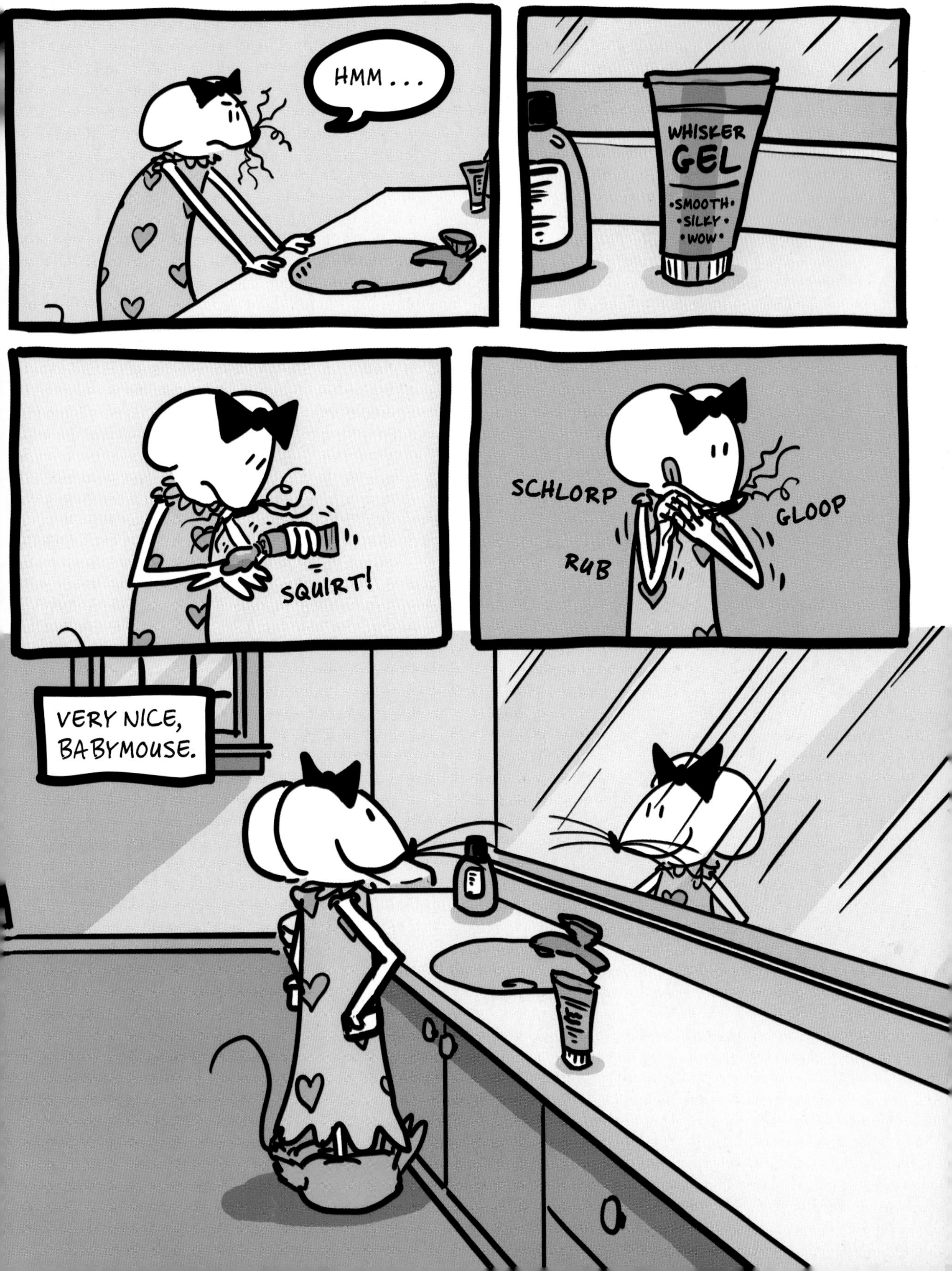
HMM . . .
WHISKER
GEL
•SMOOTH•
•SILKY•
•WOW•
SQUIRT!
SCHLORP
GLOOP
RUB
VERY NICE,
BABYMOUSE.

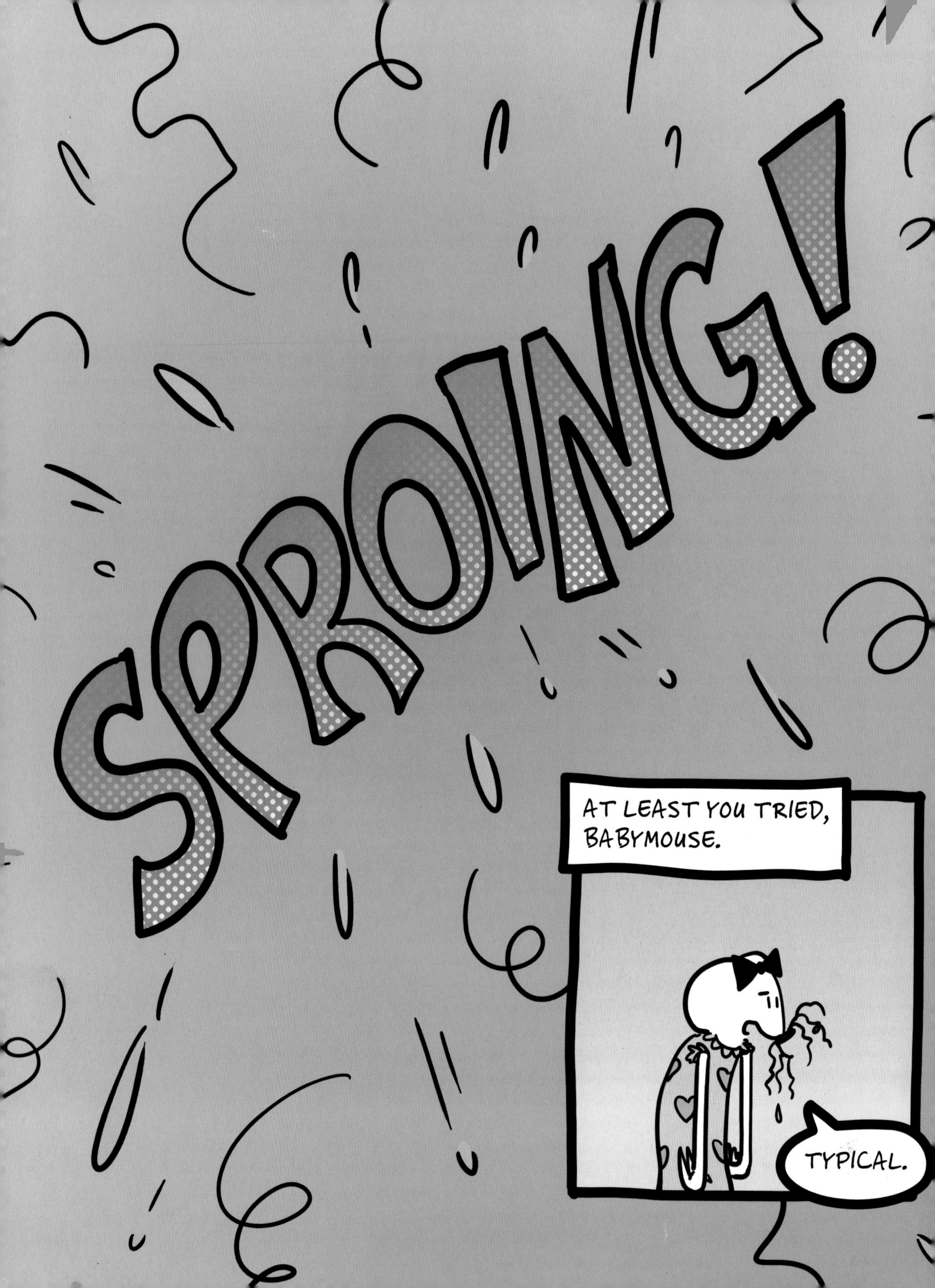
SPROING!
AT LEAST YOU TRIED, BABYMOUSE.
TYPICAL.

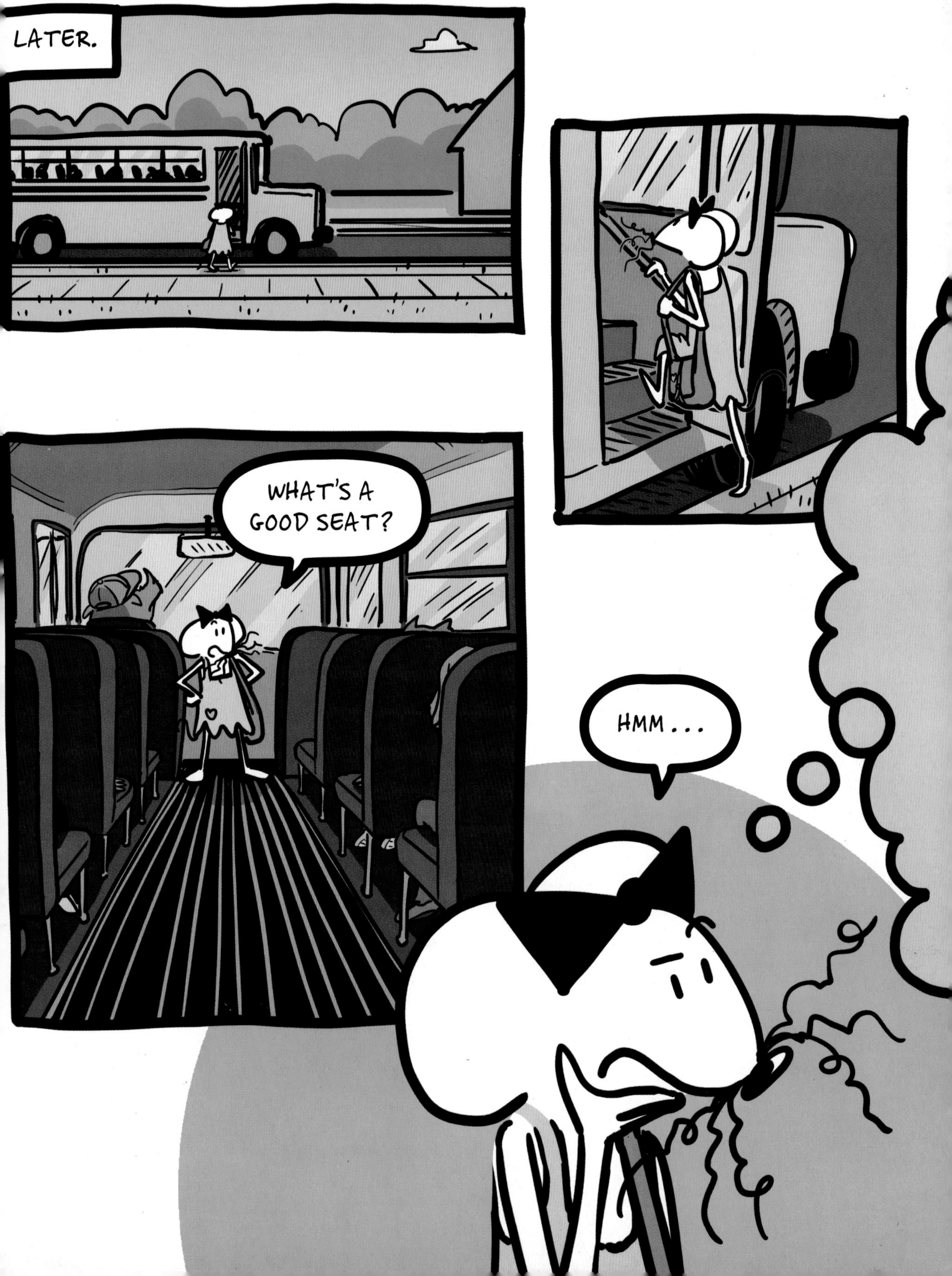
LATER.
WHAT'S A GOOD SEAT?
HMM...

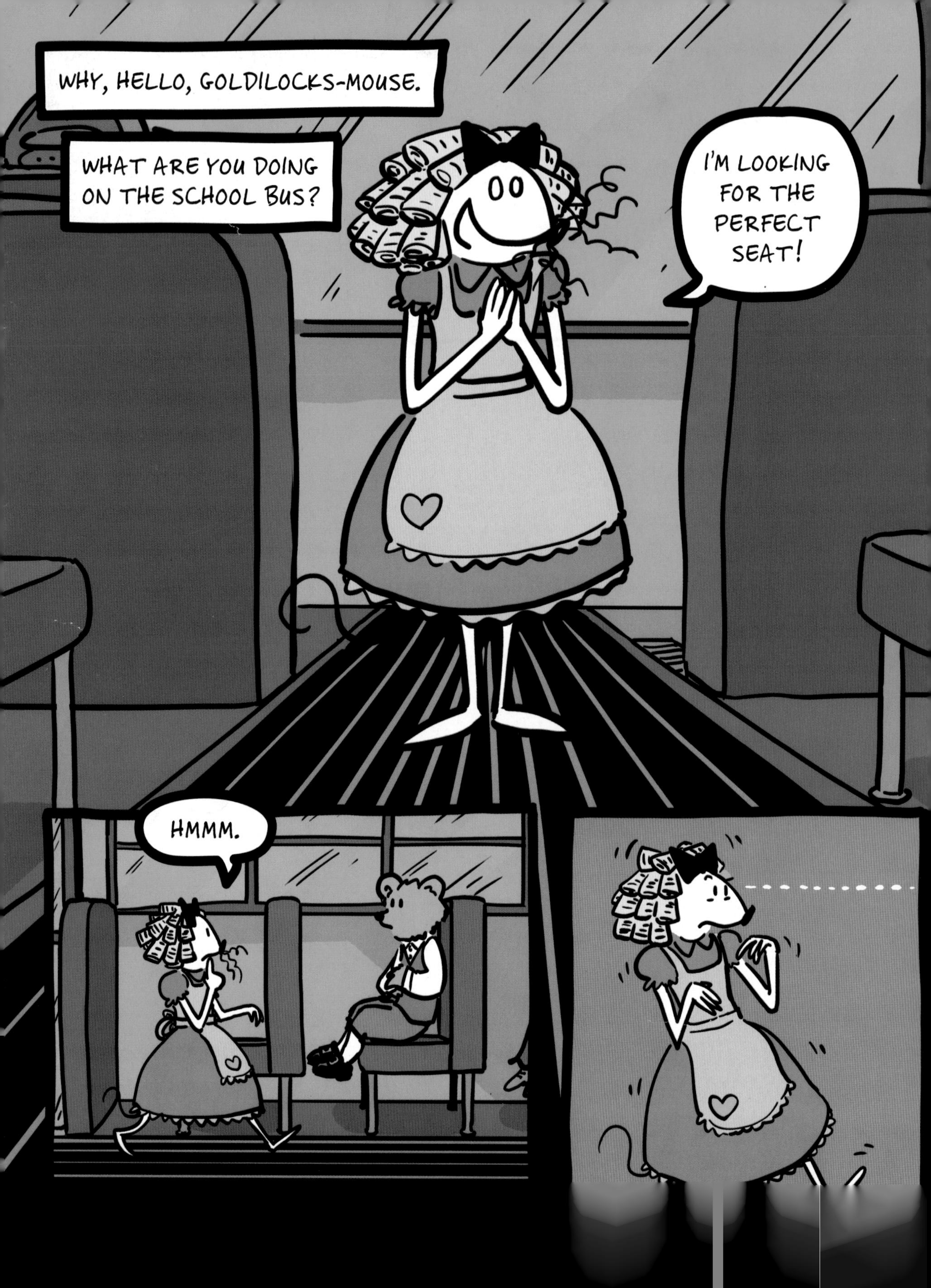
WHY, HELLO, GOLDILOCKS-MOUSE.
WHAT ARE YOU DOING ON THE SCHOOL BUS?
I'M LOOKING FOR THE PERFECT SEAT!
HMMM.

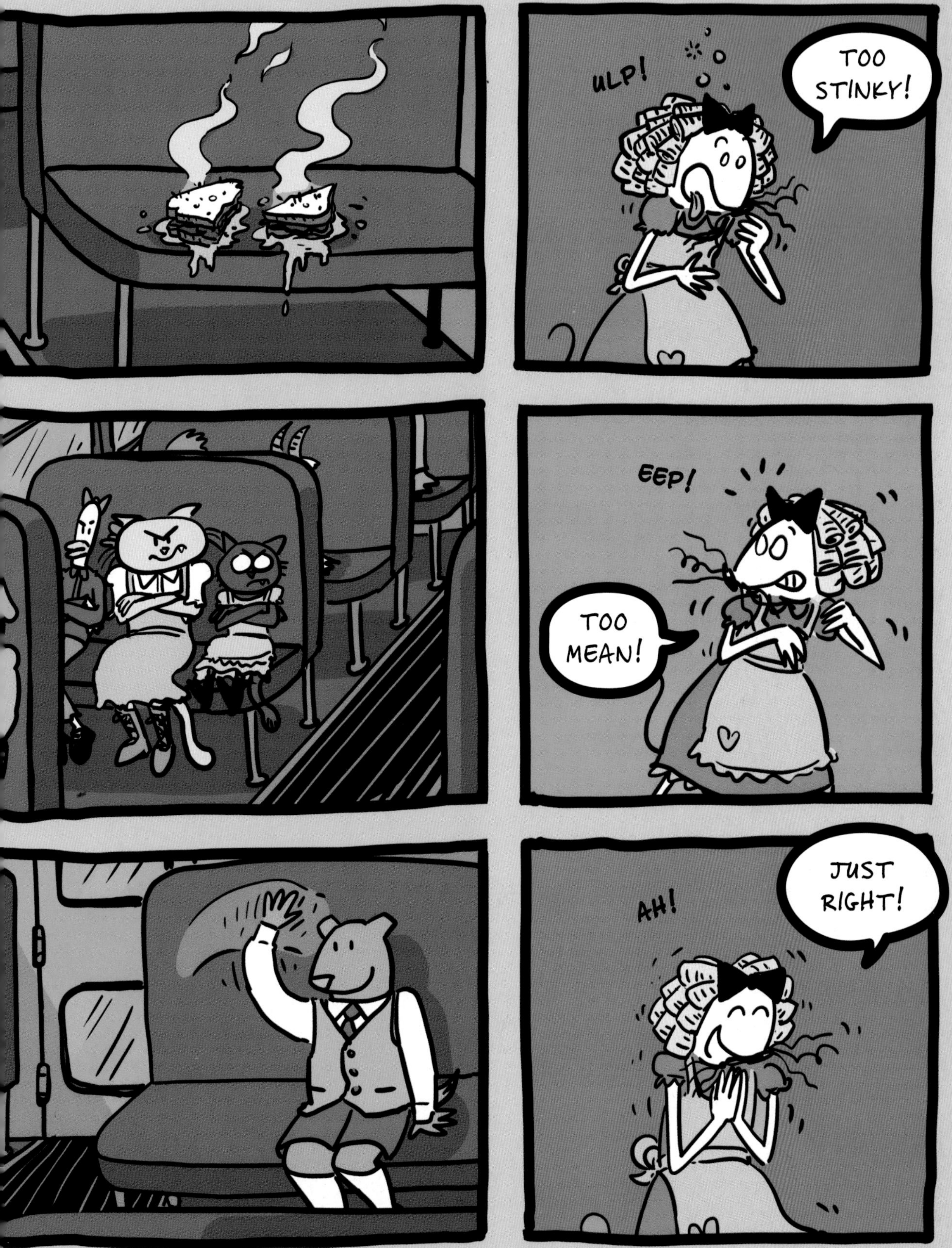
ULP!
TOO STINKY!
EEP!
TOO MEAN!
AH!
JUST RIGHT!

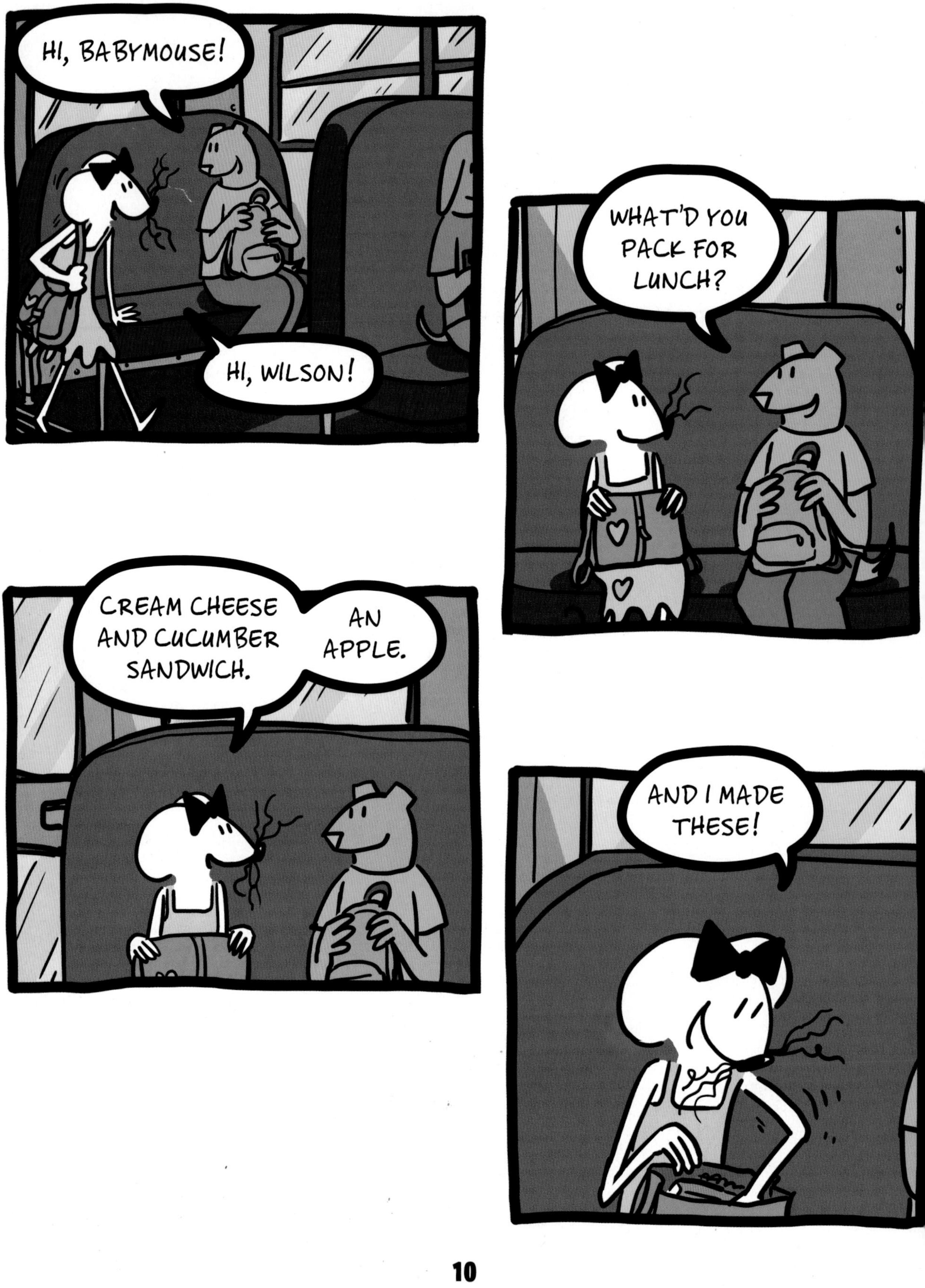
HI, BABYMOUSE!
HI, WILSON!
WHAT'D YOU PACK FOR LUNCH?
CREAM CHEESE AND CUCUMBER SANDWICH.
AN APPLE.
AND I MADE THESE!

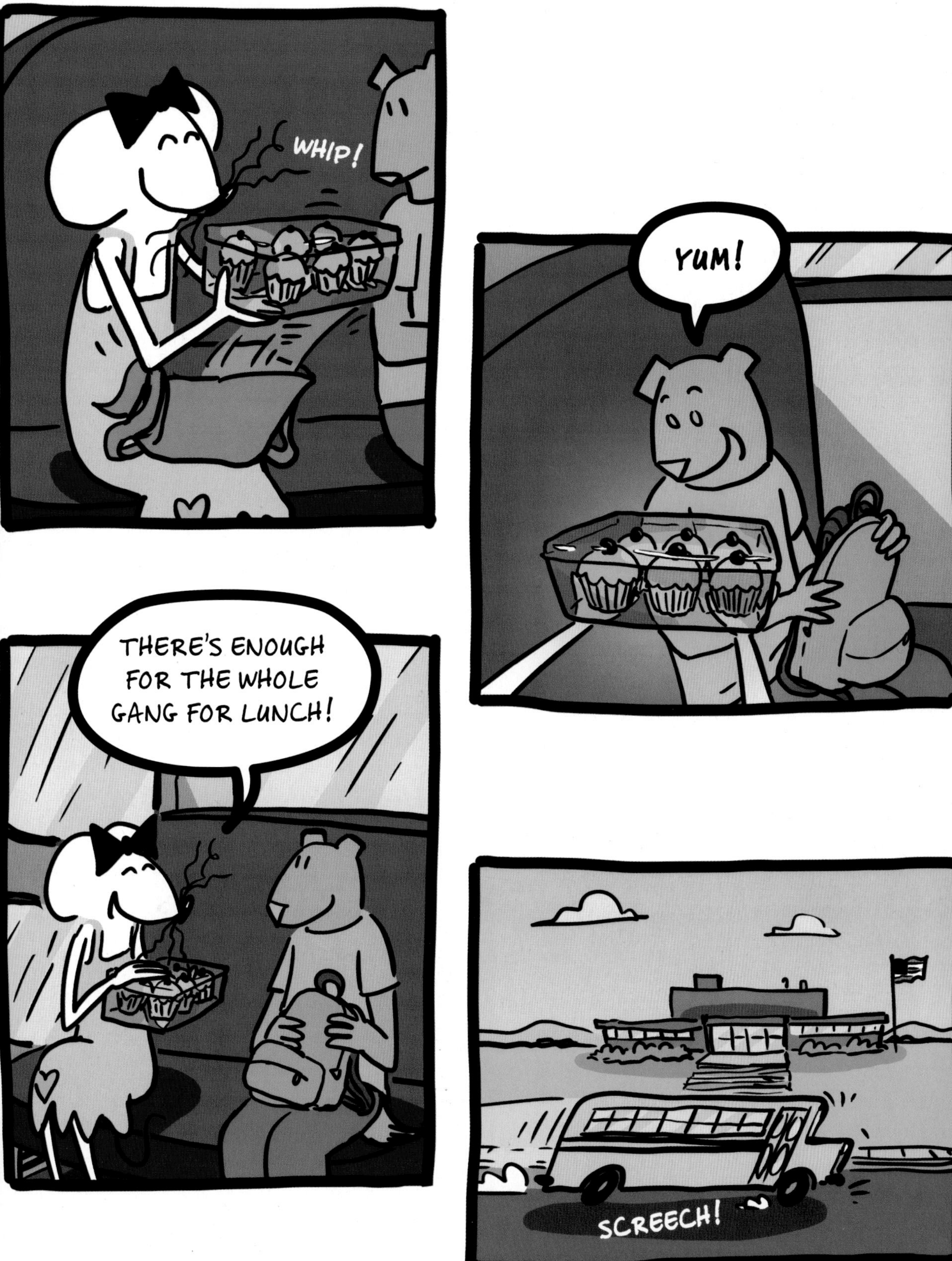
WHIP!
YUM!
THERE'S ENOUGH FOR THE WHOLE GANG FOR LUNCH!
SCREECH!

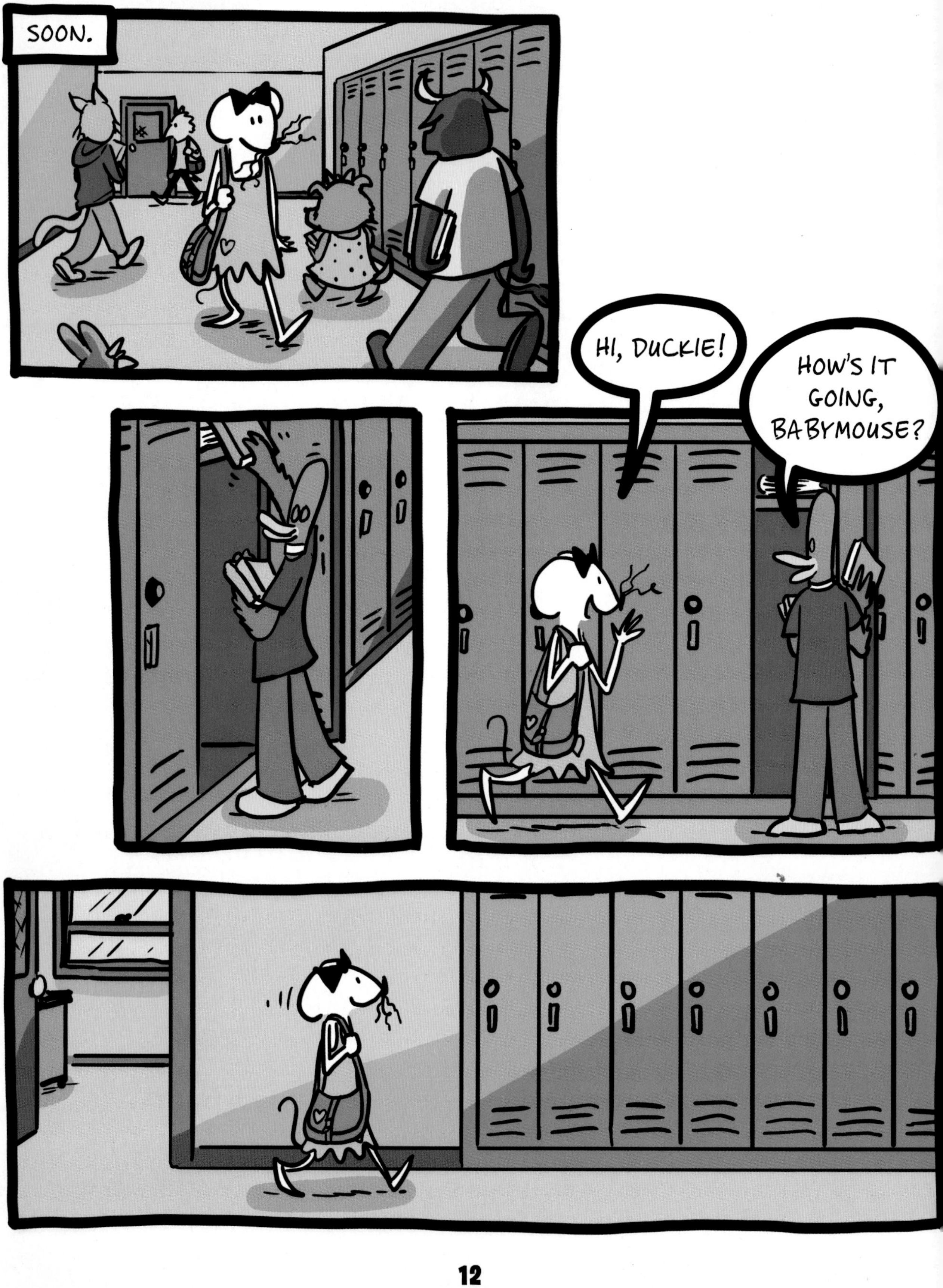
SOON.
HI, DUCKIE!
HOW'S IT GOING, BABYMOUSE?

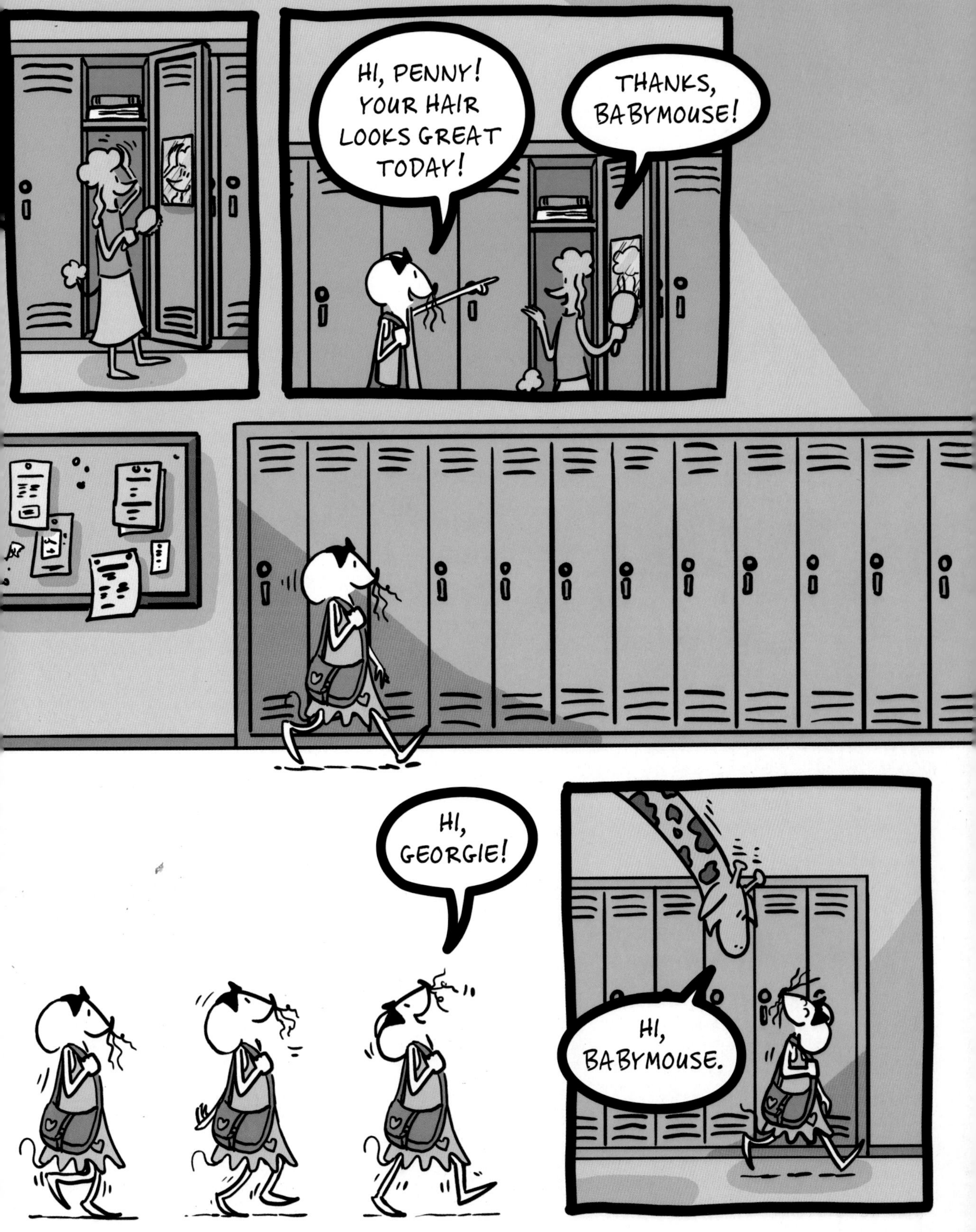
HI, PENNY! YOUR HAIR LOOKS GREAT TODAY!
THANKS, BABYMOUSE!
HI, GEORGIE!
HI, BABYMOUSE.

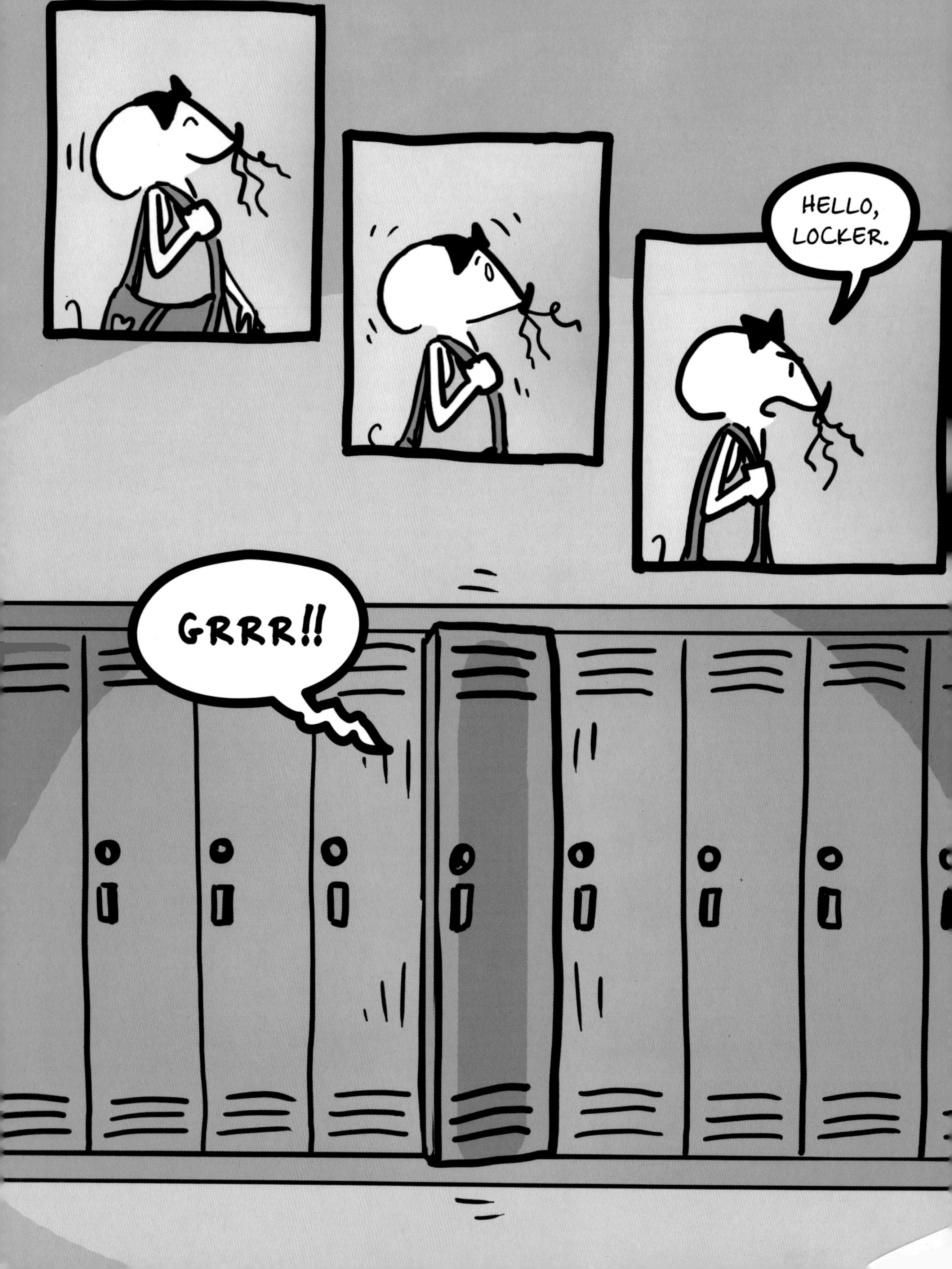
HELLO, LOCKER.
GRRRR!!

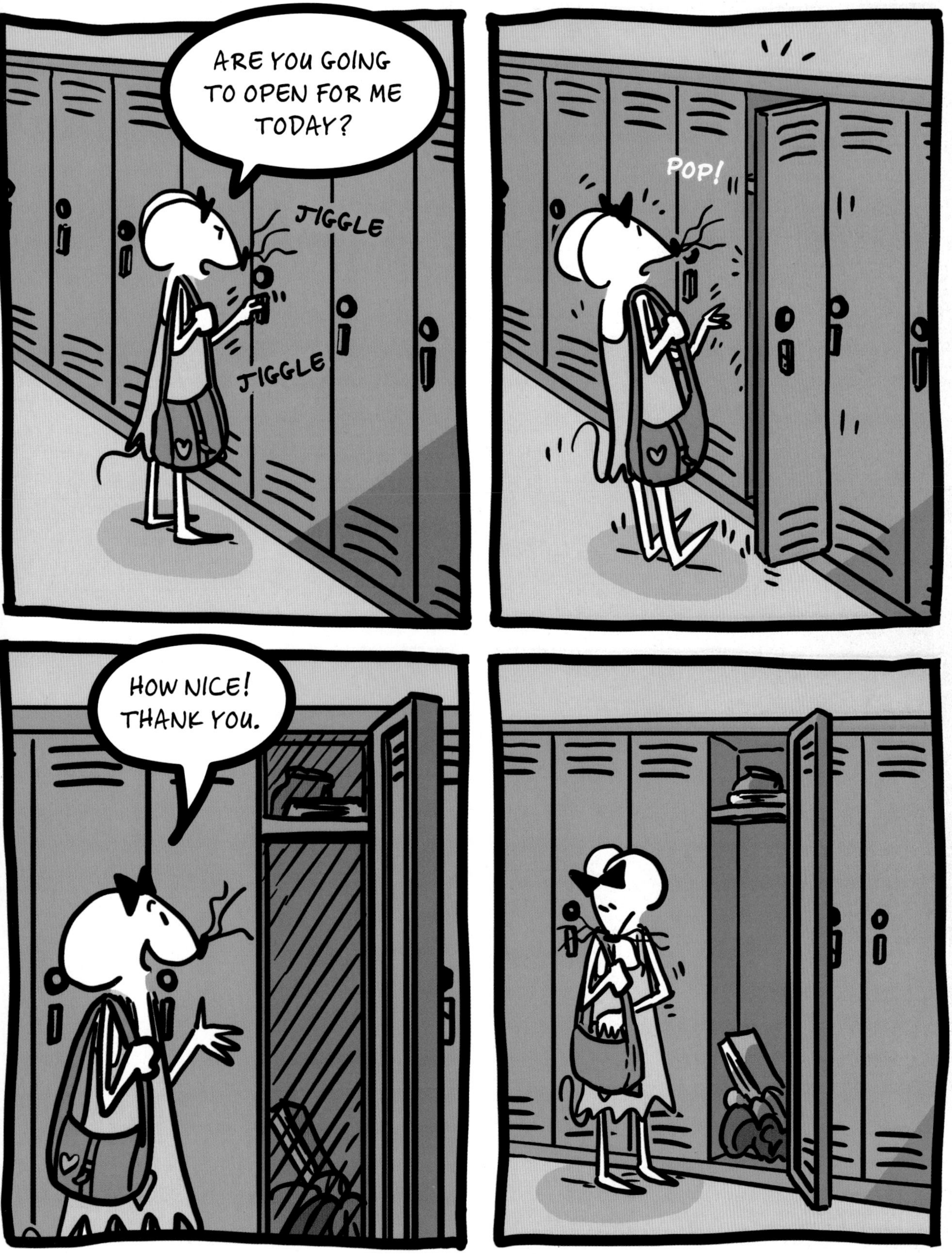
ARE YOU GOING TO OPEN FOR ME TODAY?
JIGGLE
JIGGLE
POP!
HOW NICE! THANK YOU.

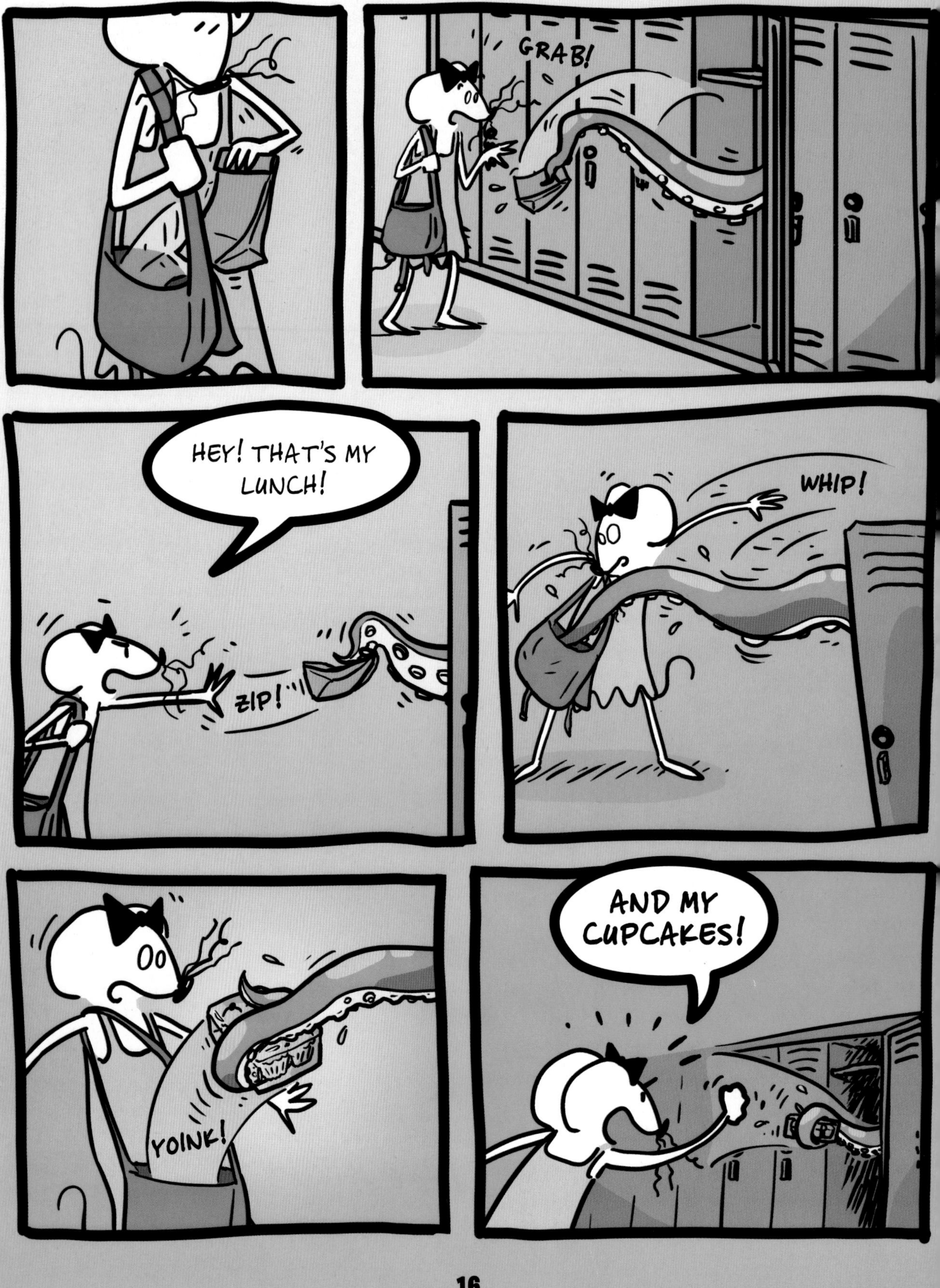
GRAB!
HEY! THAT'S MY LUNCH!
ZIP!
WHIP!
YOINK!
AND MY CUPCAKES!

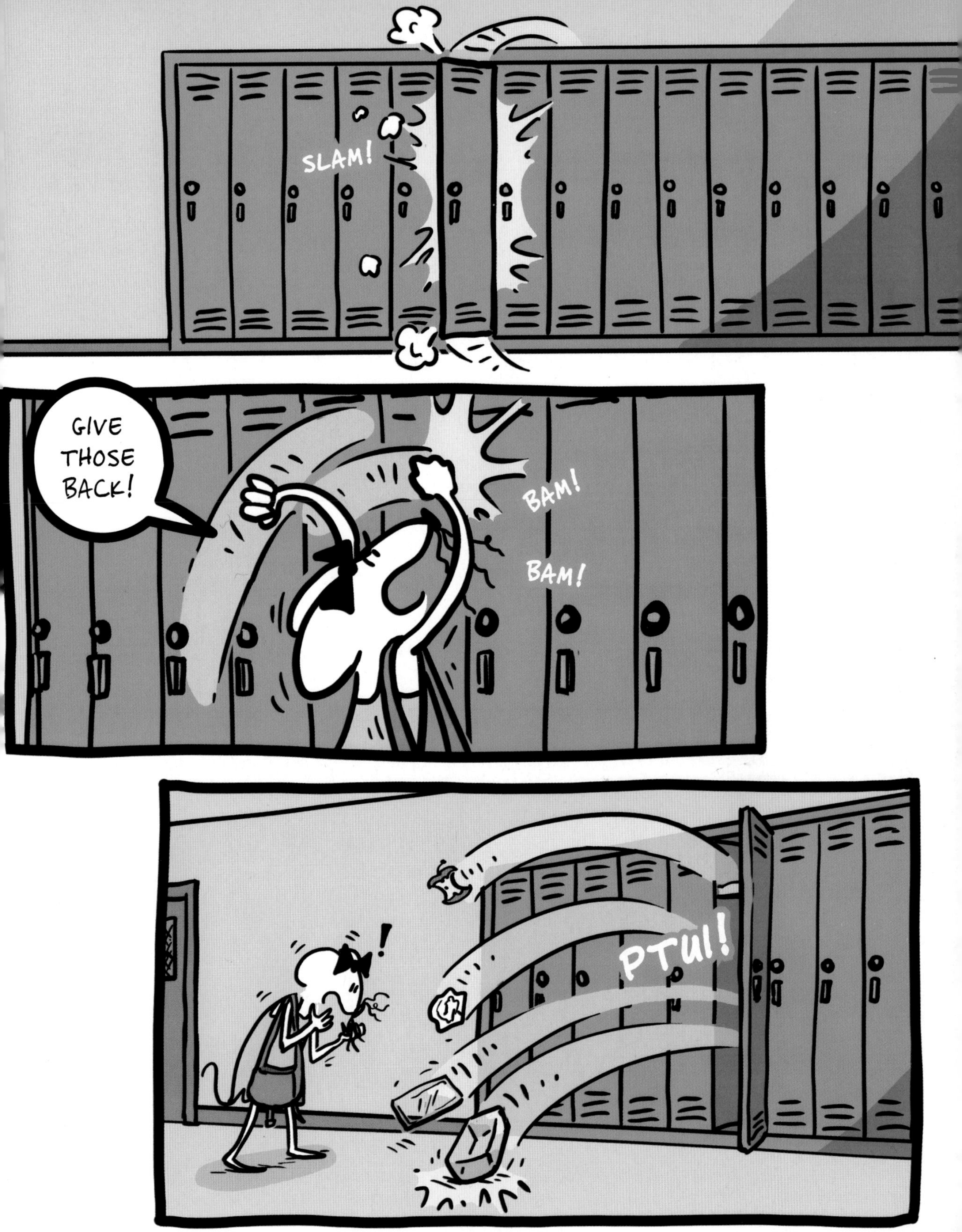
SLAM!
GIVE THOSE BACK!
BAM!
BAM!
!
PTUI!

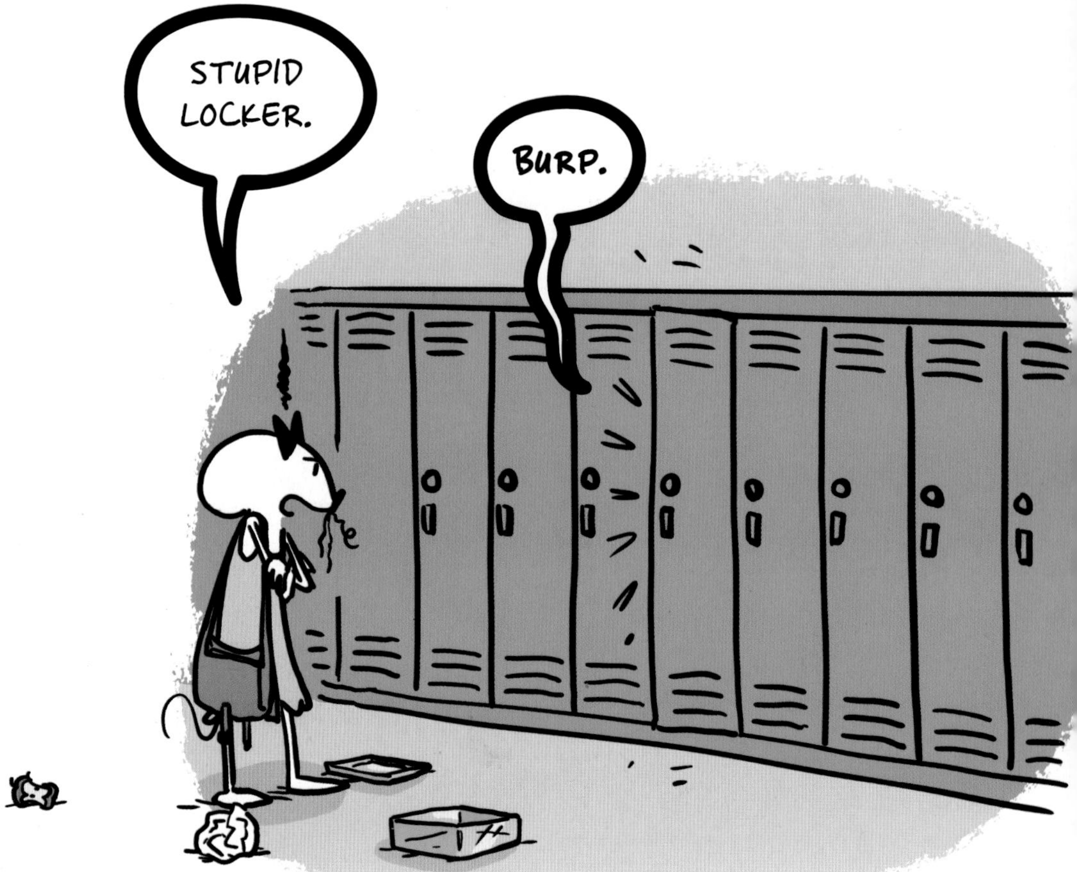
STUPID LOCKER.
BURP.

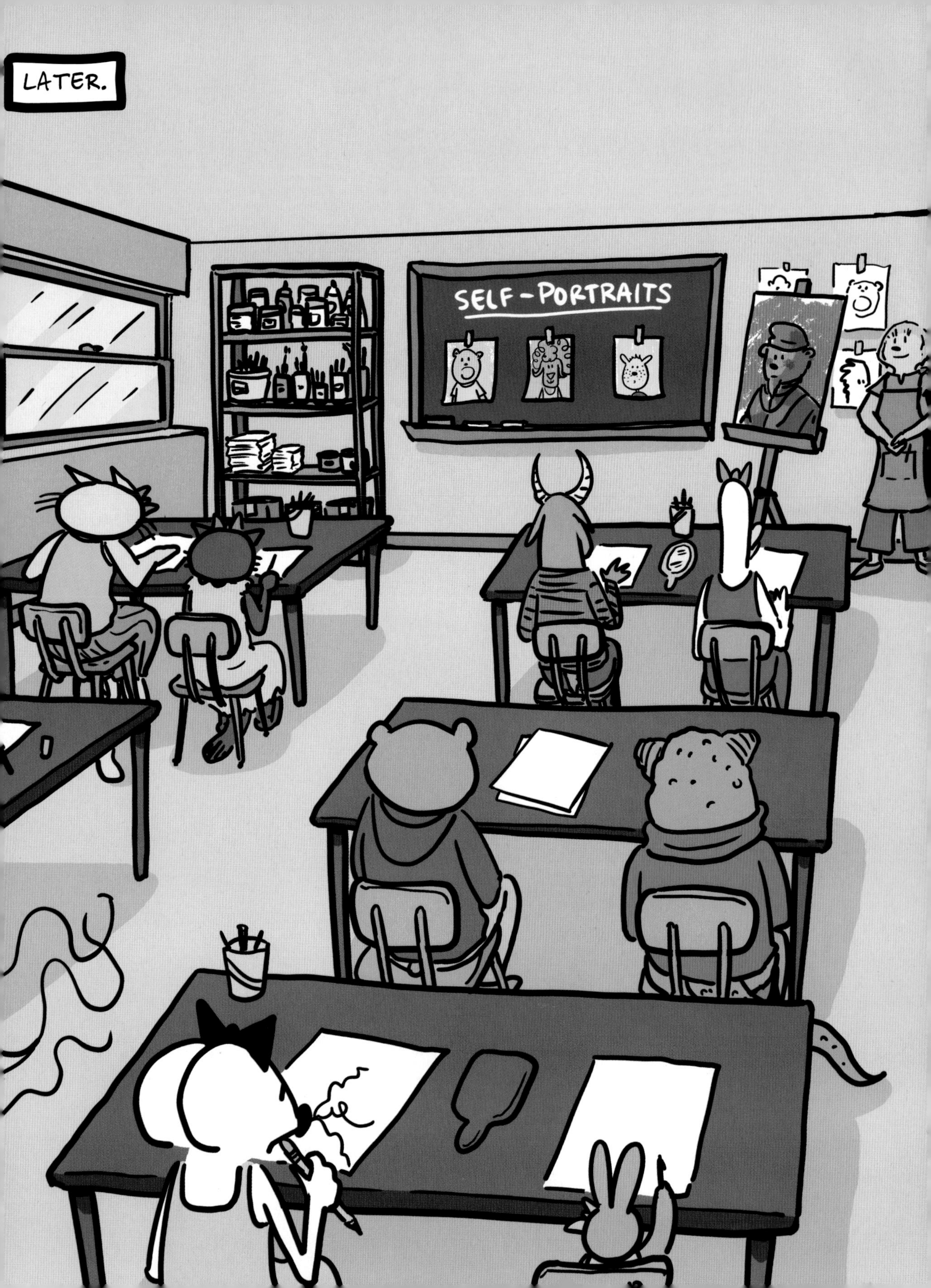
LATER.
SELF-PORTRAITS

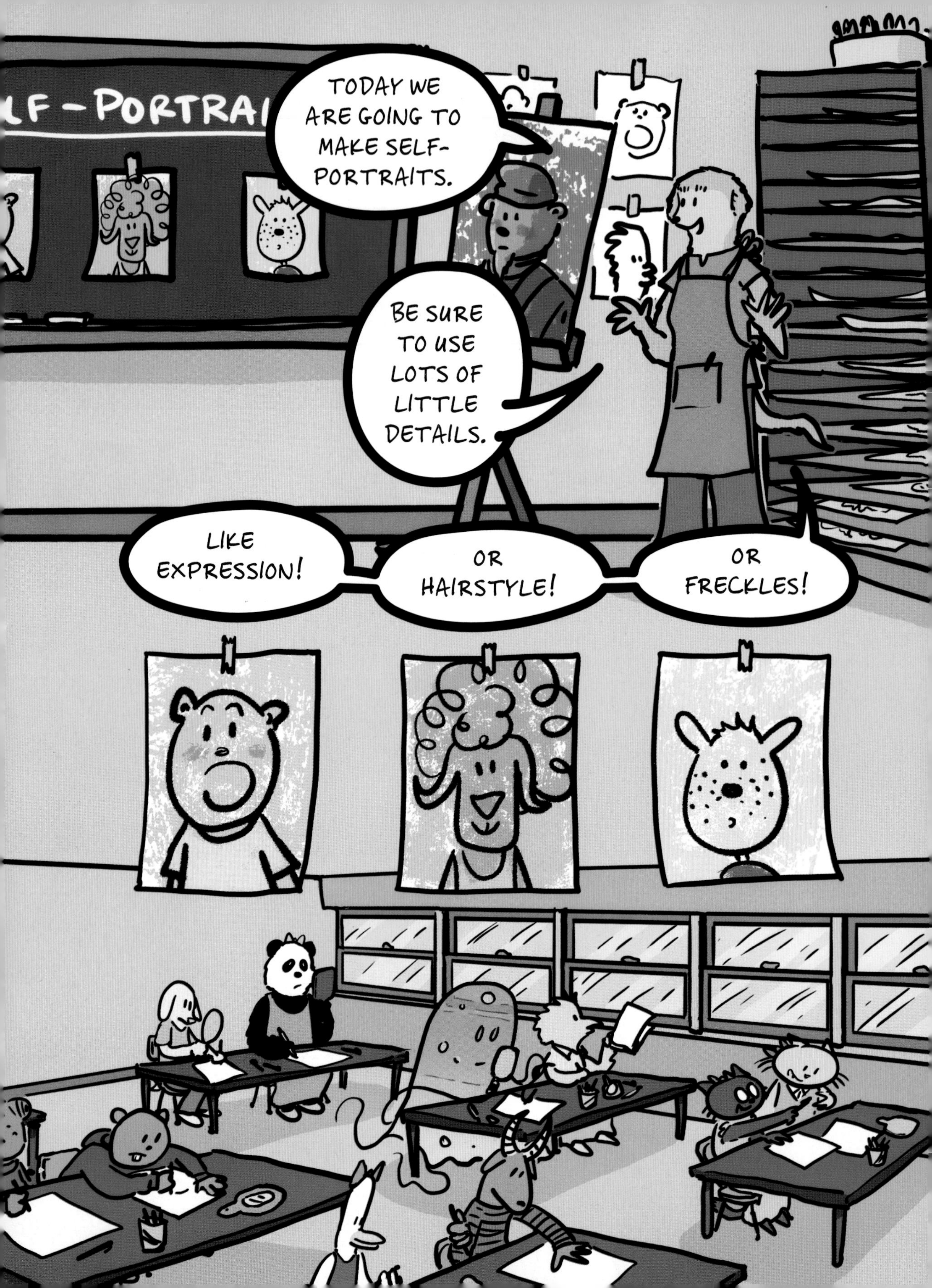

-PORTRAI
TODAY WE ARE GOING TO MAKE SELF-PORTRAITS.
BE SURE TO USE LOTS OF LITTLE DETAILS.
LIKE EXPRESSION!
OR HAIRSTYLE!
OR FRECKLES!

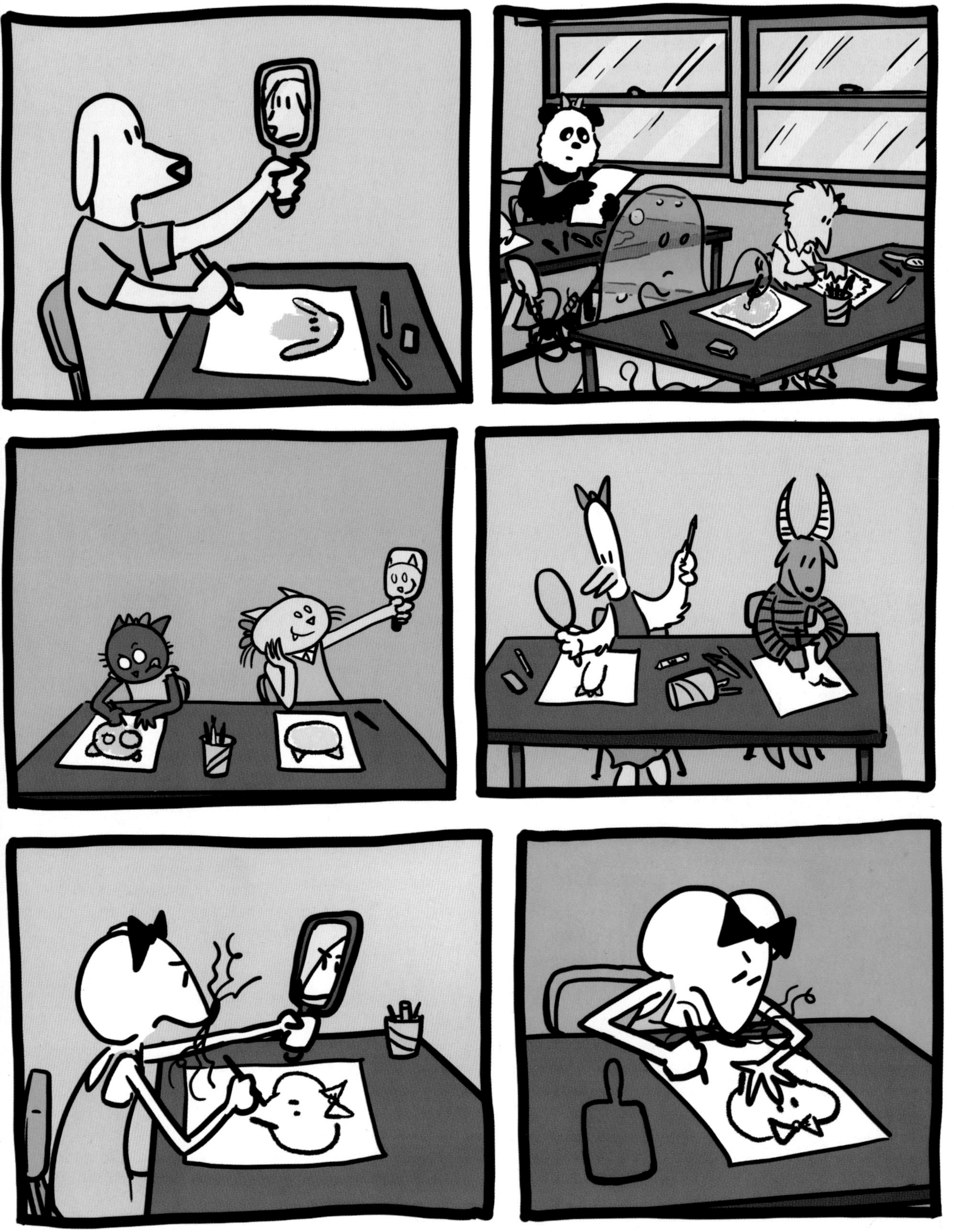

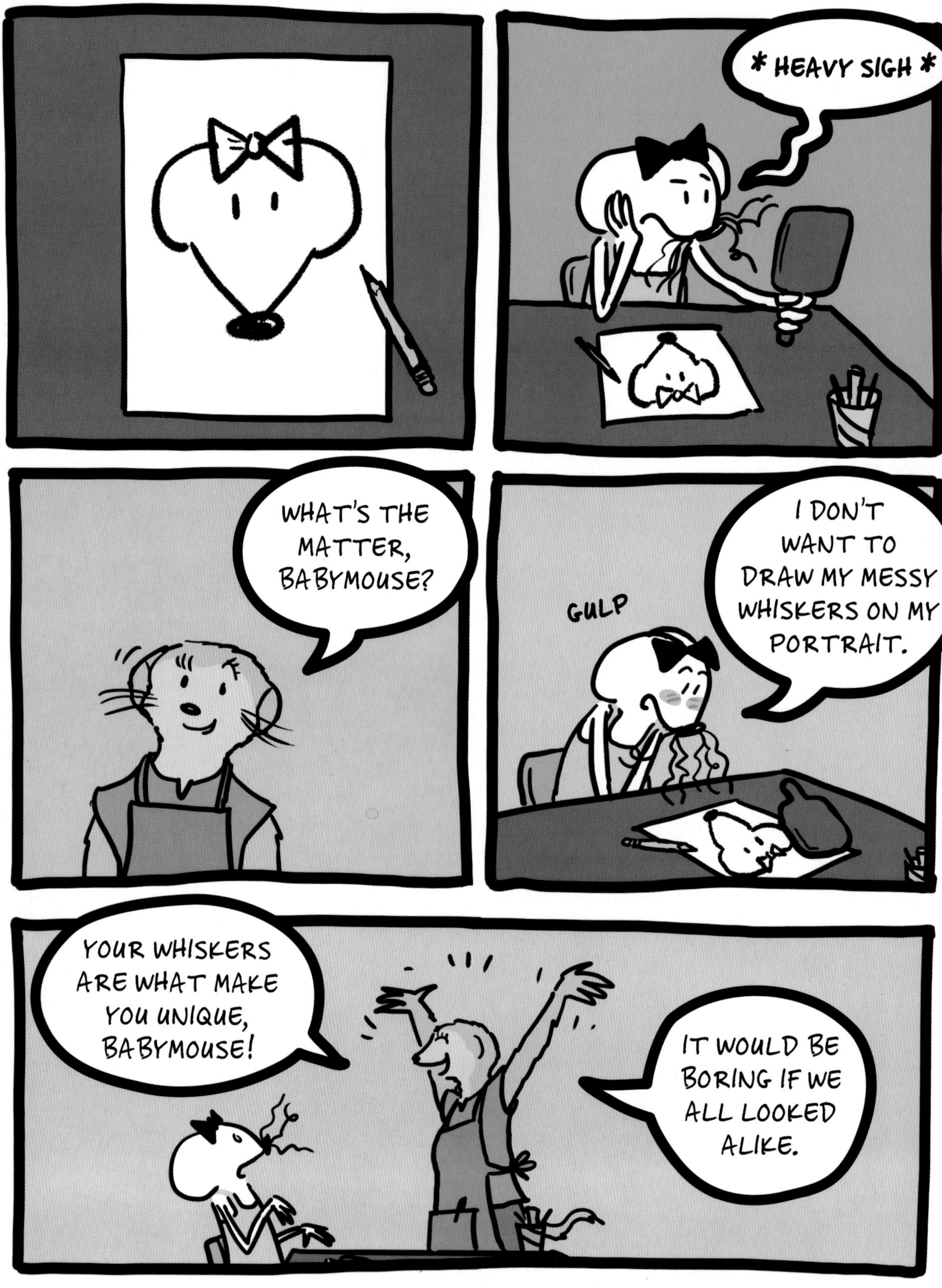
* HEAVY SIGH *
WHAT'S THE MATTER, BABYMOUSE?
GULP
I DON'T WANT TO DRAW MY MESSY WHISKERS ON MY PORTRAIT.
YOUR WHISKERS ARE WHAT MAKE YOU UNIQUE, BABYMOUSE!
IT WOULD BE BORING IF WE ALL LOOKED ALIKE.

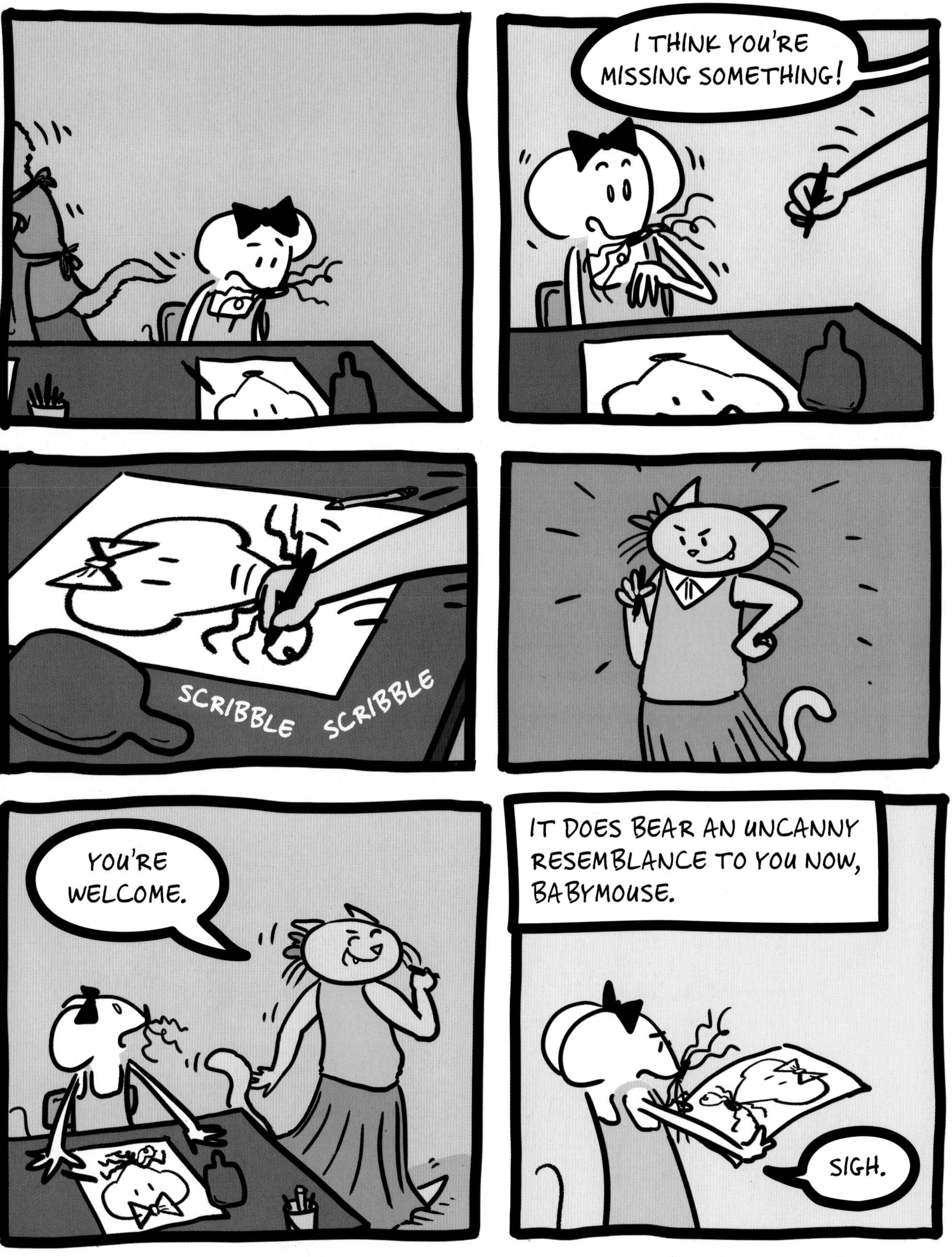
I THINK YOU'RE MISSING SOMETHING!
SCRIBBLE SCRIBBLE
YOU'RE WELCOME.
IT DOES BEAR AN UNCANNY RESEMBLANCE TO YOU NOW, BABYMOUSE.
SIGH.

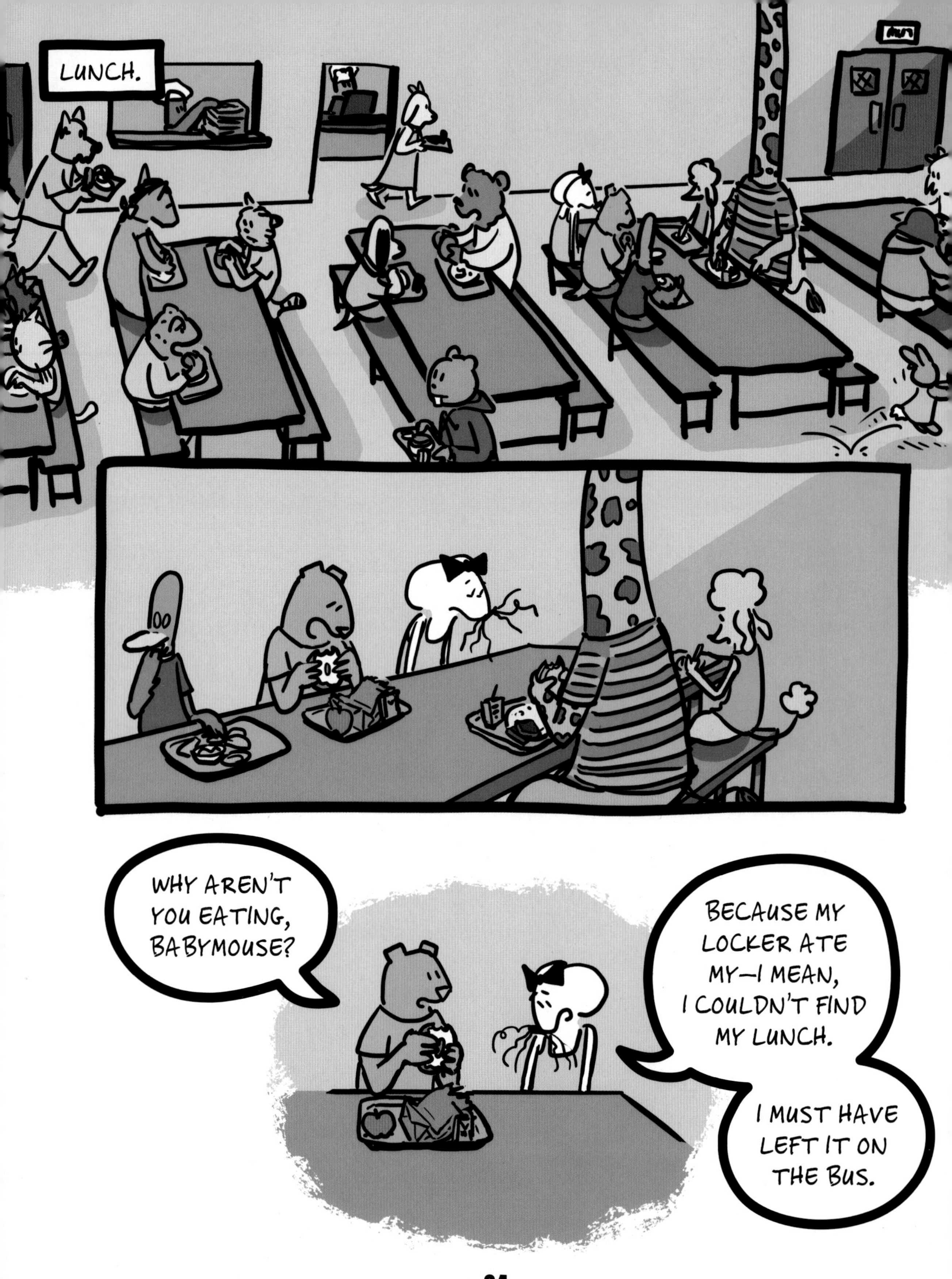
LUNCH.
WHY AREN'T YOU EATING, BABYMOUSE?
BECAUSE MY LOCKER ATE MY—I MEAN, I COULDN'T FIND MY LUNCH.
I MUST HAVE LEFT IT ON THE BUS.

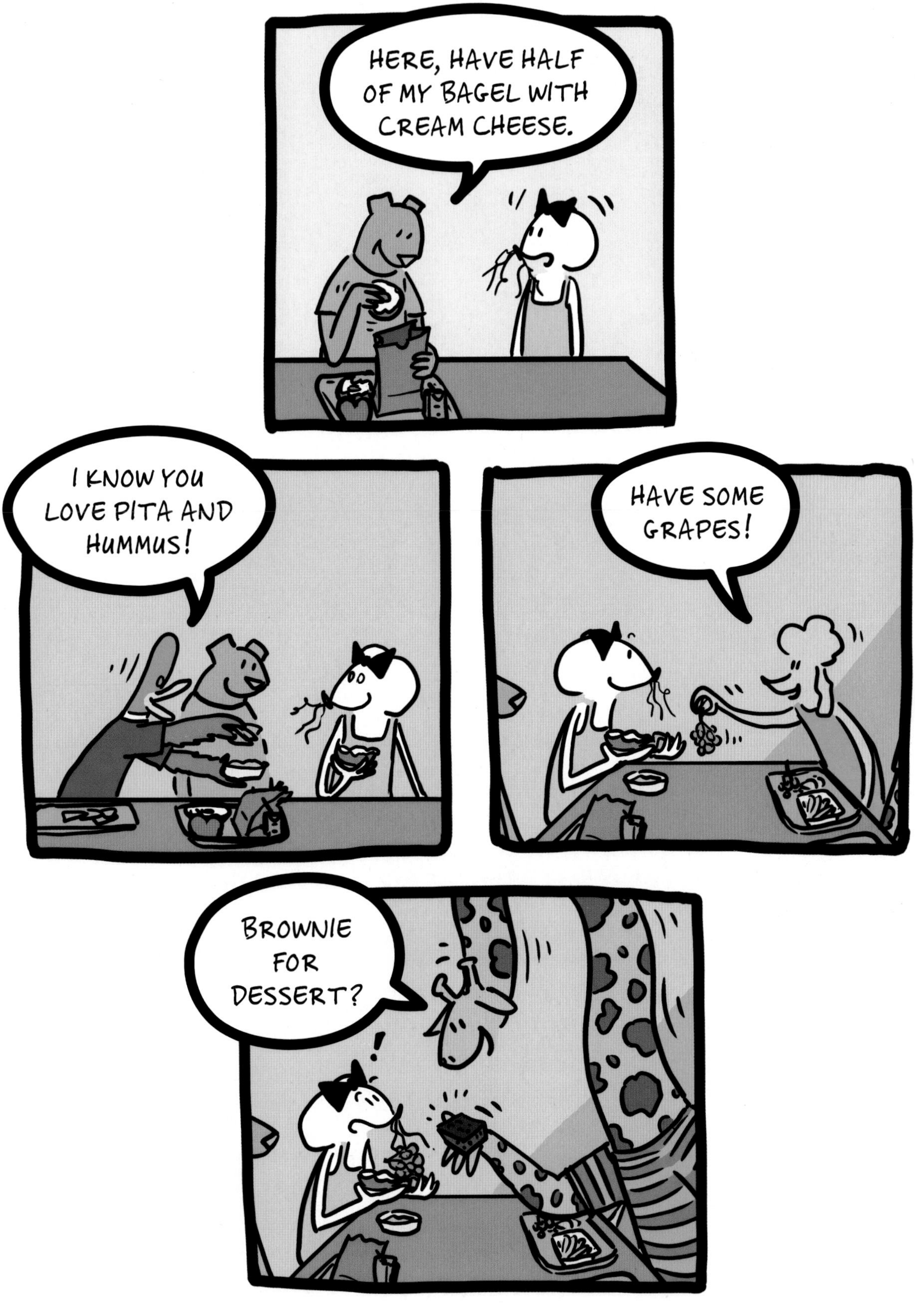
HERE, HAVE HALF OF MY BAGEL WITH CREAM CHEESE.
I KNOW YOU LOVE PITA AND HUMMUS!
HAVE SOME GRAPES!
BROWNIE FOR DESSERT?
!

THANKS!
ANY CHANCE YOU WOULD LIKE TO SHARE THAT BROWNIE WITH ME, BABYMOUSE?
I AM YOUR FAVORITE NARRATOR.

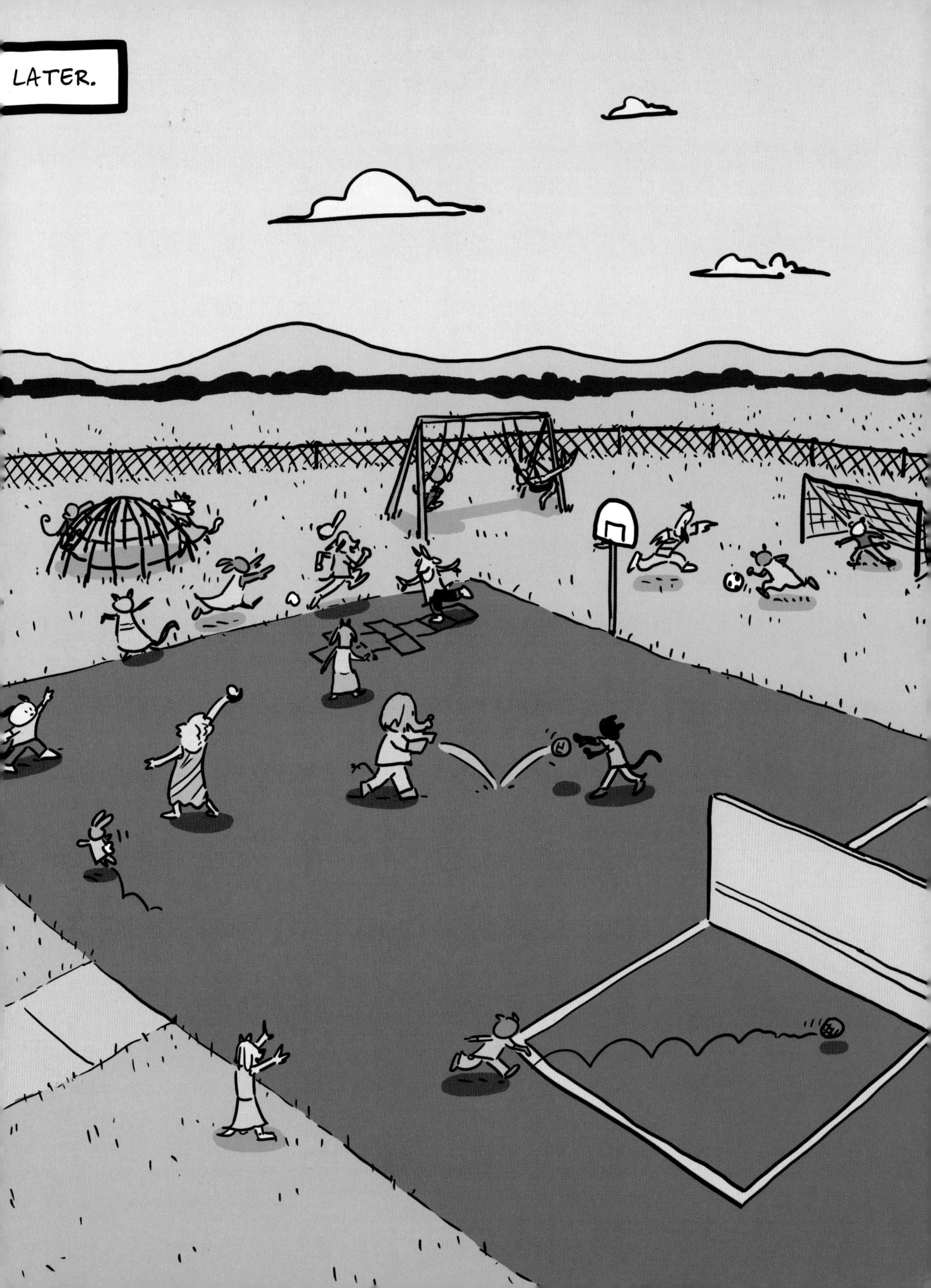
LATER.

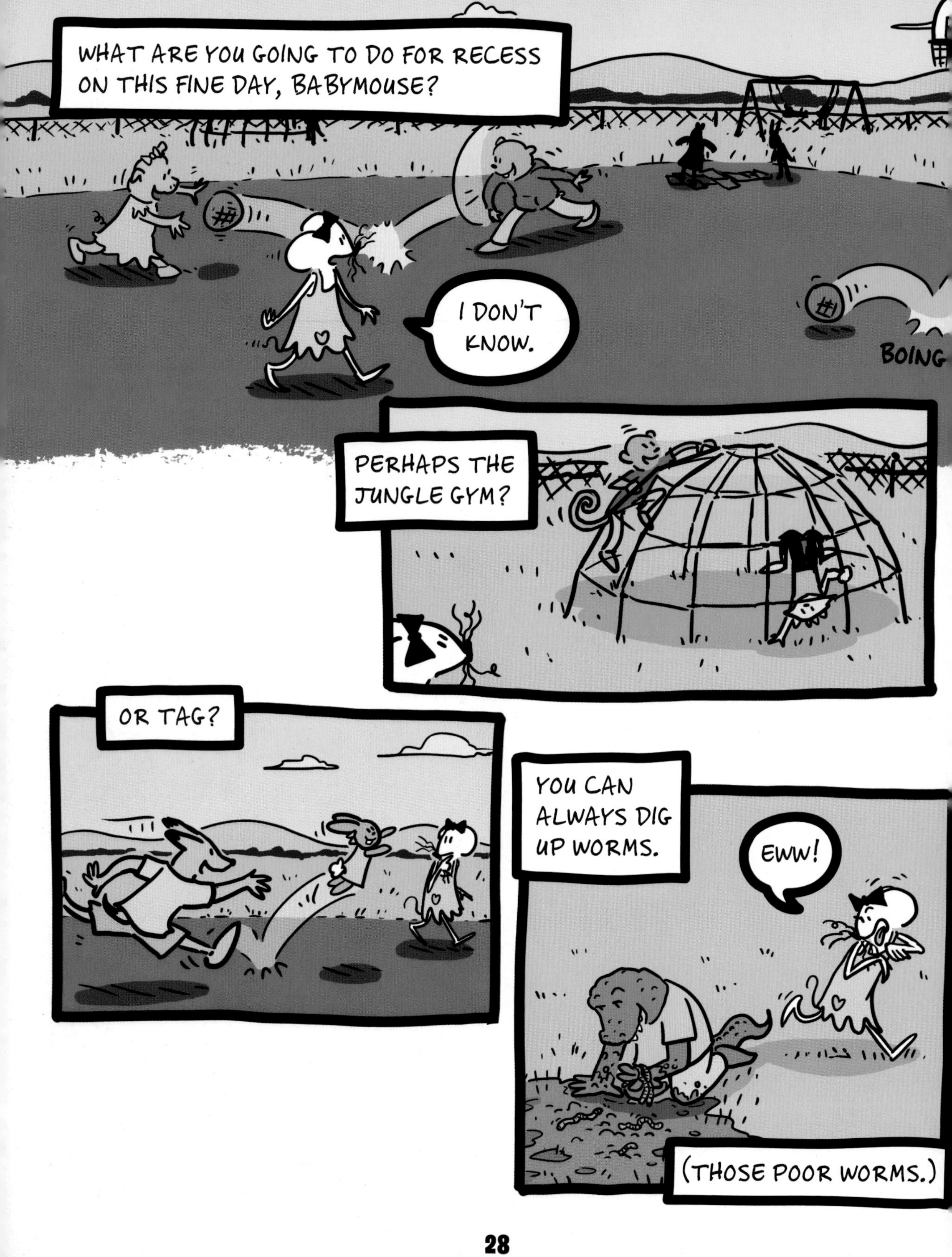

WHAT ARE YOU GOING TO DO FOR RECESS ON THIS FINE DAY, BABYMOUSE?
I DON'T KNOW.
BOING
PERHAPS THE JUNGLE GYM?
OR TAG?
YOU CAN ALWAYS DIG UP WORMS.
EWW!
(THOSE POOR WORMS.)

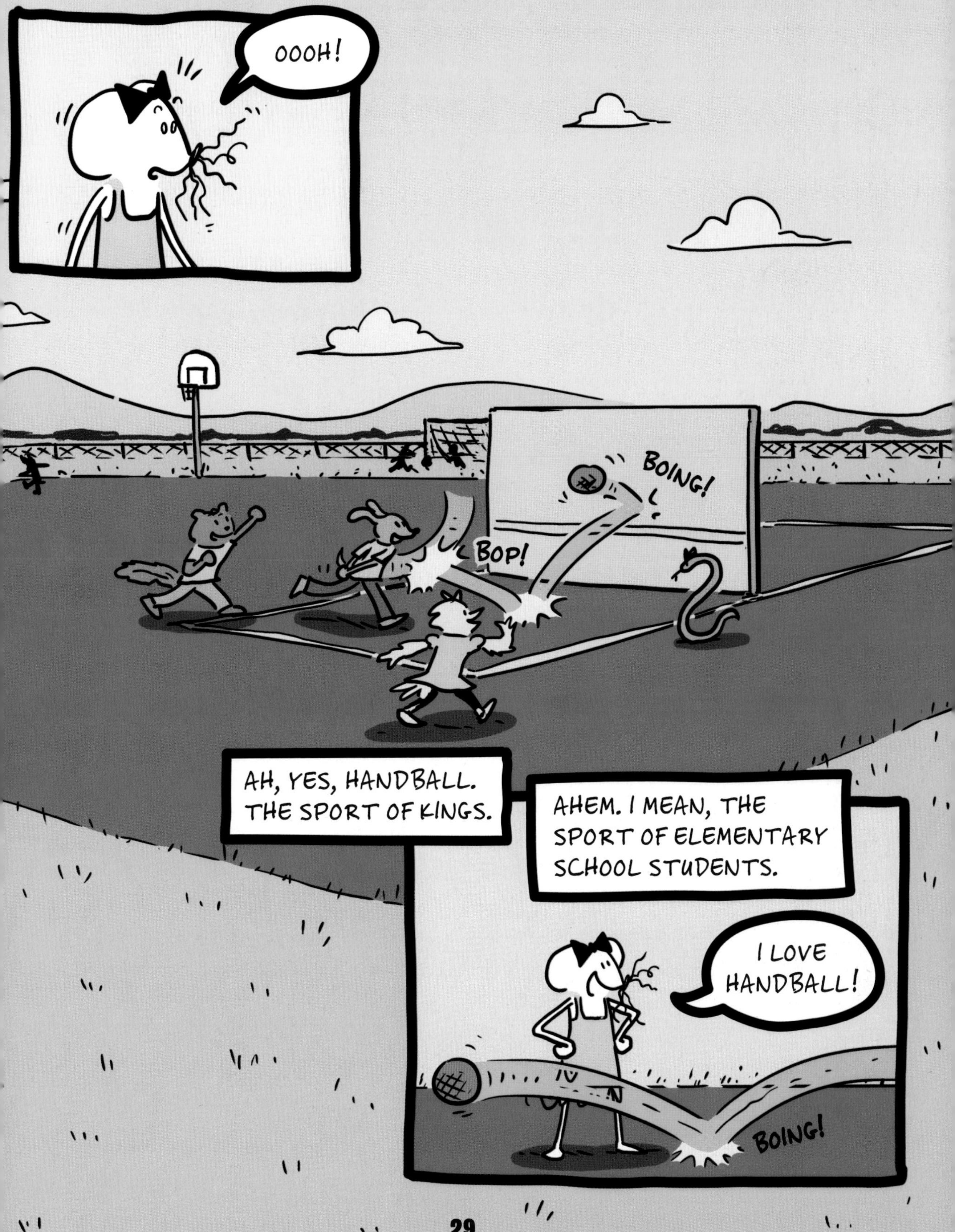
OOOH!
BOING!
BOP!
AH, YES, HANDBALL. THE SPORT OF KINGS.
AHEM. I MEAN, THE SPORT OF ELEMENTARY SCHOOL STUDENTS.
I LOVE HANDBALL!
BOING!

WHY HANDBALL IS SUPERIOR!

YOU DON'T NEED A FIELD!

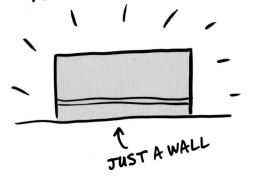

↑
JUST A WALL

YOU DON'T HAVE TO BE TALL!

NO FAIR!

SORRY, BABYMOUSE.

YOU DON'T HAVE TO PICK A TEAM!

I PICK ANYONE **BUT** BABYMOUSE.

YOU DON'T NEED A LOT OF EQUIPMENT!

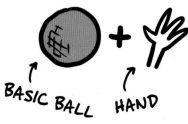

↑
BASIC BALL

↑
HAND

OOH! I HAVE **TWO** HANDS!

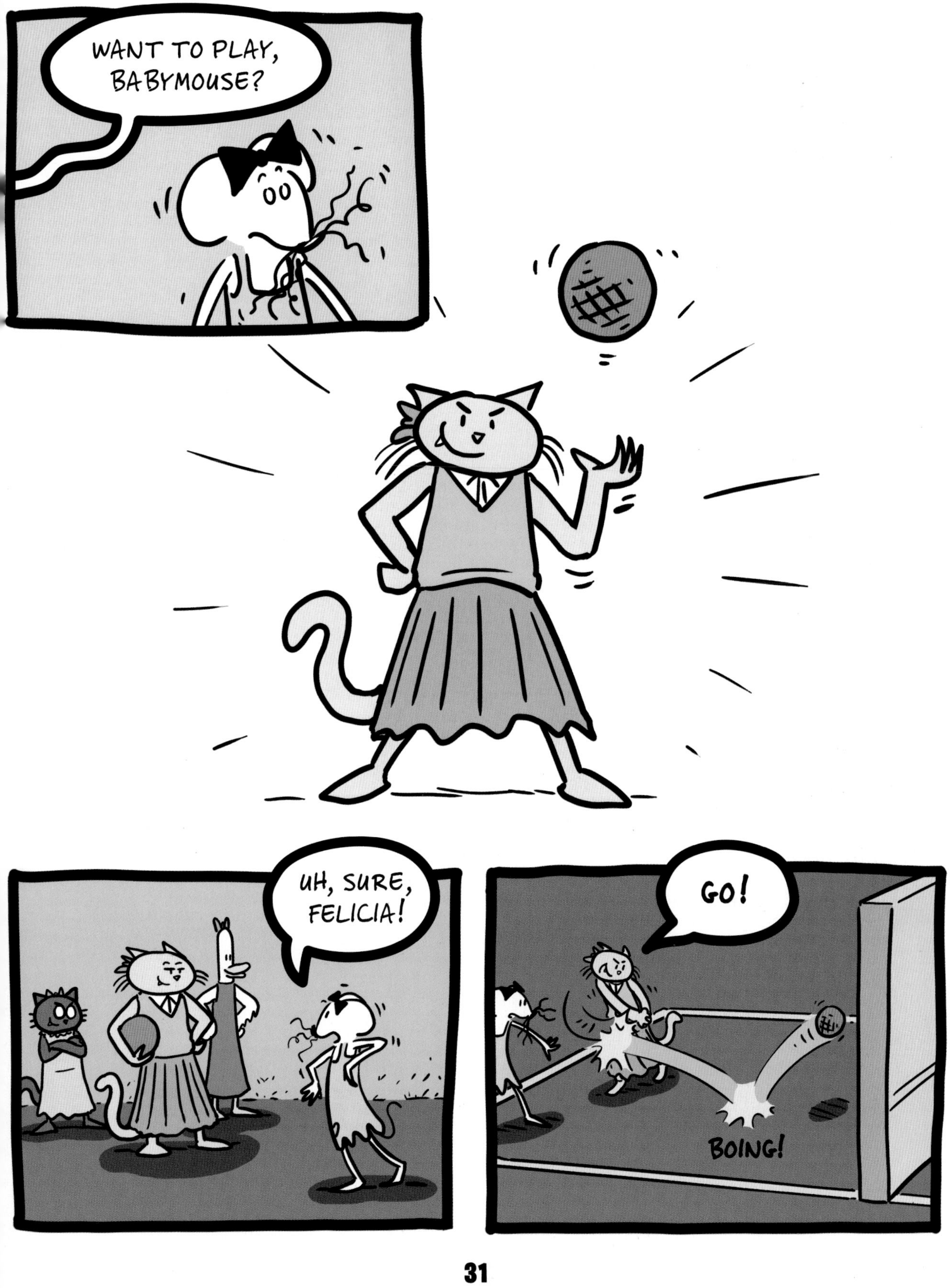
WANT TO PLAY, BABYMOUSE?
UH, SURE, FELICIA!
GO!
BOING!

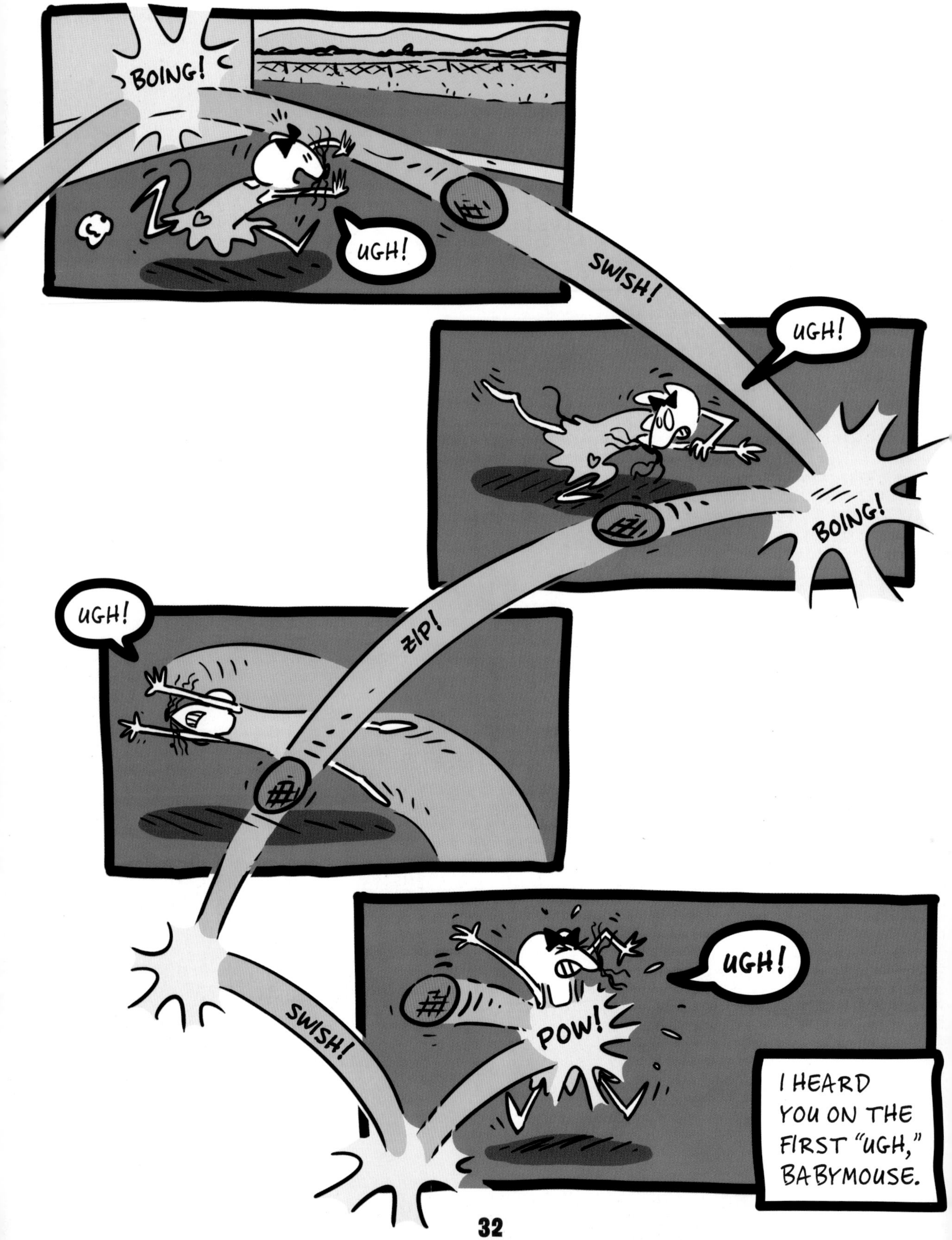
BOING!
UGH!
SWISH!
UGH!
BOING!
UGH!
ZIP!
SWISH!
UGH!
POW!
I HEARD YOU ON THE FIRST "UGH," BABYMOUSE.

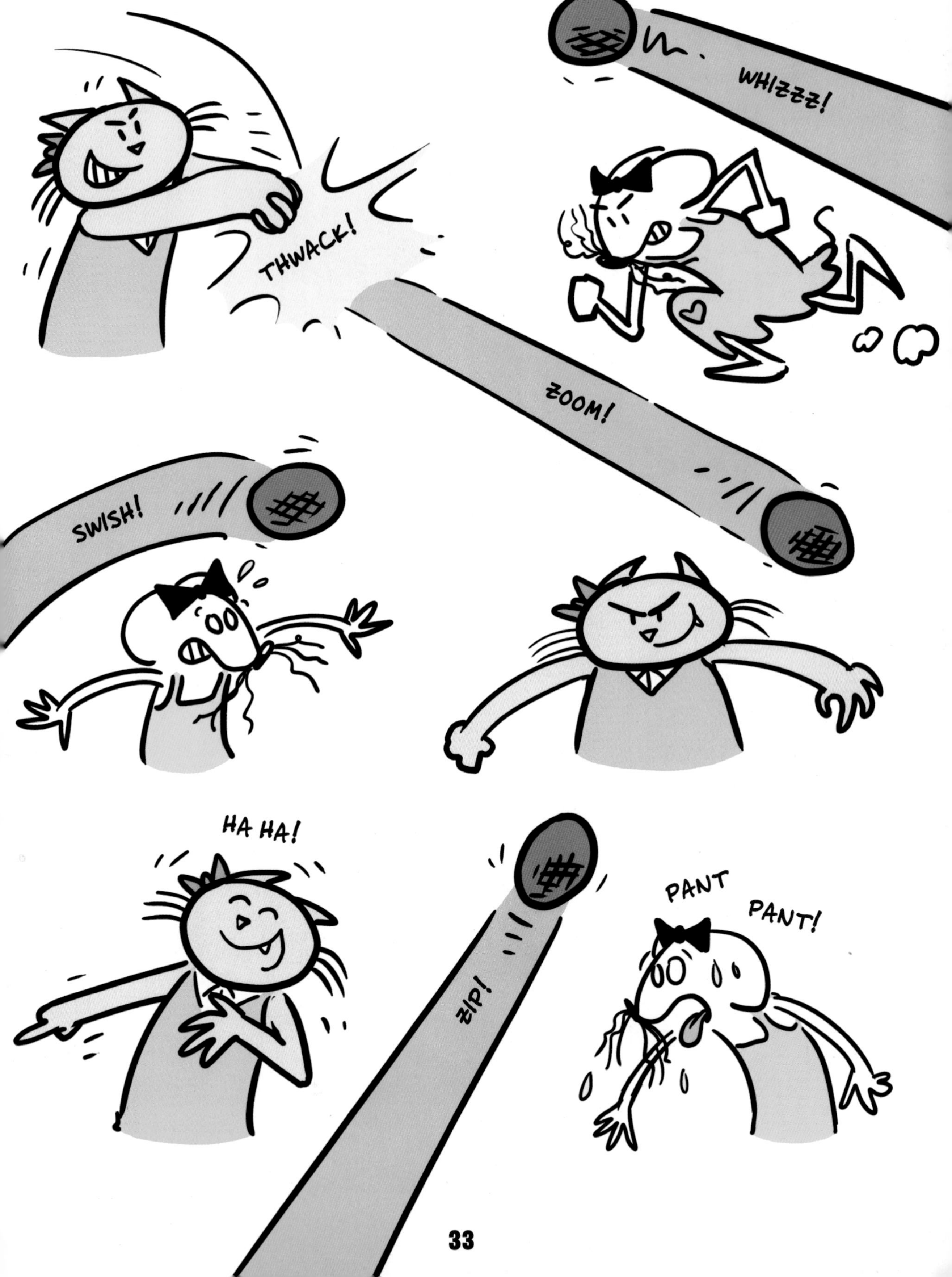
THWACK!
WHIZZZZ!
ZOOM!
SWISH!
HA HA!
ZIP!
PANT
PANT!

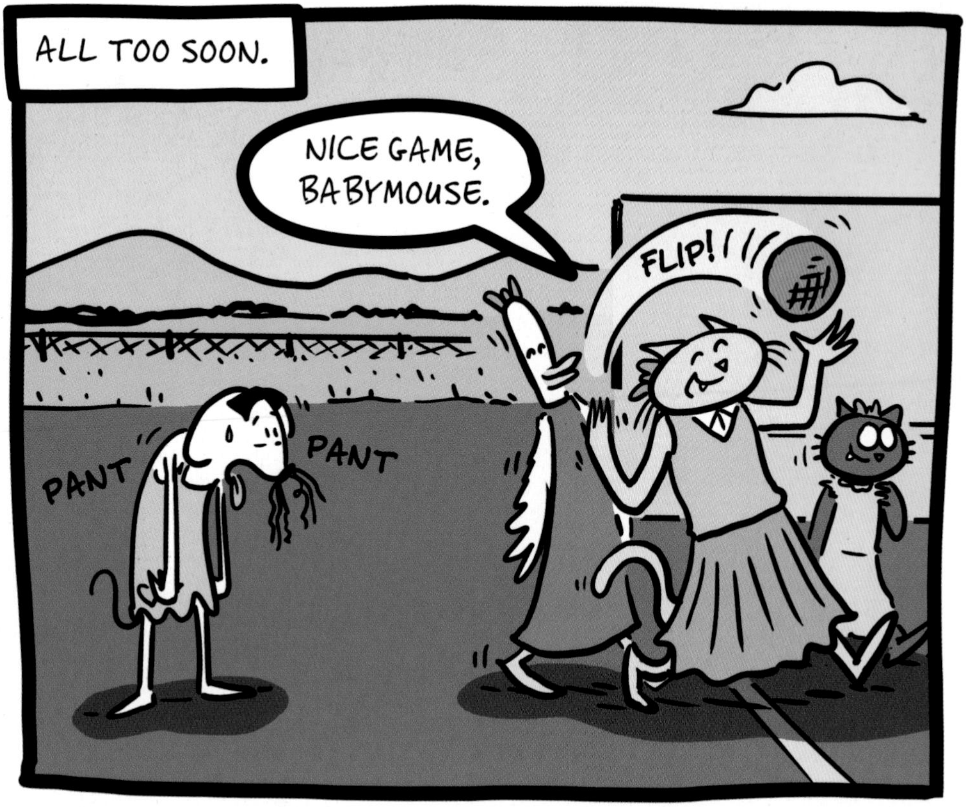
ALL TOO SOON.
NICE GAME, BABYMOUSE.
FLIP!
PANT
PANT

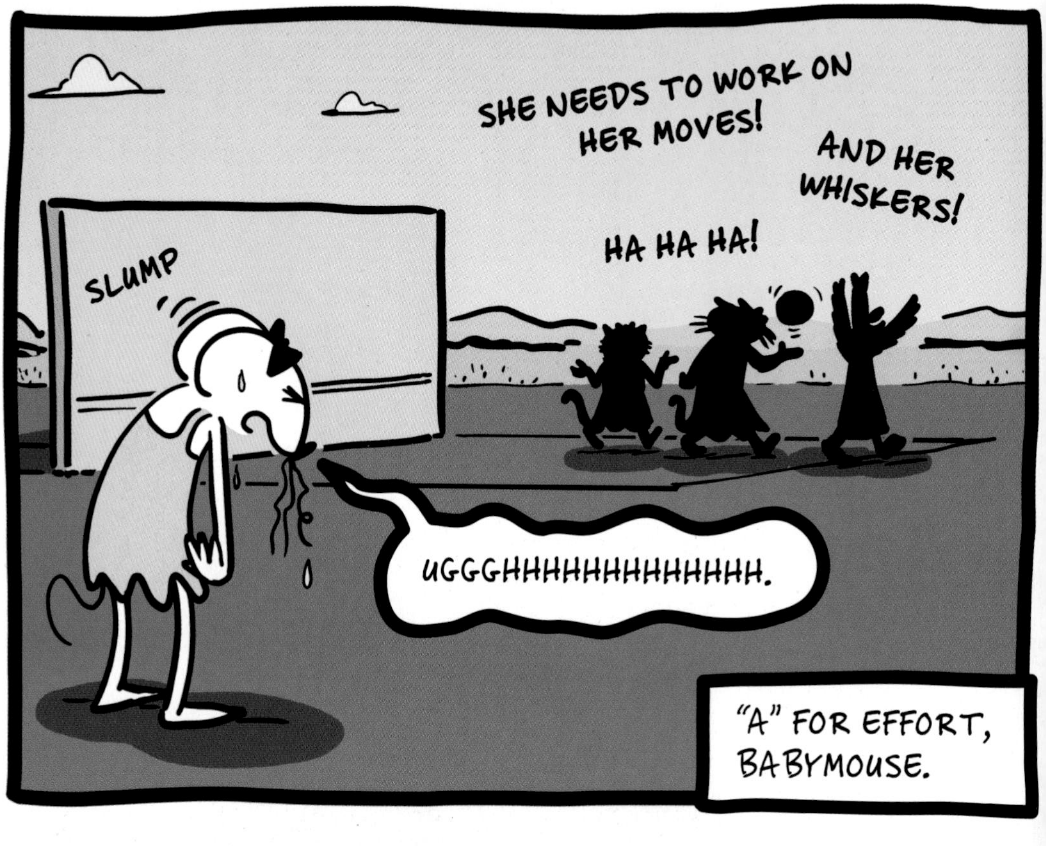
SHE NEEDS TO WORK ON HER MOVES!
AND HER WHISKERS!
HA HA HA!
SLUMP
UGGGHHHHHHHHHHHHH.
"A" FOR EFFORT, BABYMOUSE.

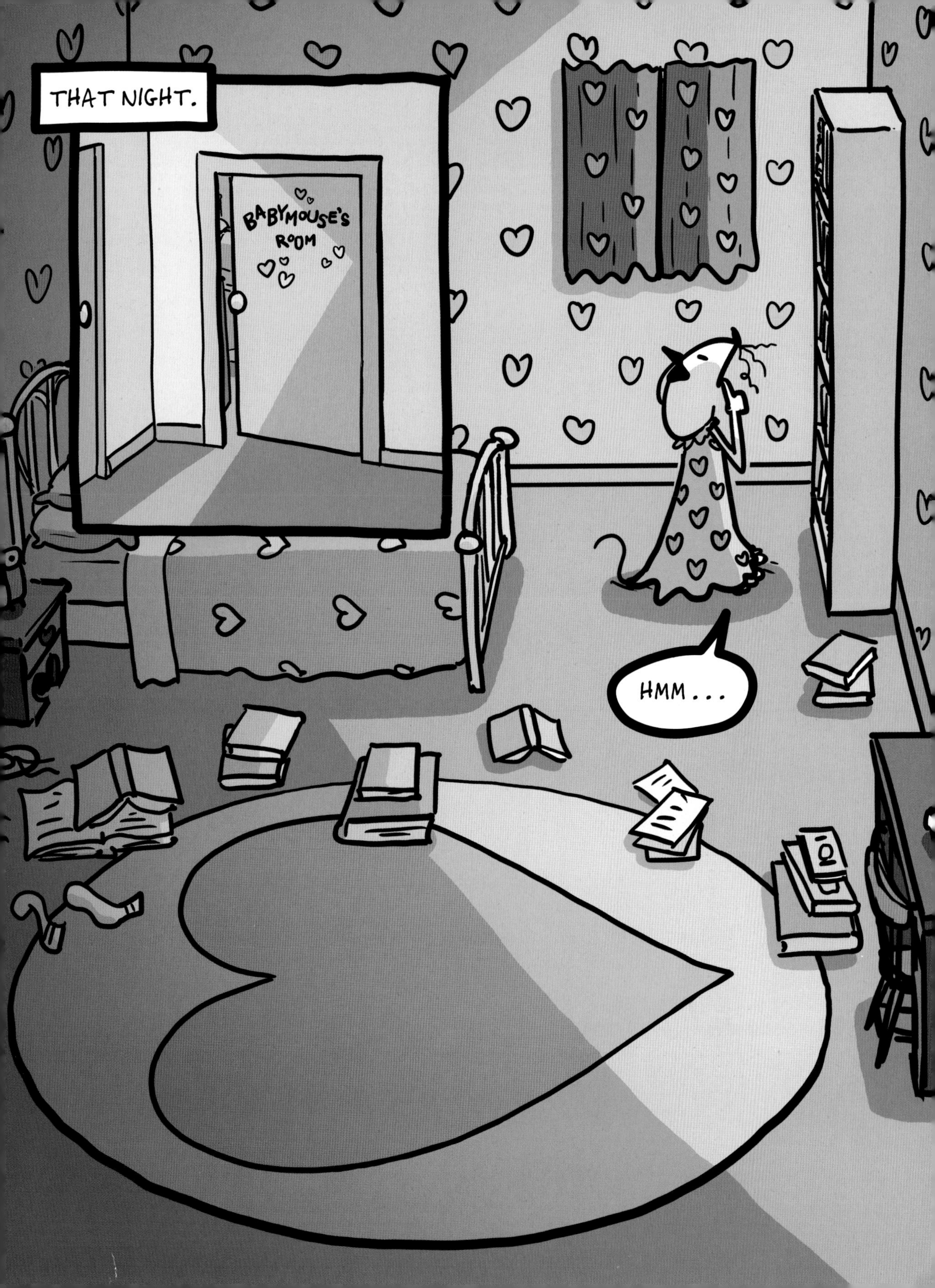
THAT NIGHT.
BABYMOUSE'S ROOM
HMM . . .

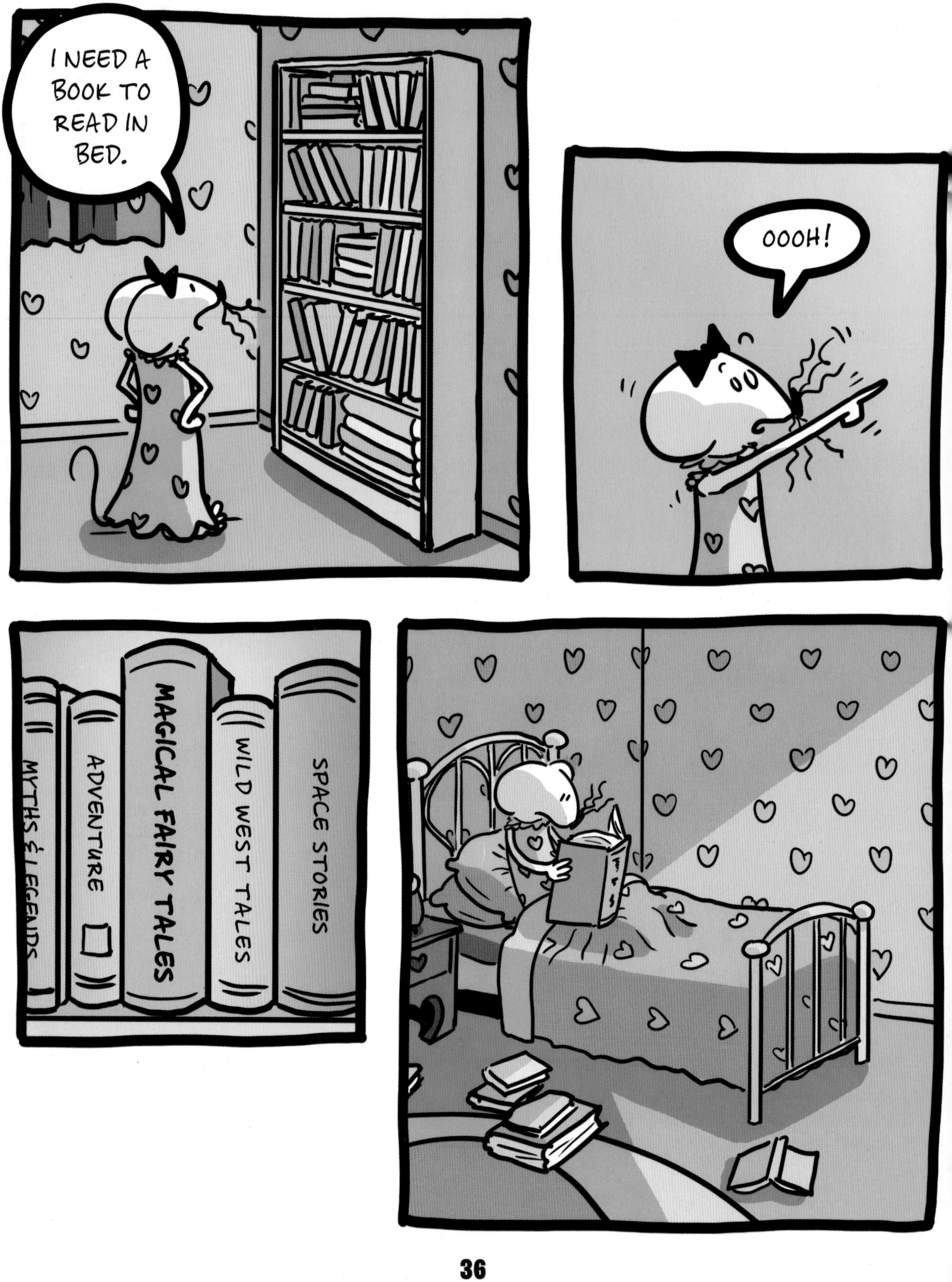
I NEED A BOOK TO READ IN BED.
OOOH!
MYTHS & LEGENDS
ADVENTURE
MAGICAL FAIRY TALES
WILD WEST TALES
SPACE STORIES

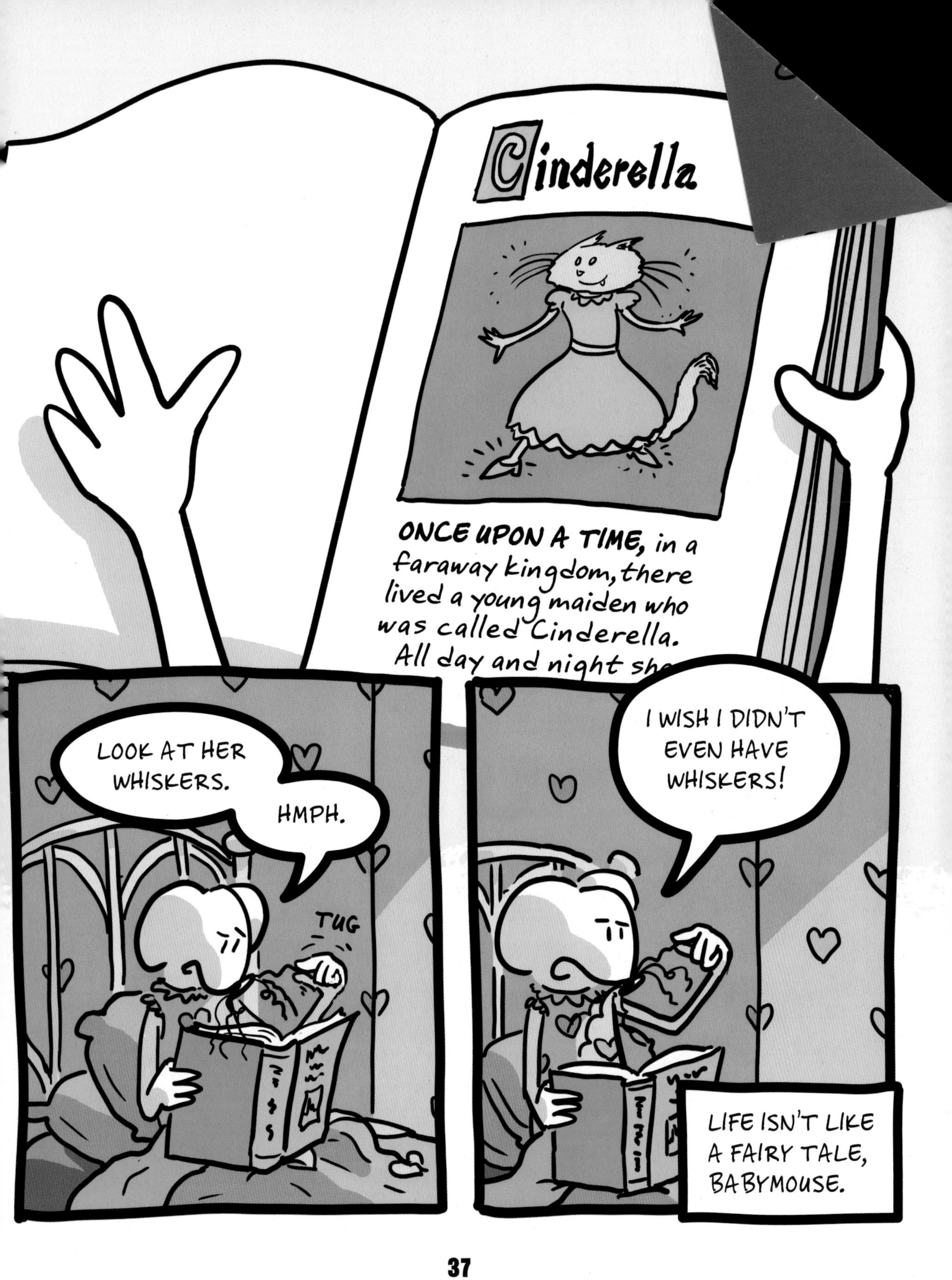

Cinderella
ONCE UPON A TIME, in a faraway kingdom, there lived a young maiden who was called Cinderella. All day and night she
LOOK AT HER WHISKERS.
HMPH.
TUG
I WISH I DIDN'T EVEN HAVE WHISKERS!
LIFE ISN'T LIKE A FAIRY TALE, BABYMOUSE.

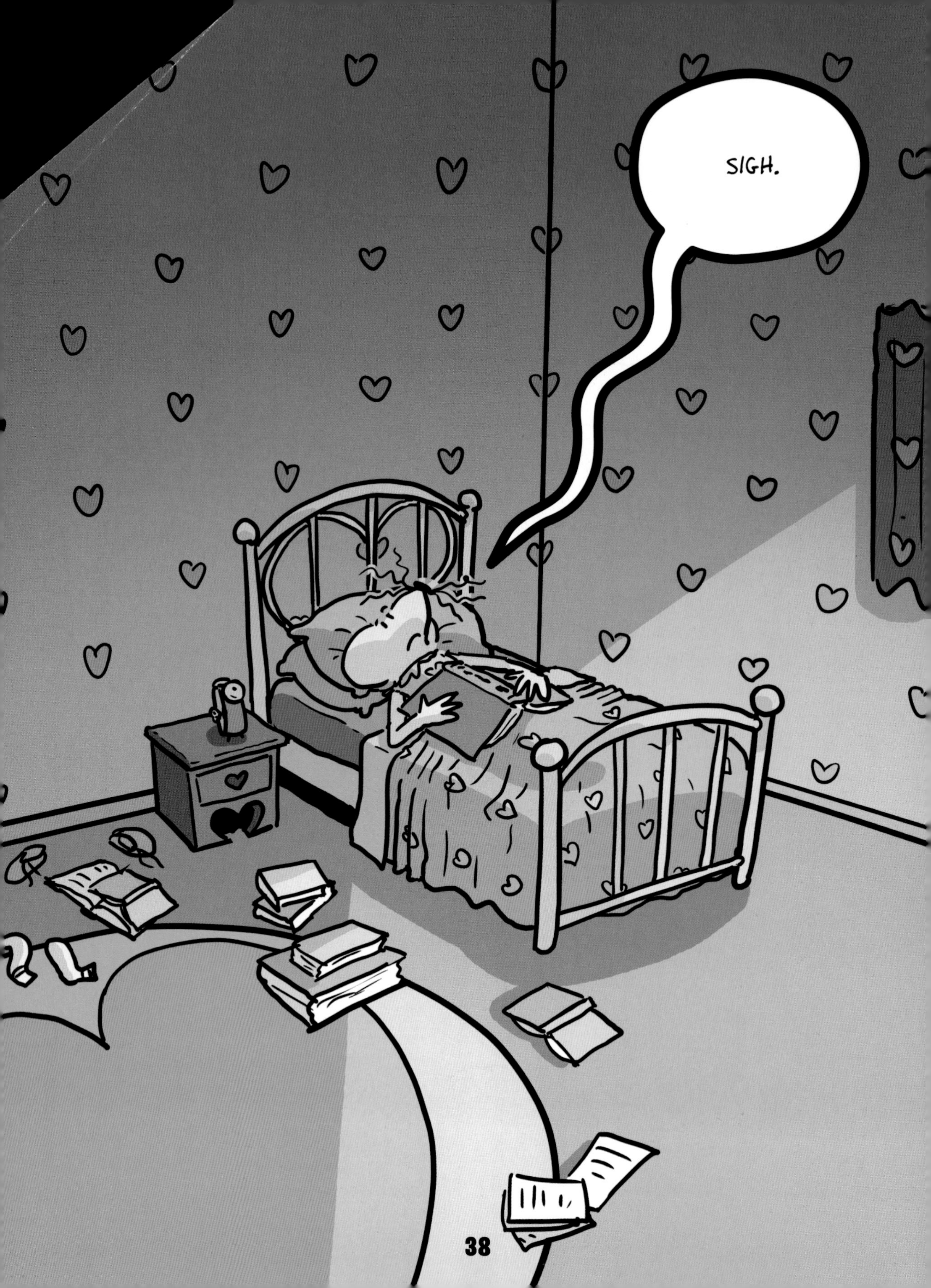
SIGH.

PART TWO

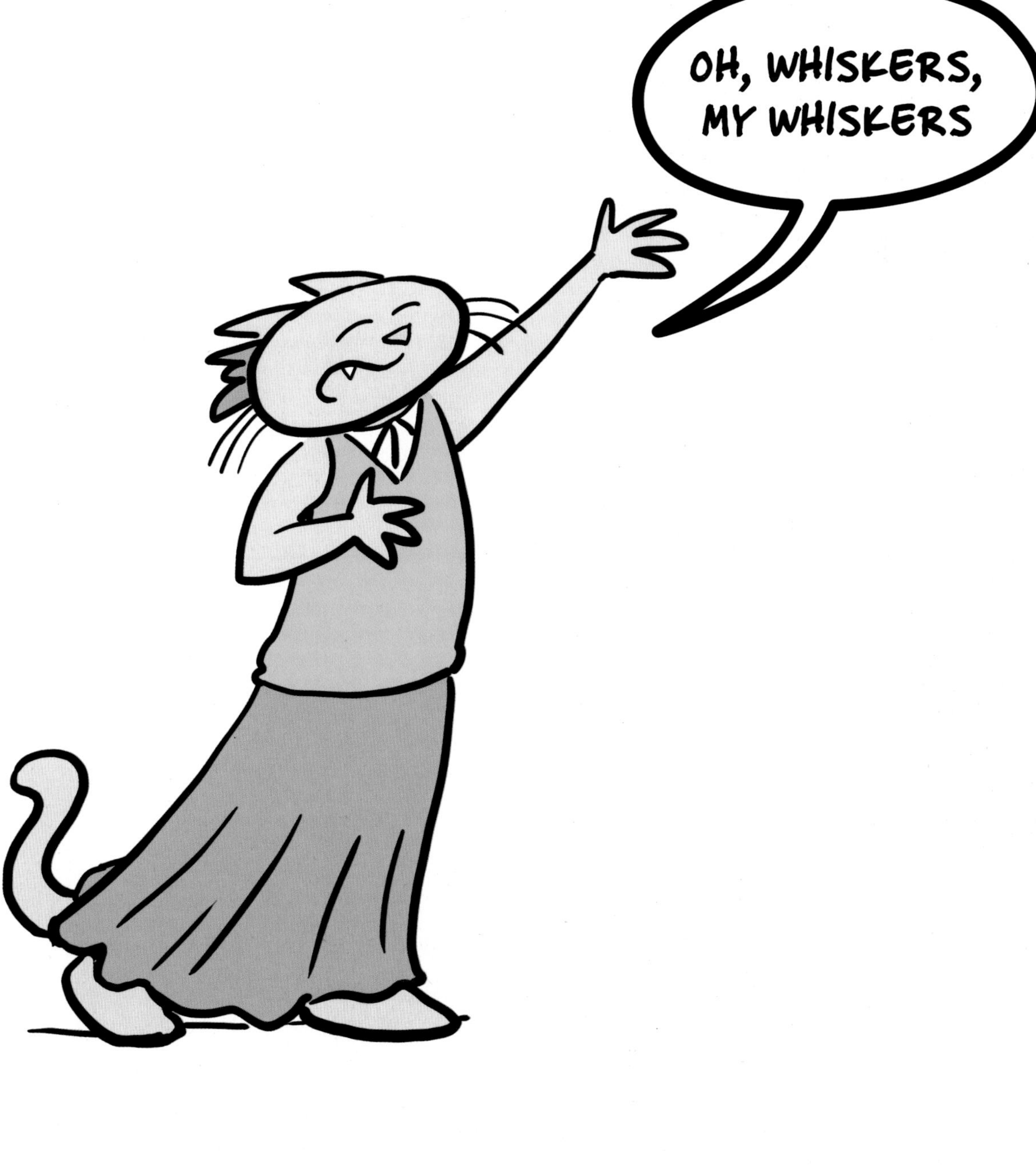
OH, WHISKERS, MY WHISKERS

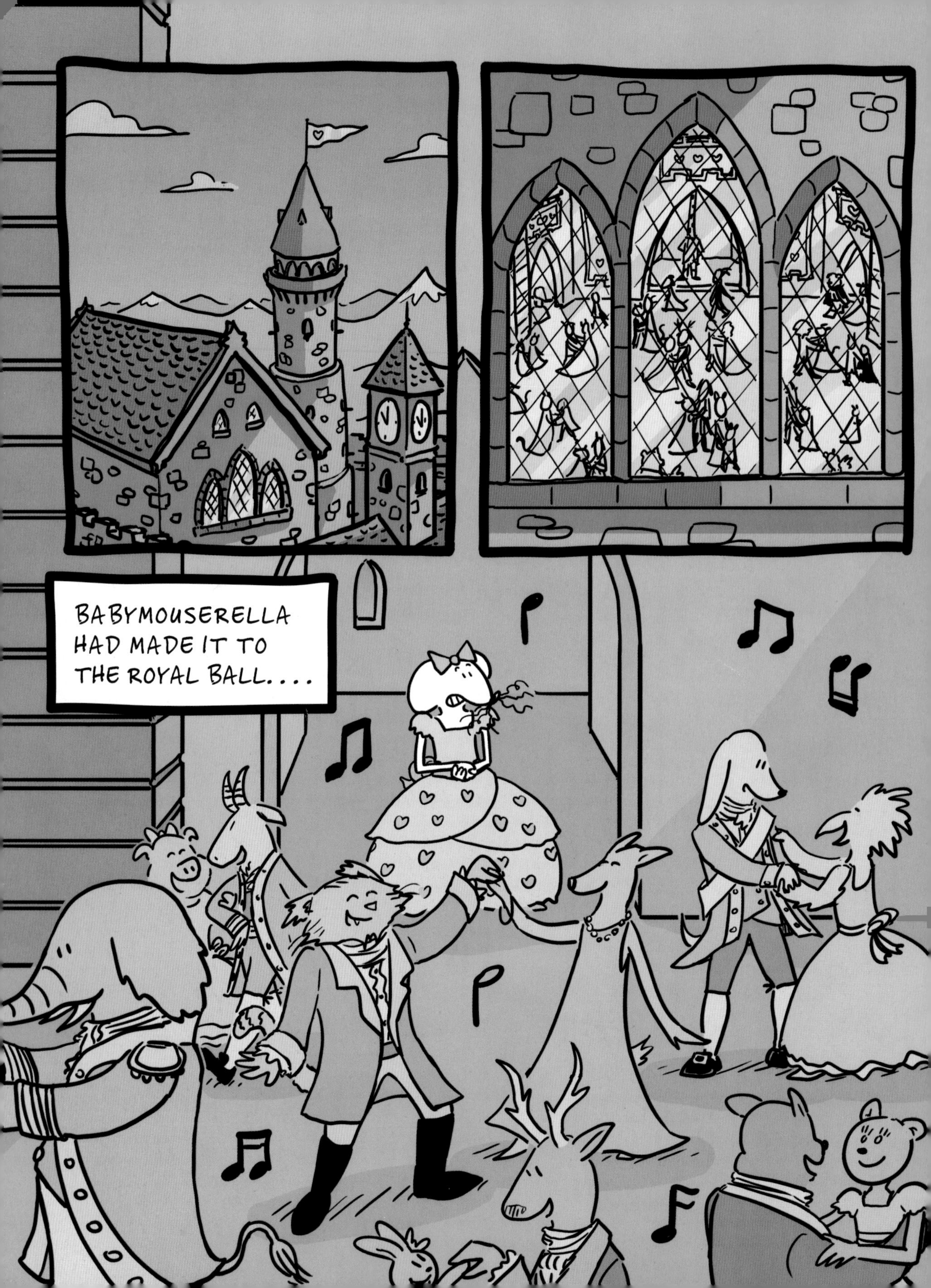
BABYMOUSERELLA HAD MADE IT TO THE ROYAL BALL....

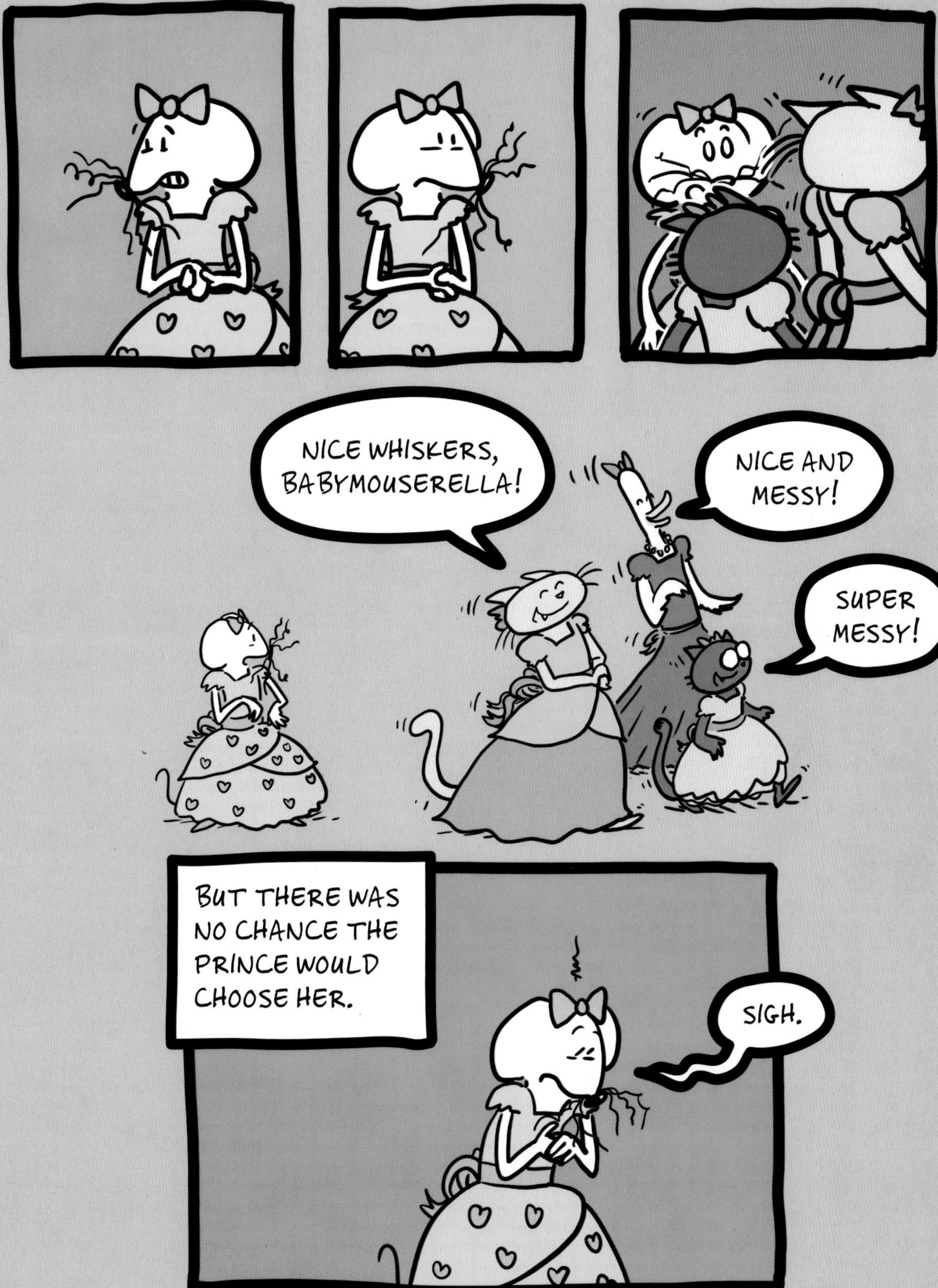
NICE WHISKERS, BABYMOUSERELLA!
NICE AND MESSY!
SUPER MESSY!
BUT THERE WAS NO CHANCE THE PRINCE WOULD CHOOSE HER.
SIGH.

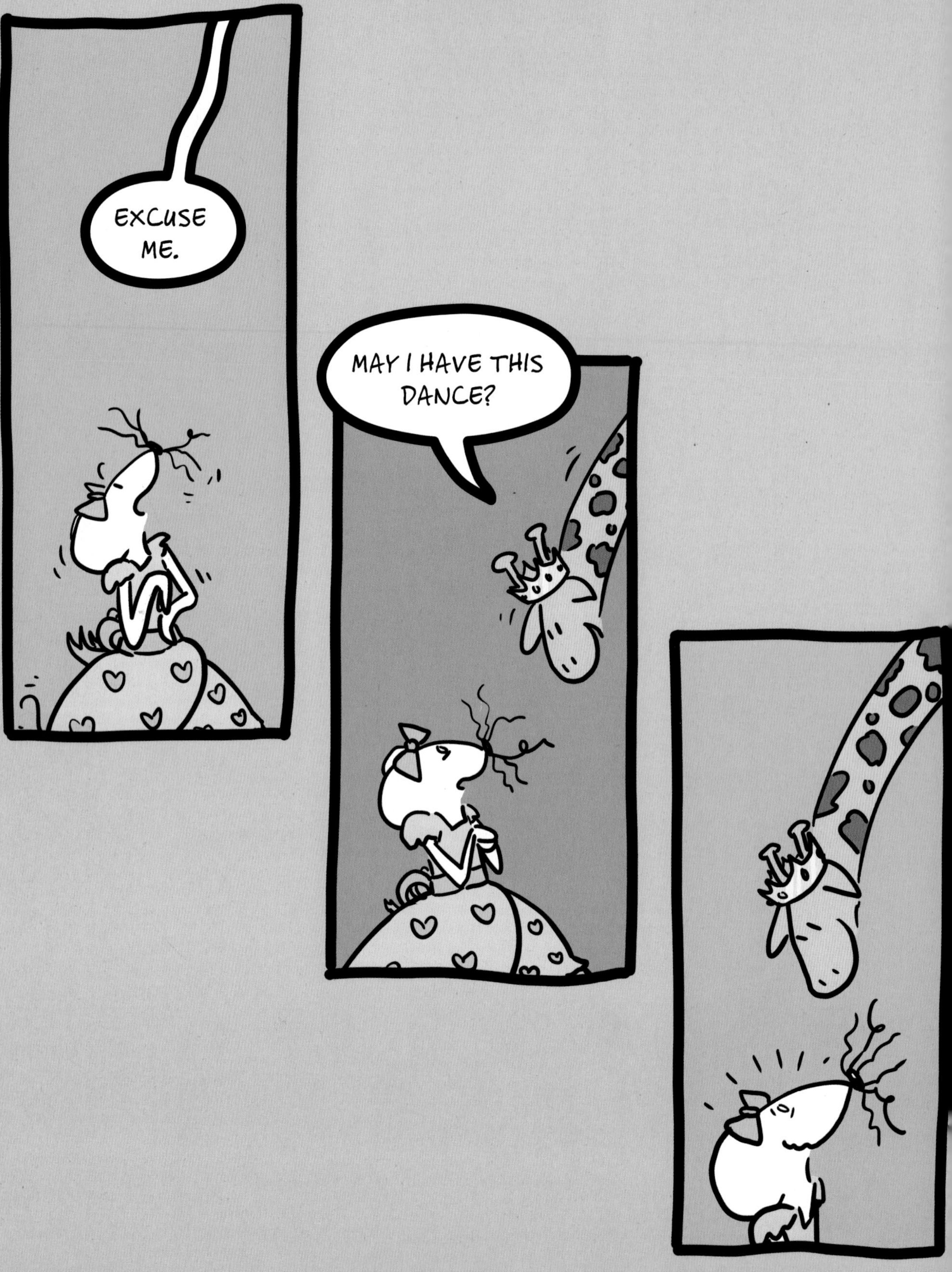
EXCUSE ME.
MAY I HAVE THIS DANCE?

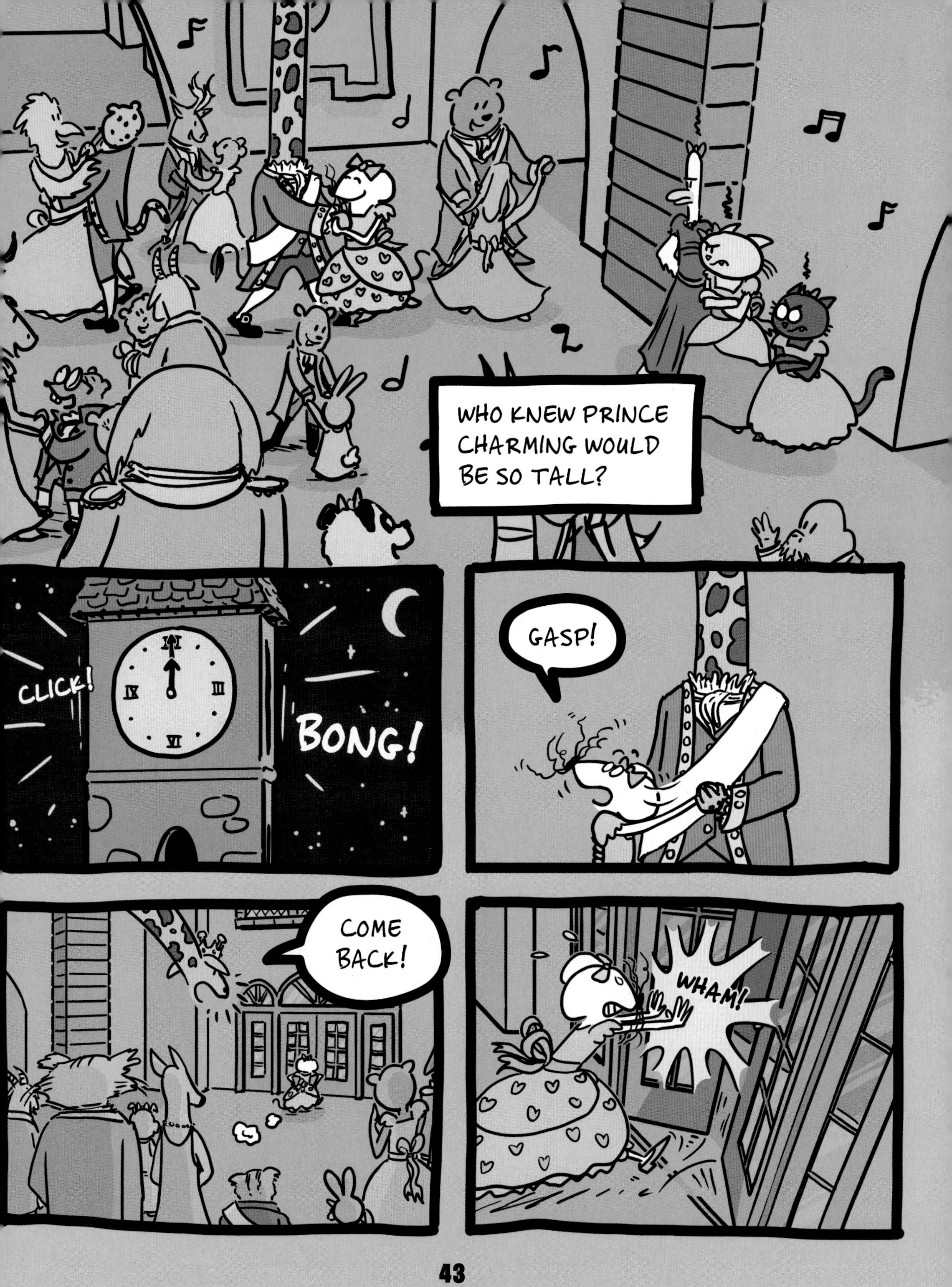
WHO KNEW PRINCE CHARMING WOULD BE SO TALL?
CLICK!
BONG!
GASP!
COME BACK!
WHAM!

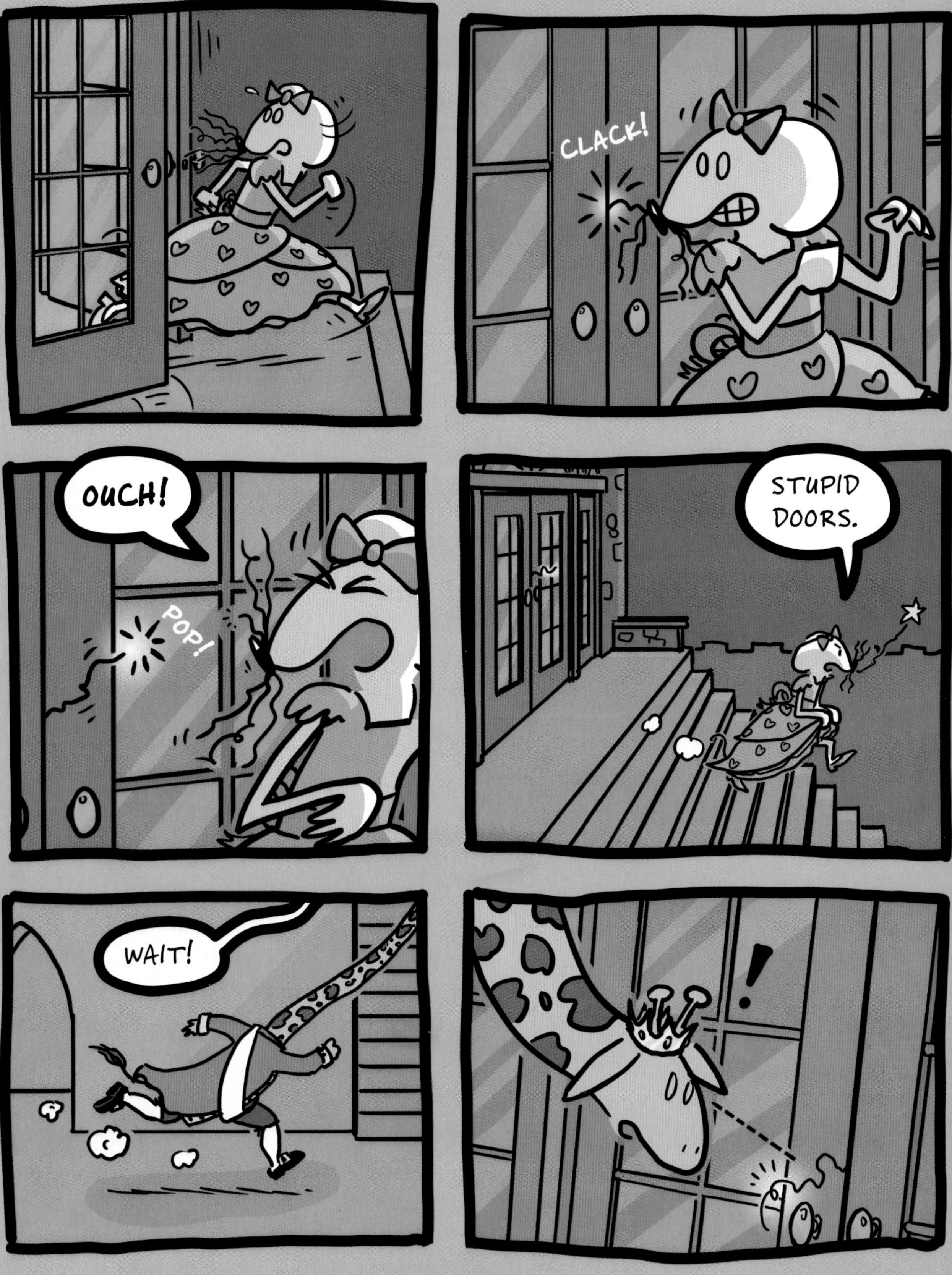
CLACK!
OUCH!
POP!
STUPID DOORS.
WAIT!
!

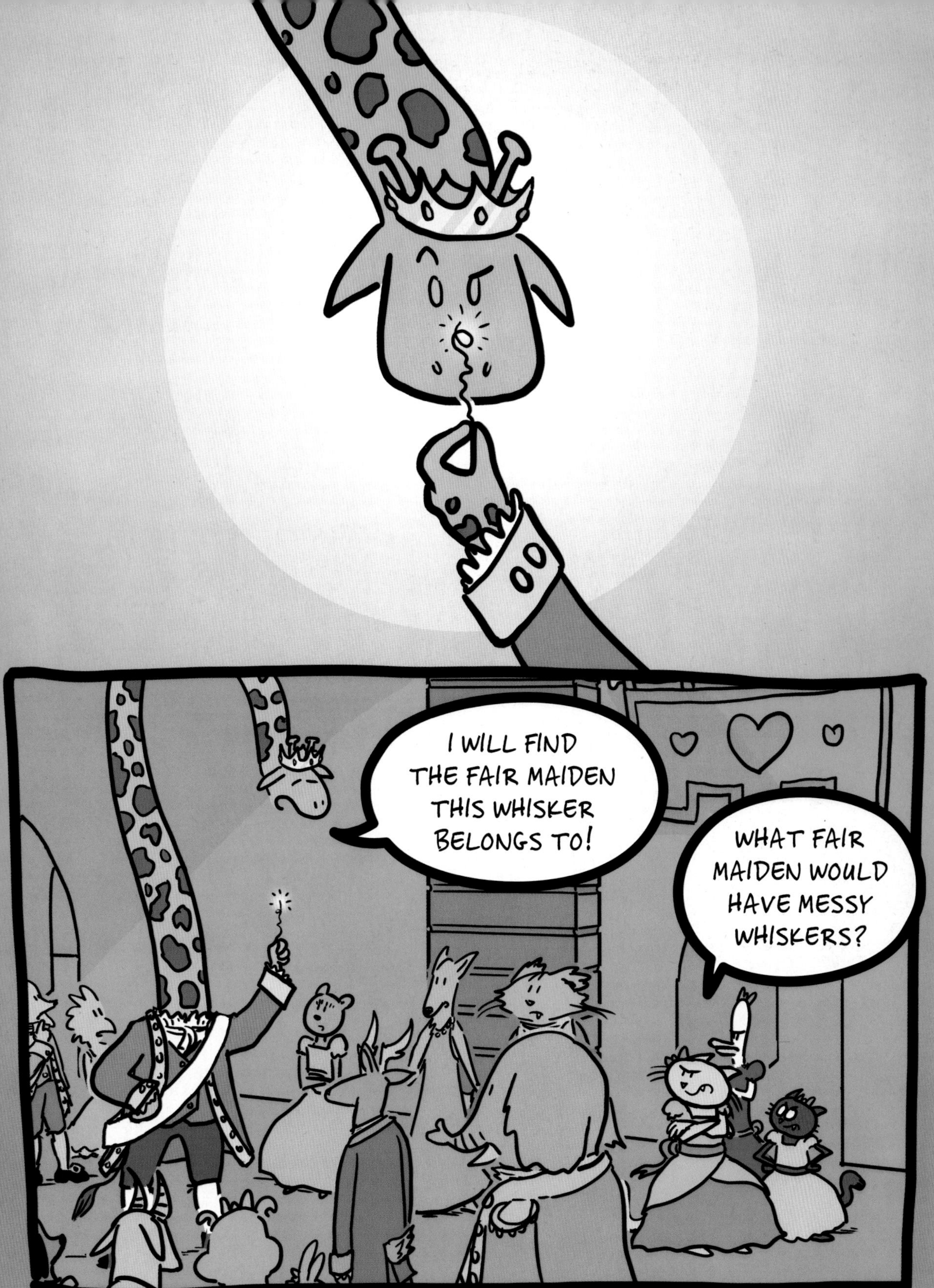
I WILL FIND THE FAIR MAIDEN THIS WHISKER BELONGS TO!
WHAT FAIR MAIDEN WOULD HAVE MESSY WHISKERS?

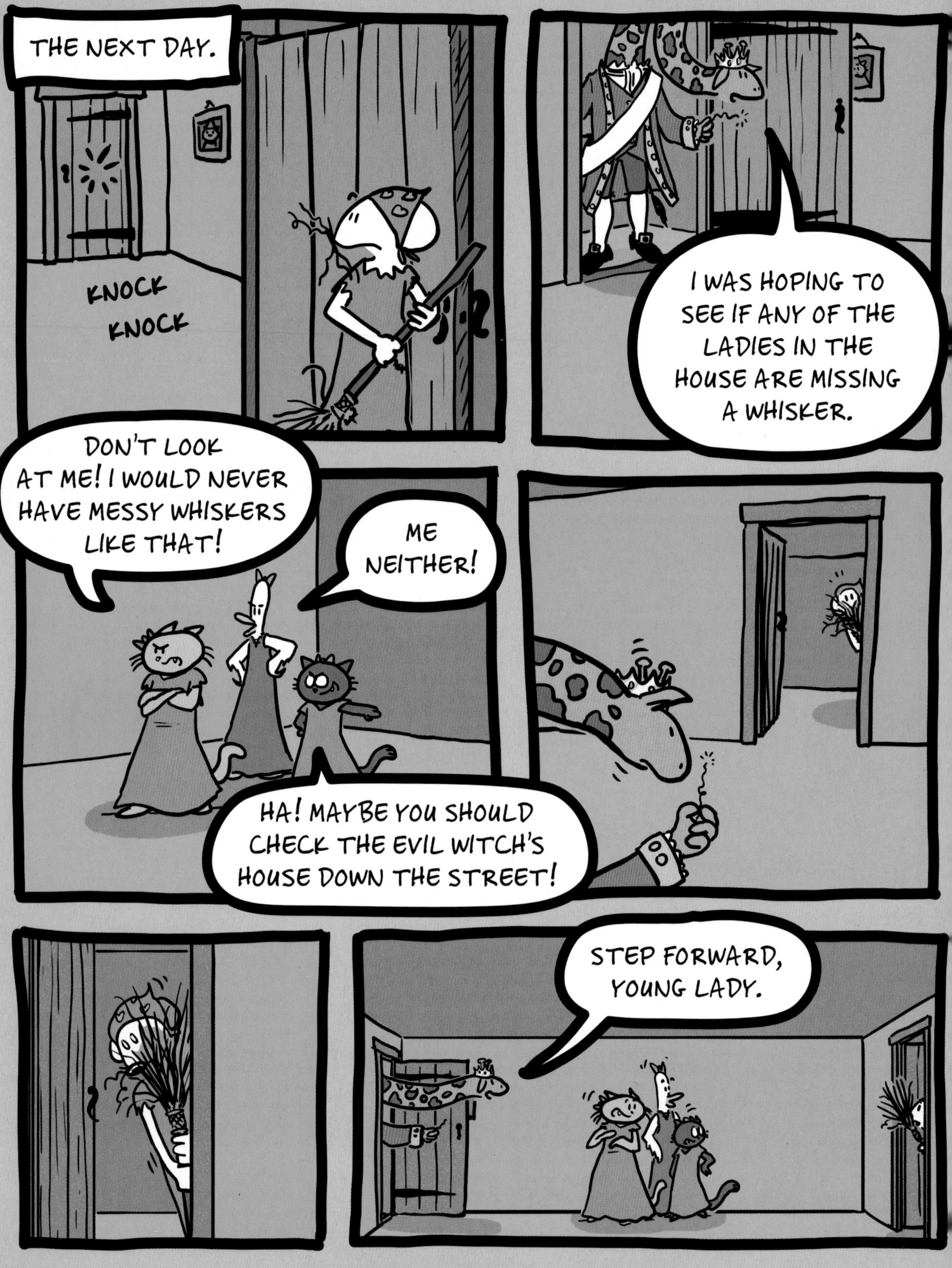
THE NEXT DAY.
KNOCK KNOCK
I WAS HOPING TO SEE IF ANY OF THE LADIES IN THE HOUSE ARE MISSING A WHISKER.
DON'T LOOK AT ME! I WOULD NEVER HAVE MESSY WHISKERS LIKE THAT!
ME NEITHER!
HA! MAYBE YOU SHOULD CHECK THE EVIL WITCH'S HOUSE DOWN THE STREET!
STEP FORWARD, YOUNG LADY.

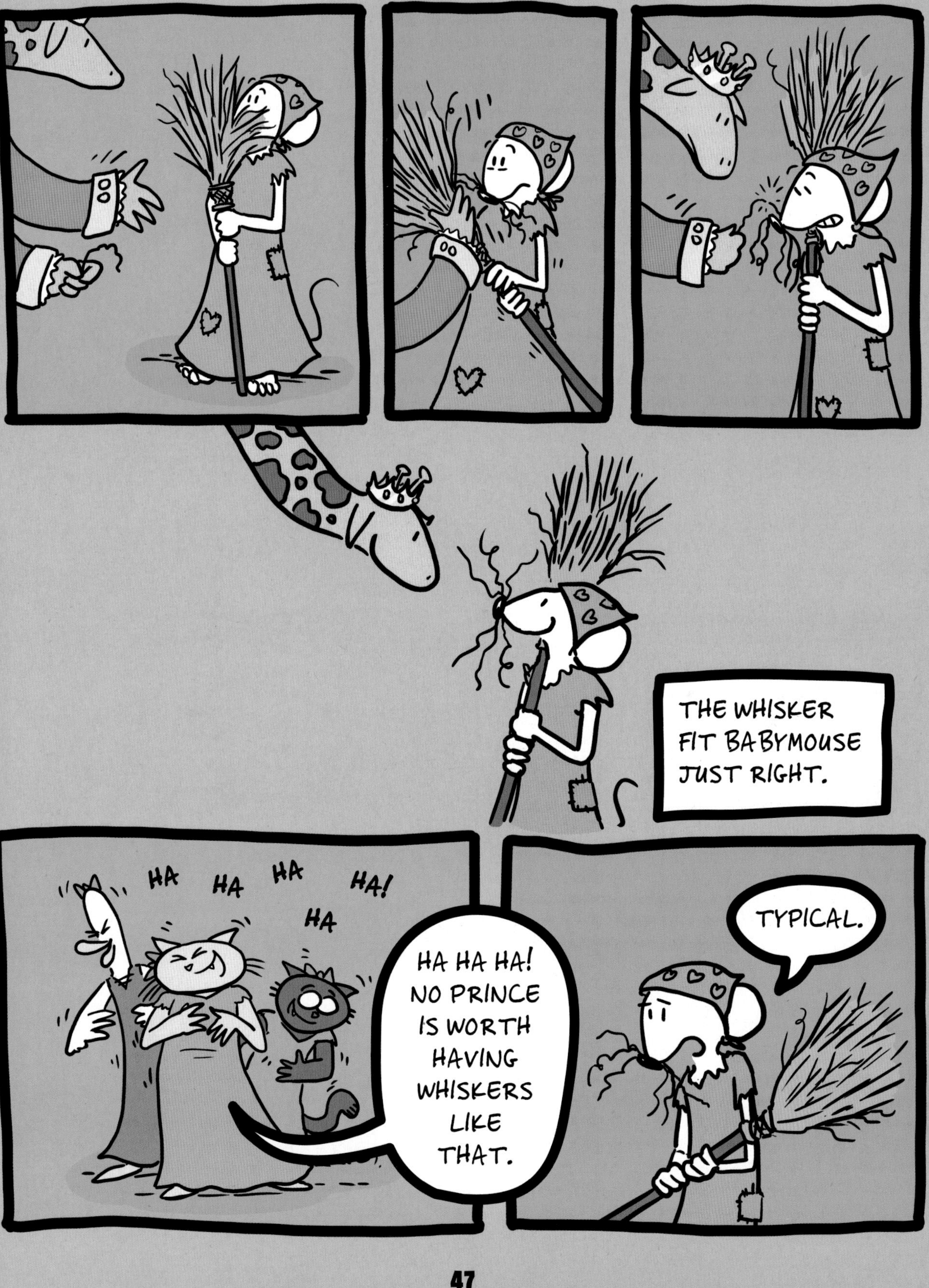
THE WHISKER FIT BABYMOUSE JUST RIGHT.
HA HA HA HA! HA
HA HA HA! NO PRINCE IS WORTH HAVING WHISKERS LIKE THAT.
TYPICAL.

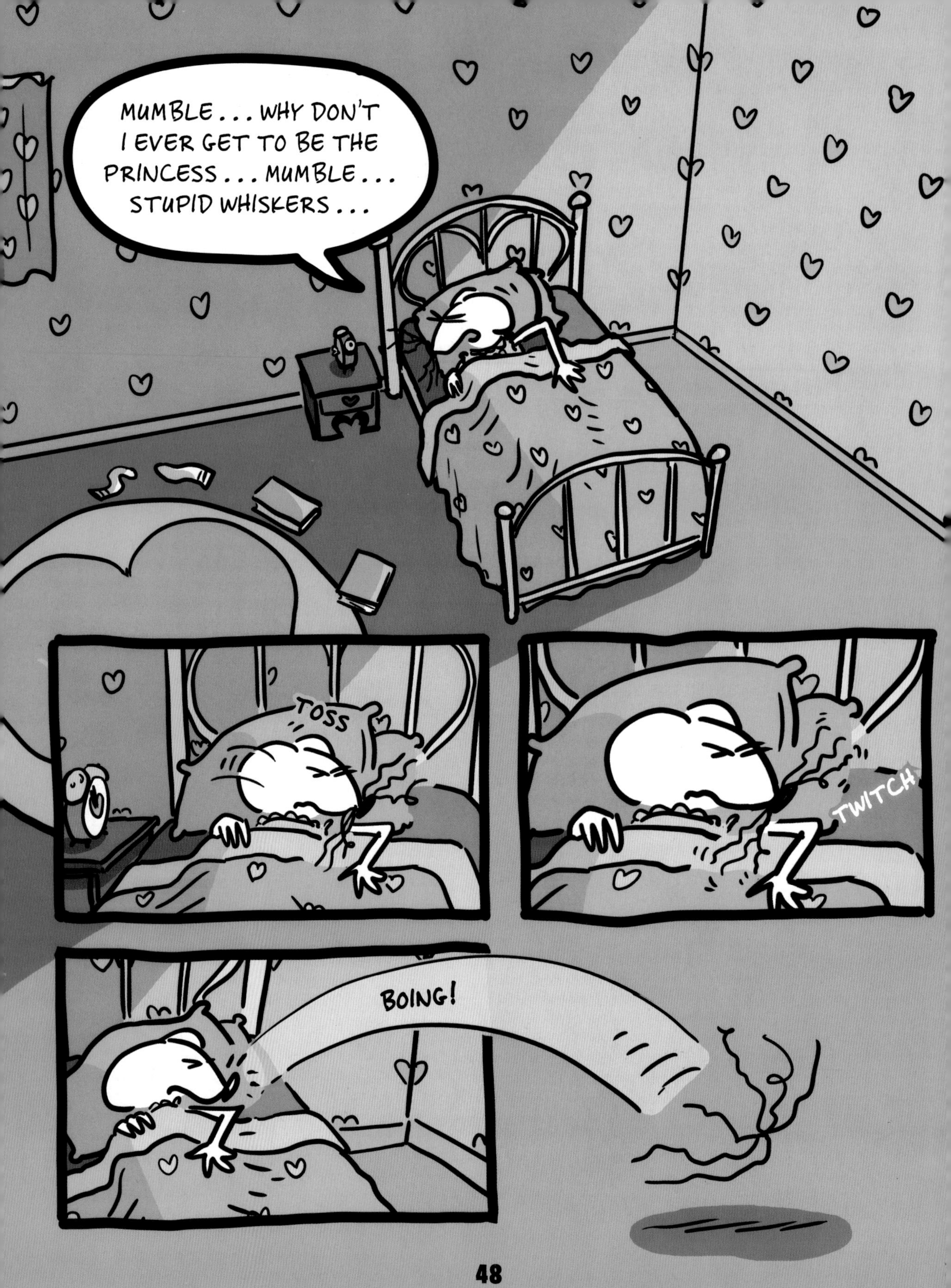
MUMBLE . . . WHY DON'T I EVER GET TO BE THE PRINCESS . . . MUMBLE . . . STUPID WHISKERS . . .
TOSS
TWITCH
BOING!

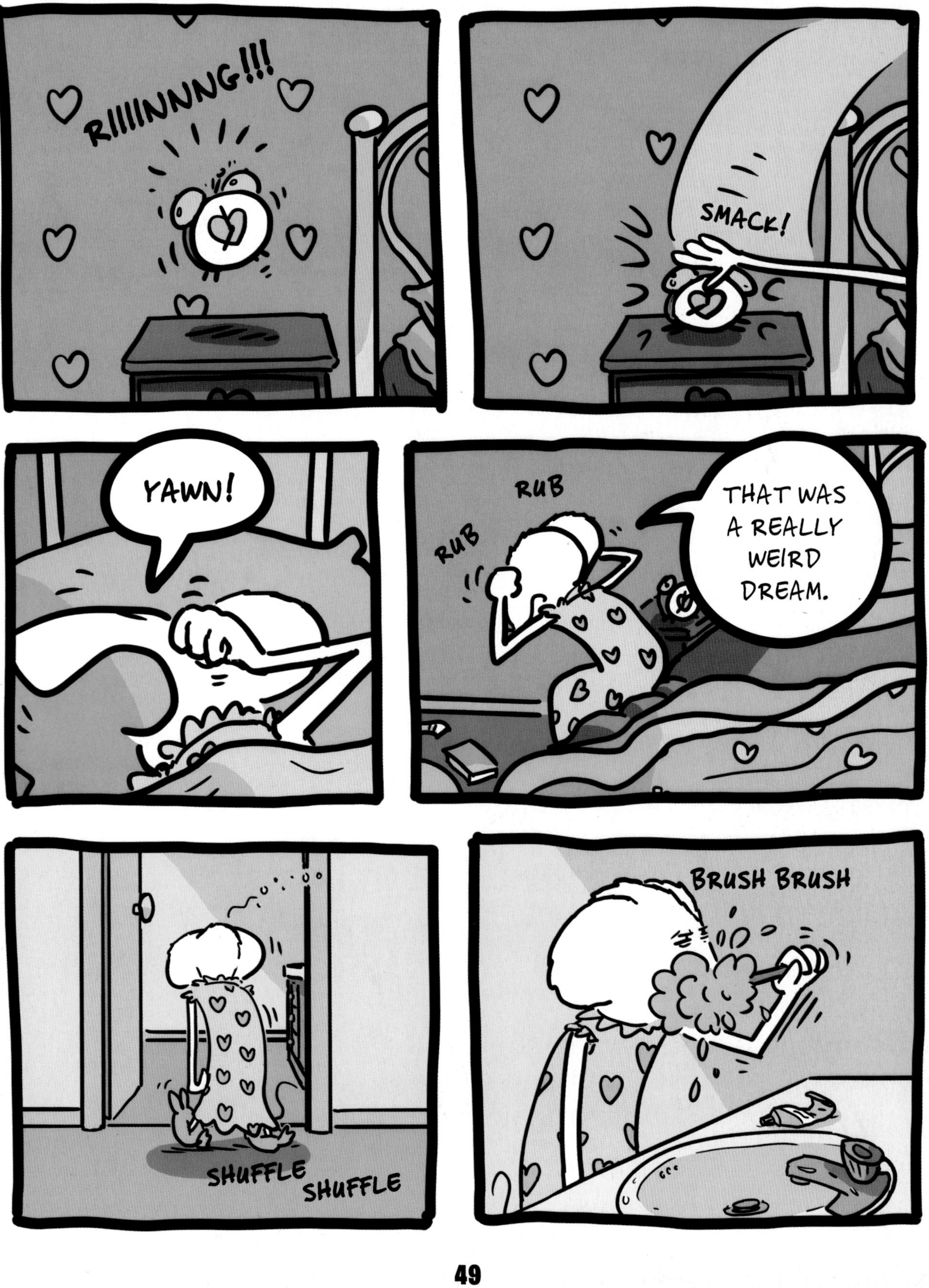
RIIIINNNG!!!
SMACK!
YAWN!
RUB
RUB
THAT WAS A REALLY WEIRD DREAM.
SHUFFLE
SHUFFLE
BRUSH BRUSH

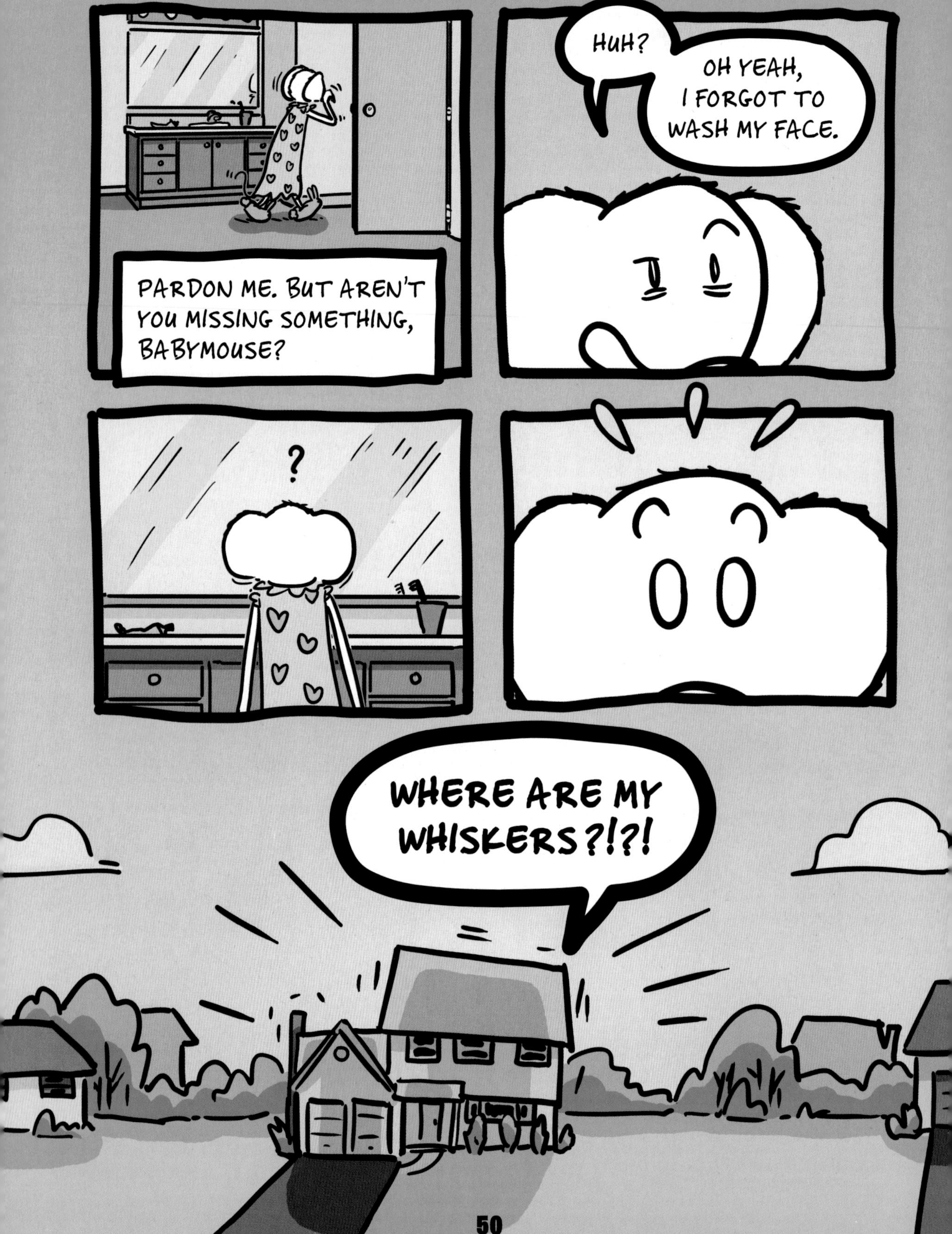
PARDON ME. BUT AREN'T YOU MISSING SOMETHING, BABYMOUSE?
HUH?
OH YEAH, I FORGOT TO WASH MY FACE.
?
WHERE ARE MY WHISKERS?!?!

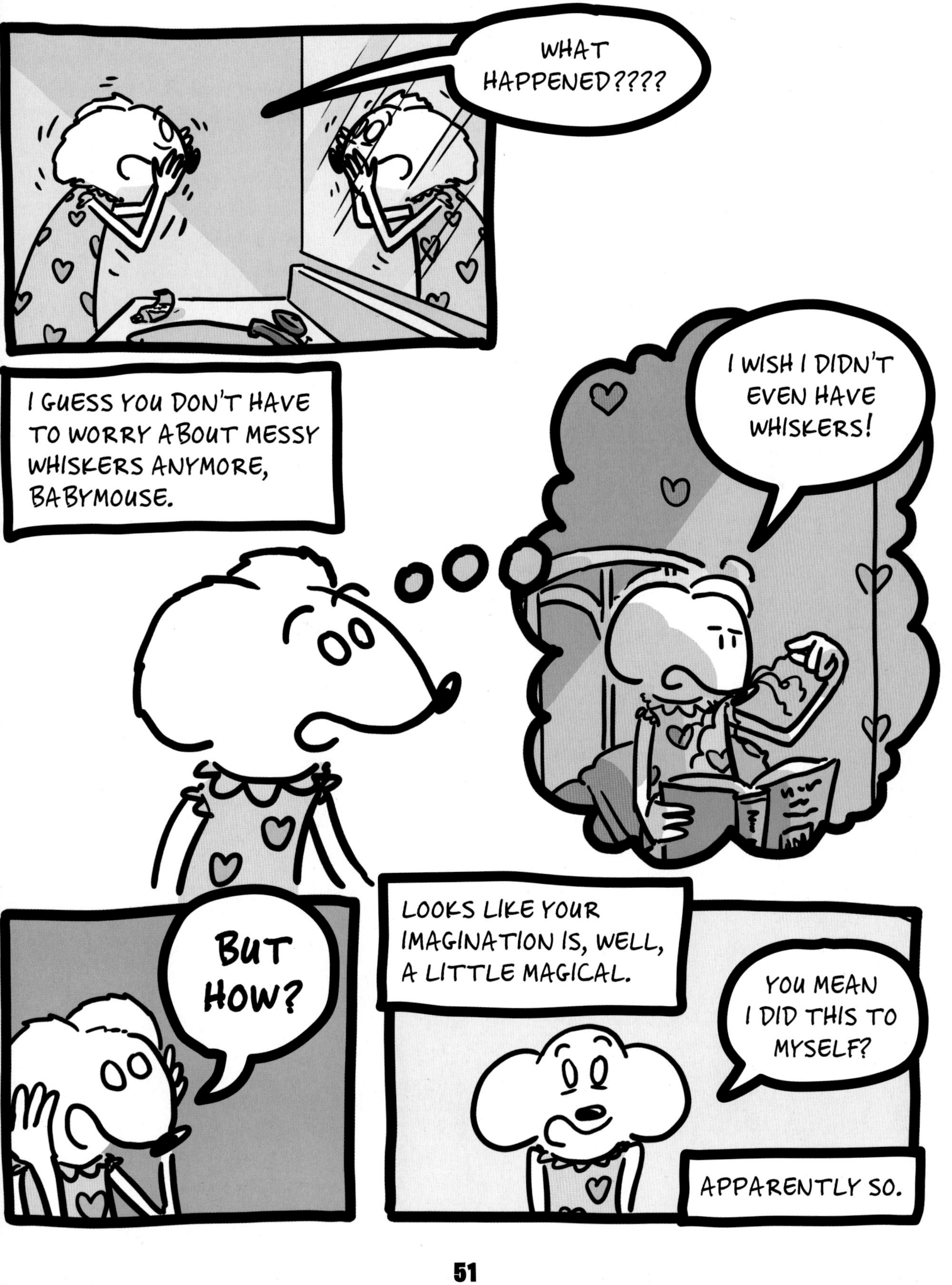
WHAT HAPPENED????
I GUESS YOU DON'T HAVE TO WORRY ABOUT MESSY WHISKERS ANYMORE, BABYMOUSE.
I WISH I DIDN'T EVEN HAVE WHISKERS!
BUT HOW?
LOOKS LIKE YOUR IMAGINATION IS, WELL, A LITTLE MAGICAL.
YOU MEAN I DID THIS TO MYSELF?
APPARENTLY SO.

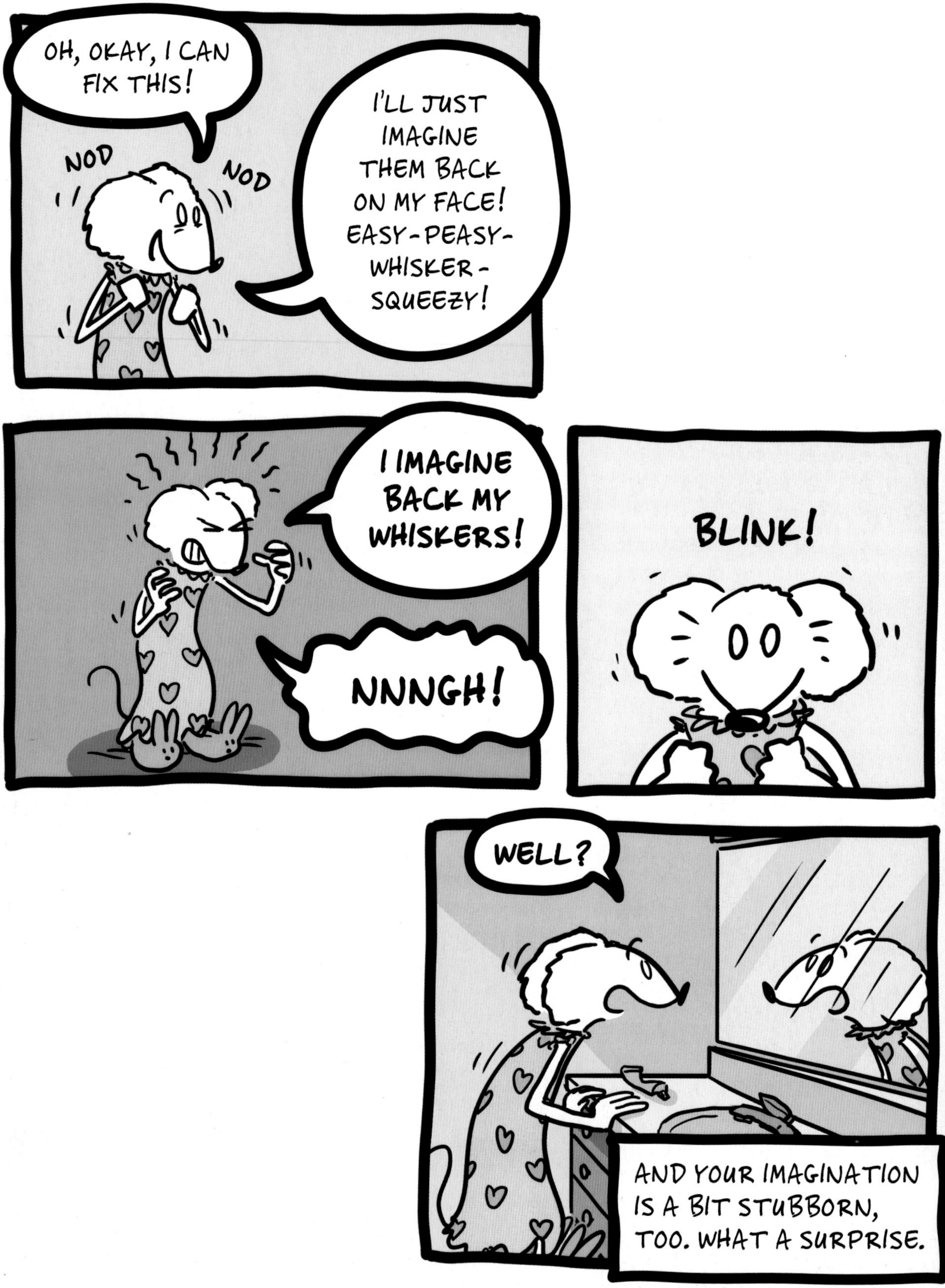

OH, OKAY, I CAN FIX THIS!
NOD NOD
I'LL JUST IMAGINE THEM BACK ON MY FACE! EASY-PEASY-WHISKER-SQUEEZY!
I IMAGINE BACK MY WHISKERS!
NNNGH!
BLINK!
WELL?
AND YOUR IMAGINATION IS A BIT STUBBORN, TOO. WHAT A SURPRISE.

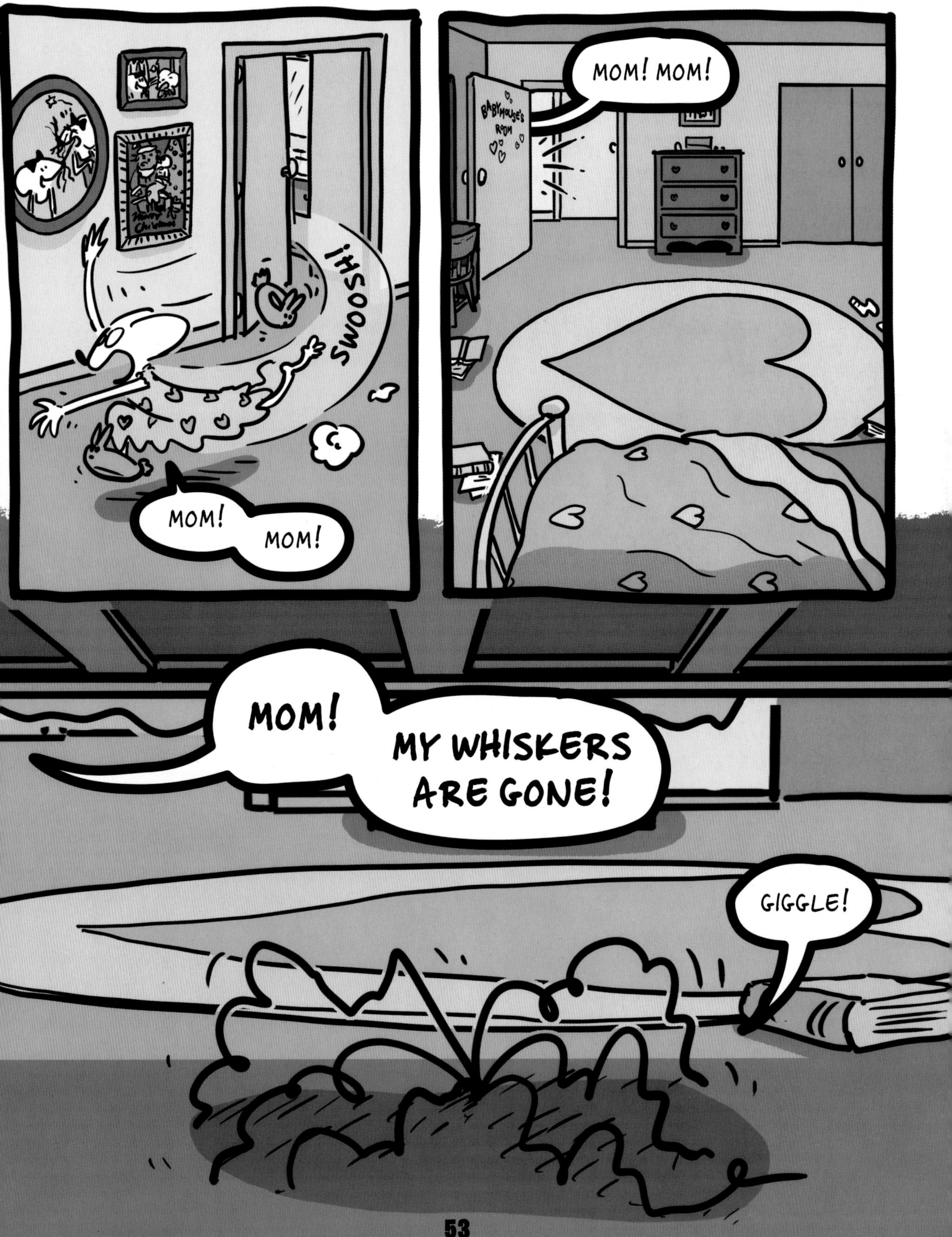
SWOOSH!
MOM!
MOM!
MOM! MOM!
BABYMOUSE'S ROOM
MOM!
MY WHISKERS ARE GONE!
GIGGLE!

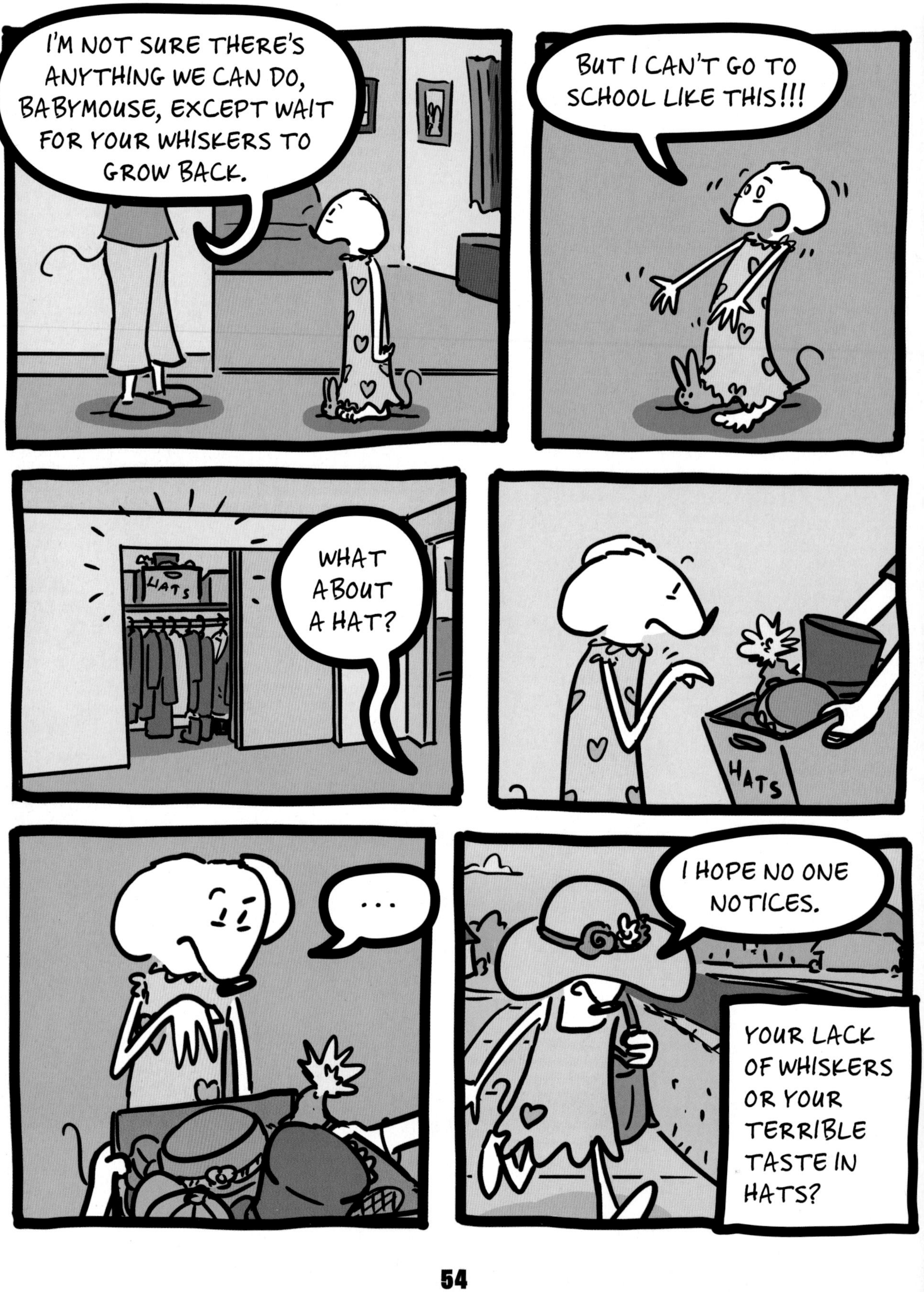
I'M NOT SURE THERE'S ANYTHING WE CAN DO, BABYMOUSE, EXCEPT WAIT FOR YOUR WHISKERS TO GROW BACK.
BUT I CAN'T GO TO SCHOOL LIKE THIS!!!
HATS
WHAT ABOUT A HAT?
HATS
...
I HOPE NO ONE NOTICES.
YOUR LACK OF WHISKERS OR YOUR TERRIBLE TASTE IN HATS?

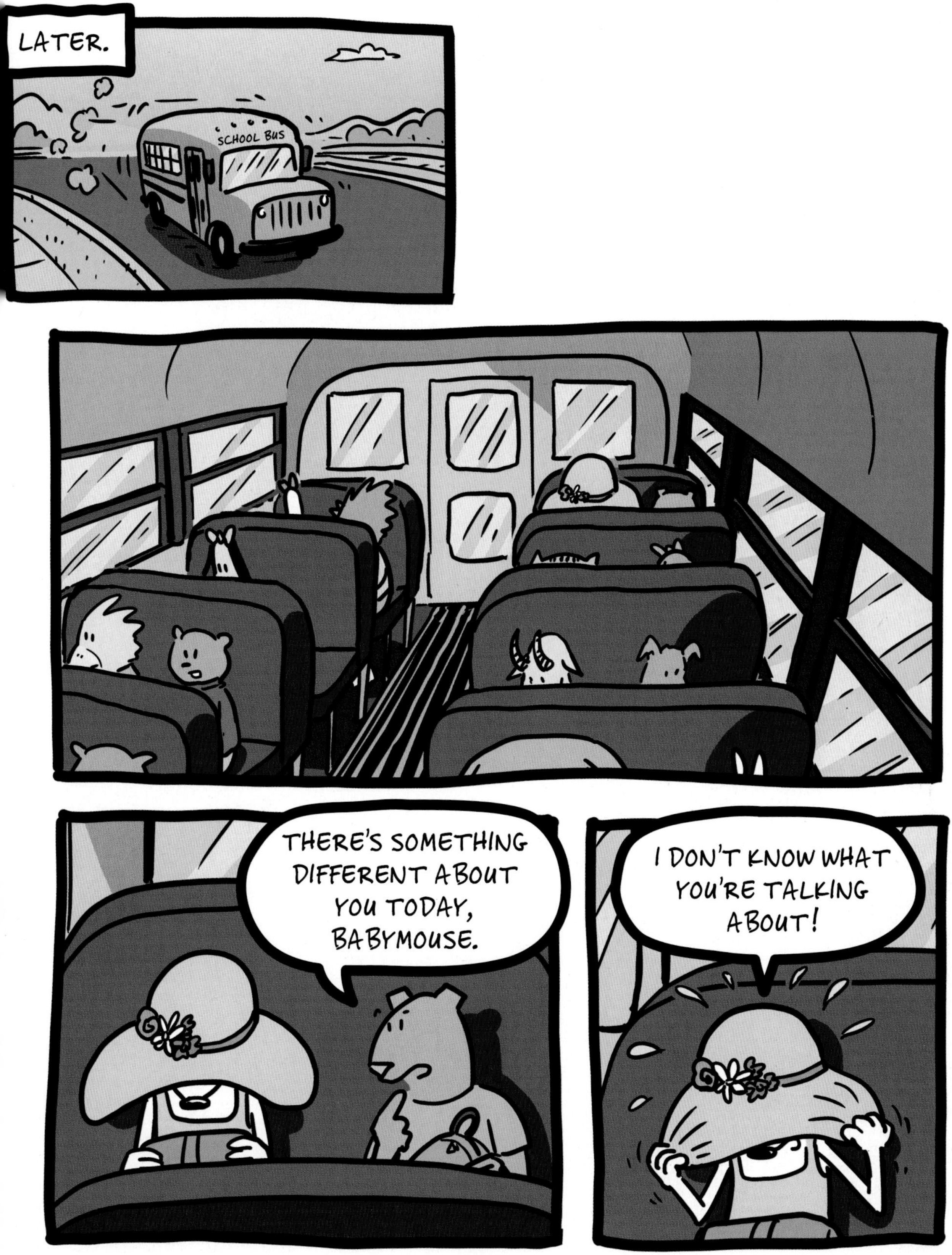
LATER.
SCHOOL BUS
THERE'S SOMETHING DIFFERENT ABOUT YOU TODAY, BABYMOUSE.
I DON'T KNOW WHAT YOU'RE TALKING ABOUT!

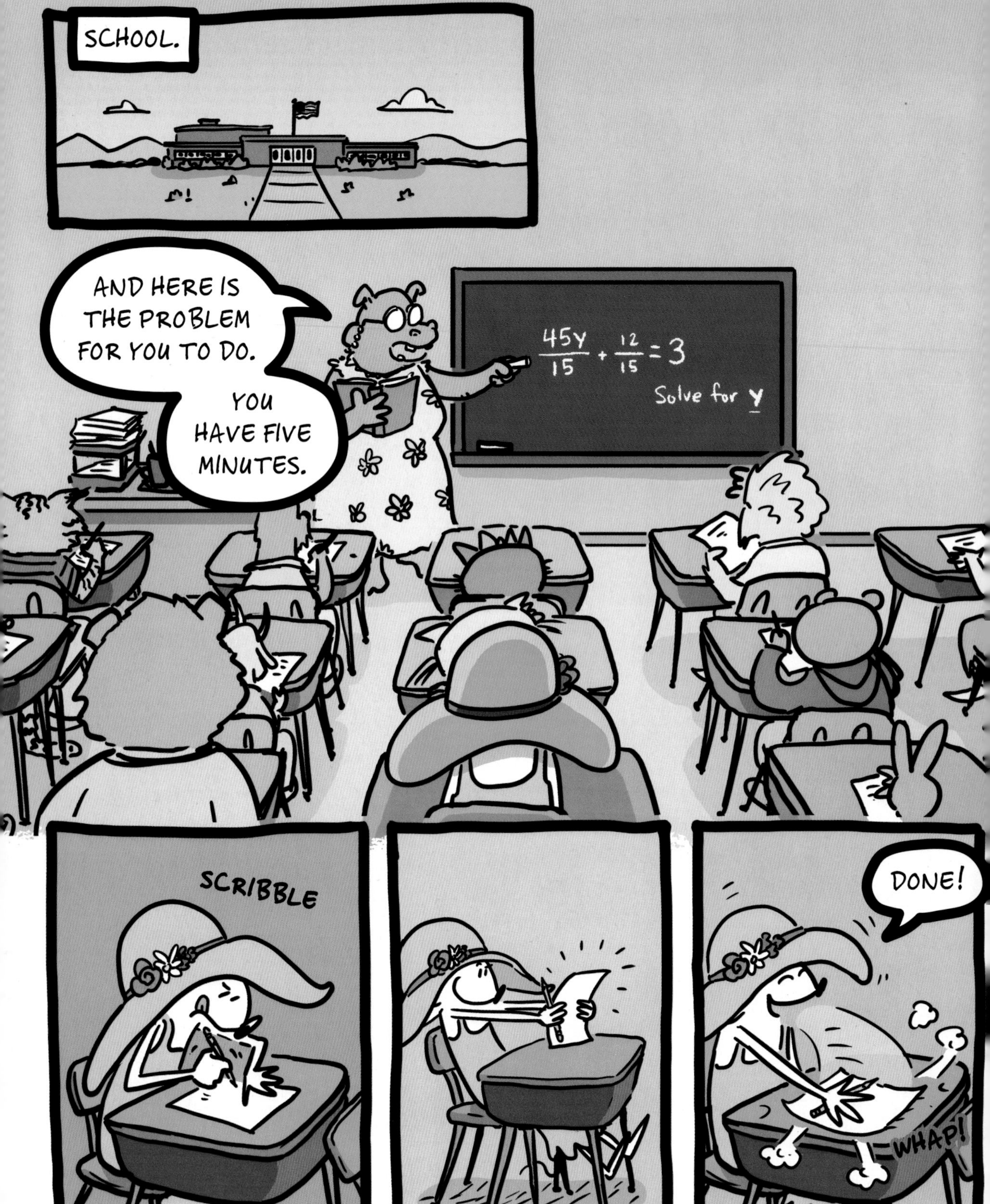
SCHOOL.
AND HERE IS THE PROBLEM FOR YOU TO DO.
YOU HAVE FIVE MINUTES.
45y/15 + 12/15 = 3
Solve for y
SCRIBBLE
DONE!
WHAP!

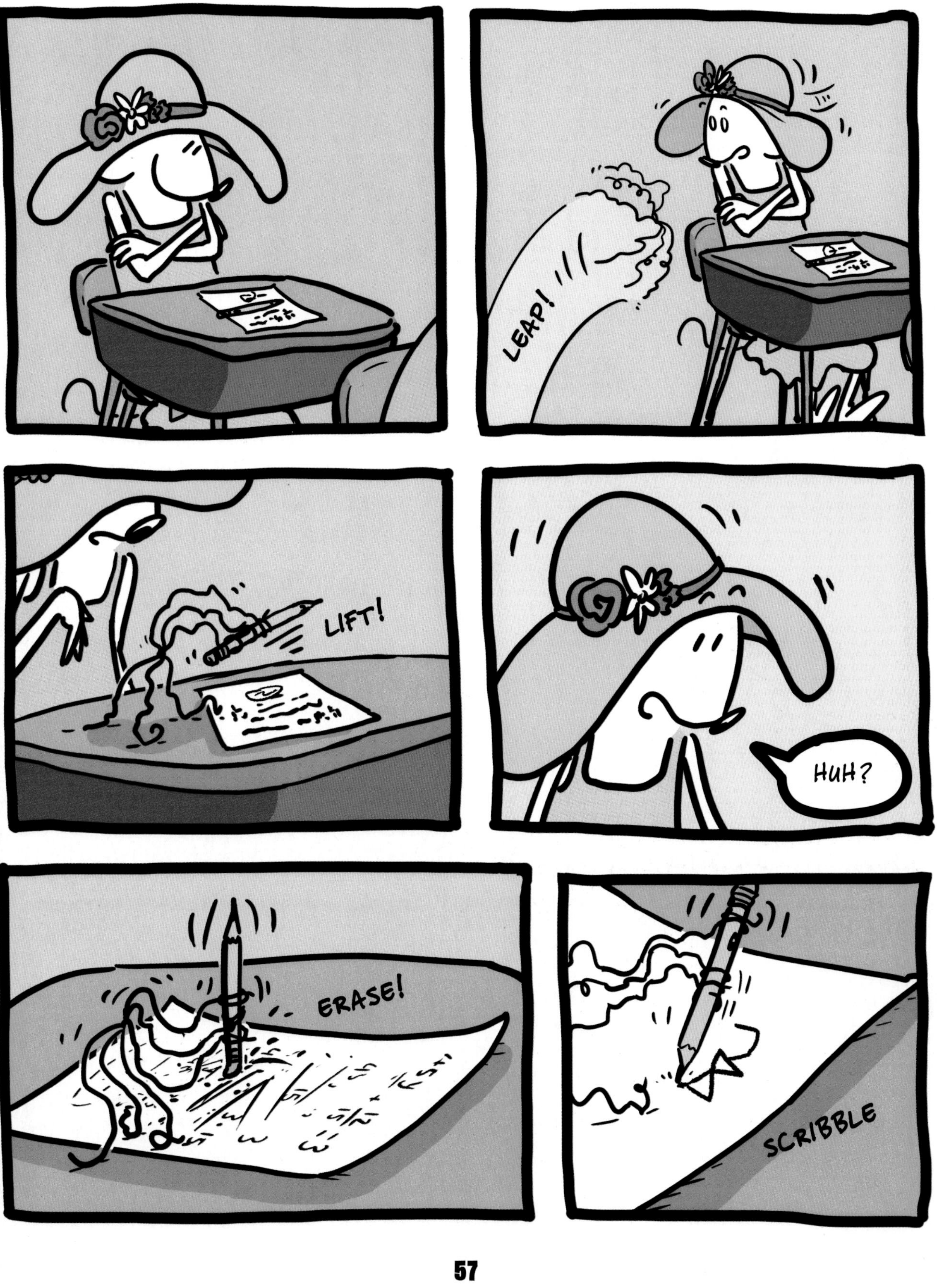
LEAP!
LIFT!
HUH?
ERASE!
SCRIBBLE

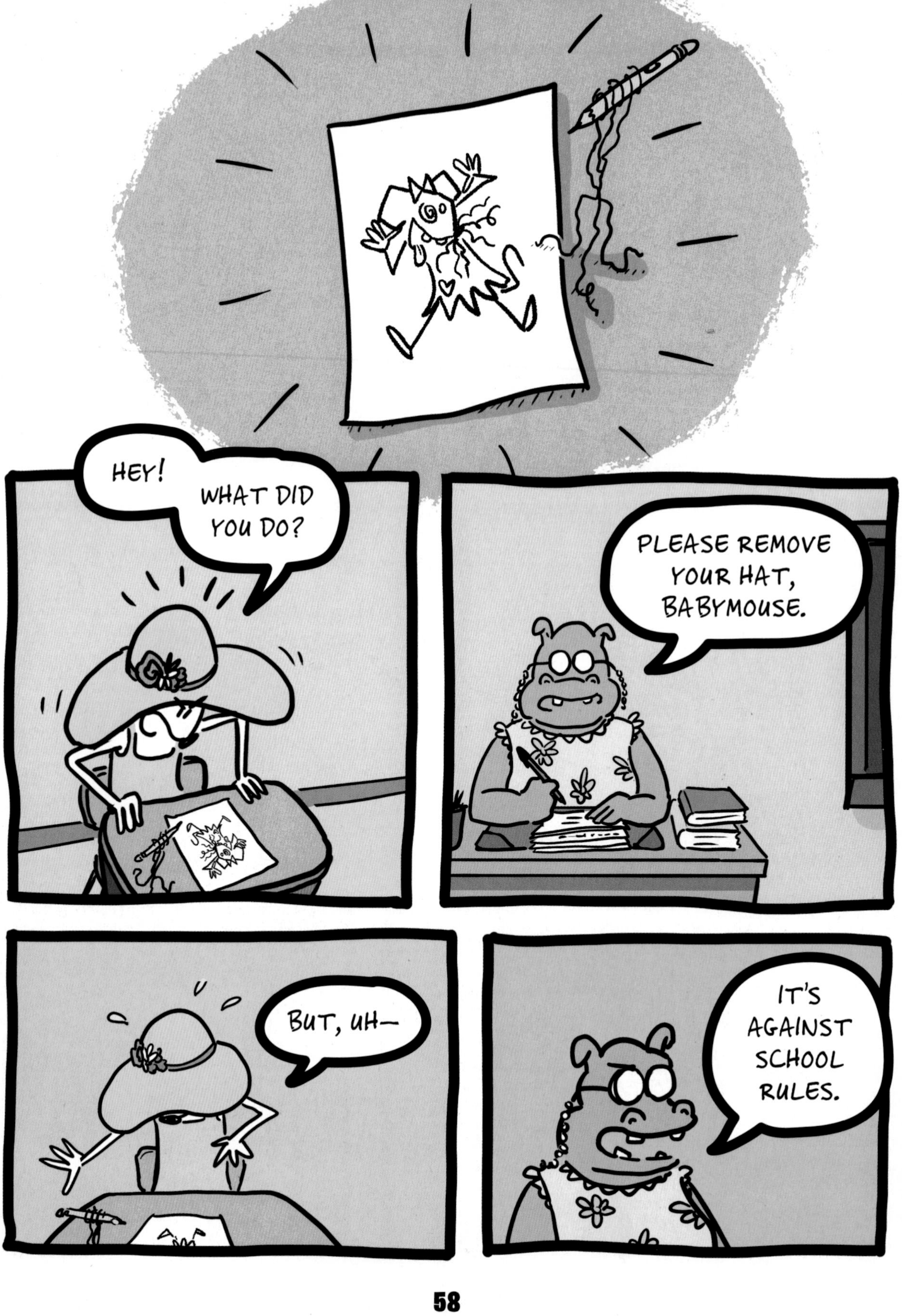
HEY!
WHAT DID YOU DO?
PLEASE REMOVE YOUR HAT, BABYMOUSE.
BUT, UH—
IT'S AGAINST SCHOOL RULES.

HA HA HA HA HA HA HA HA HA!!

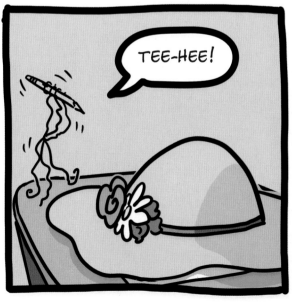

TEE-HEE!

HA   HA   HA   HA!
HA
SIGH.
SNICKER!

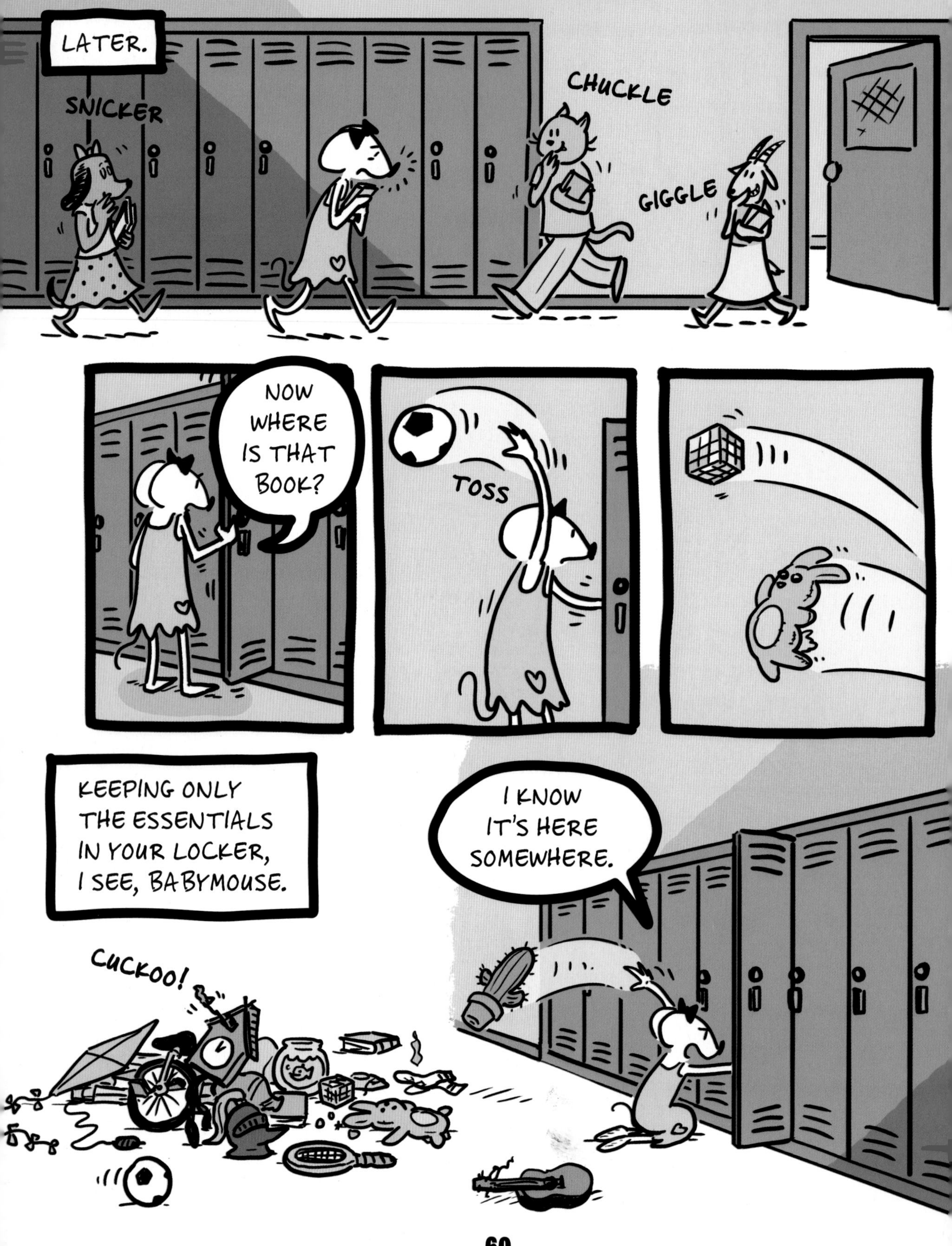
LATER.
SNICKER
CHUCKLE
GIGGLE
NOW WHERE IS THAT BOOK?
TOSS
KEEPING ONLY THE ESSENTIALS IN YOUR LOCKER, I SEE, BABYMOUSE.
I KNOW IT'S HERE SOMEWHERE.
CUCKOO!

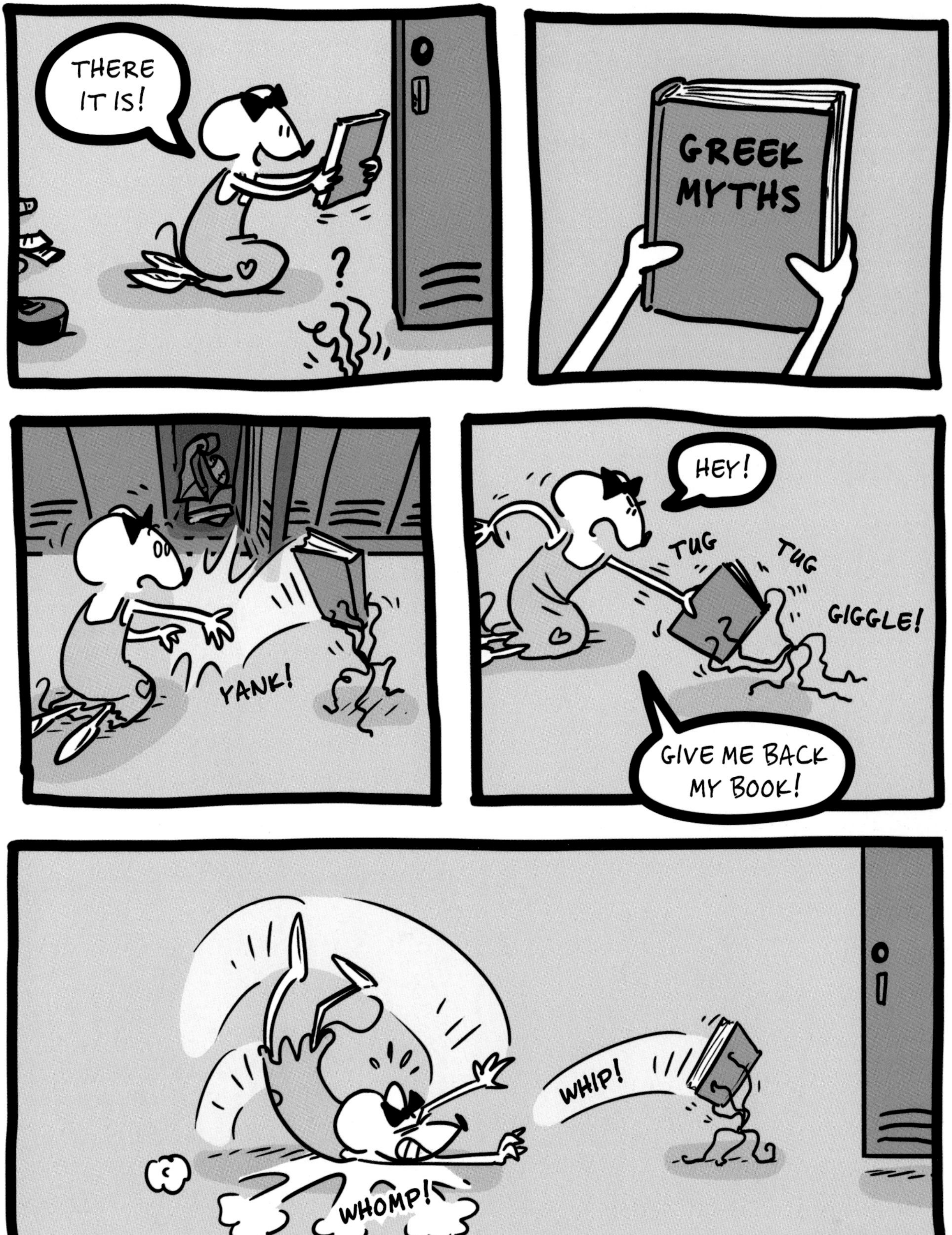
THERE IT IS!
?
GREEK MYTHS
YANK!
HEY!
TUG
TUG
GIGGLE!
GIVE ME BACK MY BOOK!
WHIP!
WHOMP!

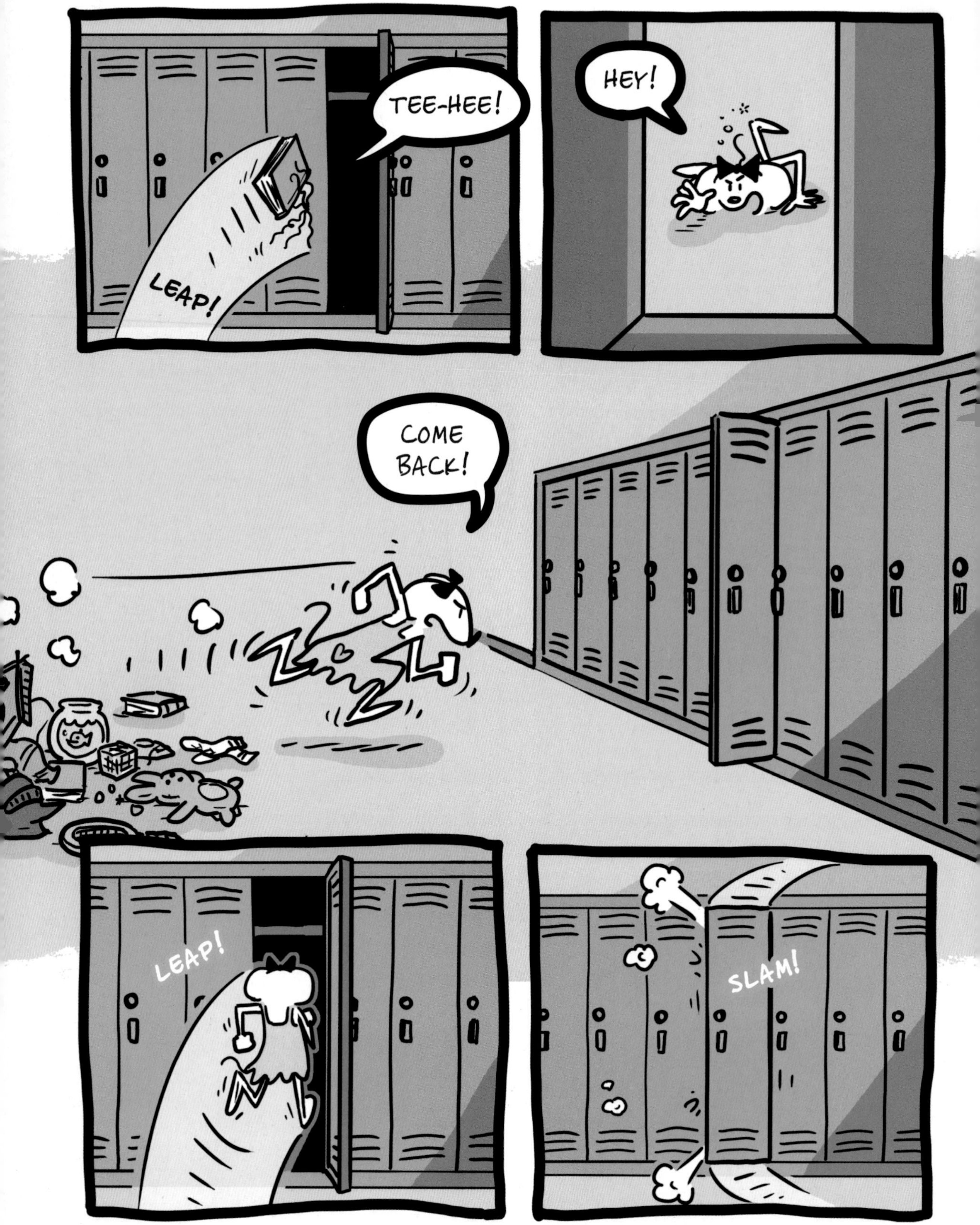
TEE-HEE!
LEAP!
HEY!
COME BACK!
LEAP!
SLAM!

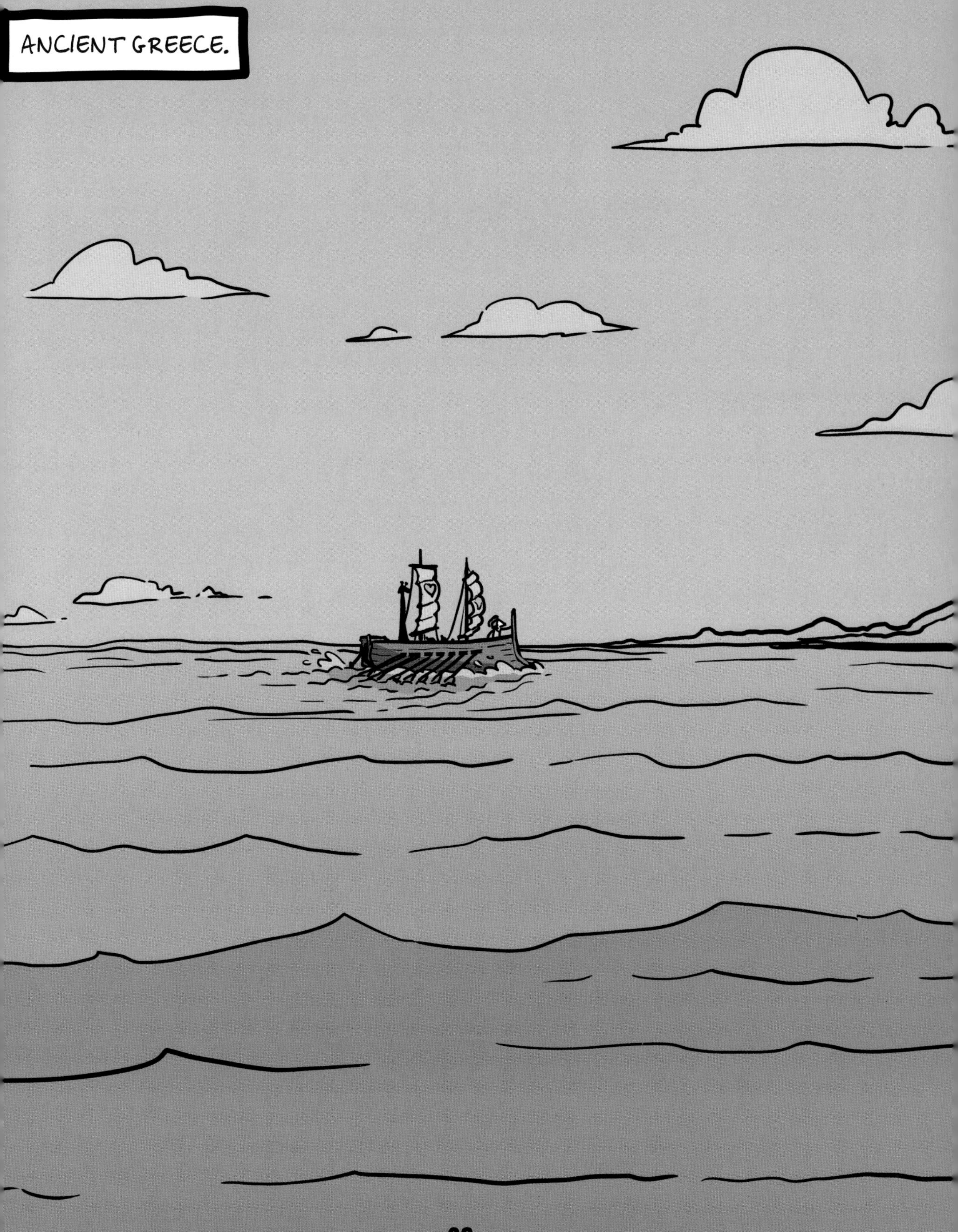
ANCIENT GREECE.

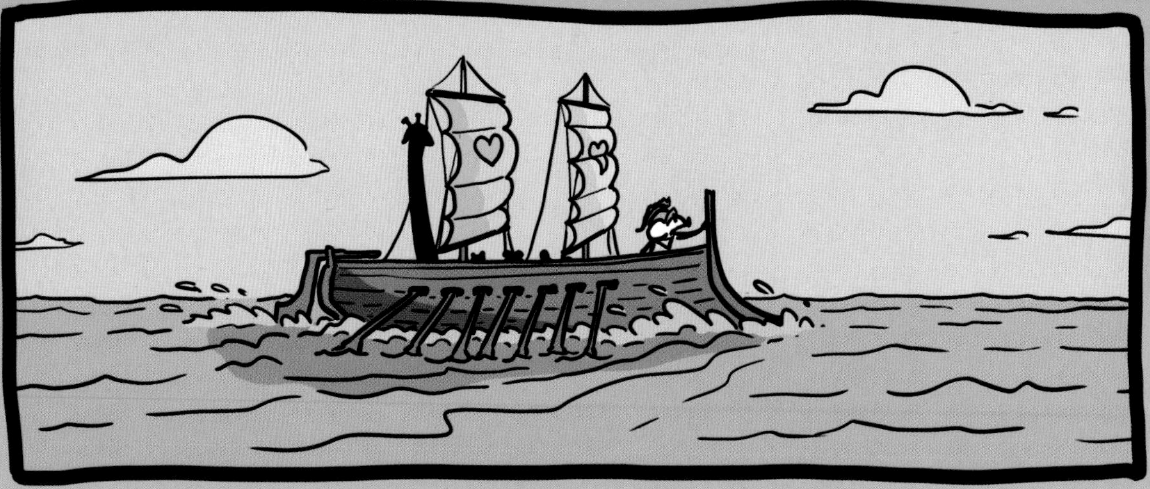

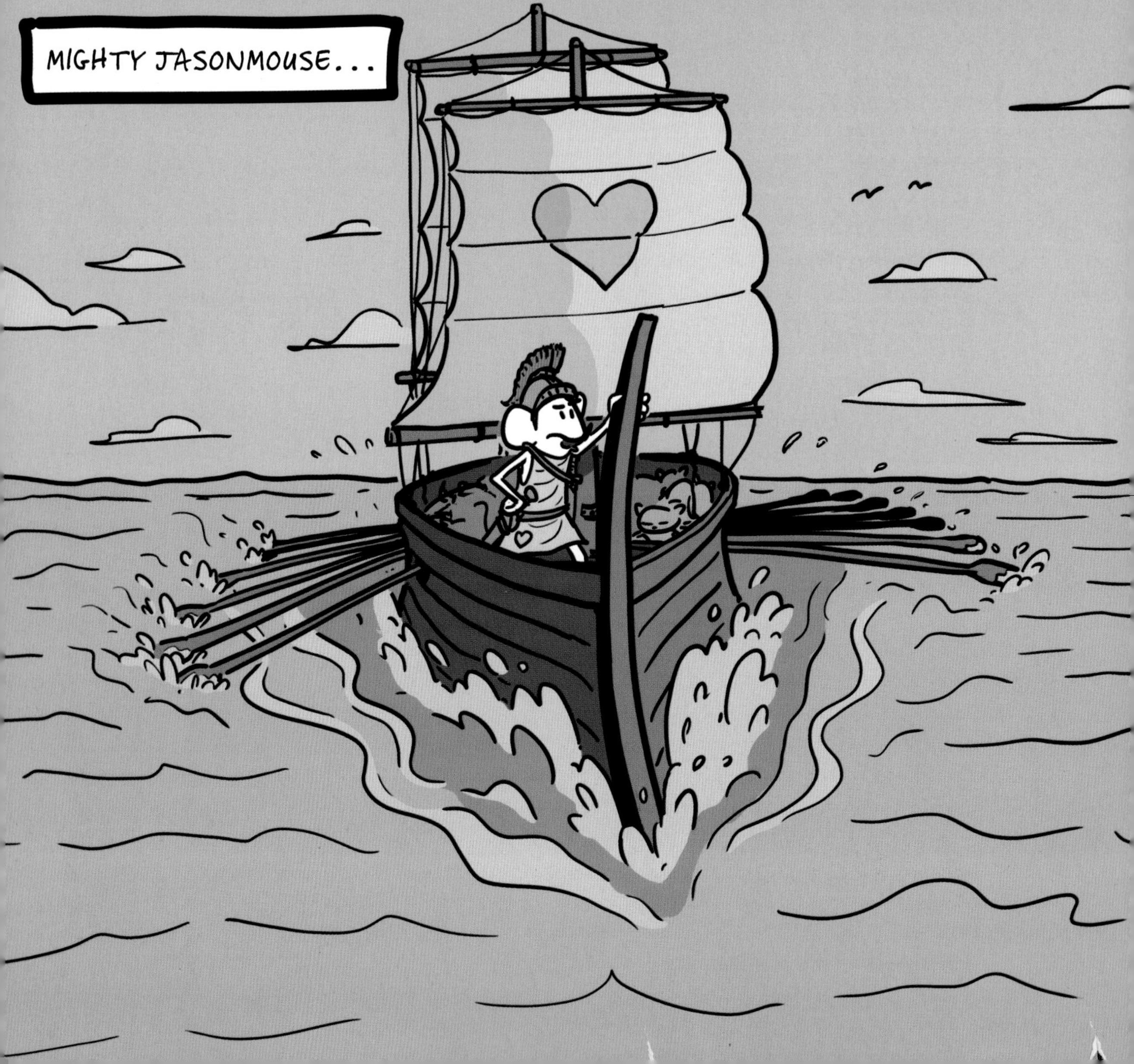
MIGHTY JASONMOUSE...

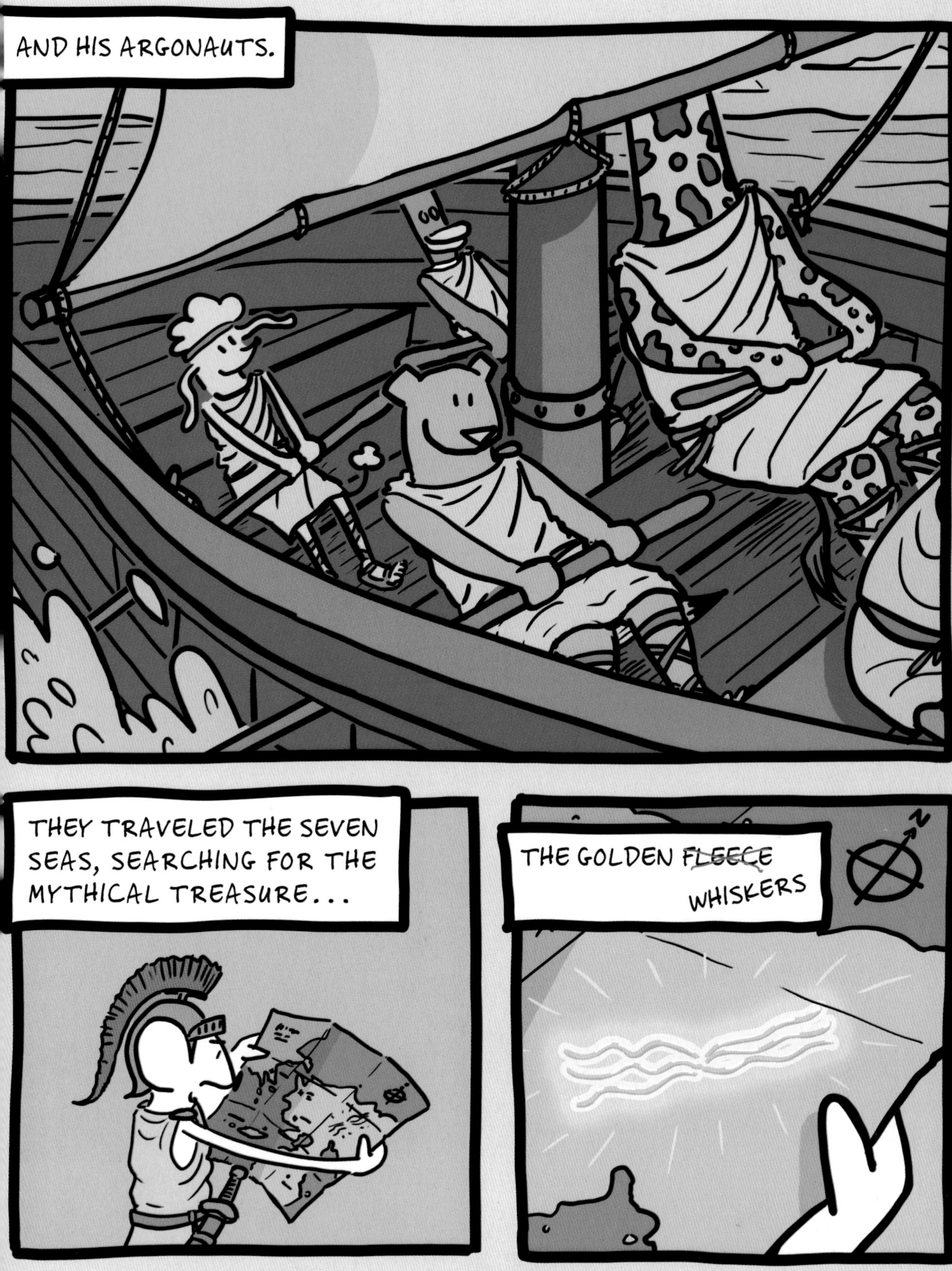
AND HIS ARGONAUTS.
THEY TRAVELED THE SEVEN SEAS, SEARCHING FOR THE MYTHICAL TREASURE...
THE GOLDEN ~~FLEECE~~ WHISKERS
N

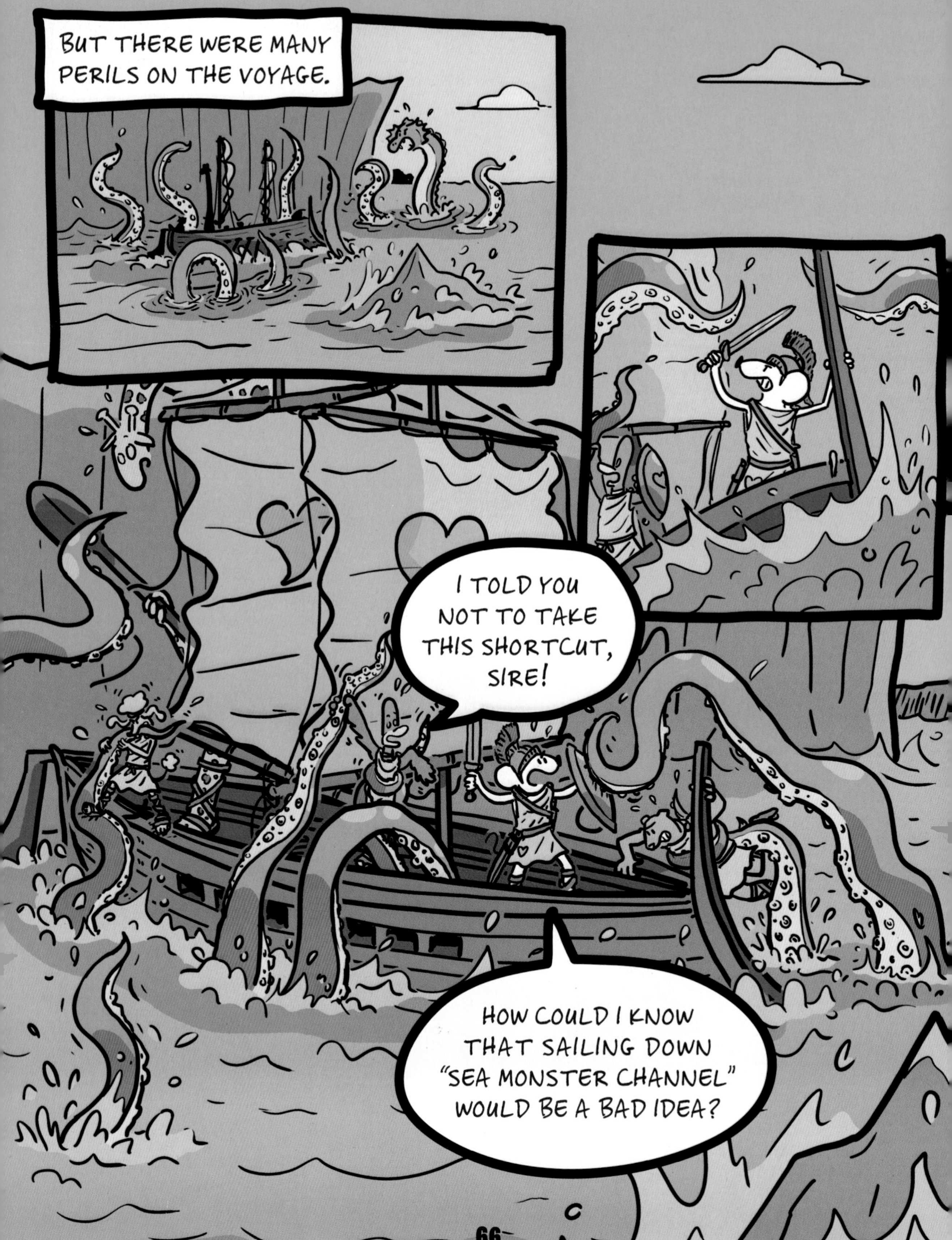
BUT THERE WERE MANY PERILS ON THE VOYAGE.
I TOLD YOU NOT TO TAKE THIS SHORTCUT, SIRE!
HOW COULD I KNOW THAT SAILING DOWN "SEA MONSTER CHANNEL" WOULD BE A BAD IDEA?

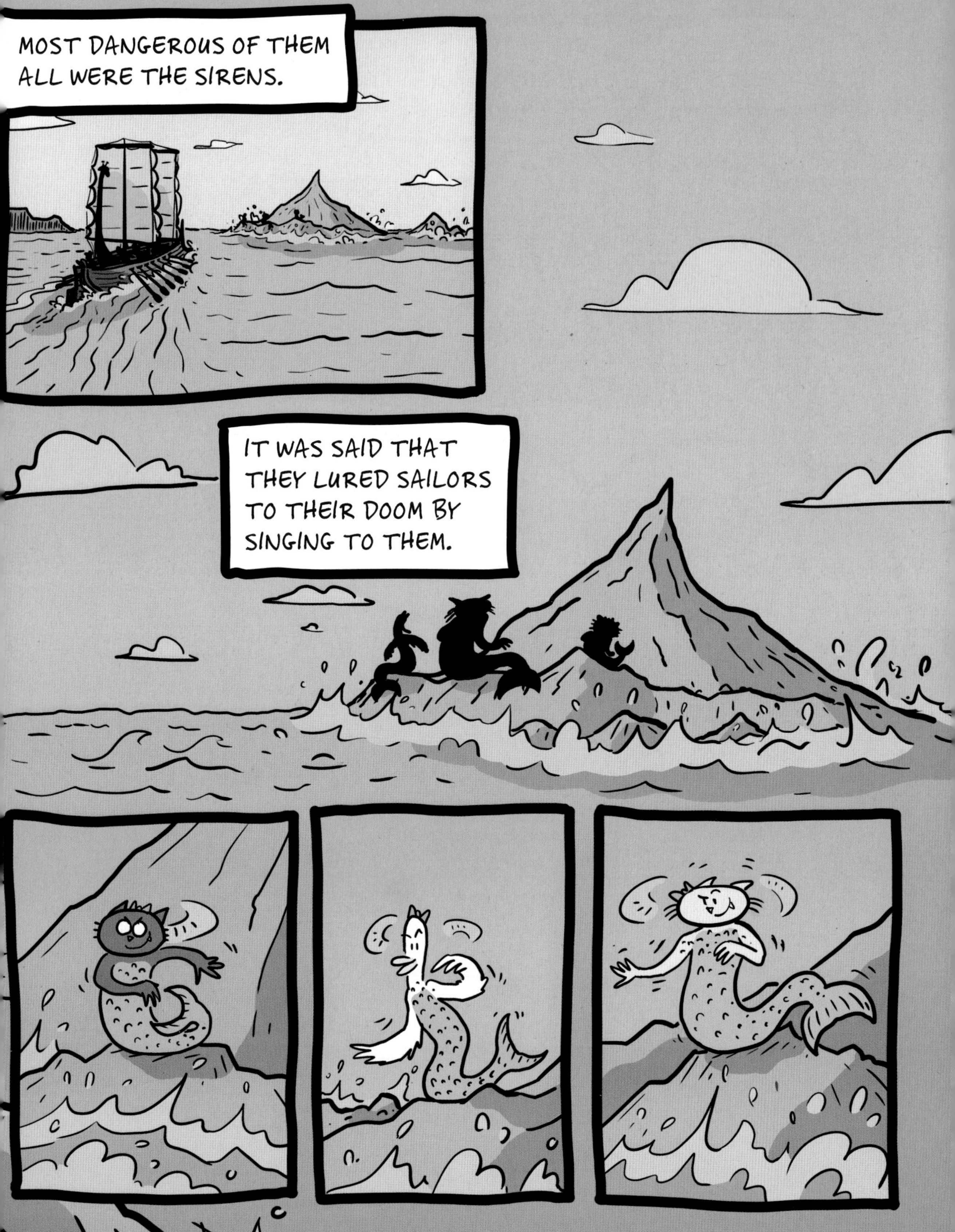
MOST DANGEROUS OF THEM ALL WERE THE SIRENS.
IT WAS SAID THAT THEY LURED SAILORS TO THEIR DOOM BY SINGING TO THEM.

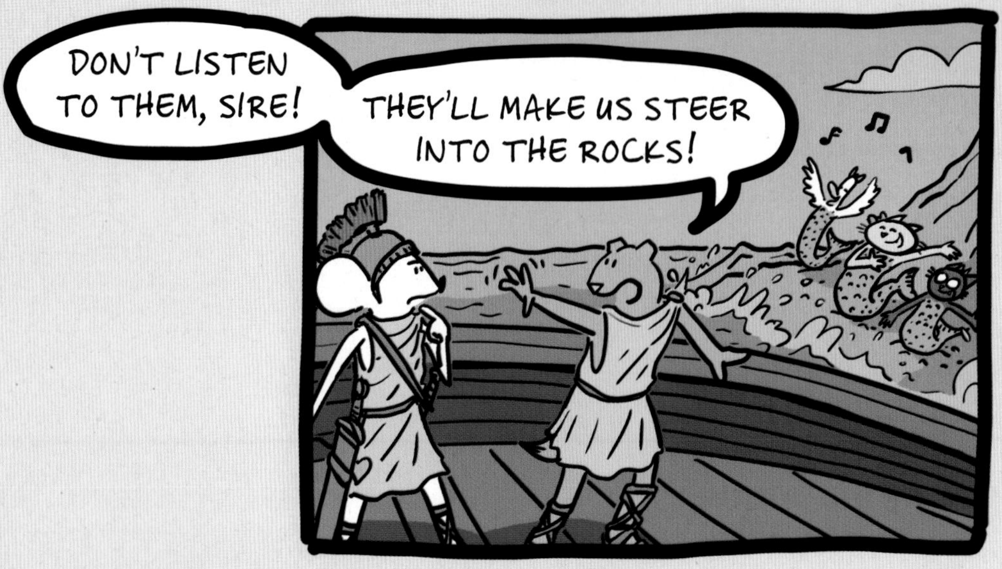
DON'T LISTEN TO THEM, SIRE!
THEY'LL MAKE US STEER INTO THE ROCKS!

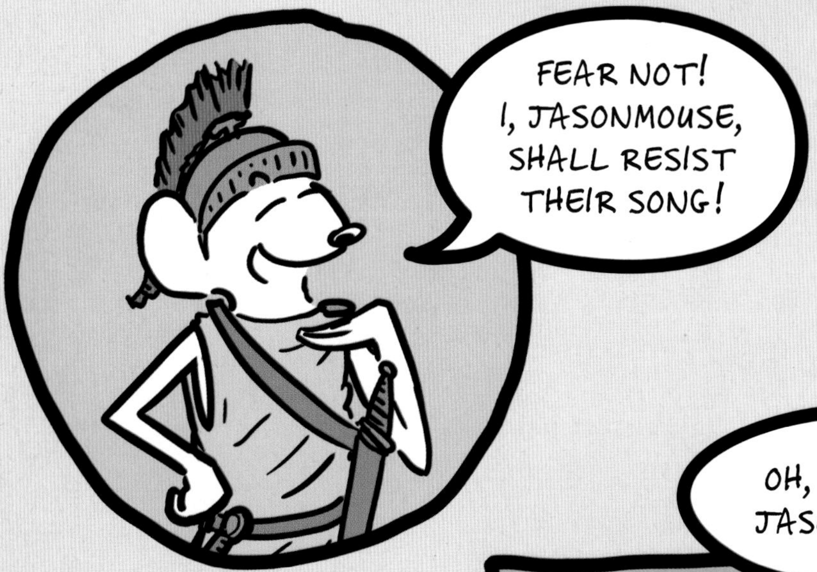
FEAR NOT! I, JASONMOUSE, SHALL RESIST THEIR SONG!

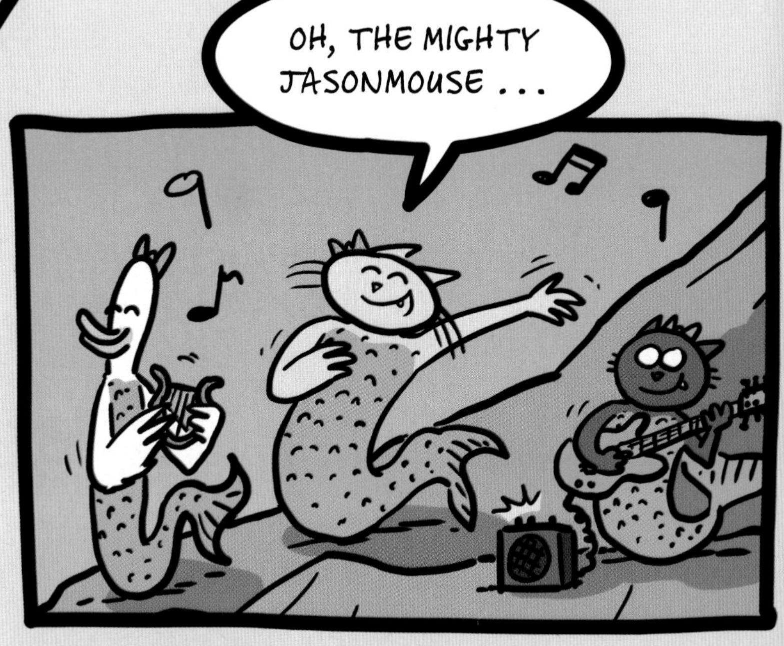
OH, THE MIGHTY JASONMOUSE . . .

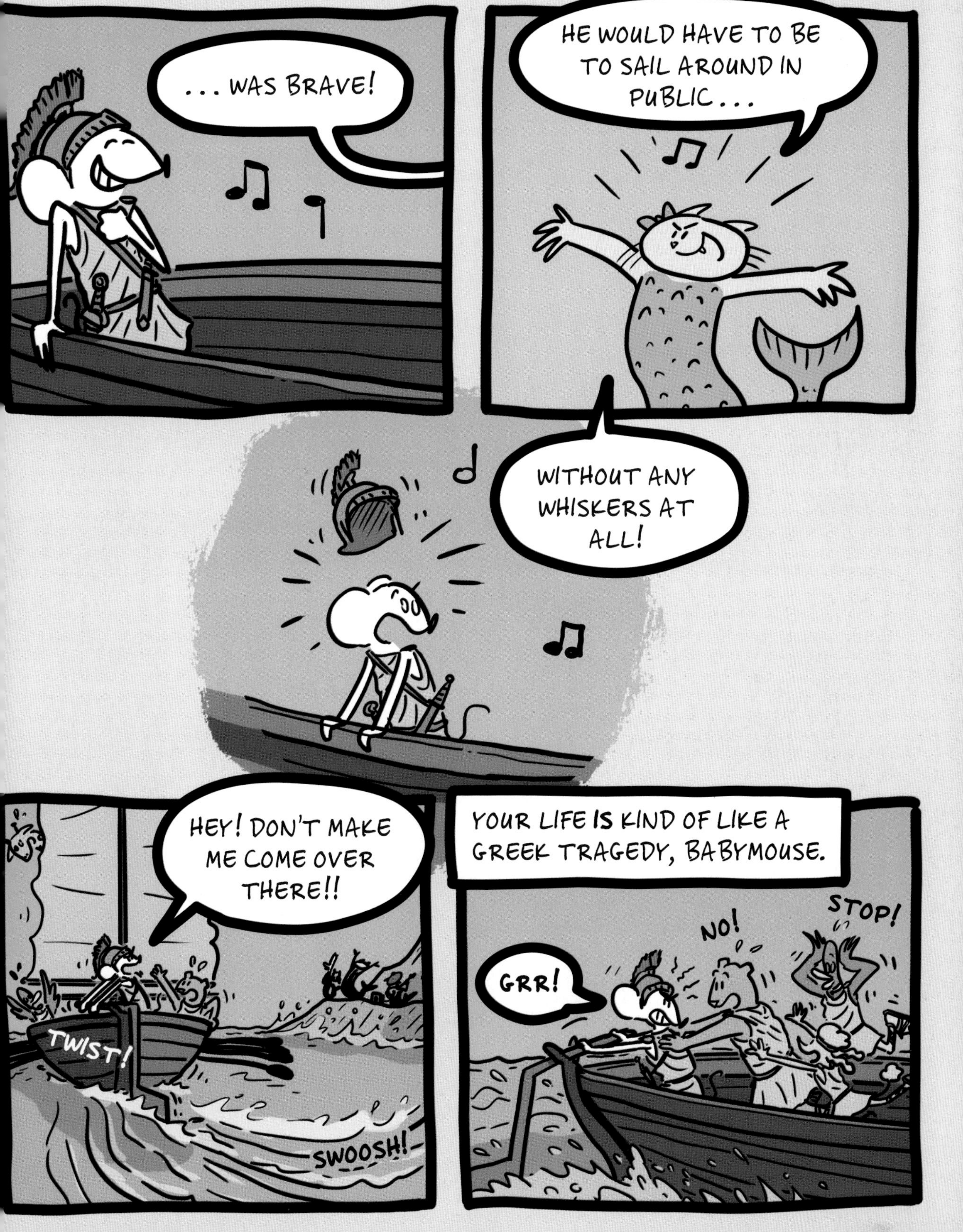
. . . WAS BRAVE!
HE WOULD HAVE TO BE TO SAIL AROUND IN PUBLIC . . .
WITHOUT ANY WHISKERS AT ALL!
HEY! DON'T MAKE ME COME OVER THERE!!
TWIST!
SWOOSH!
YOUR LIFE IS KIND OF LIKE A GREEK TRAGEDY, BABYMOUSE.
GRR!
NO!
STOP!

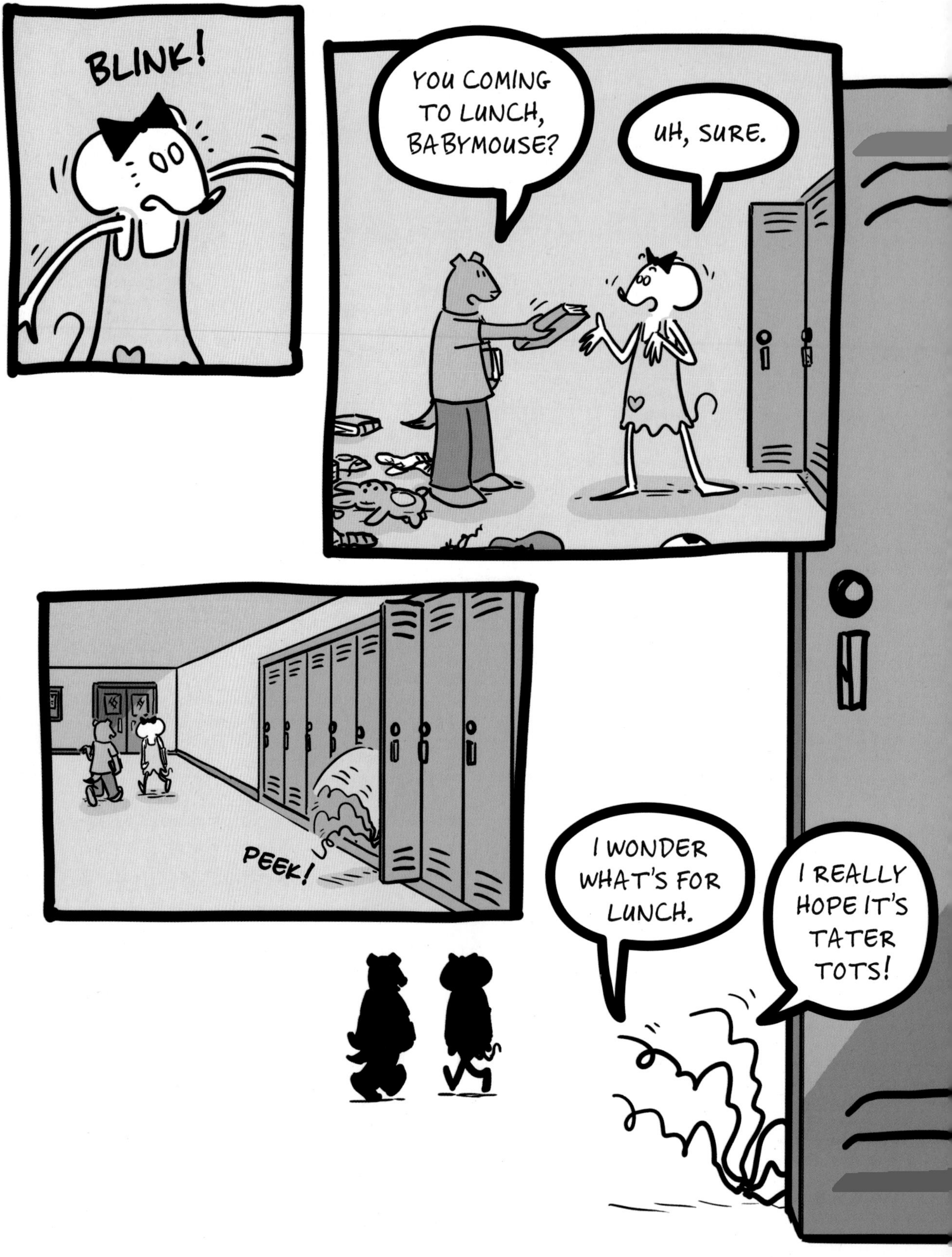
BLINK!
YOU COMING TO LUNCH, BABYMOUSE?
UH, SURE.
PEEK!
I WONDER WHAT'S FOR LUNCH.
I REALLY HOPE IT'S TATER TOTS!

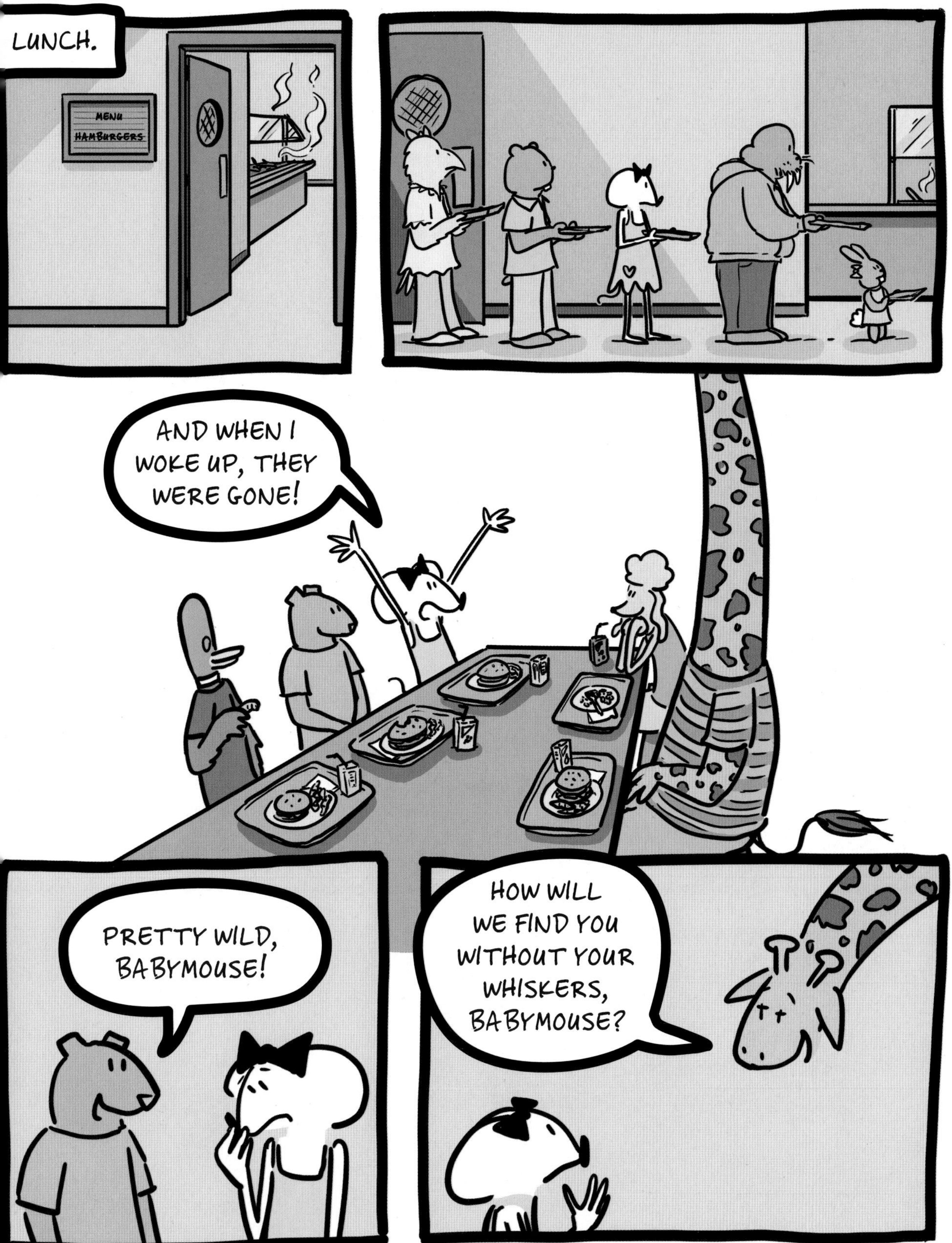
LUNCH.
MENU
HAMBURGERS
AND WHEN I WOKE UP, THEY WERE GONE!
PRETTY WILD, BABYMOUSE!
HOW WILL WE FIND YOU WITHOUT YOUR WHISKERS, BABYMOUSE?

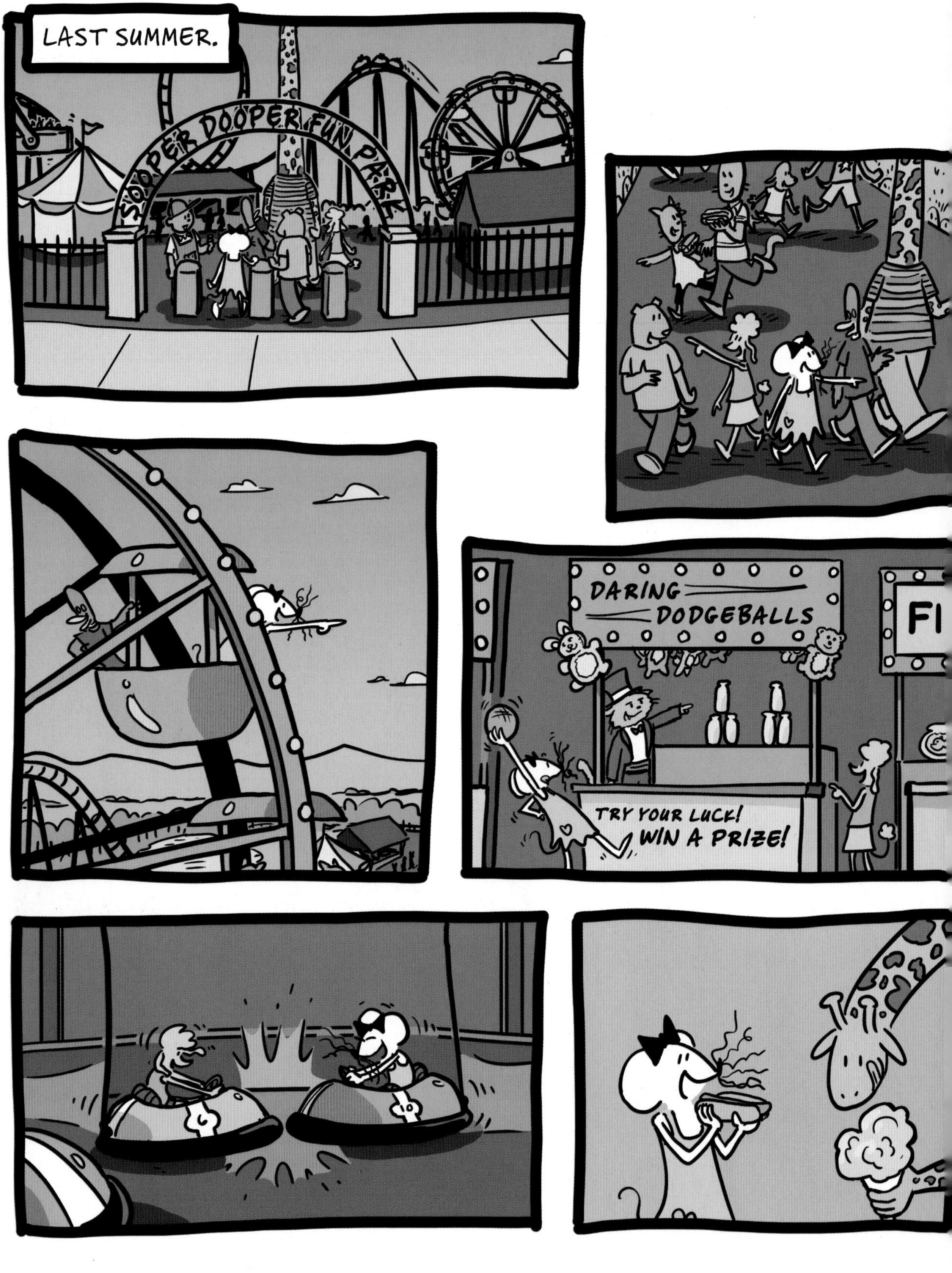
LAST SUMMER.
SOOPER DOOPER FUN PARK
DARING DODGEBALLS
TRY YOUR LUCK! WIN A PRIZE!

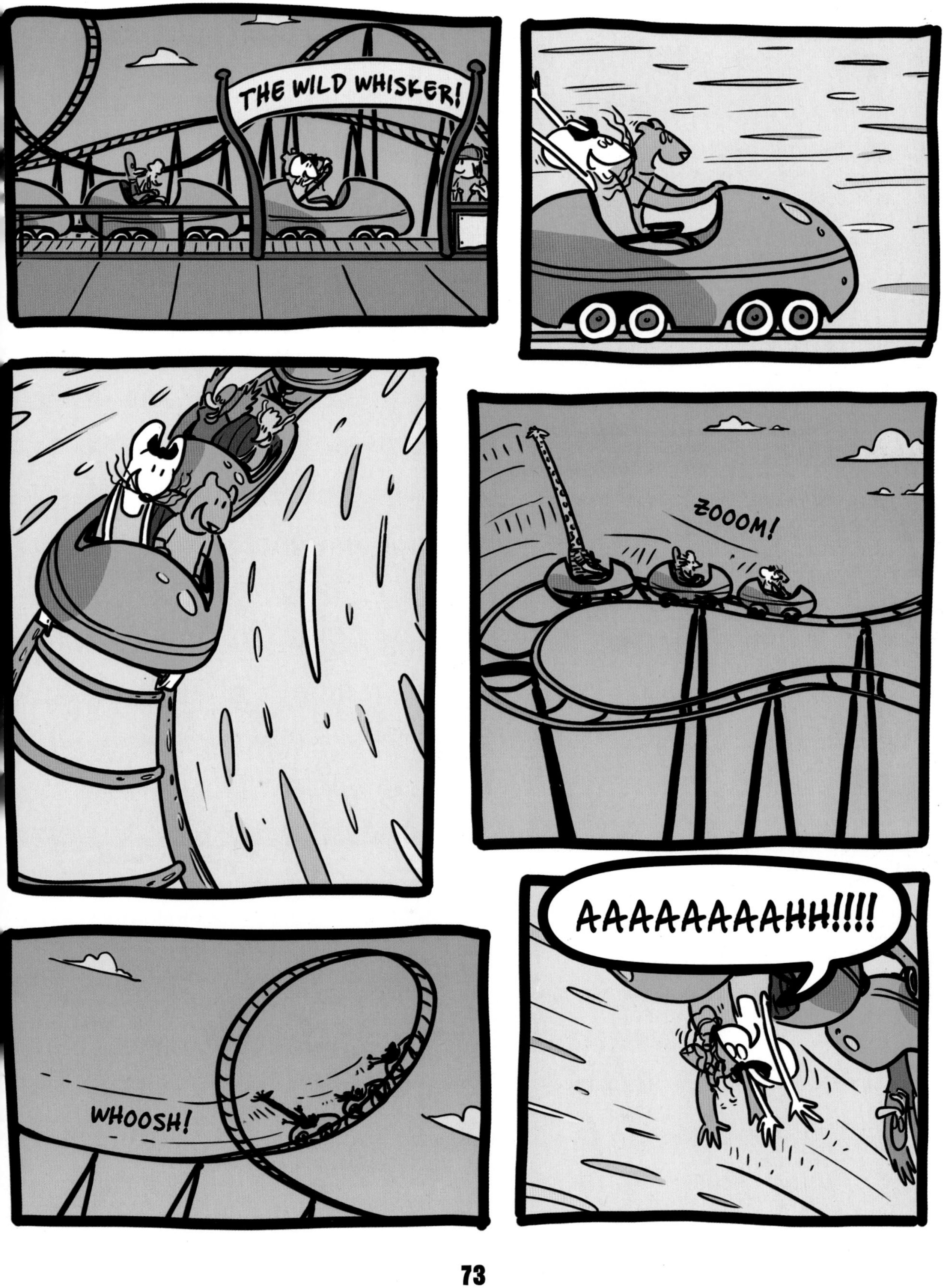
THE WILD WHISKER!
ZOOOM!
WHOOSH!
AAAAAAAAAHH!!!!

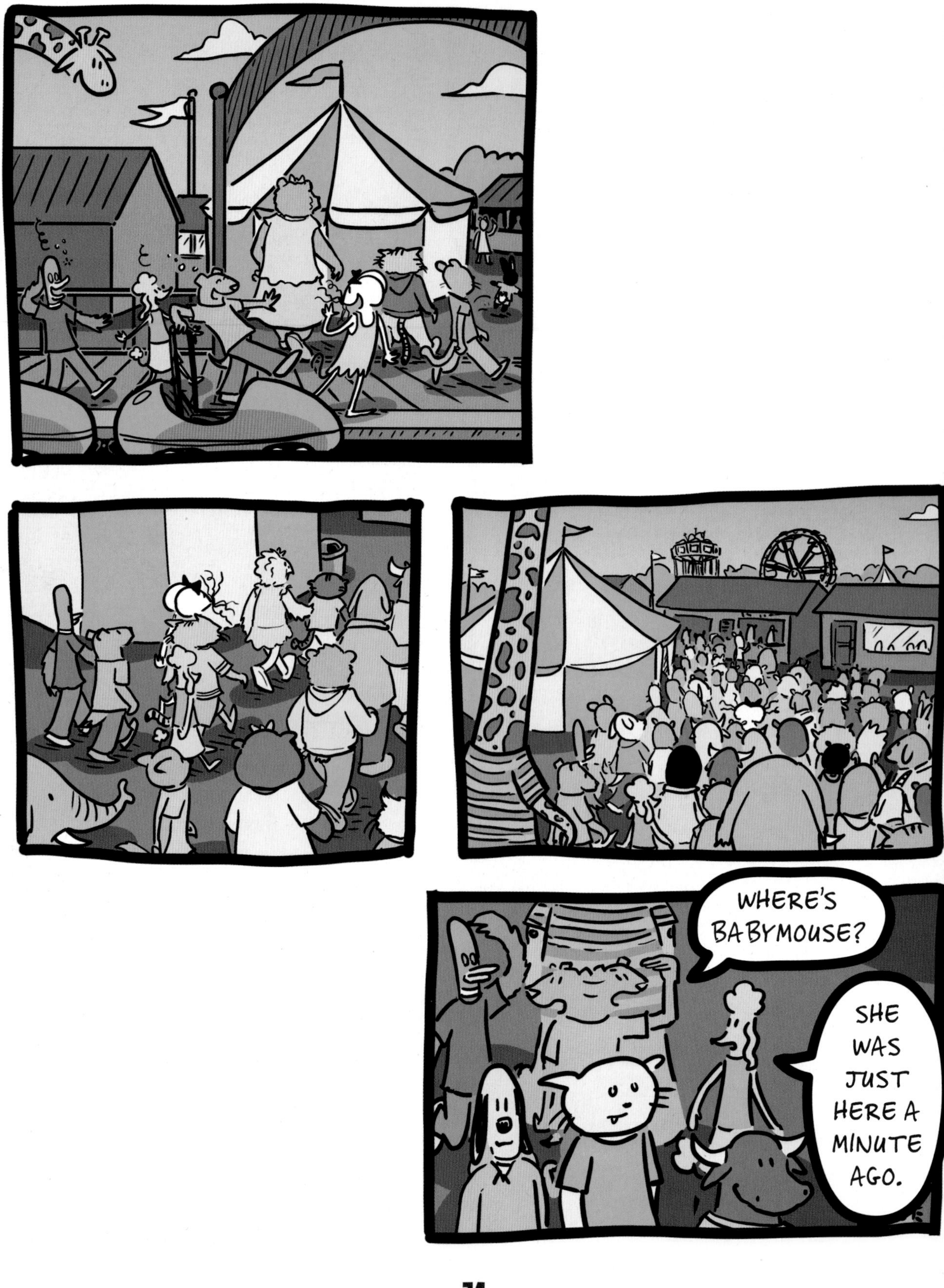
WHERE'S BABYMOUSE?
SHE WAS JUST HERE A MINUTE AGO.

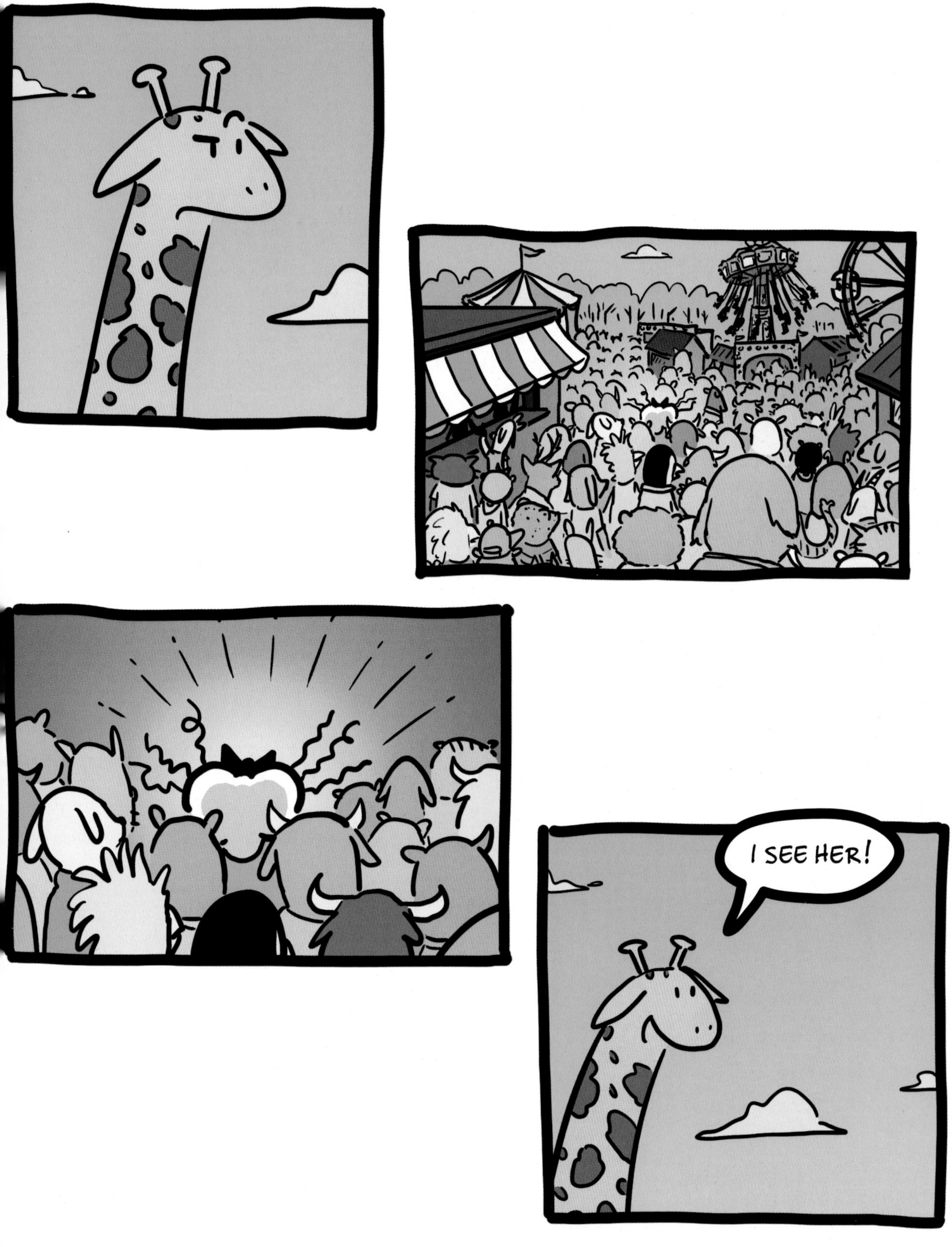
I SEE HER!

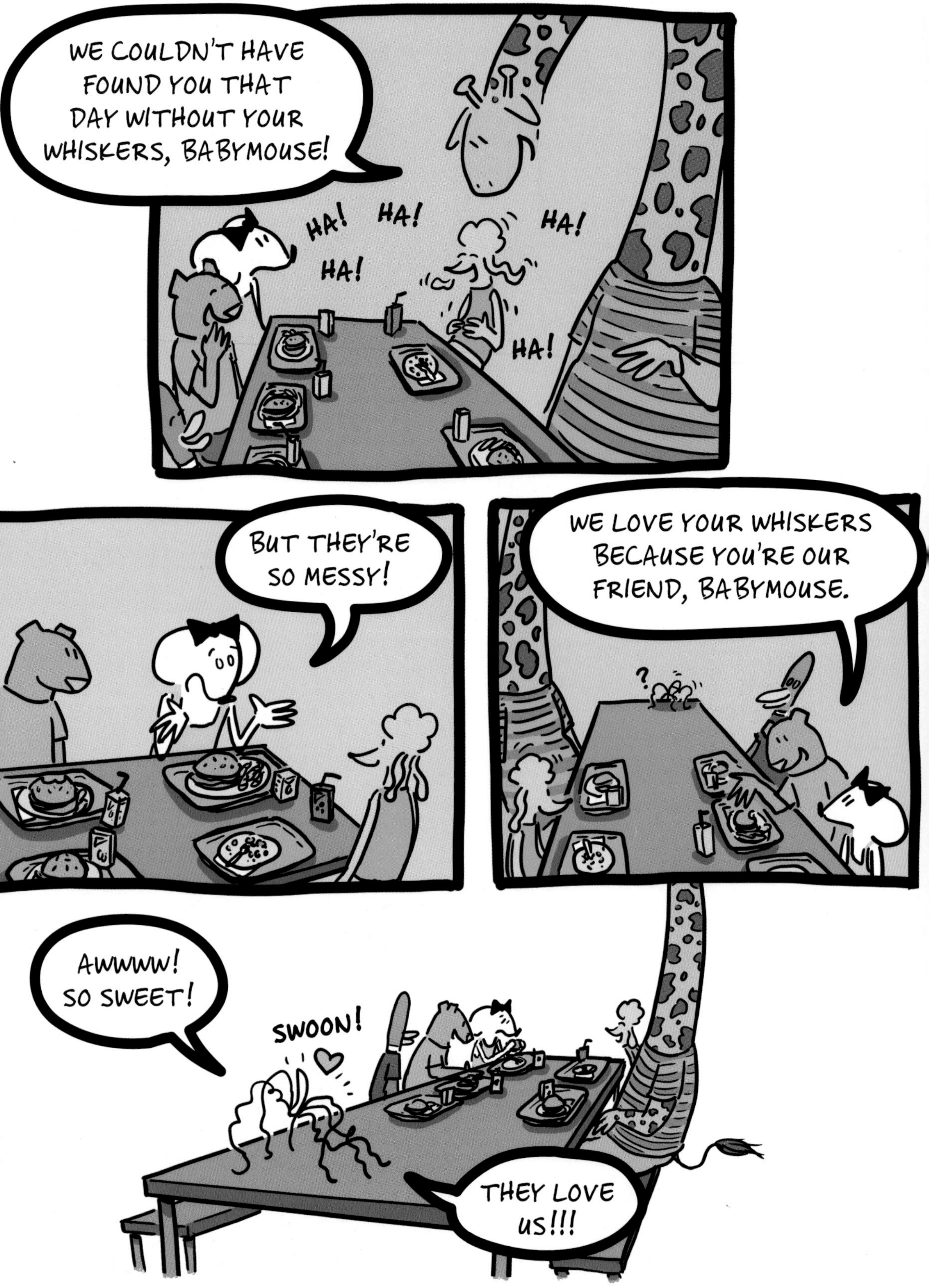
WE COULDN'T HAVE FOUND YOU THAT DAY WITHOUT YOUR WHISKERS, BABYMOUSE!
HA! HA! HA! HA! HA!
BUT THEY'RE SO MESSY!
WE LOVE YOUR WHISKERS BECAUSE YOU'RE OUR FRIEND, BABYMOUSE.
?
AWWWW! SO SWEET!
SWOON!
THEY LOVE US!!!

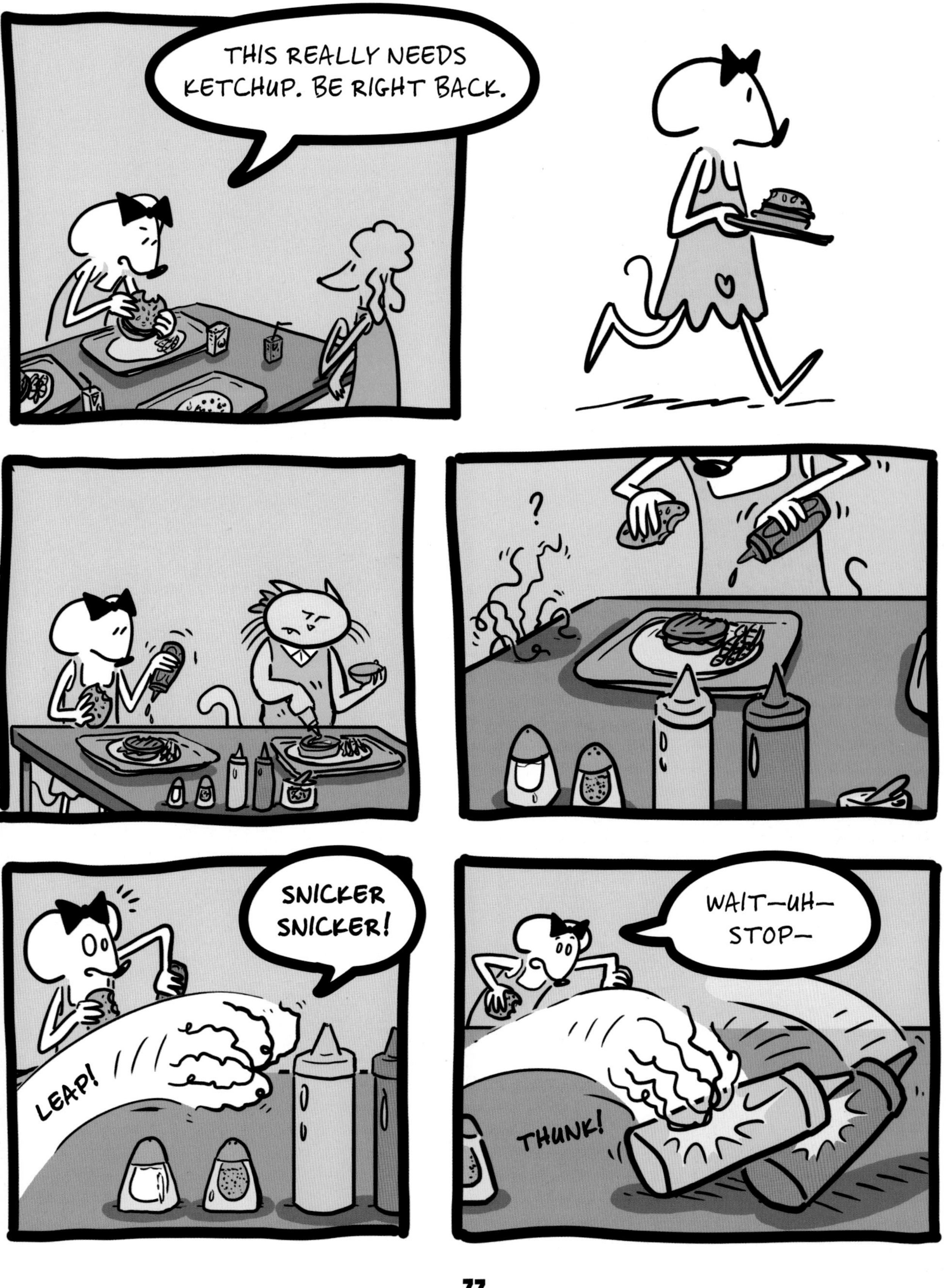
THIS REALLY NEEDS KETCHUP. BE RIGHT BACK.
?
SNICKER SNICKER!
LEAP!
WAIT—UH— STOP—
THUNK!

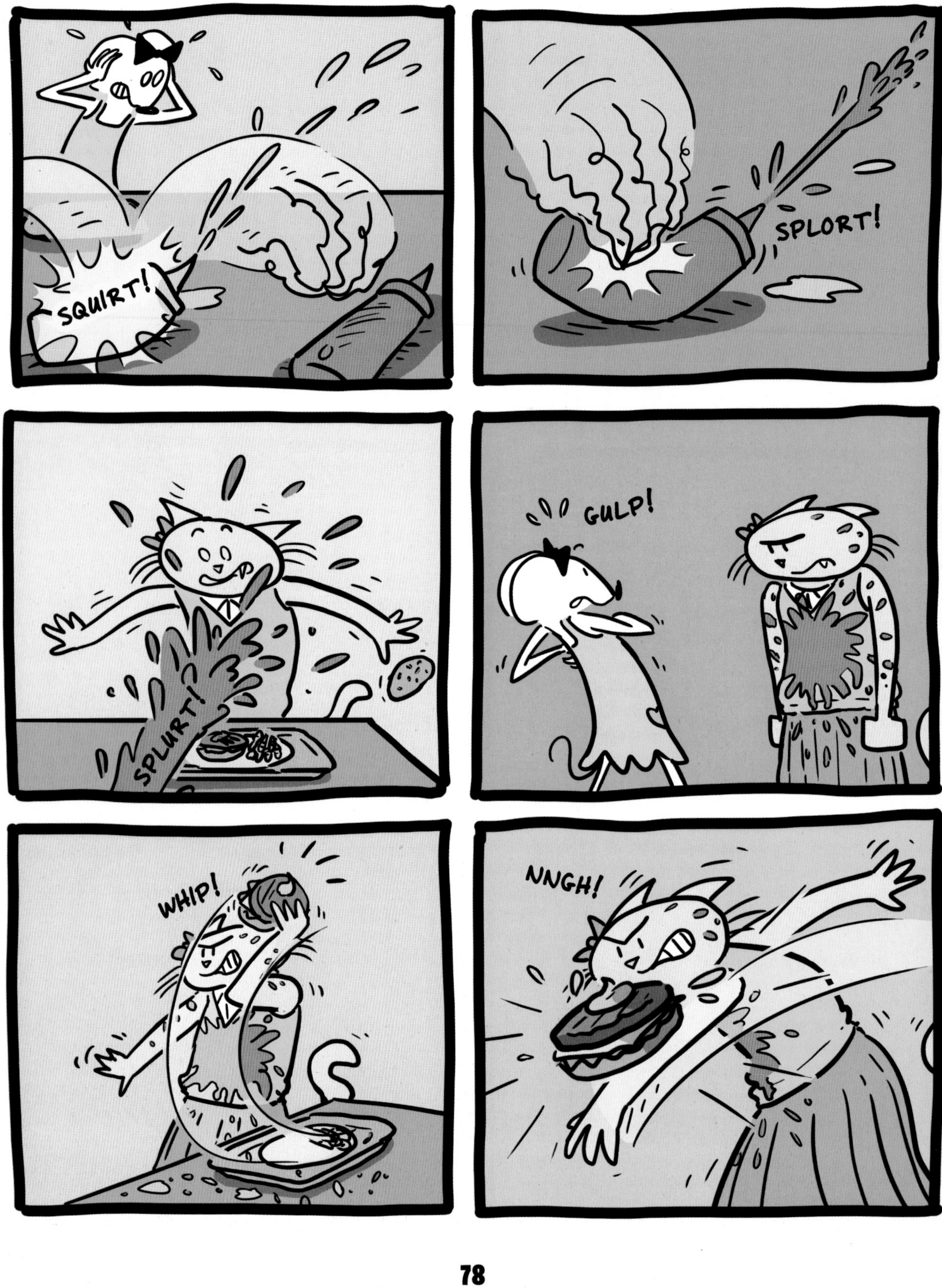
SQUIRT!
SPLORT!
SPLURT!
GULP!
WHIP!
NNGH!

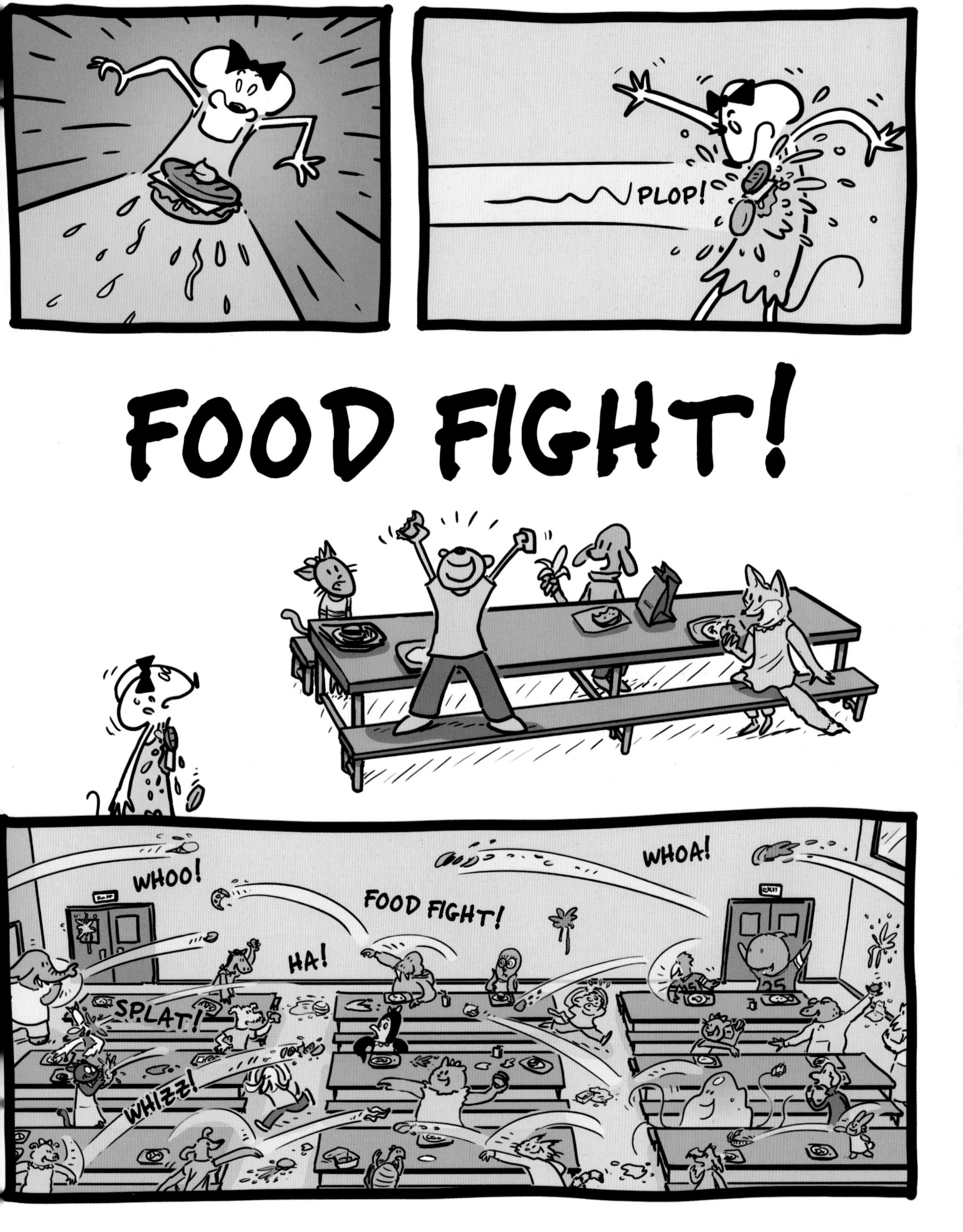
PLOP!
FOOD FIGHT!
WHOO!
FOOD FIGHT!
WHOA!
HA!
SPLAT!
WHIZZ!

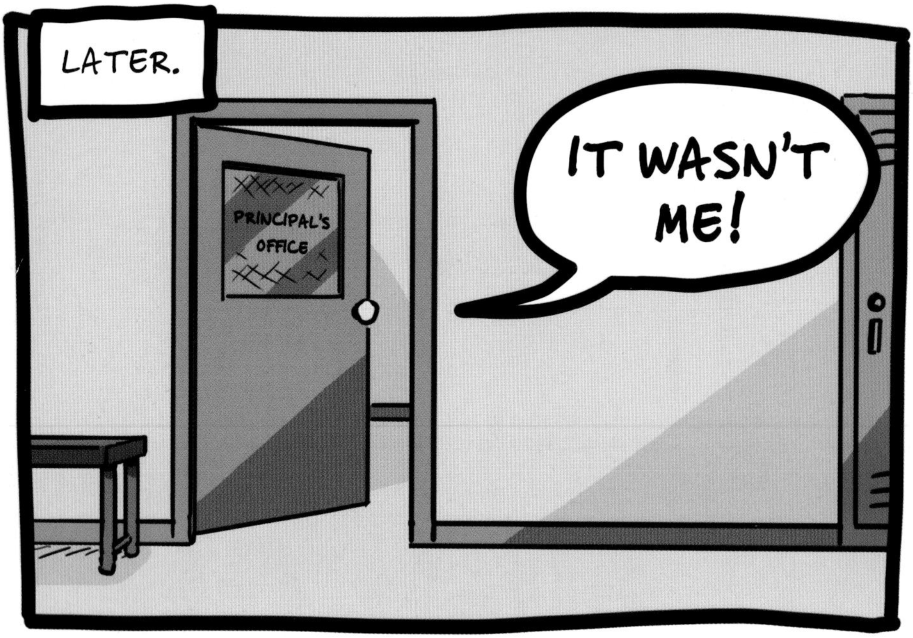
LATER.
PRINCIPAL'S OFFICE
IT WASN'T ME!

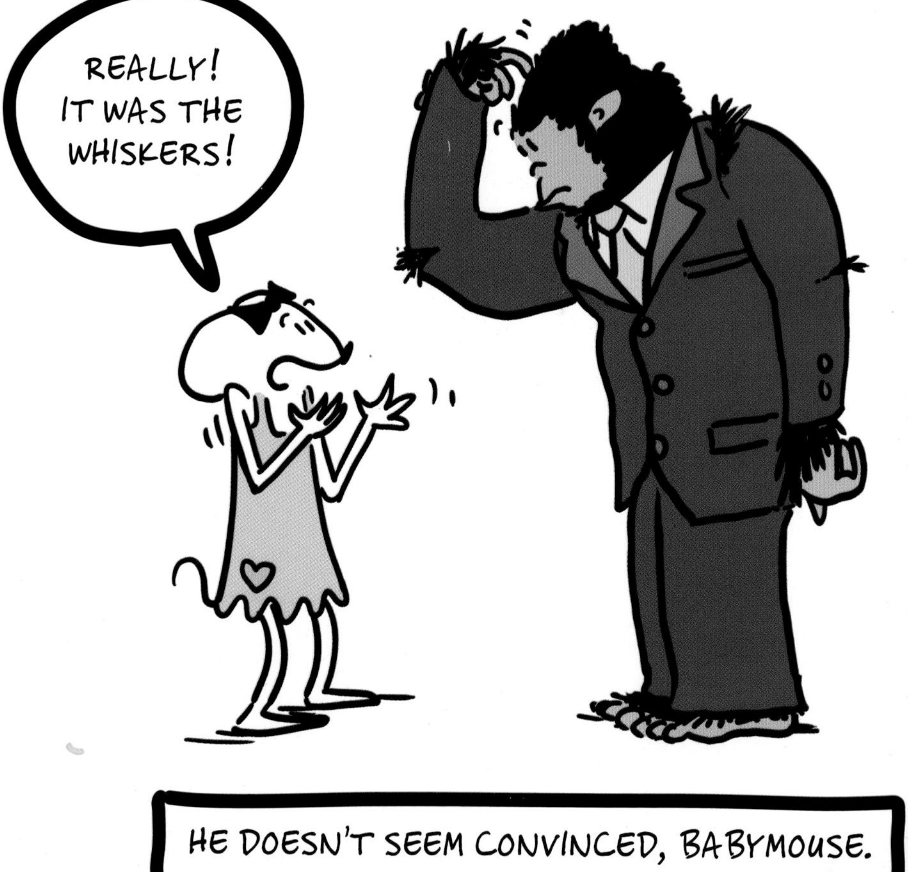
REALLY! IT WAS THE WHISKERS!
HE DOESN'T SEEM CONVINCED, BABYMOUSE.

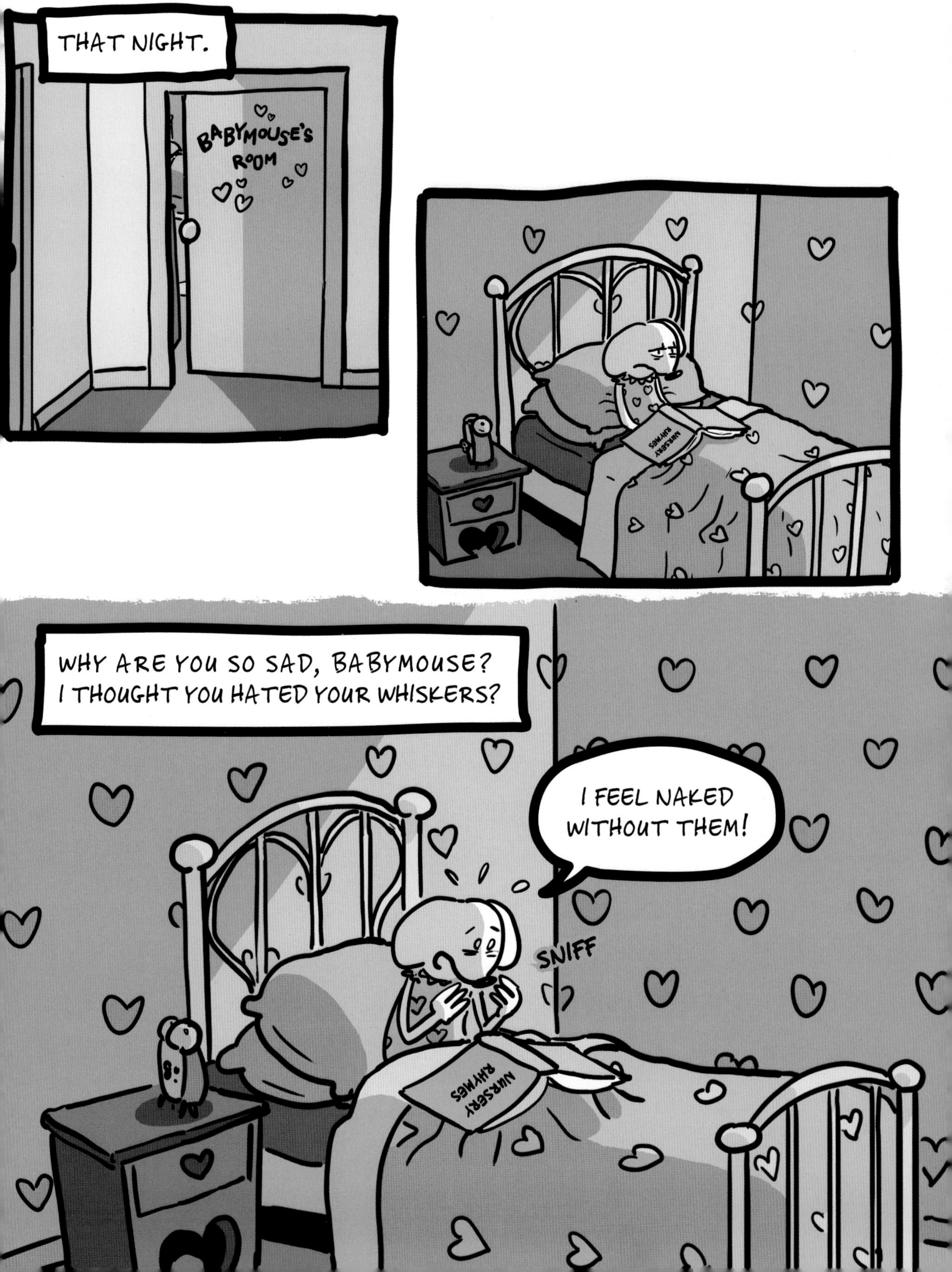
THAT NIGHT.
BABYMOUSE'S ROOM
NURSERY RHYMES
WHY ARE YOU SO SAD, BABYMOUSE? I THOUGHT YOU HATED YOUR WHISKERS?
I FEEL NAKED WITHOUT THEM!
SNIFF
NURSERY RHYMES

The Three Little Kittens

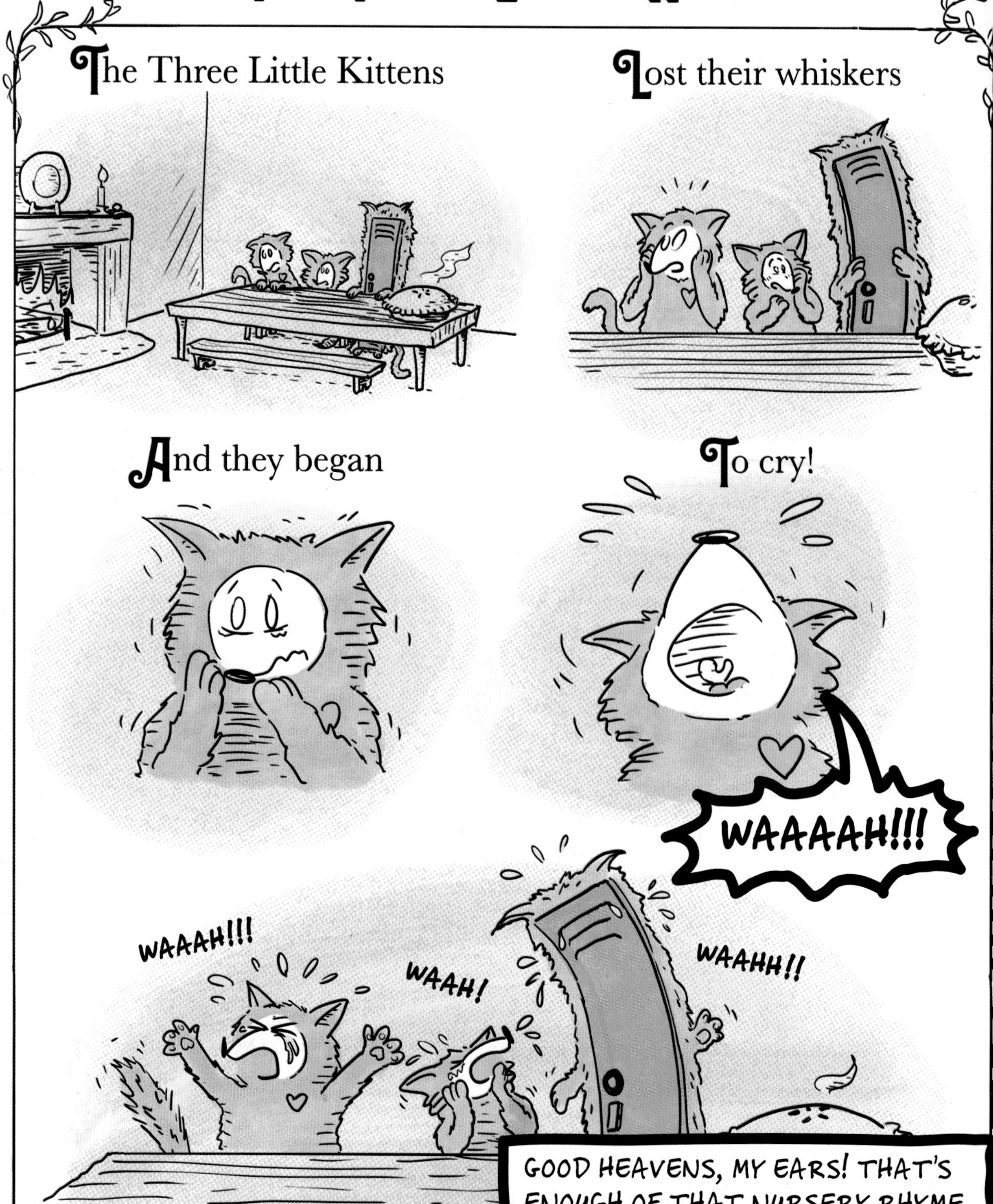
The Three Little Kittens
Lost their whiskers
And they began
To cry!
WAAAAH!!!
WAAAH!!!
WAAH!
WAAHH!!
GOOD HEAVENS, MY EARS! THAT'S ENOUGH OF THAT NURSERY RHYME.

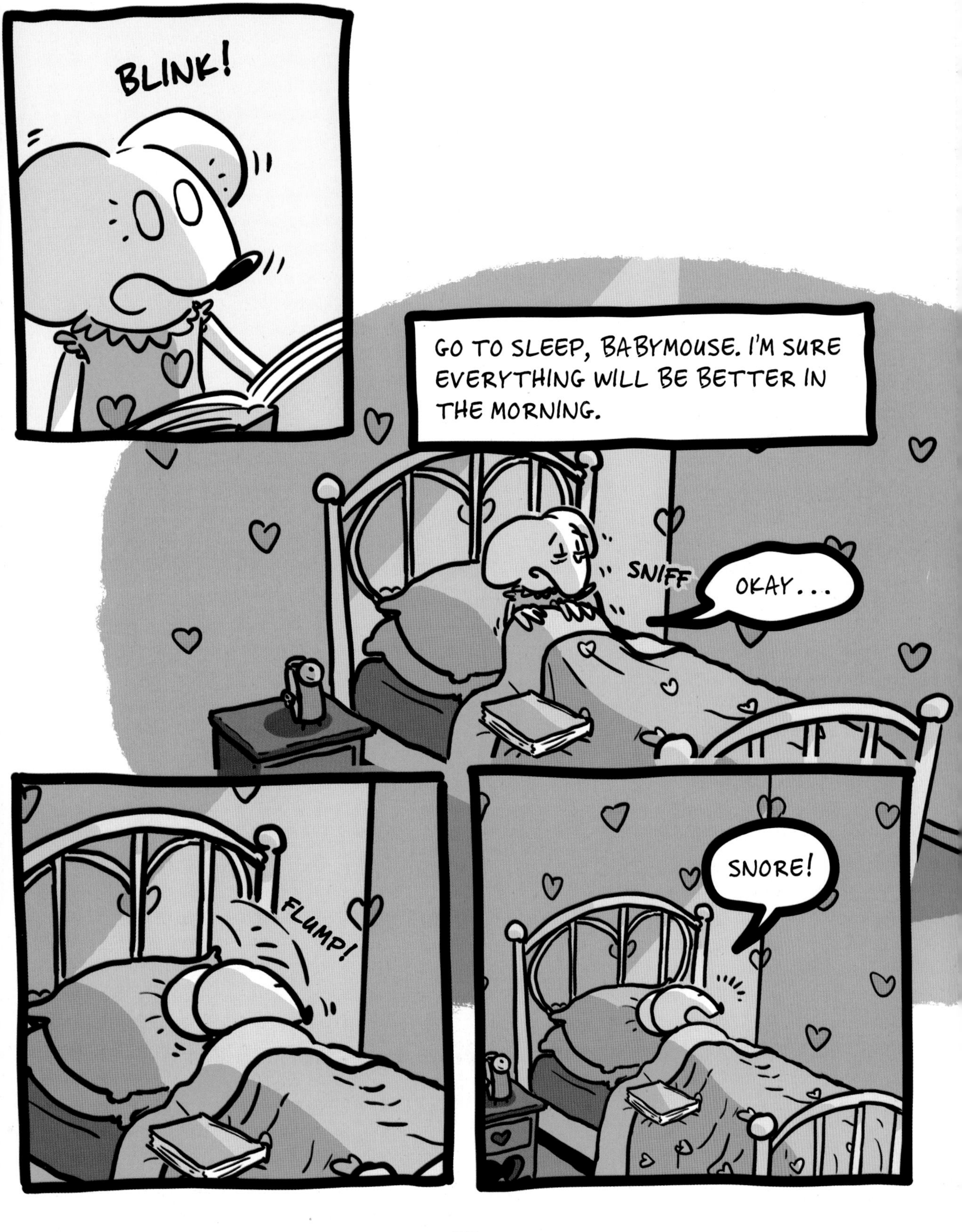
BLINK!
GO TO SLEEP, BABYMOUSE. I'M SURE EVERYTHING WILL BE BETTER IN THE MORNING.
SNIFF
OKAY...
FLUMP!
SNORE!

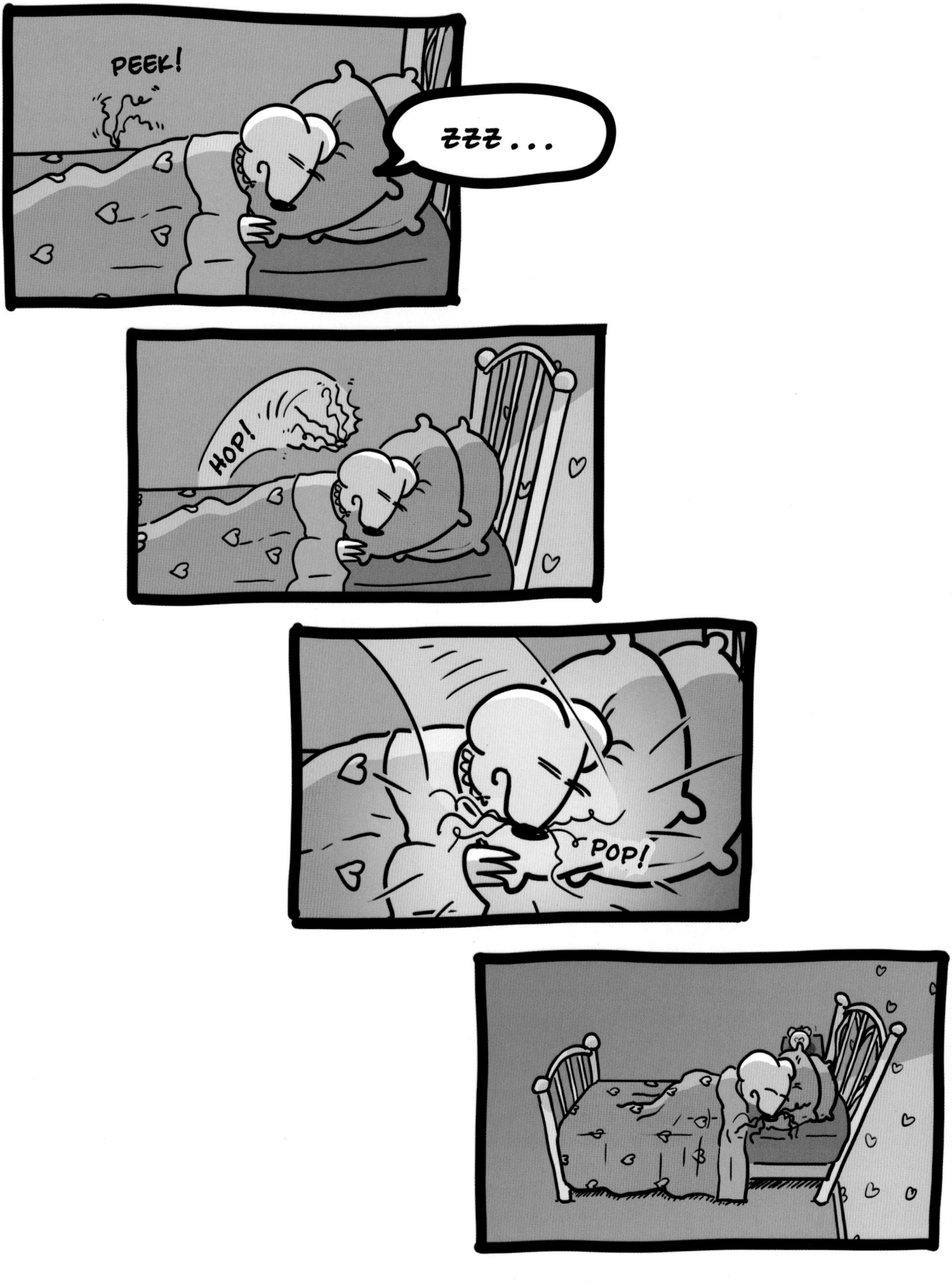
PEEK!
ZZZ...
HOP!
POP!

PART THREE

THE LONG & ~~SHORT~~ LONGER OF IT

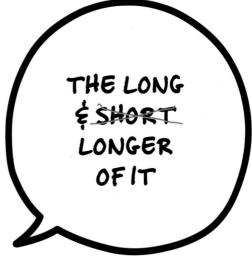

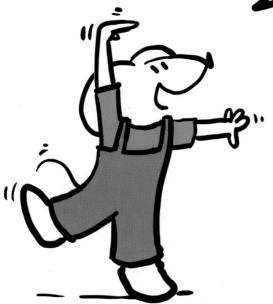

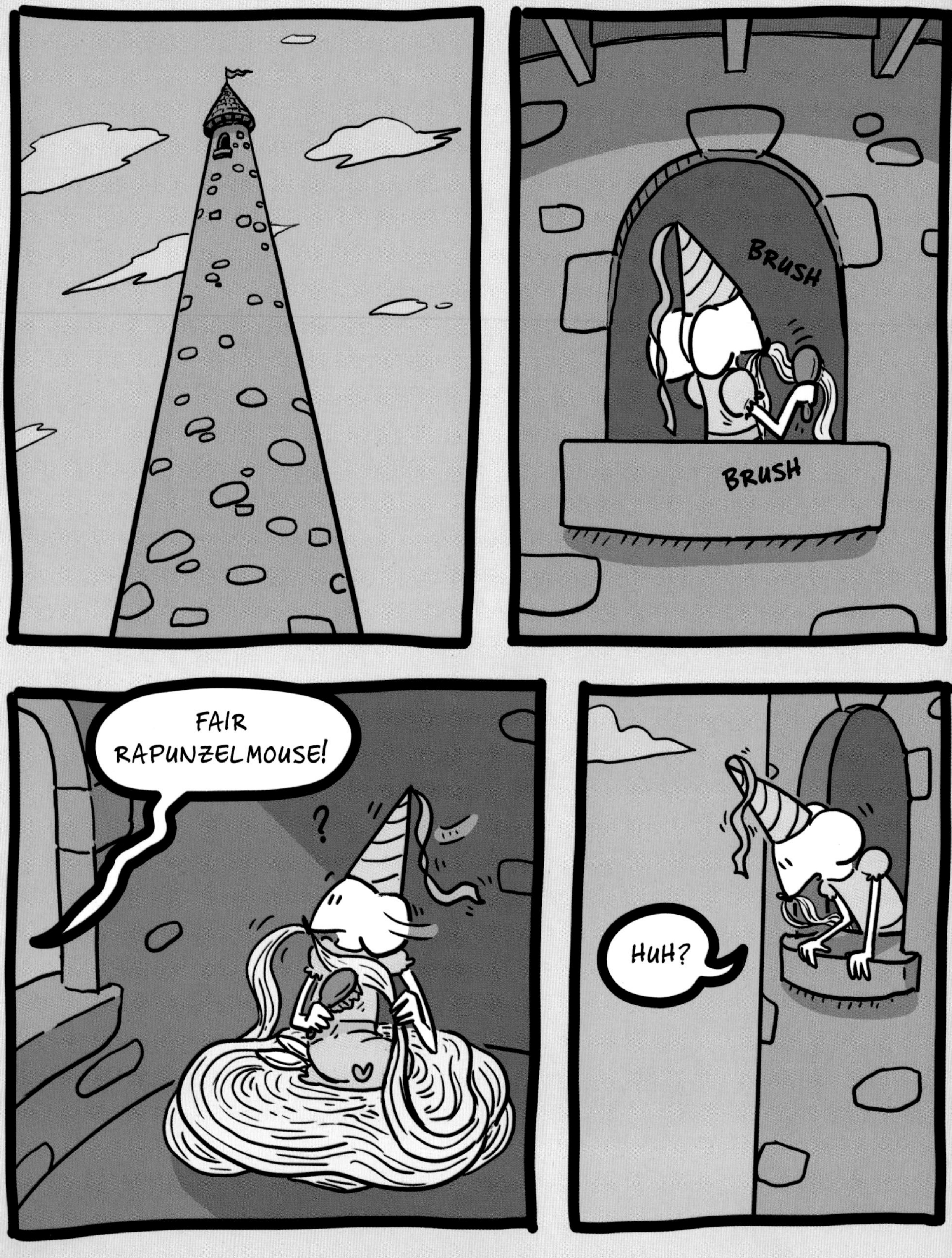
BRUSH
BRUSH
FAIR RAPUNZELMOUSE!
?
HUH?

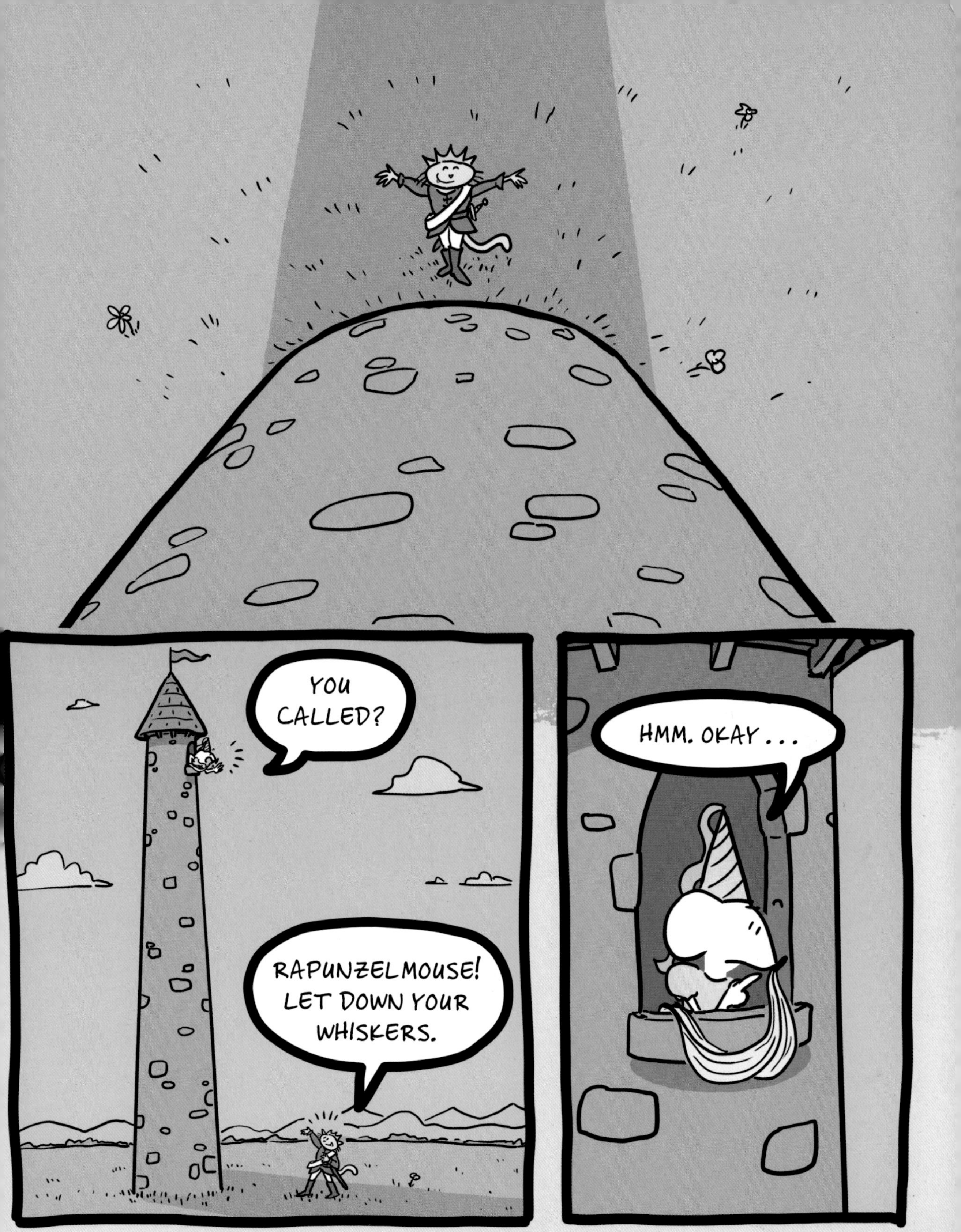
RAPUNZELMOUSE! LET DOWN YOUR WHISKERS.
YOU CALLED?
HMM. OKAY . . .

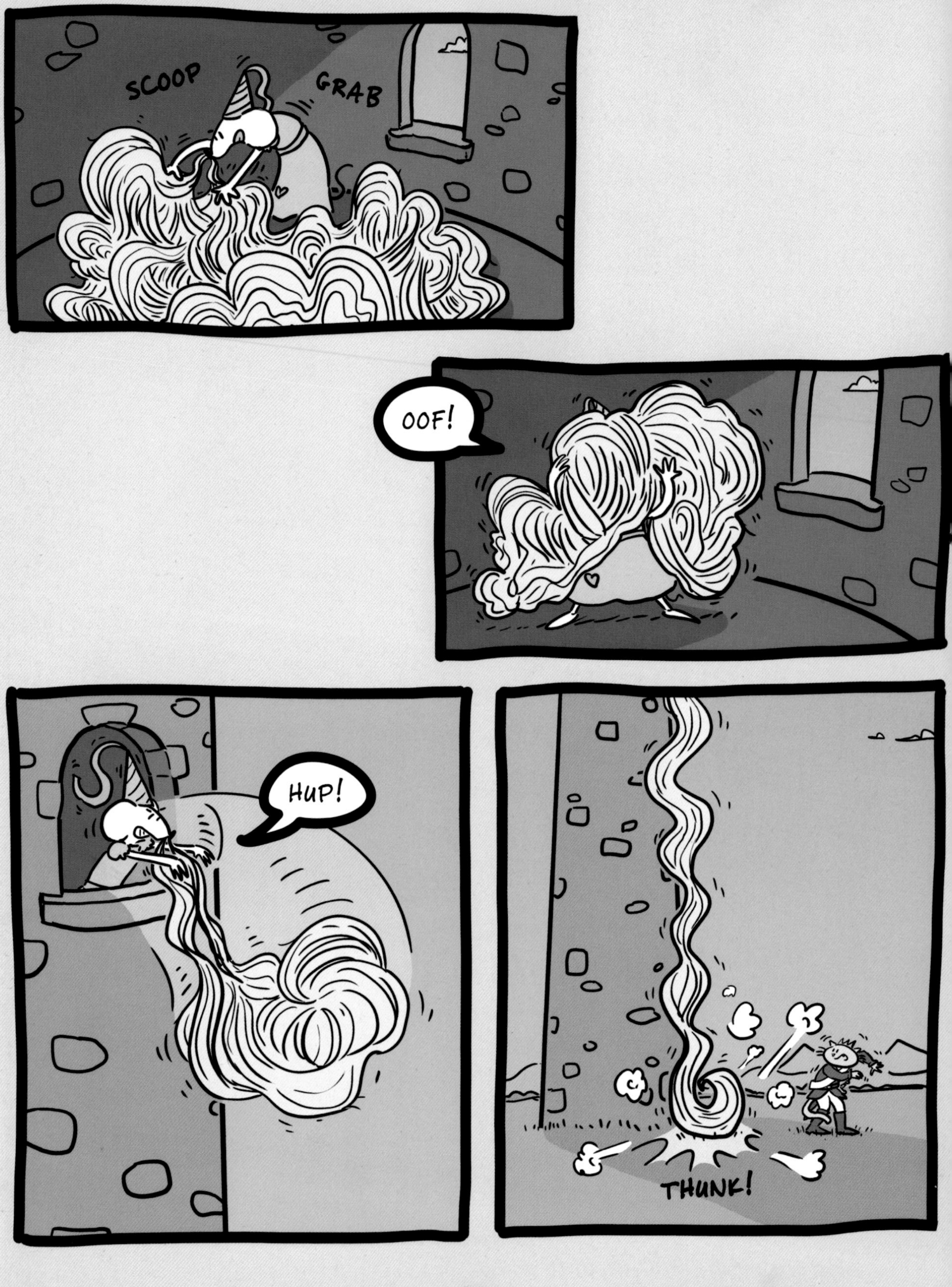
SCOOP
GRAB
OOF!
HUP!
THUNK!

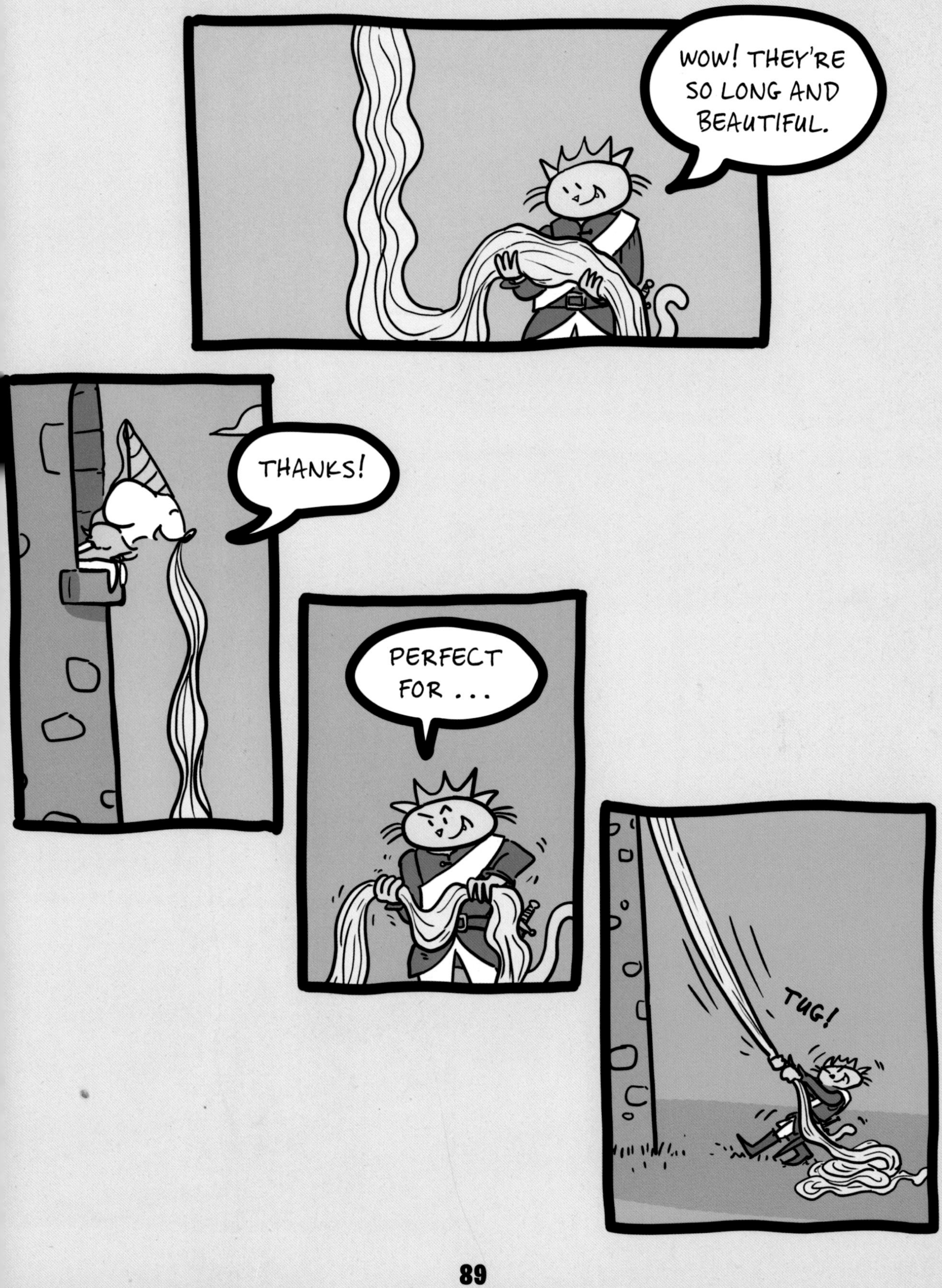
WOW! THEY'RE SO LONG AND BEAUTIFUL.
THANKS!
PERFECT FOR . . .
TUG!

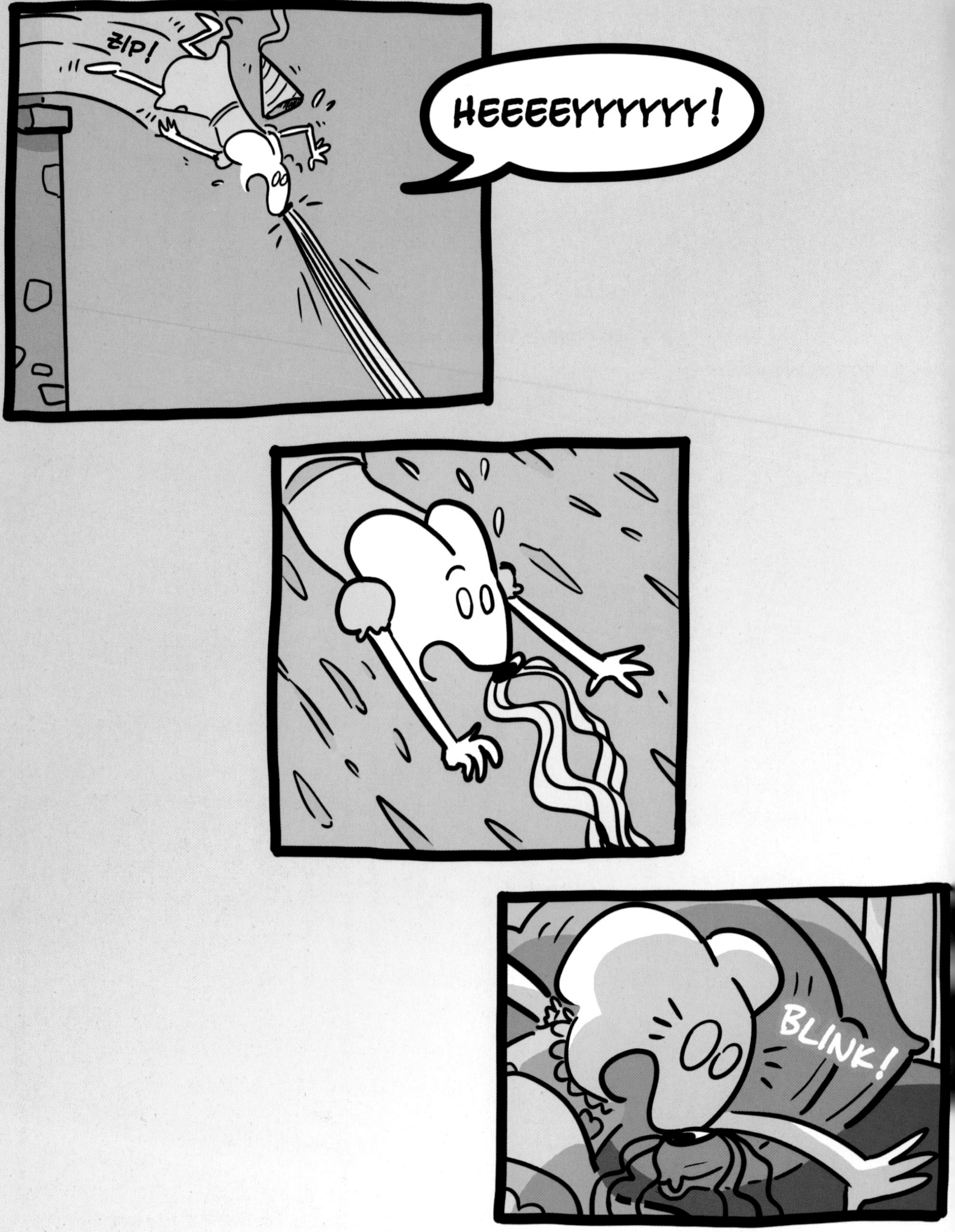
ZIP!
HEEEEYYYYYY!
BLINK!

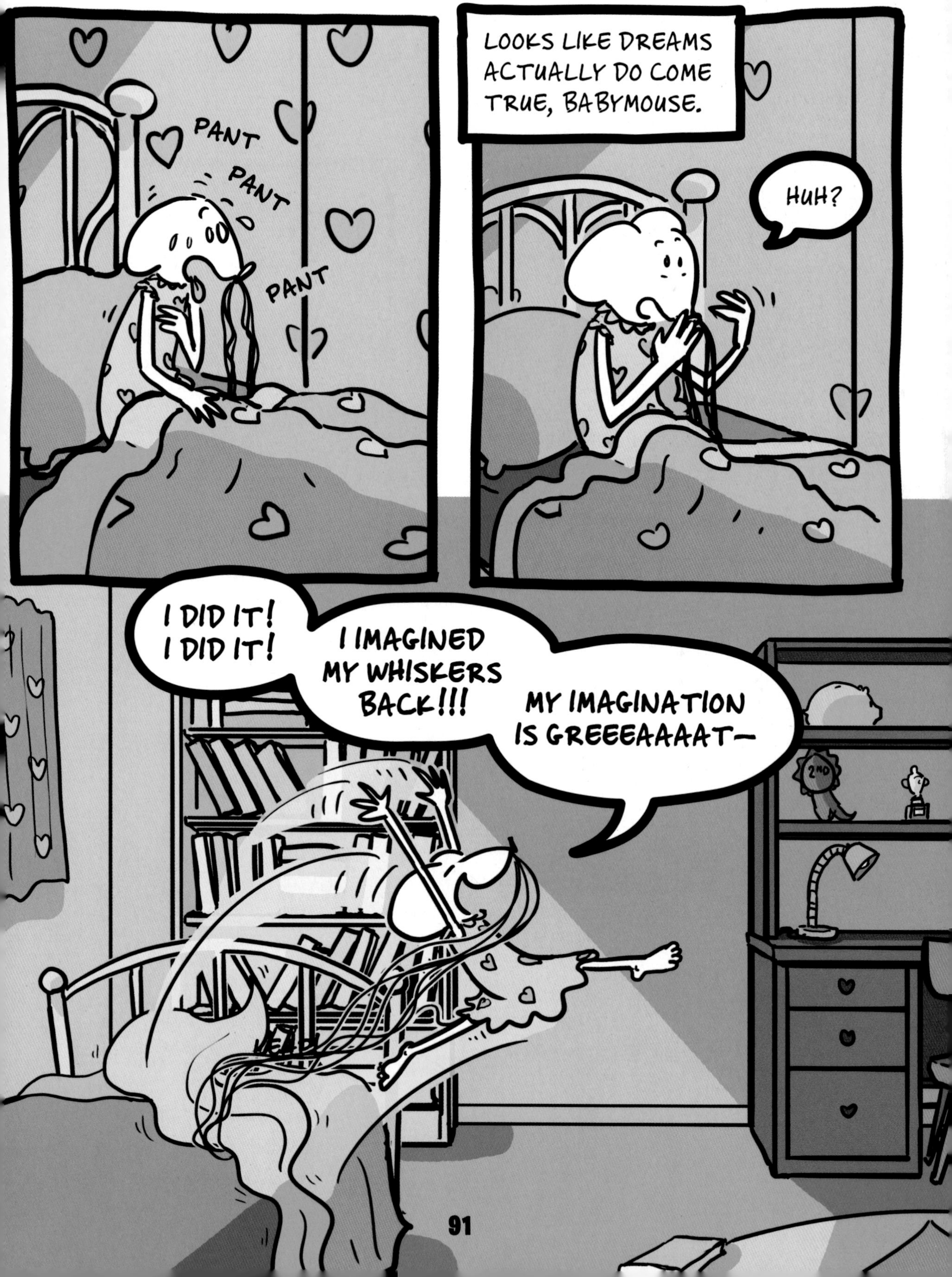
PANT
PANT
PANT
LOOKS LIKE DREAMS ACTUALLY DO COME TRUE, BABYMOUSE.
HUH?
I DID IT! I DID IT!
I IMAGINED MY WHISKERS BACK!!!
MY IMAGINATION IS GREEEAAAAT—
2ND

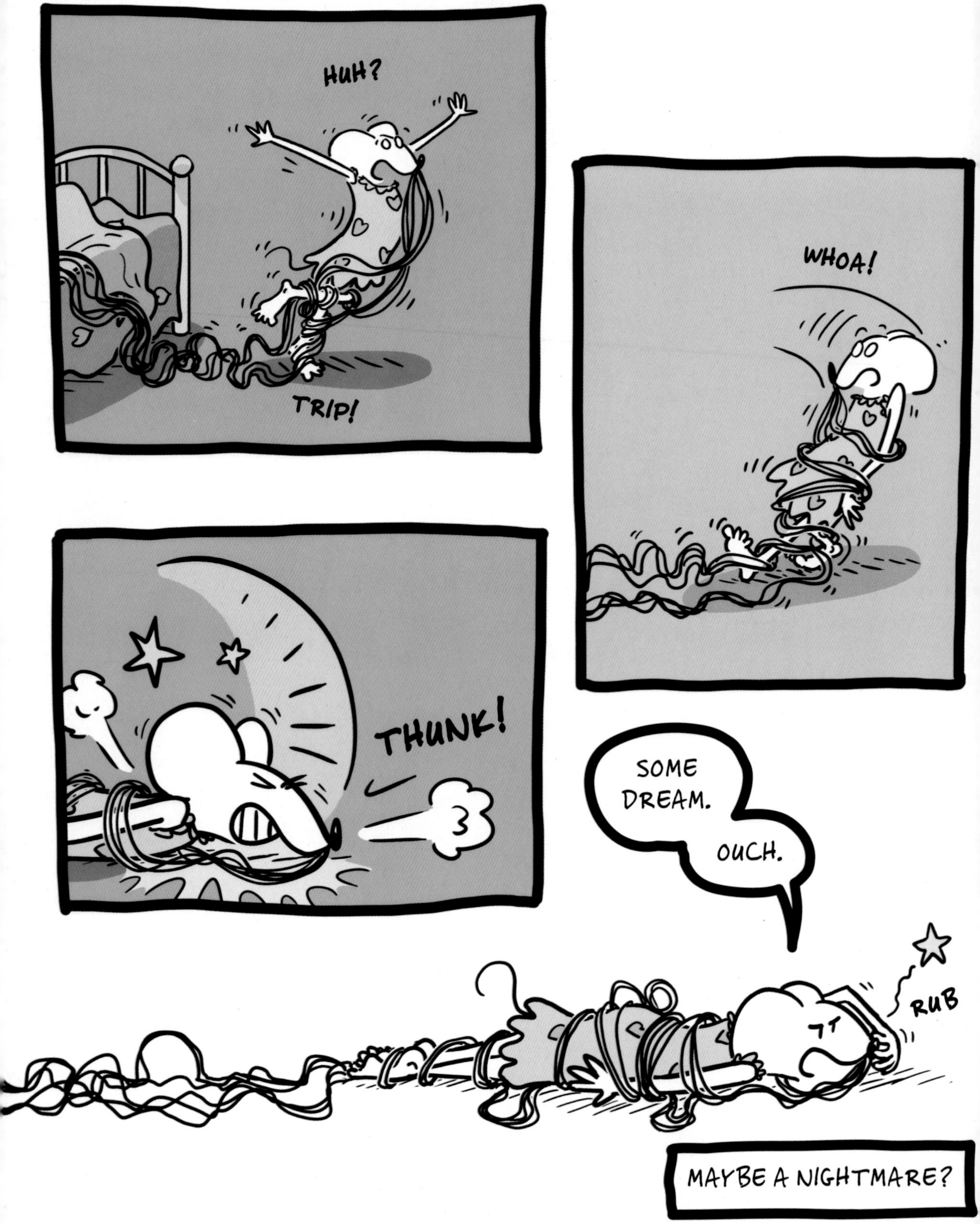
HUH?
TRIP!
WHOA!
THUNK!
SOME DREAM.
OUCH.
RUB
MAYBE A NIGHTMARE?

THOSE ARE VERY SHARP SCISSORS, BABYMOUSE.

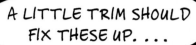
A LITTLE TRIM SHOULD FIX THESE UP. . . .

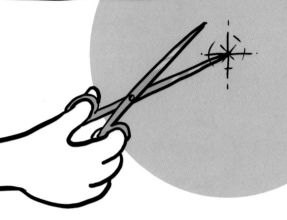

SNIP!

SNIP!

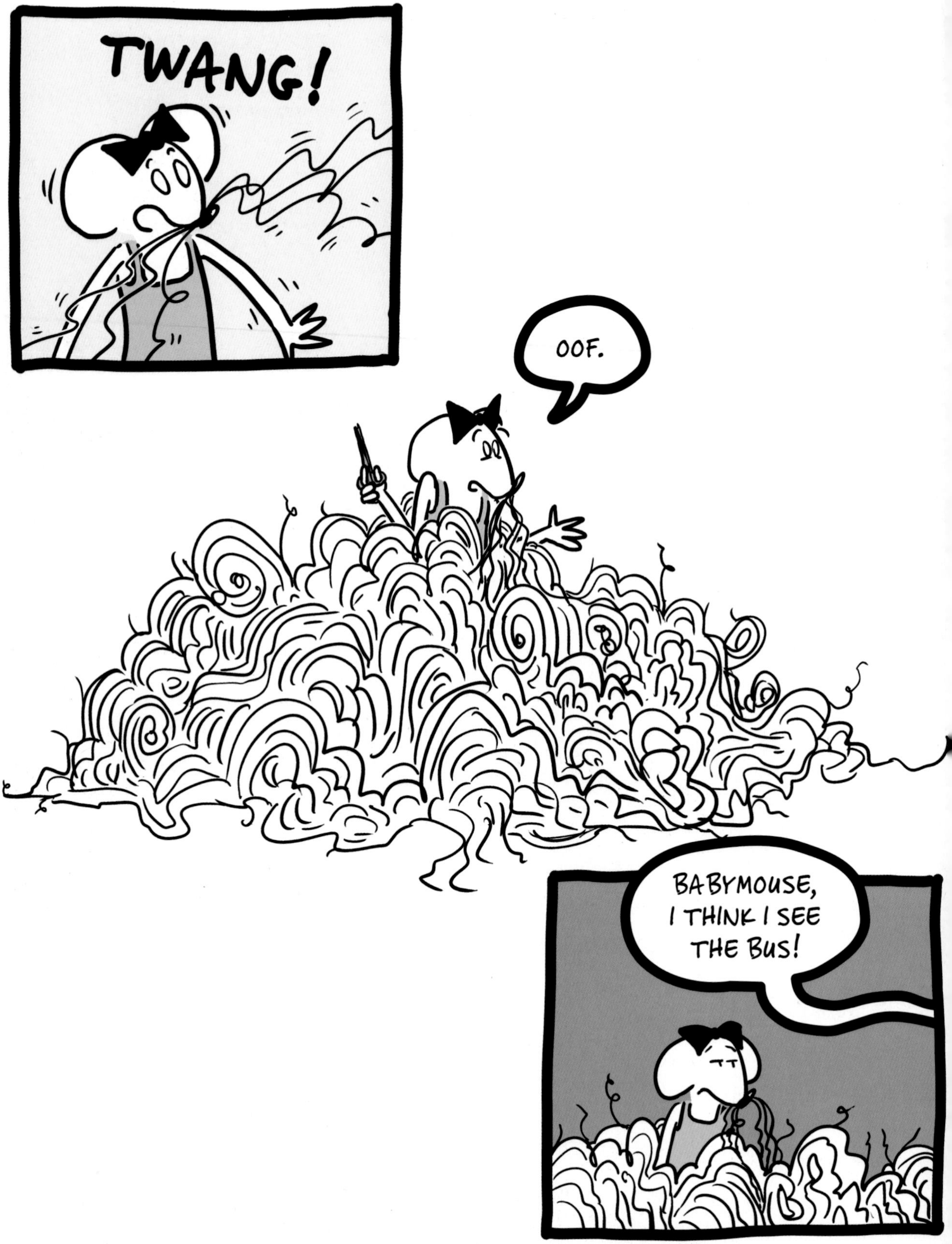
TWANG!
OOF.
BABYMOUSE, I THINK I SEE THE BUS!

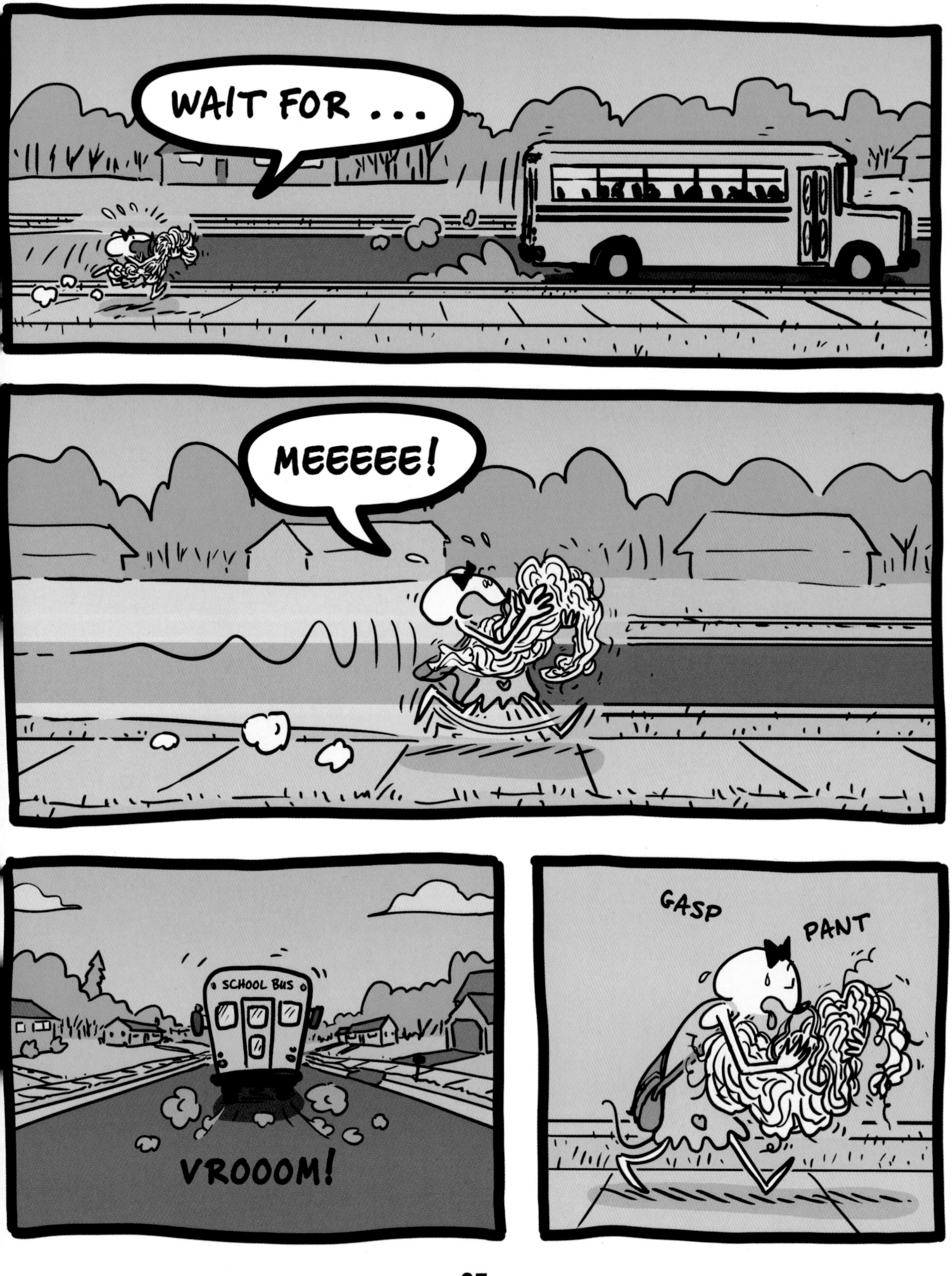
WAIT FOR . . .
MEEEEEE!
SCHOOL BUS
VROOOM!
GASP
PANT

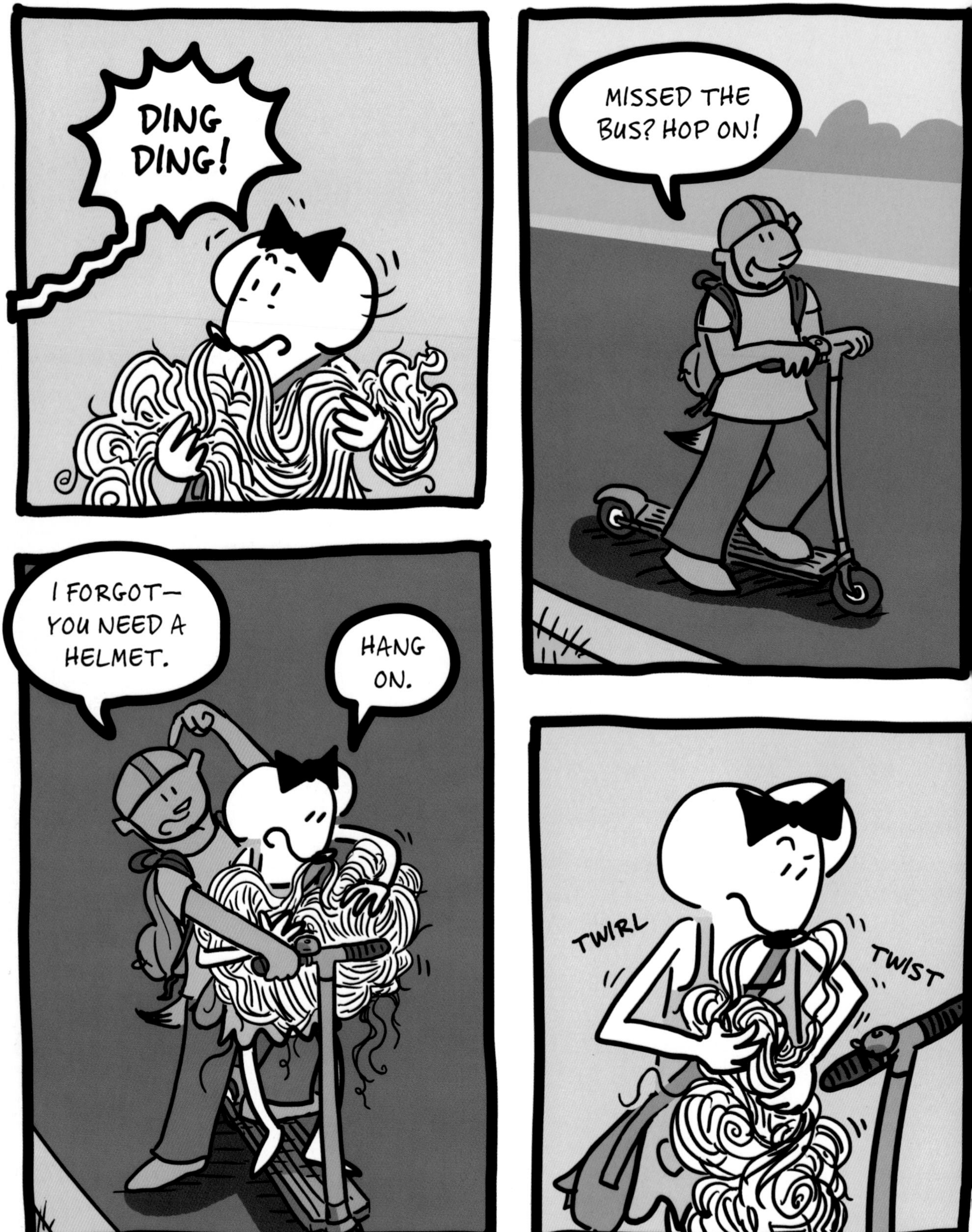
DING DING!
MISSED THE BUS? HOP ON!
I FORGOT— YOU NEED A HELMET.
HANG ON.
TWIRL
TWIST

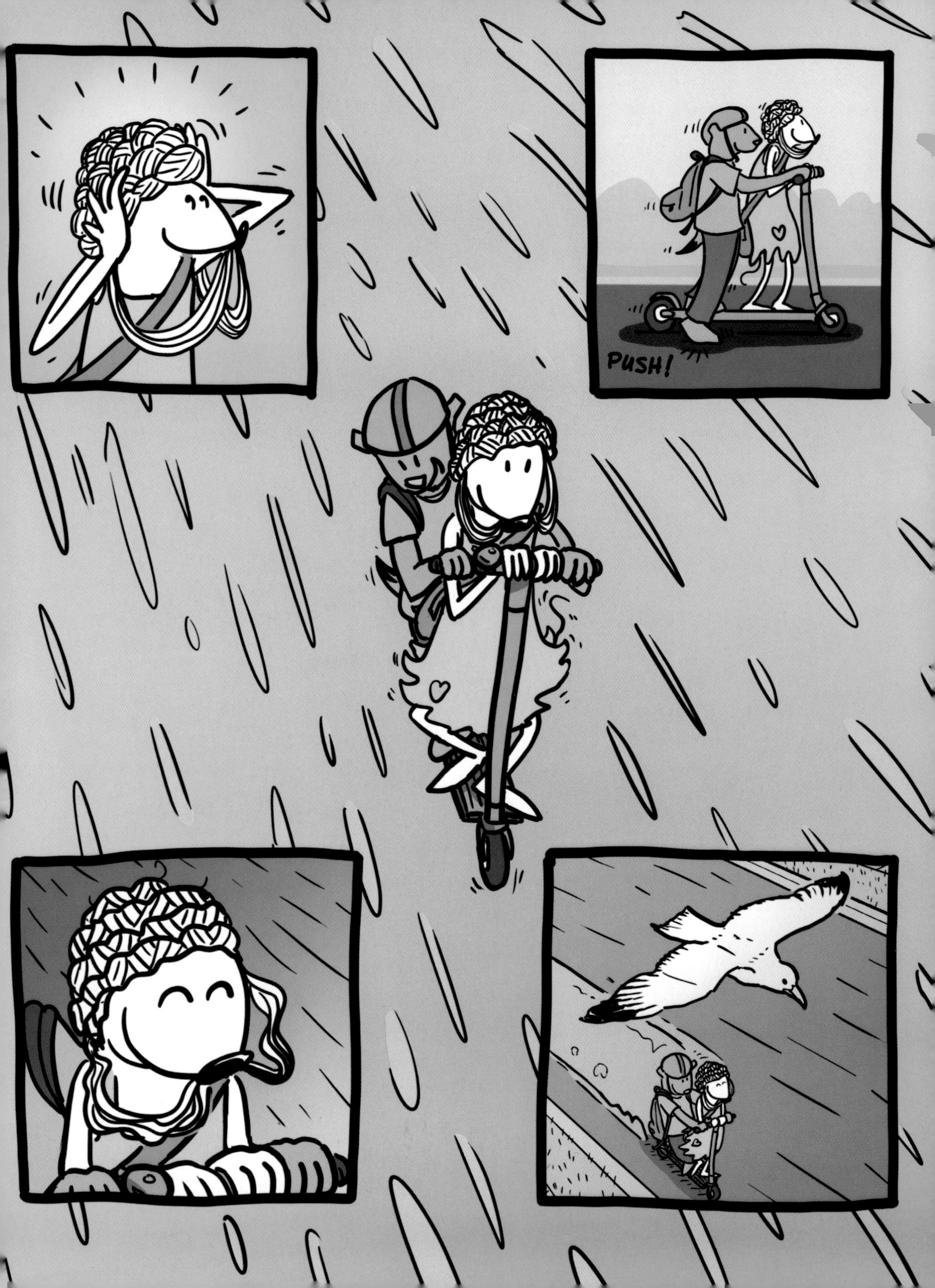
PUSH!

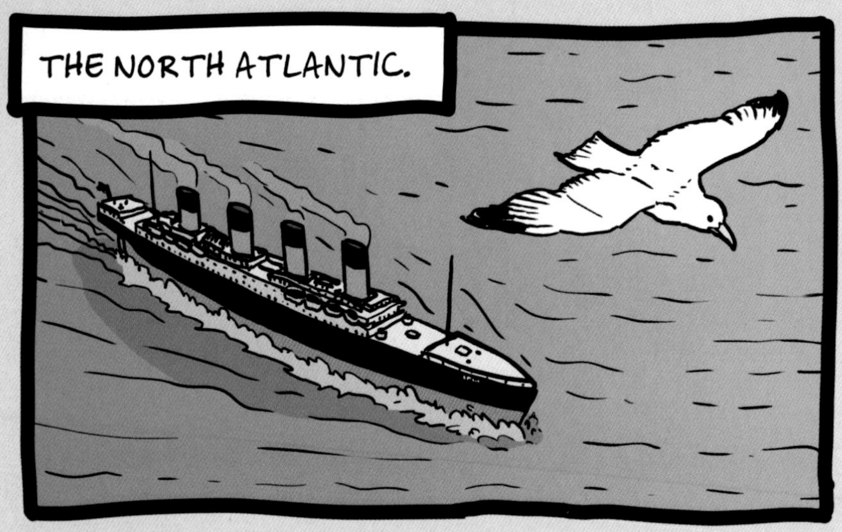
THE NORTH ATLANTIC.

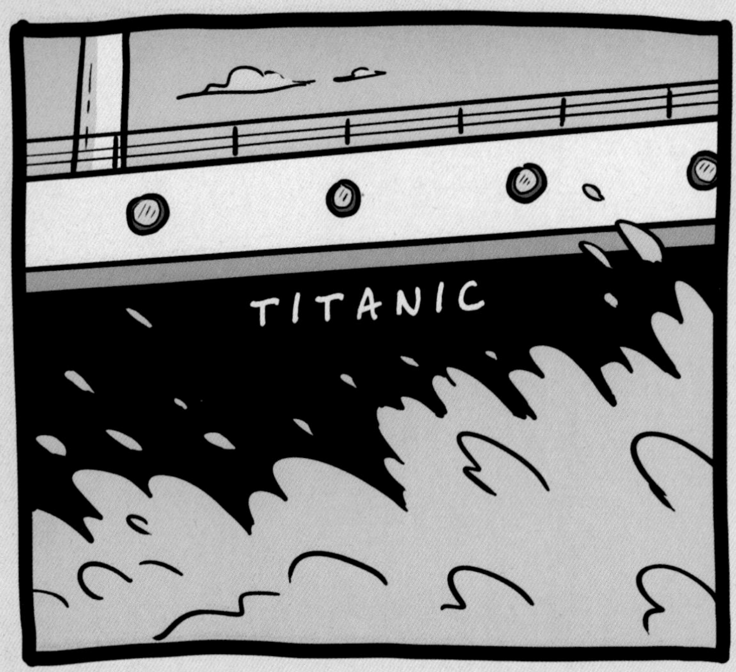
TITANIC

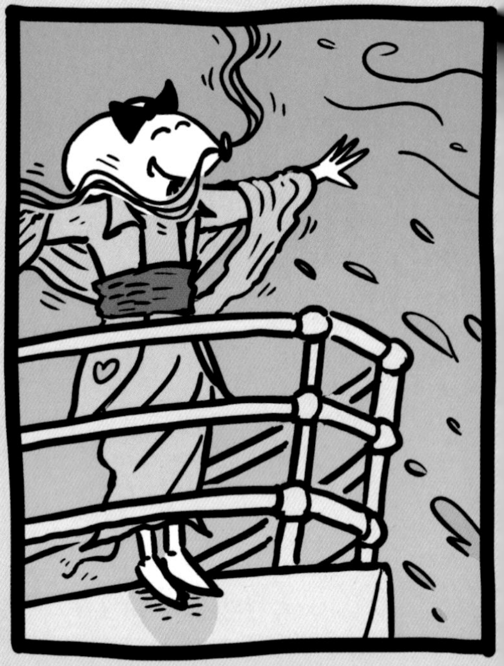

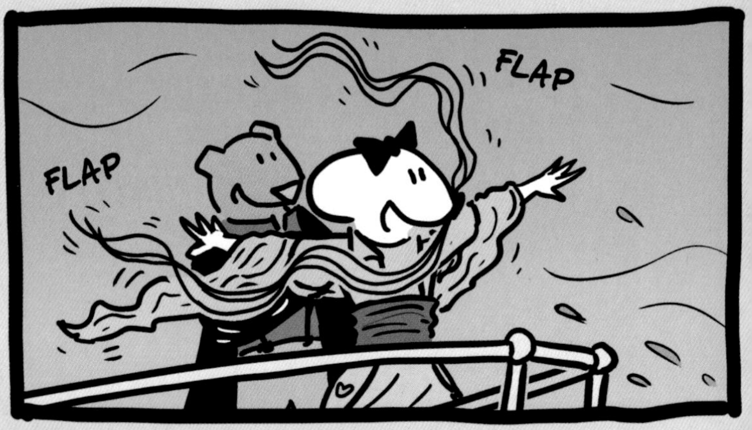
FLAP
FLAP

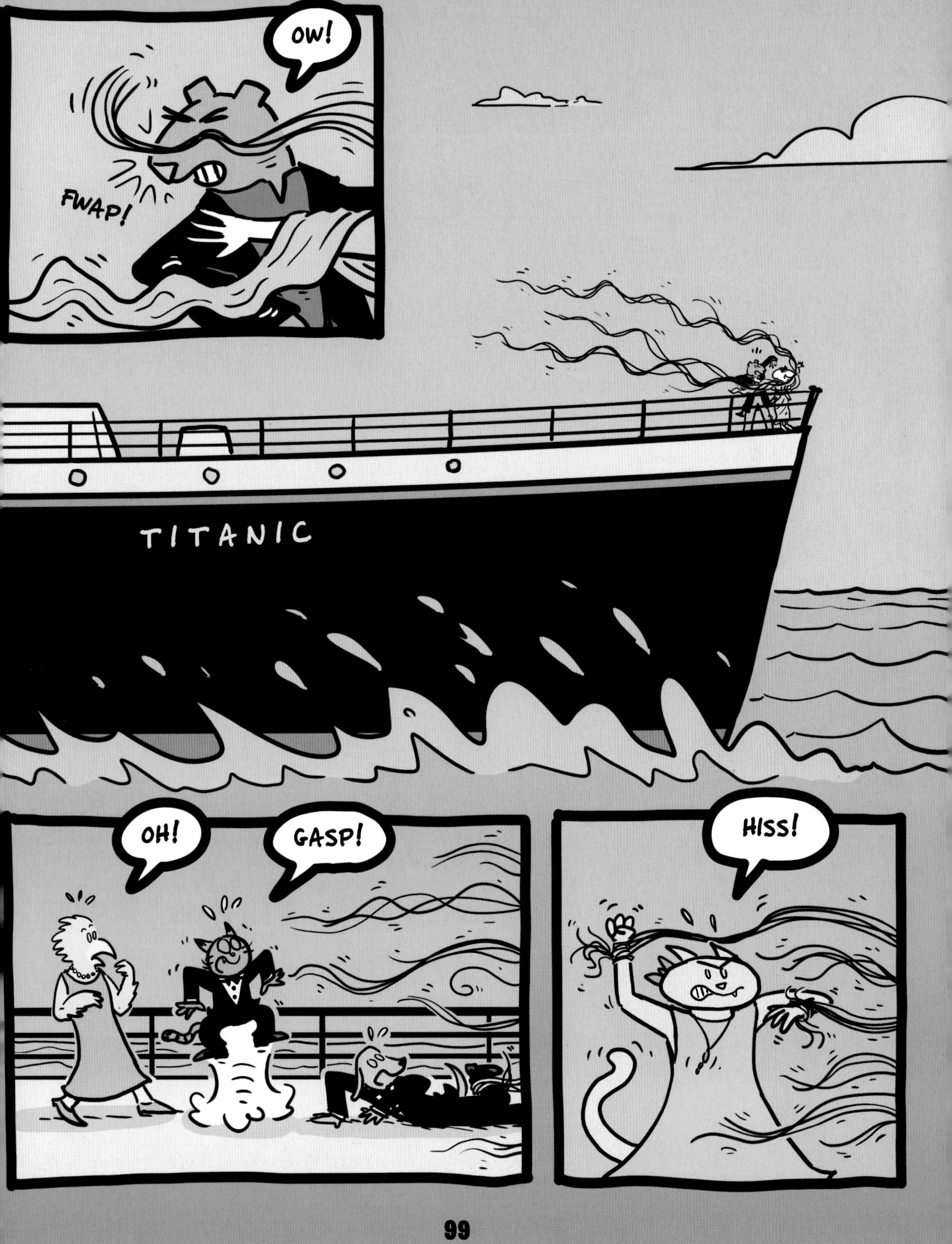
OW!
FWAP!
TITANIC
OH!
GASP!
HISS!

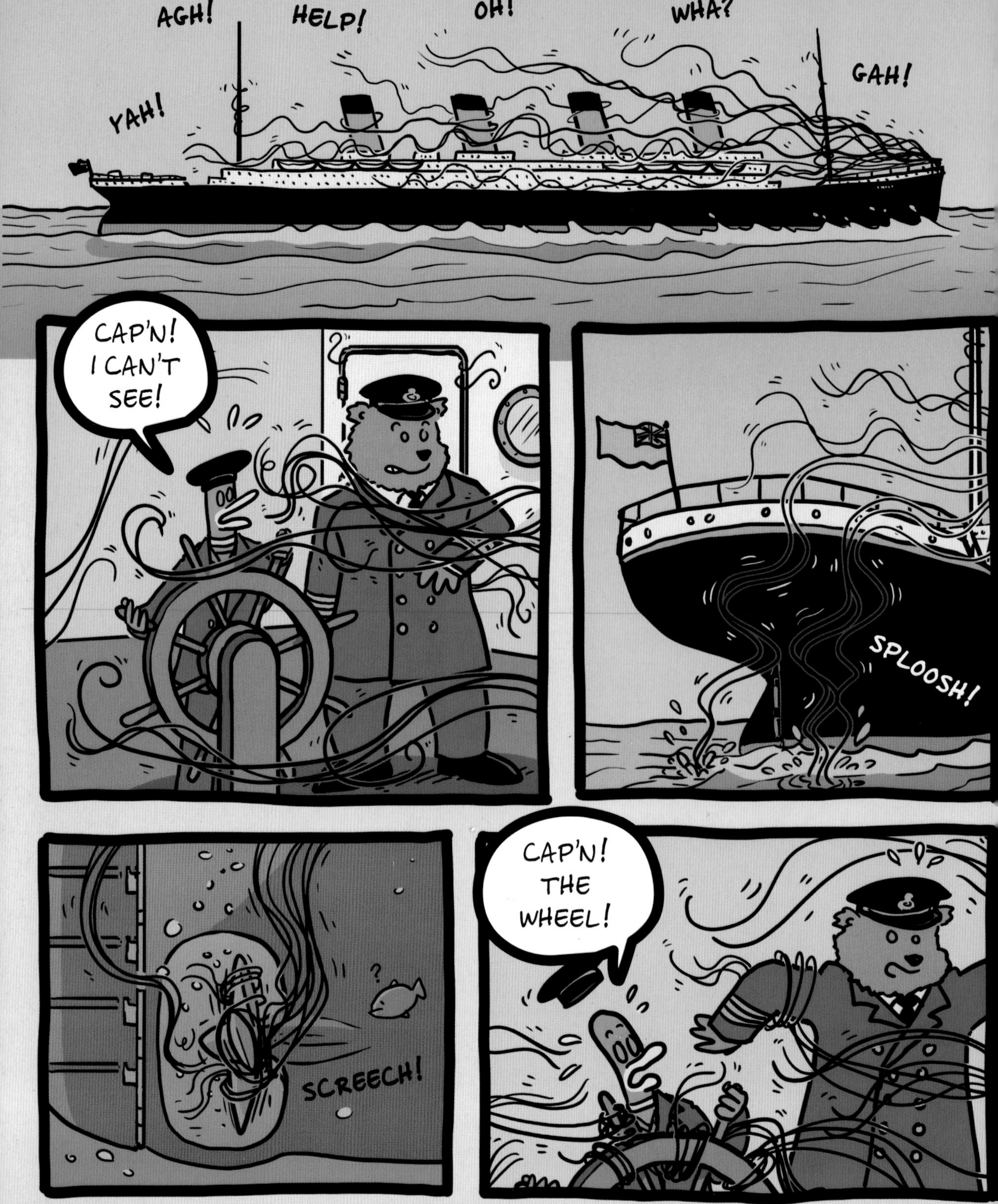
AGH!
HELP!
OH!
WHA?
YAH!
GAH!
CAP'N! I CAN'T SEE!
SPLOOSH!
SCREECH!
?
CAP'N! THE WHEEL!

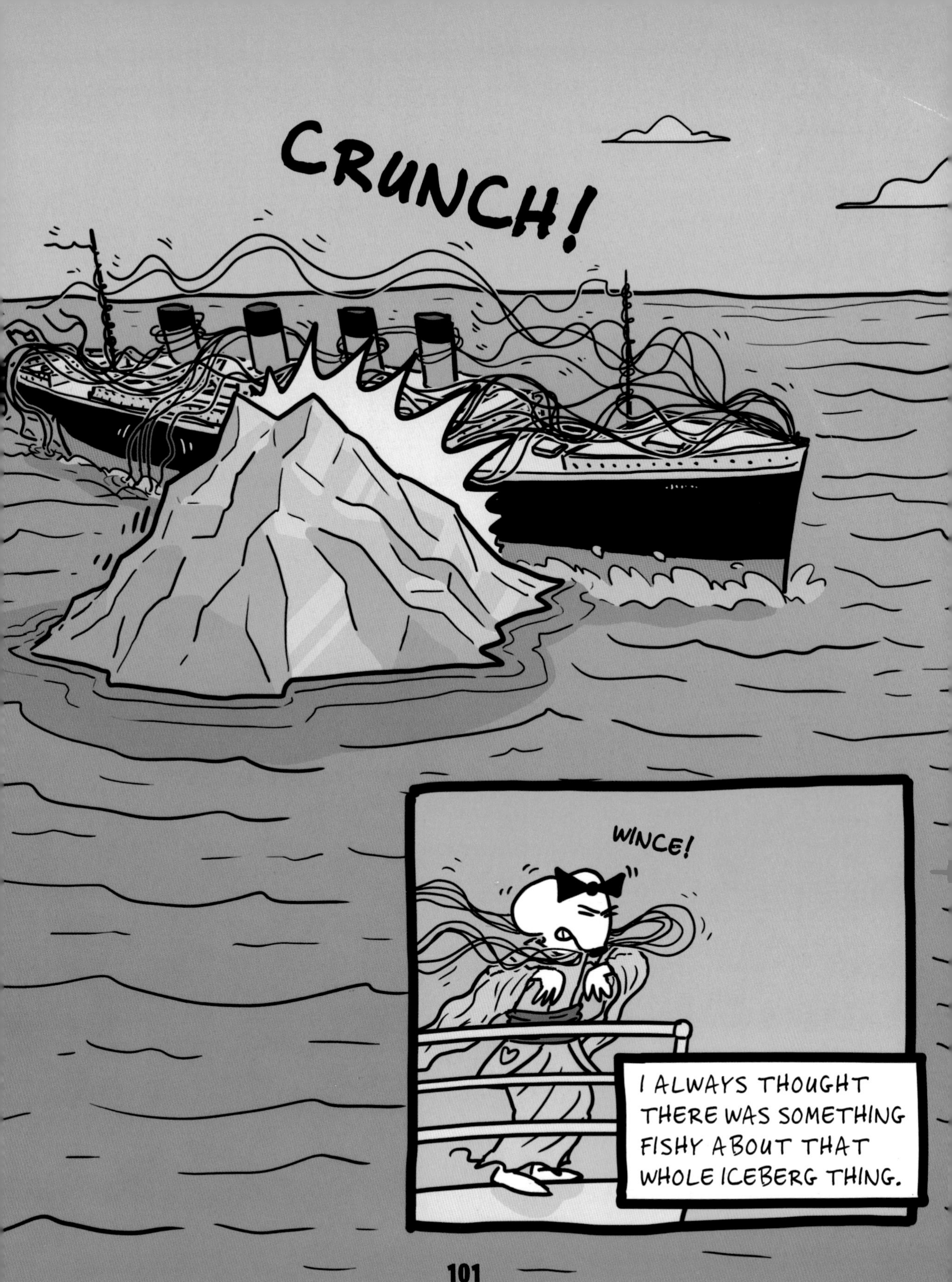
CRUNCH!
WINCE!
I ALWAYS THOUGHT THERE WAS SOMETHING FISHY ABOUT THAT WHOLE ICEBERG THING.

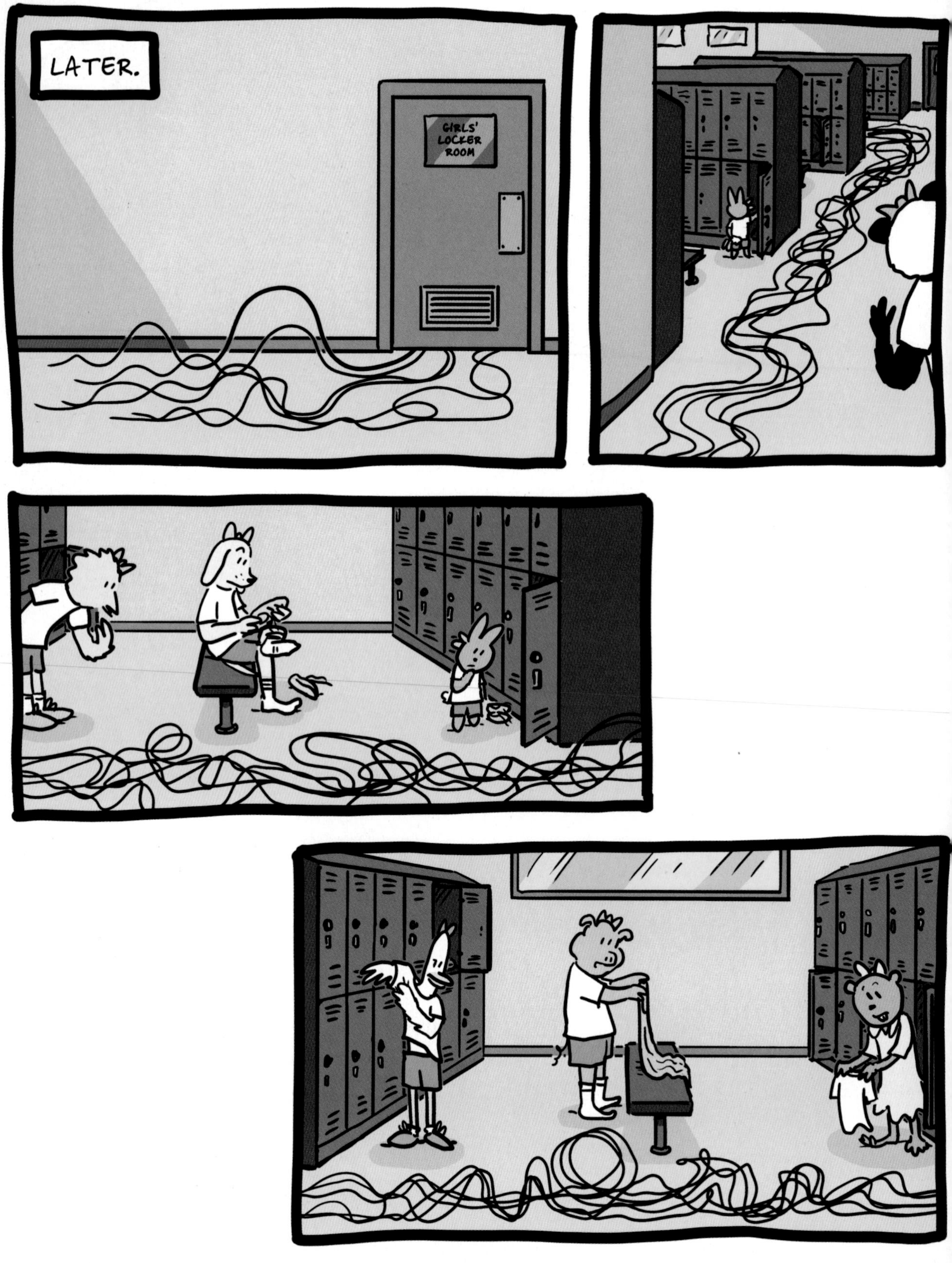
LATER.
GIRLS' LOCKER ROOM

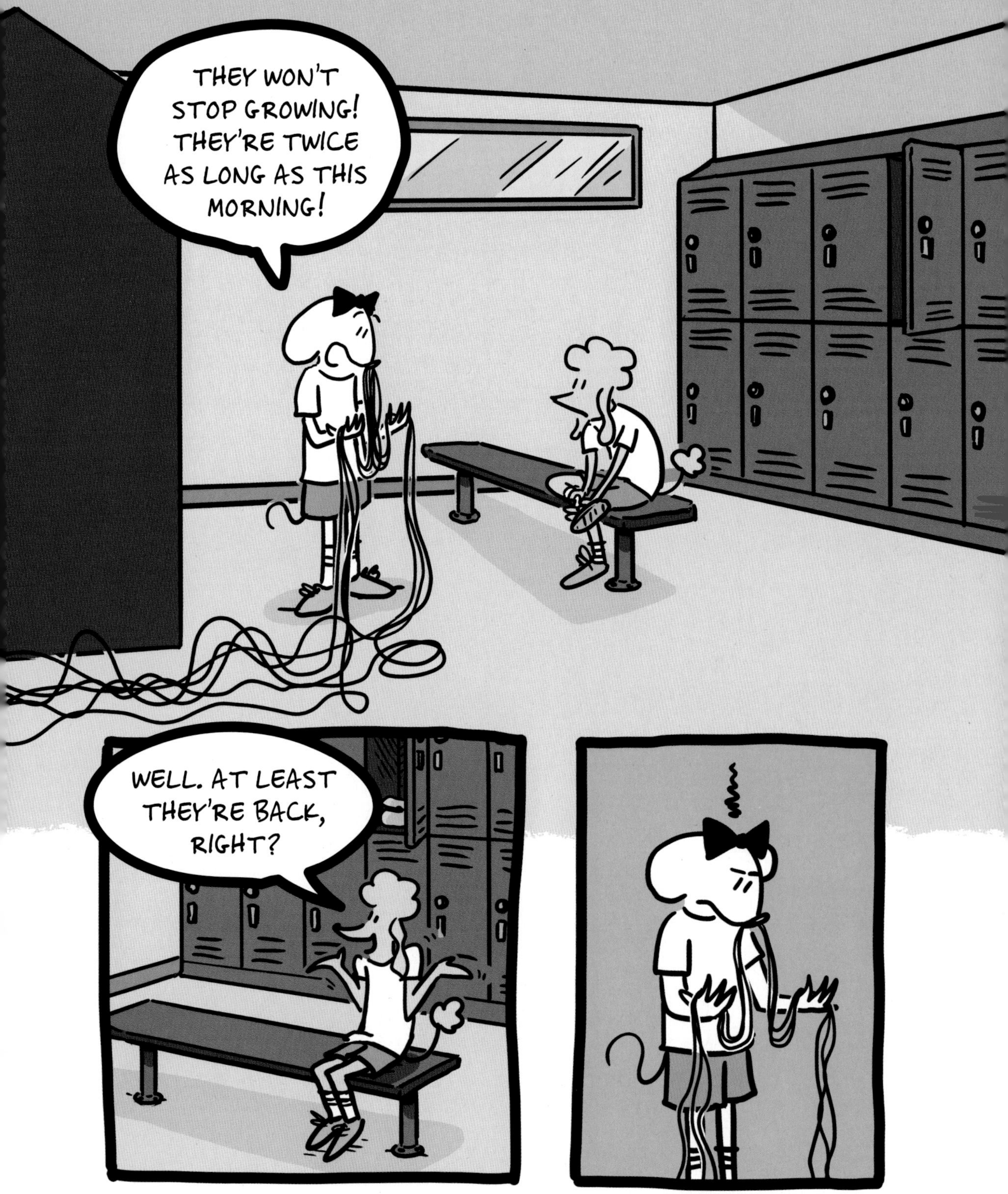
THEY WON'T STOP GROWING! THEY'RE TWICE AS LONG AS THIS MORNING!
WELL. AT LEAST THEY'RE BACK, RIGHT?

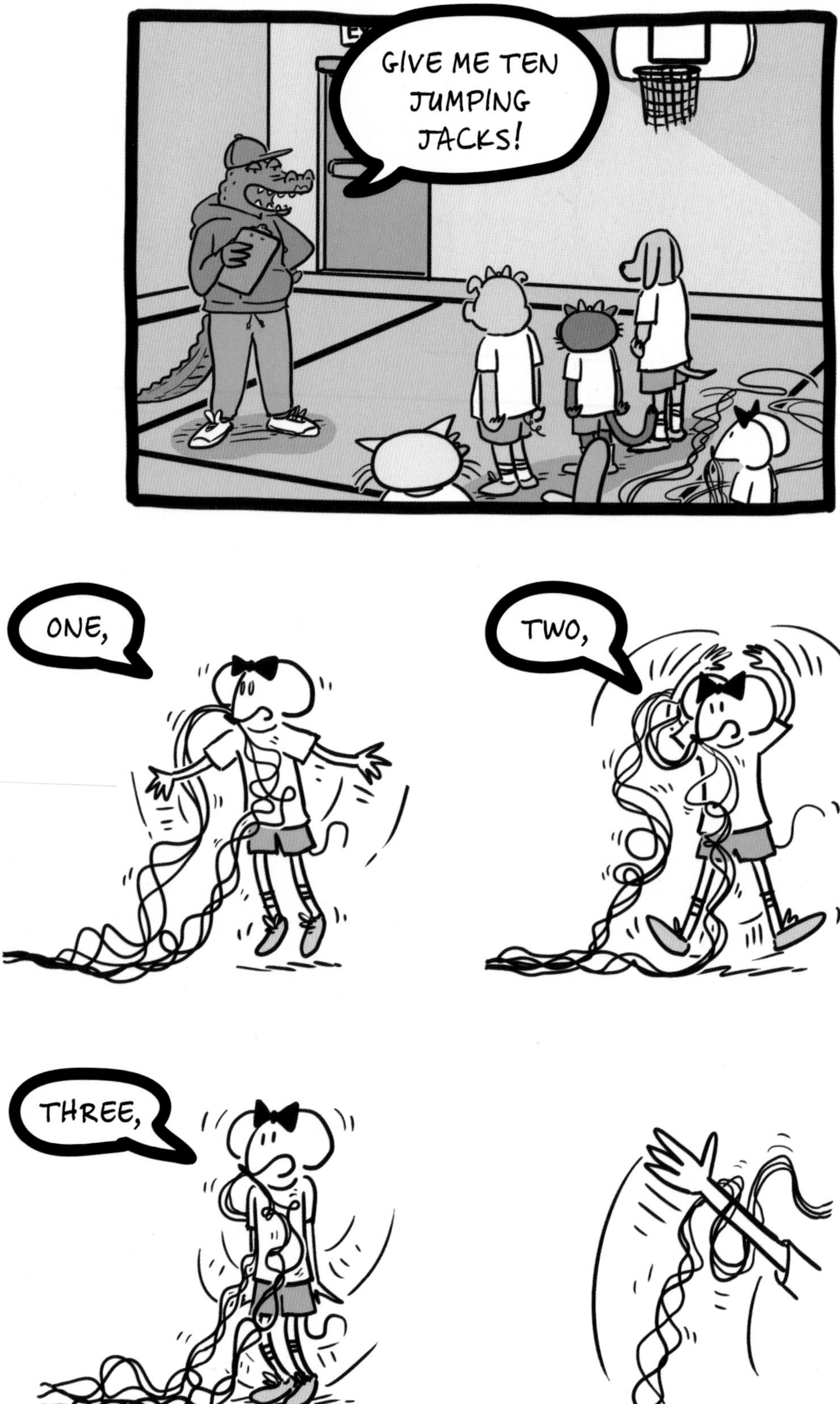
GIVE ME TEN JUMPING JACKS!
ONE,
TWO,
THREE,

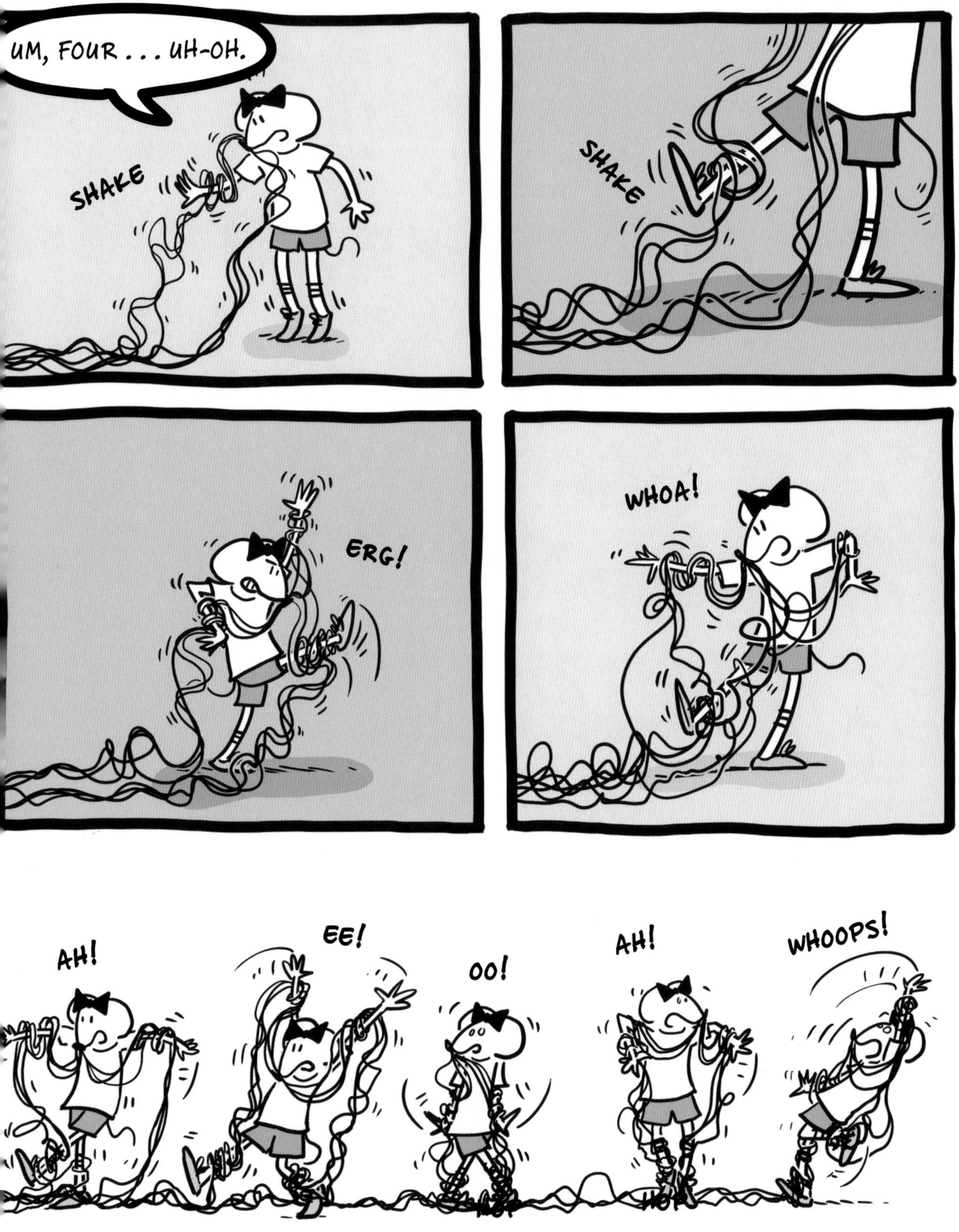
UM, FOUR . . . UH-OH.
SHAKE
SHAKE
ERG!
WHOA!
AH!
EE!
OO!
AH!
WHOOPS!

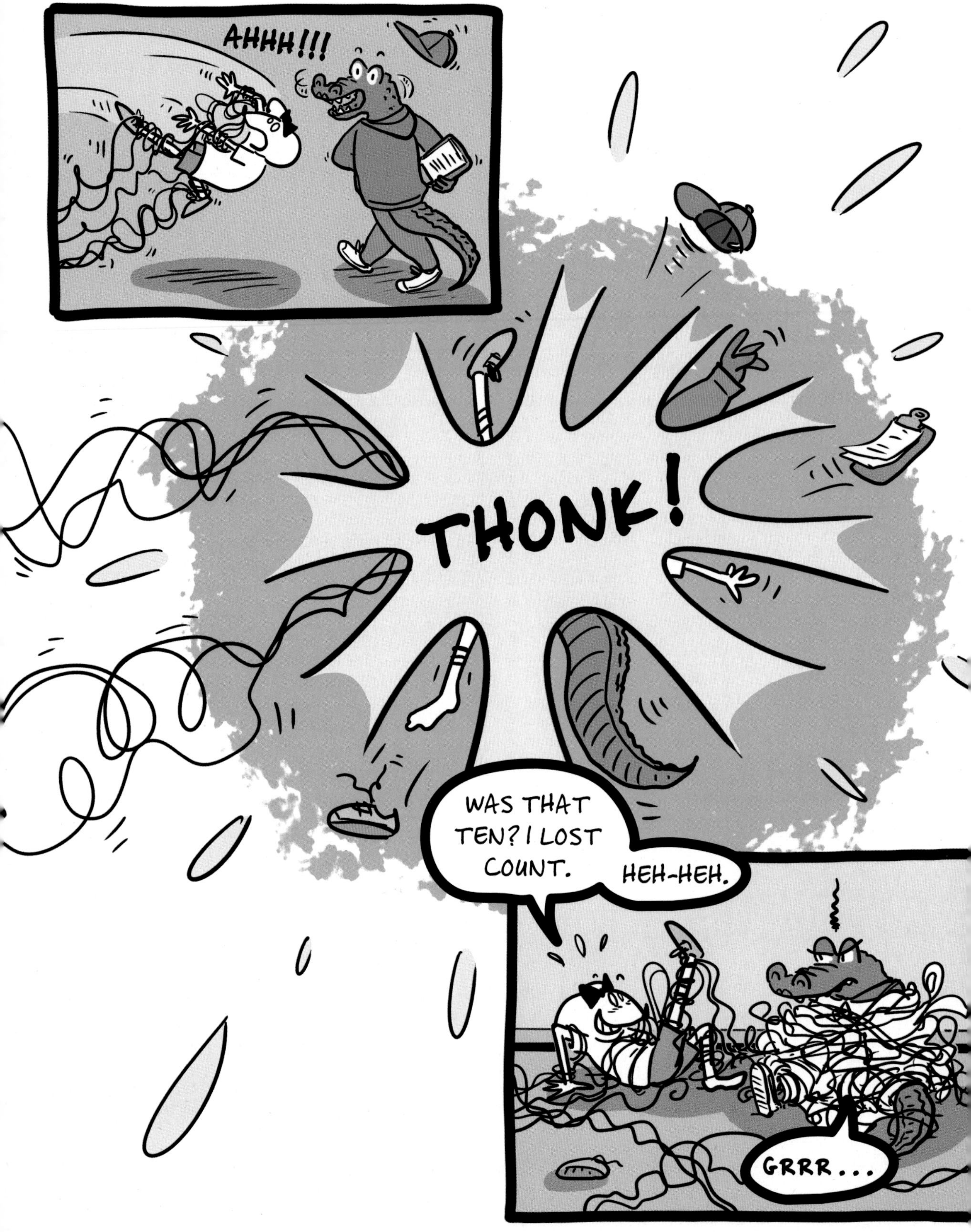
AHHH!!!
THONK!
WAS THAT TEN? I LOST COUNT.
HEH-HEH.
GRRR...

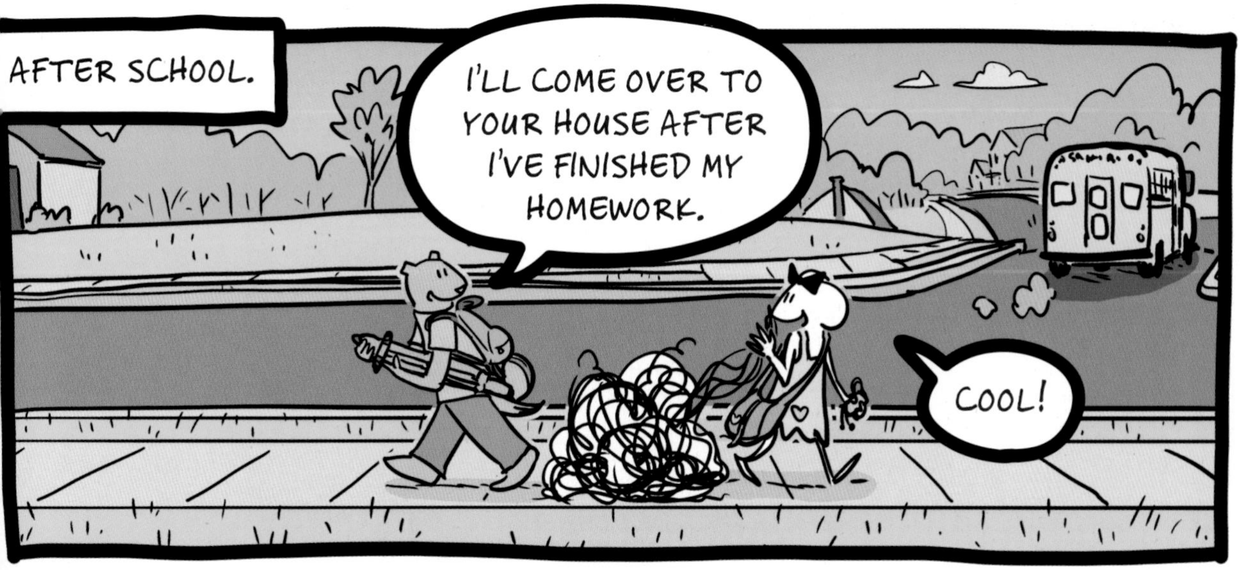
AFTER SCHOOL.
I'LL COME OVER TO YOUR HOUSE AFTER I'VE FINISHED MY HOMEWORK.
COOL!

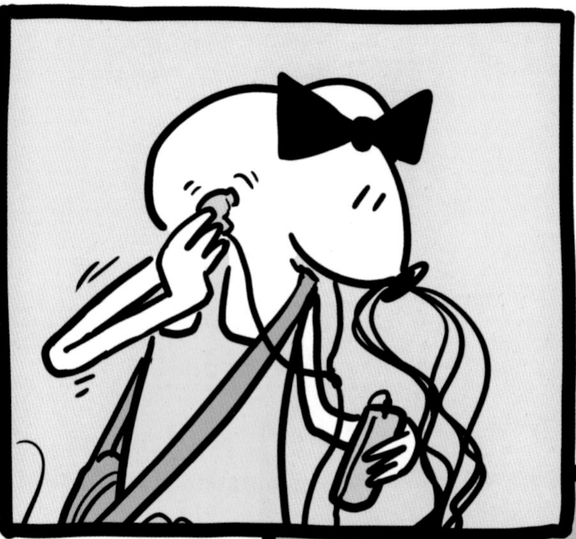

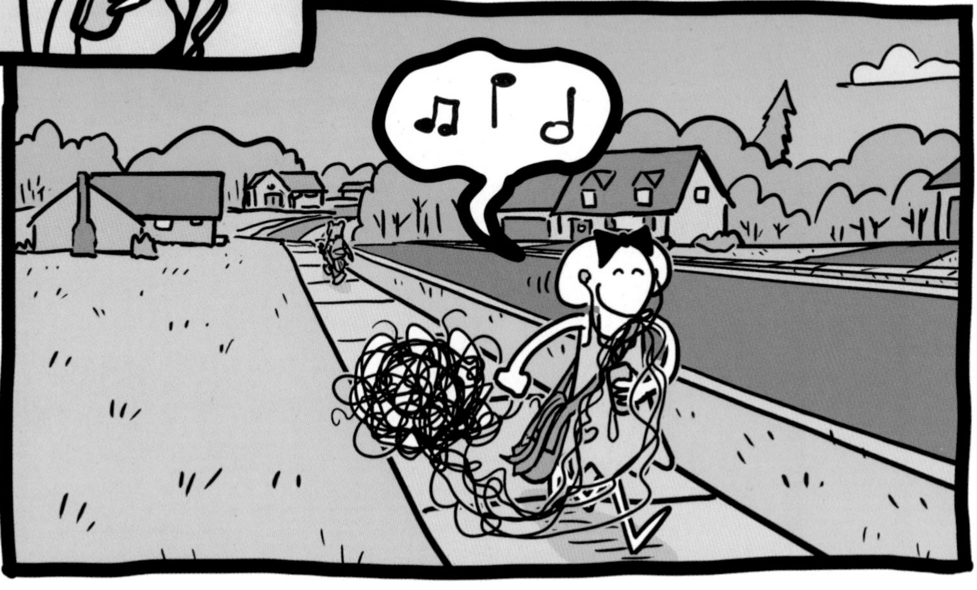

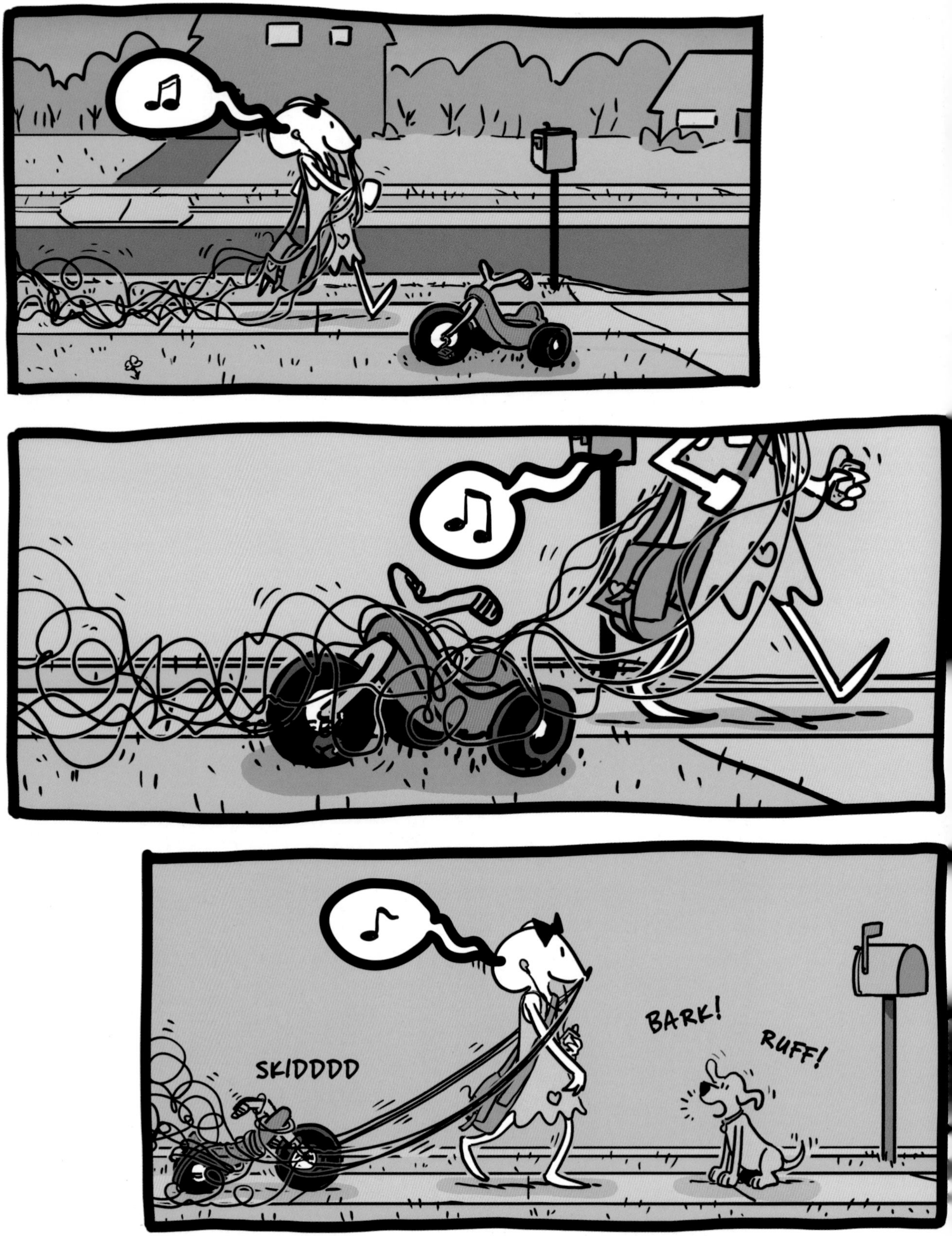
SKIDDDD
BARK!
RUFF!

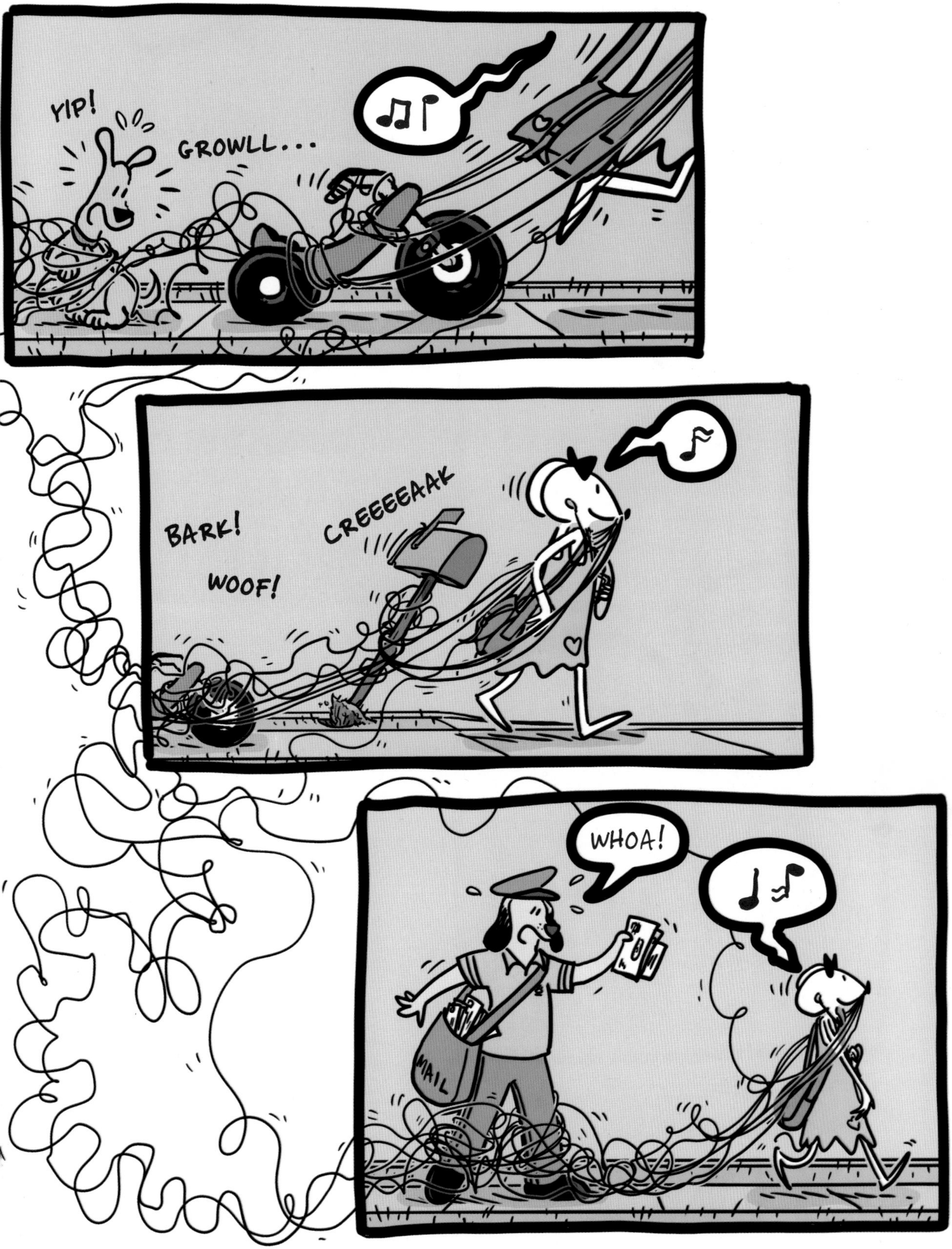
YIP!
GROWLL...
BARK!
WOOF!
CREEEEAAK
WHOA!
MAIL

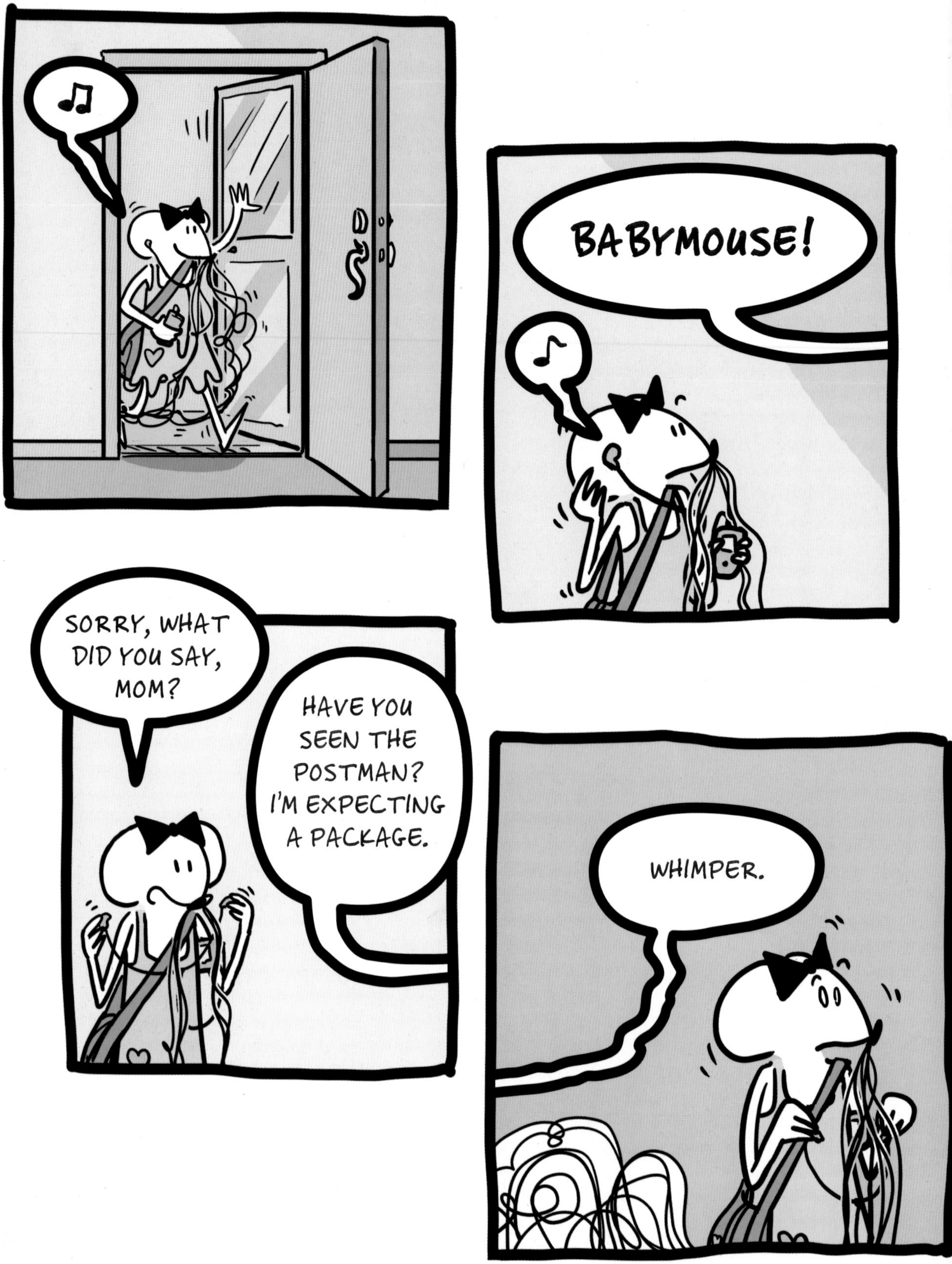
♫
BABYMOUSE!
♪
SORRY, WHAT DID YOU SAY, MOM?
HAVE YOU SEEN THE POSTMAN? I'M EXPECTING A PACKAGE.
WHIMPER.

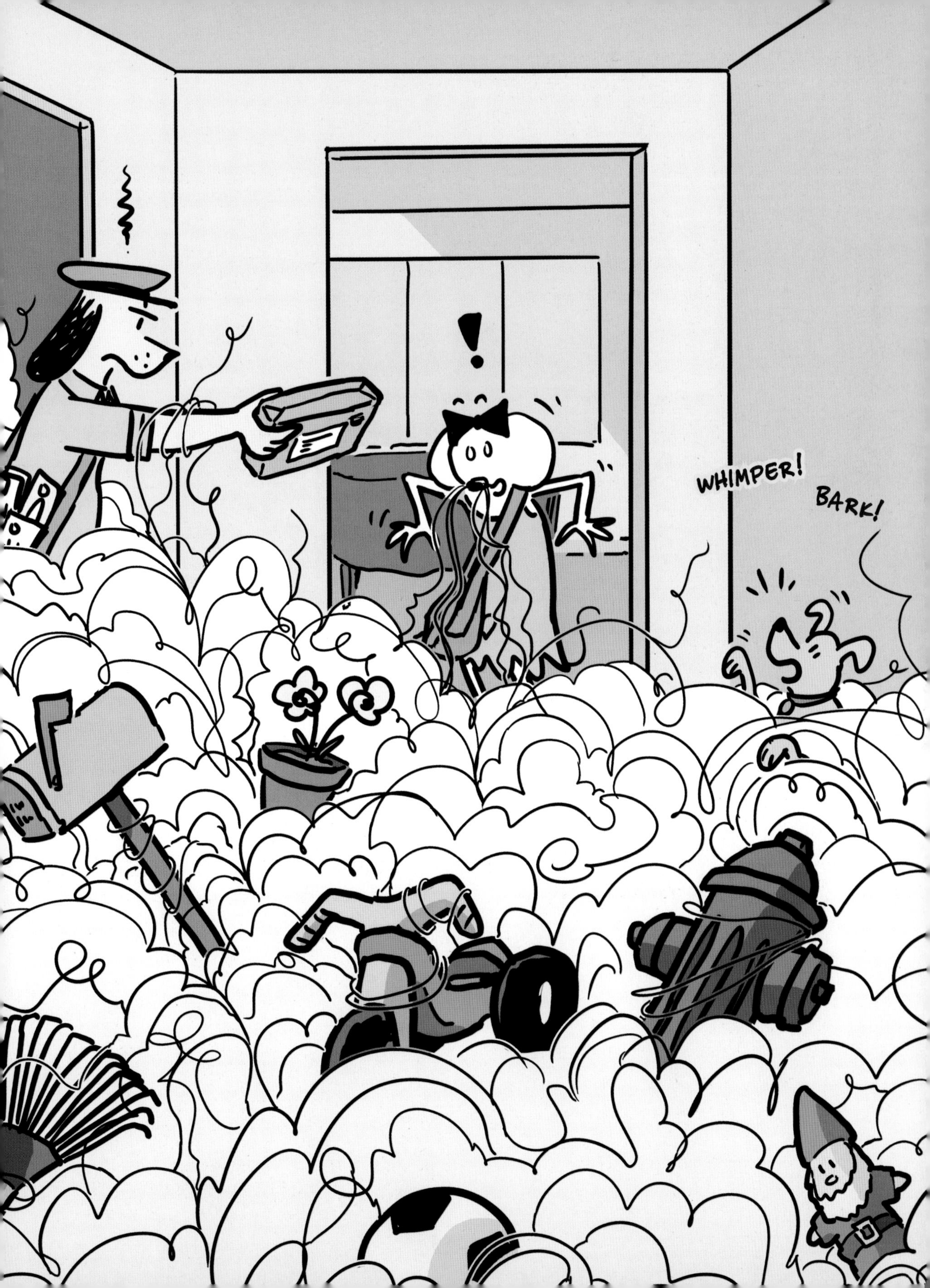
WHIMPER!
BARK!

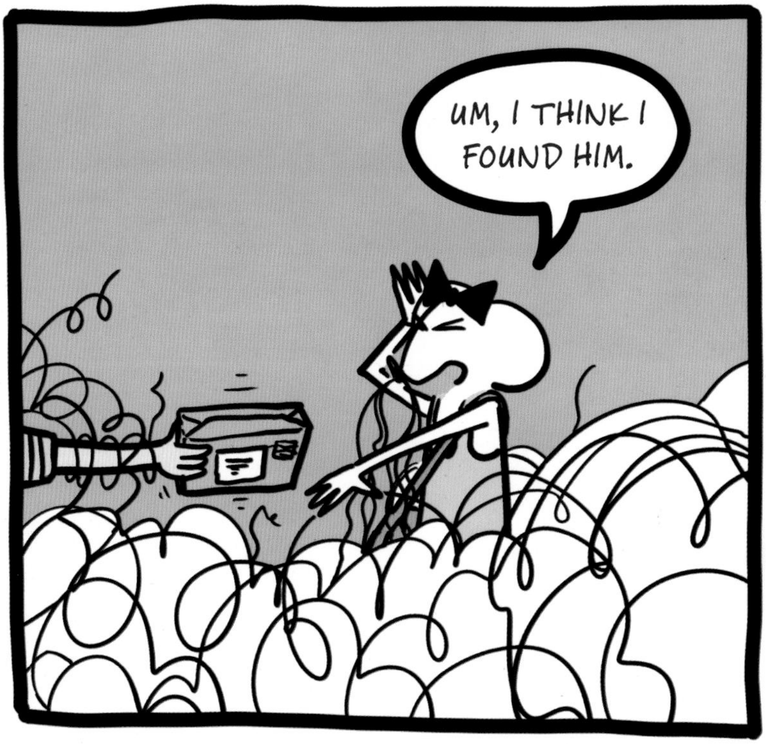
UM, I THINK I FOUND HIM.

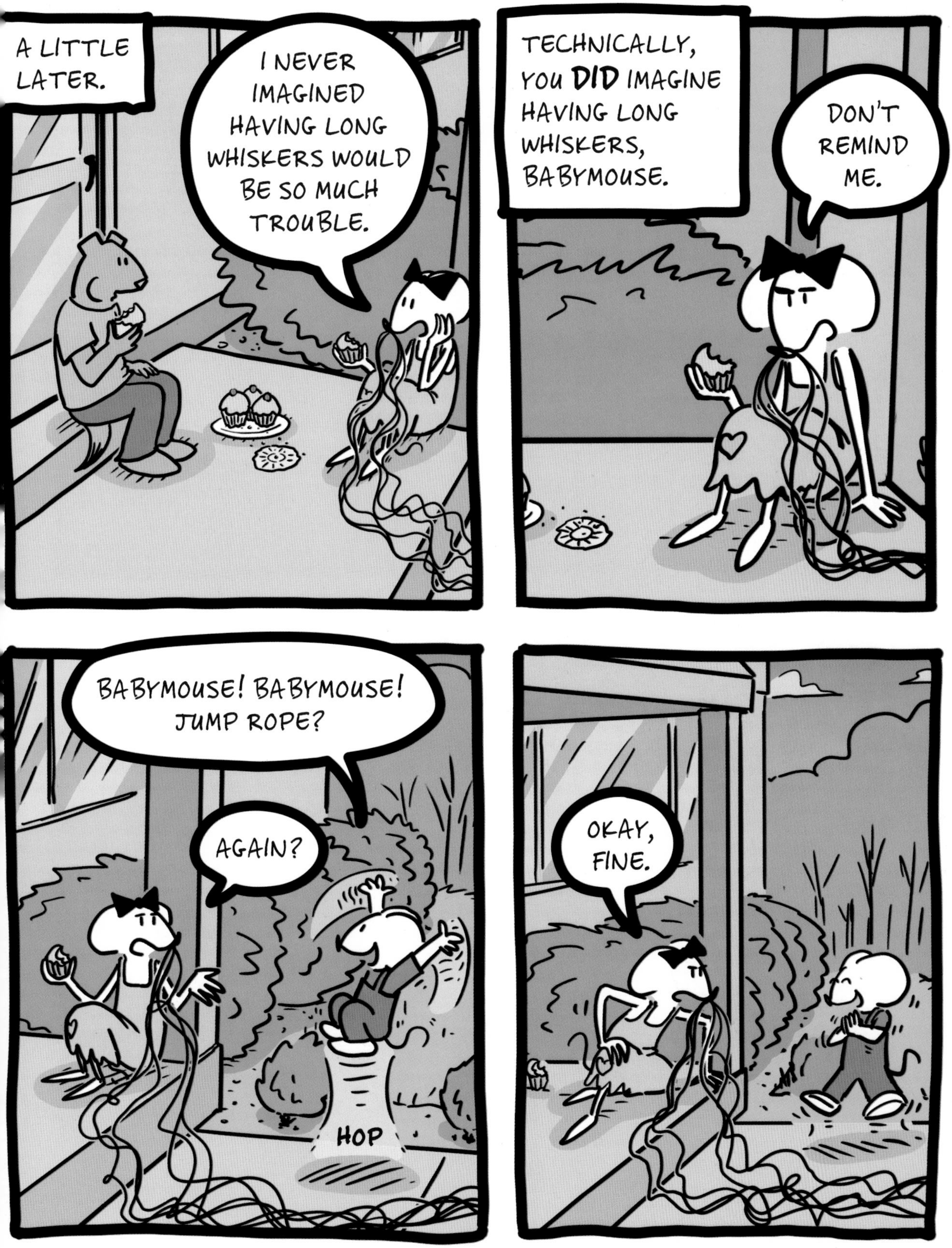
A LITTLE LATER.
I NEVER IMAGINED HAVING LONG WHISKERS WOULD BE SO MUCH TROUBLE.
TECHNICALLY, YOU **DID** IMAGINE HAVING LONG WHISKERS, BABYMOUSE.
DON'T REMIND ME.
BABYMOUSE! BABYMOUSE! JUMP ROPE?
AGAIN?
HOP
OKAY, FINE.

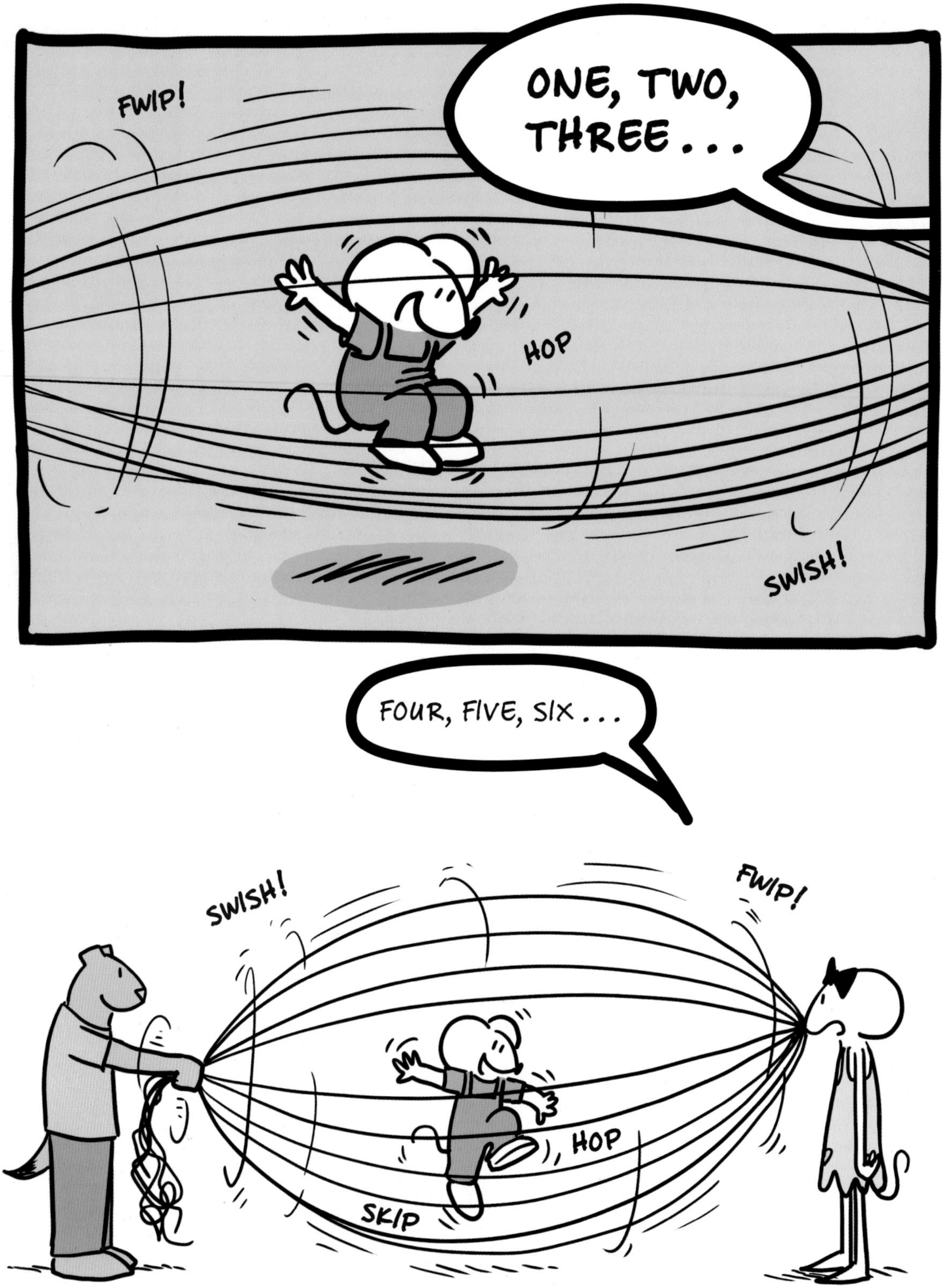
FWIP!
ONE, TWO, THREE . . .
HOP
SWISH!
FOUR, FIVE, SIX . . .
SWISH!
FWIP!
HOP
SKIP

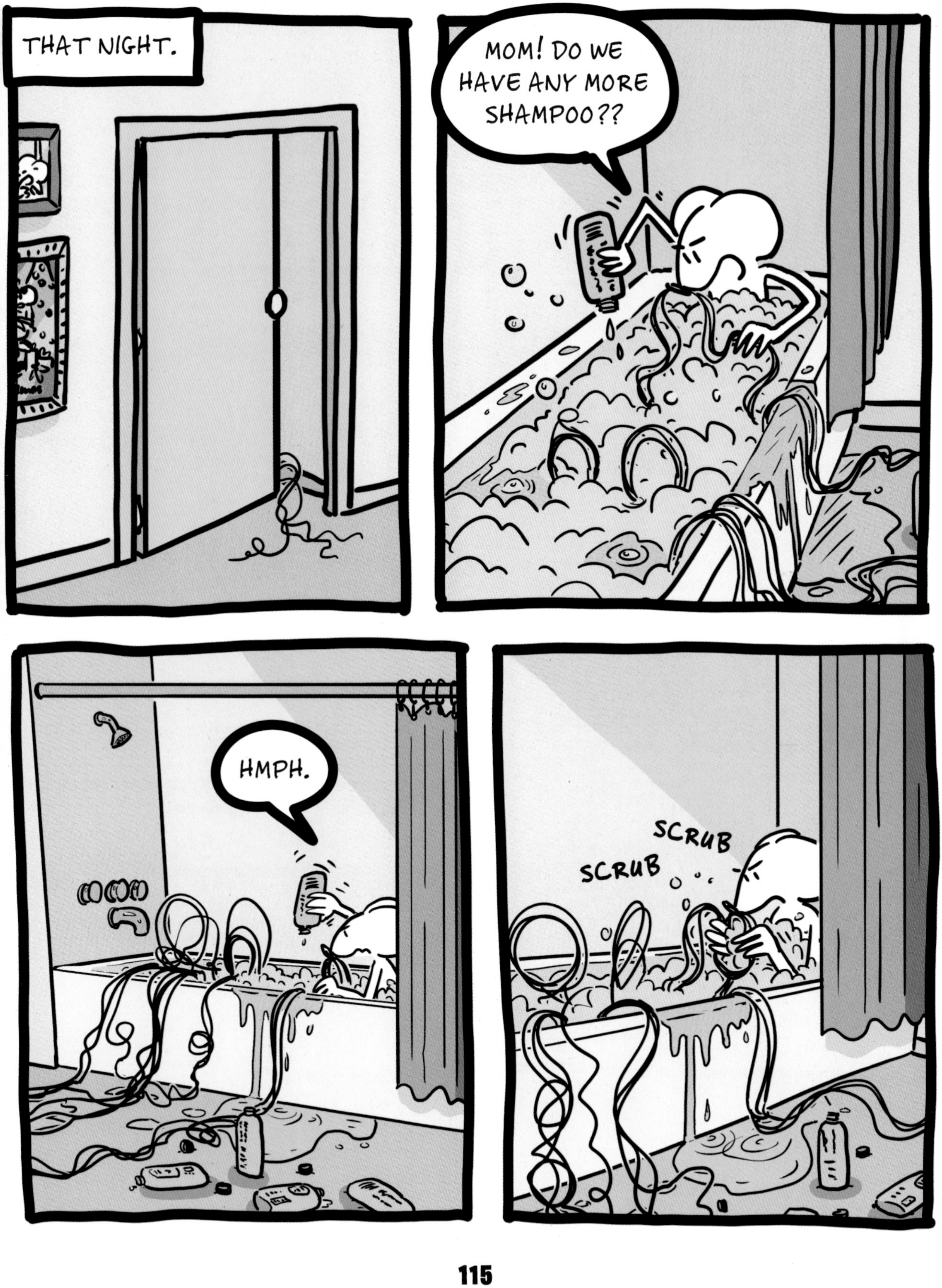
THAT NIGHT.
MOM! DO WE HAVE ANY MORE SHAMPOO??
HMPH.
SCRUB
SCRUB

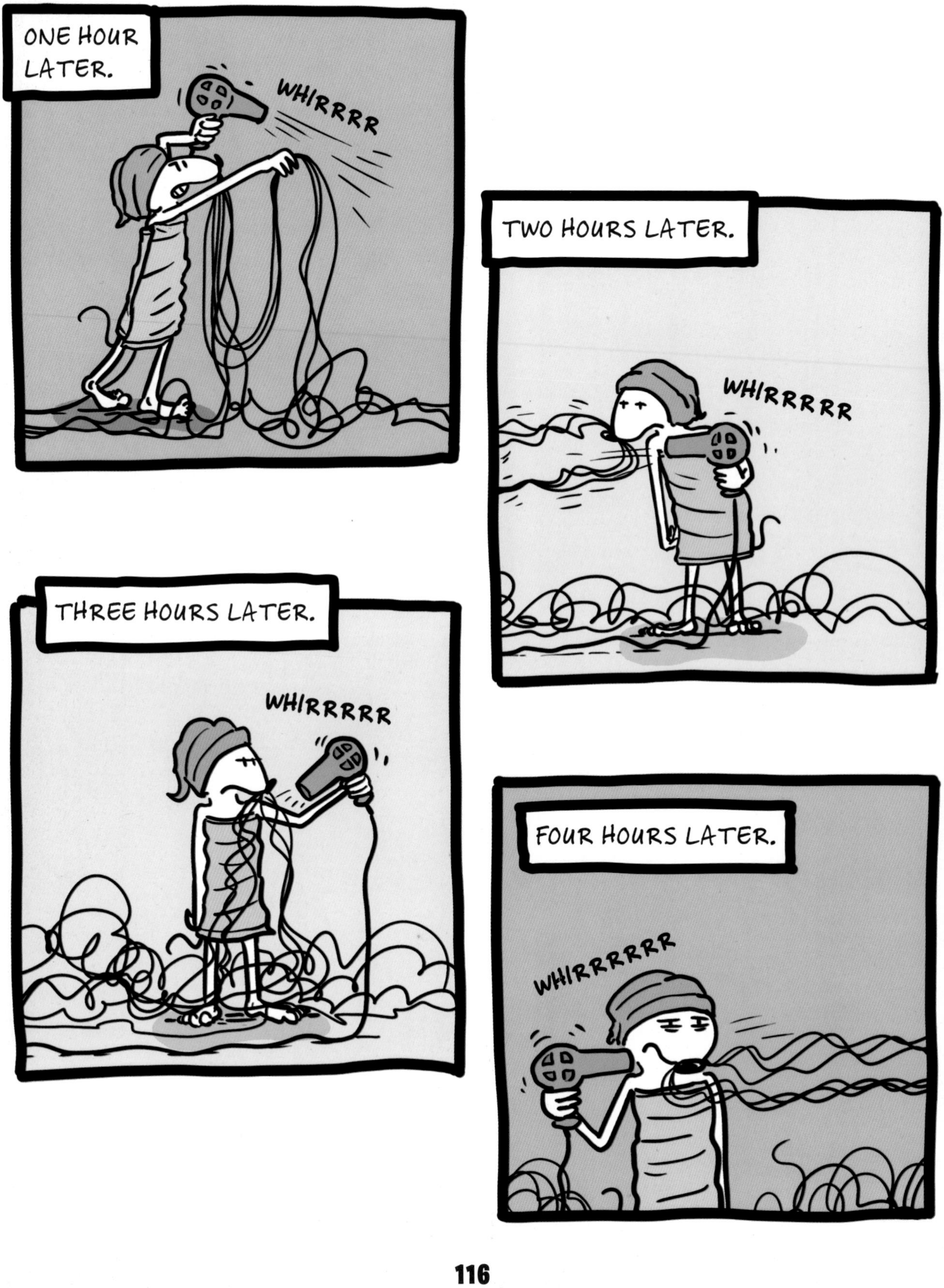
ONE HOUR LATER.
WHIRRRR
TWO HOURS LATER.
WHIRRRRR
THREE HOURS LATER.
WHIRRRRR
FOUR HOURS LATER.
WHIRRRRRR

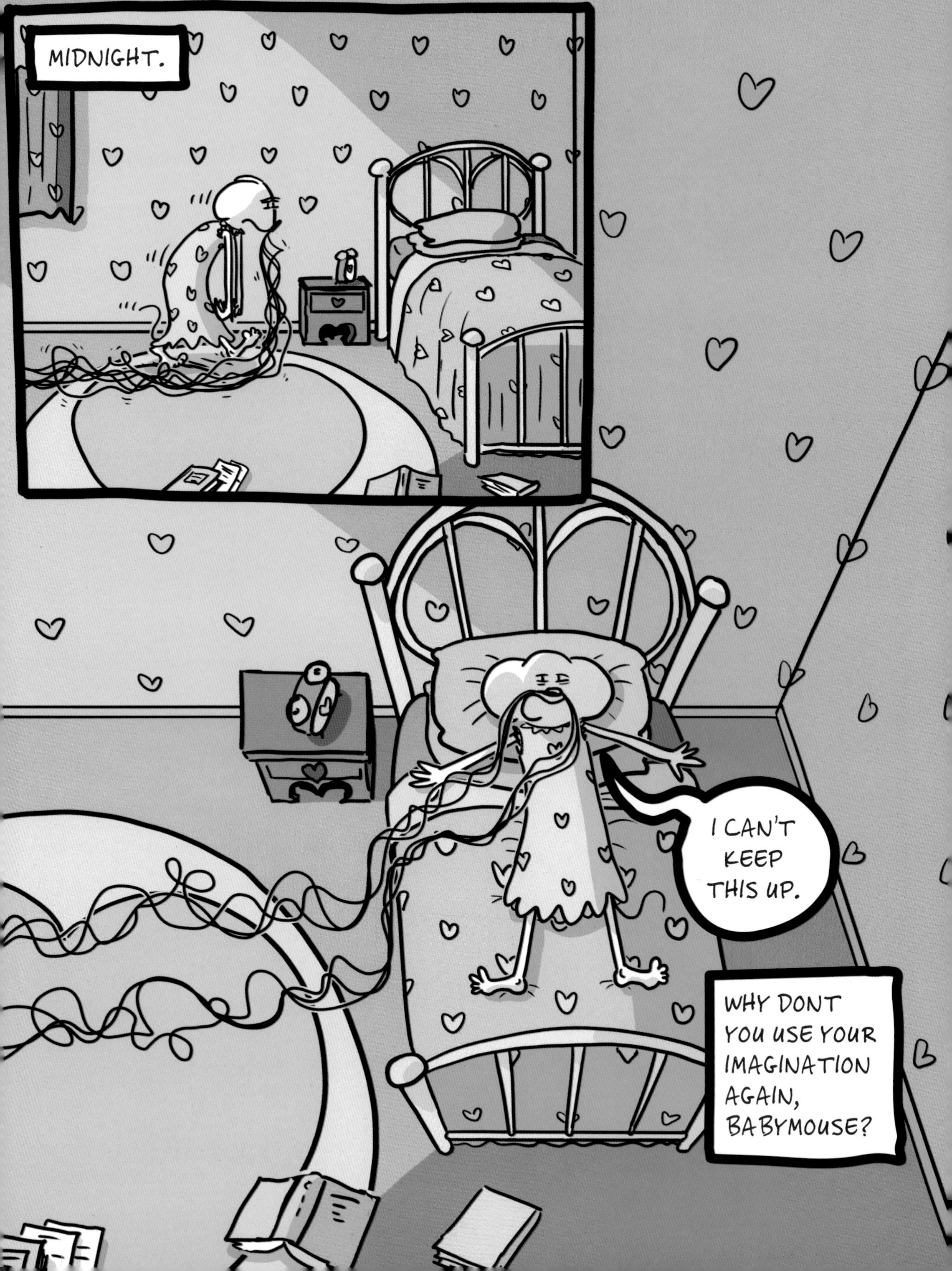
MIDNIGHT.
I CAN'T KEEP THIS UP.
WHY DONT YOU USE YOUR IMAGINATION AGAIN, BABYMOUSE?

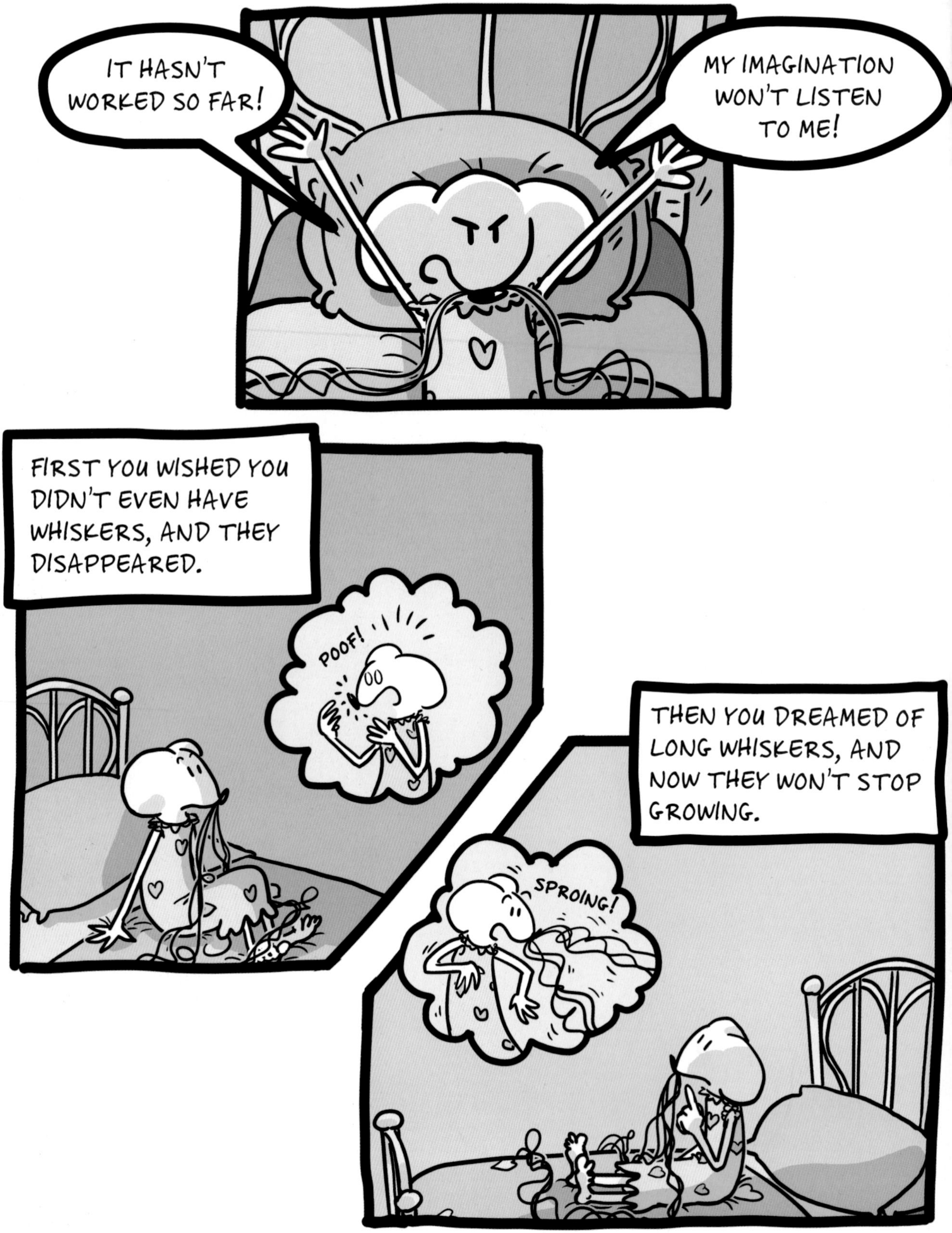
IT HASN'T WORKED SO FAR!
MY IMAGINATION WON'T LISTEN TO ME!
FIRST YOU WISHED YOU DIDN'T EVEN HAVE WHISKERS, AND THEY DISAPPEARED.
POOF!
THEN YOU DREAMED OF LONG WHISKERS, AND NOW THEY WON'T STOP GROWING.
SPROING!

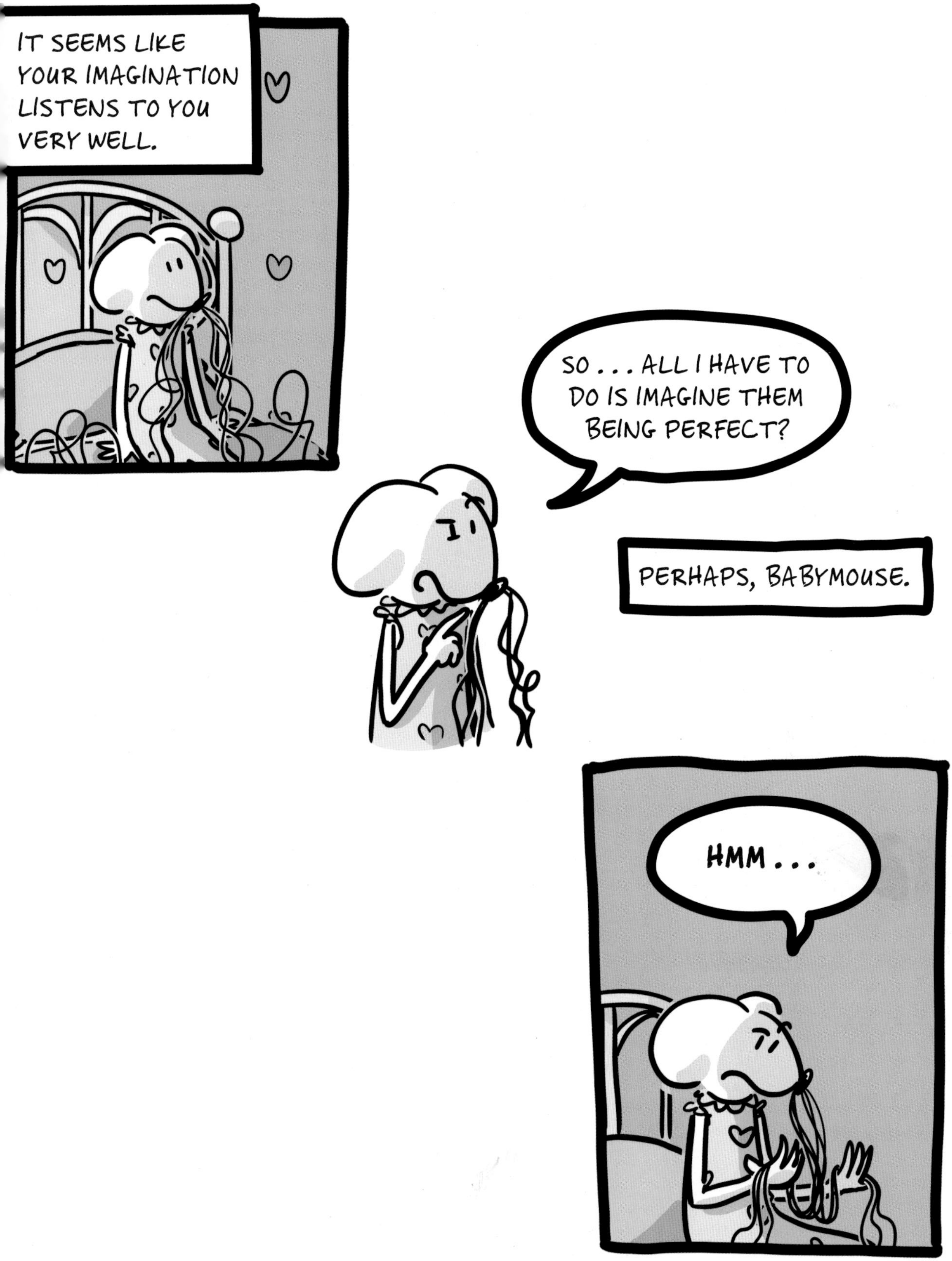
IT SEEMS LIKE YOUR IMAGINATION LISTENS TO YOU VERY WELL.
SO . . . ALL I HAVE TO DO IS IMAGINE THEM BEING PERFECT?
PERHAPS, BABYMOUSE.
HMM . . .

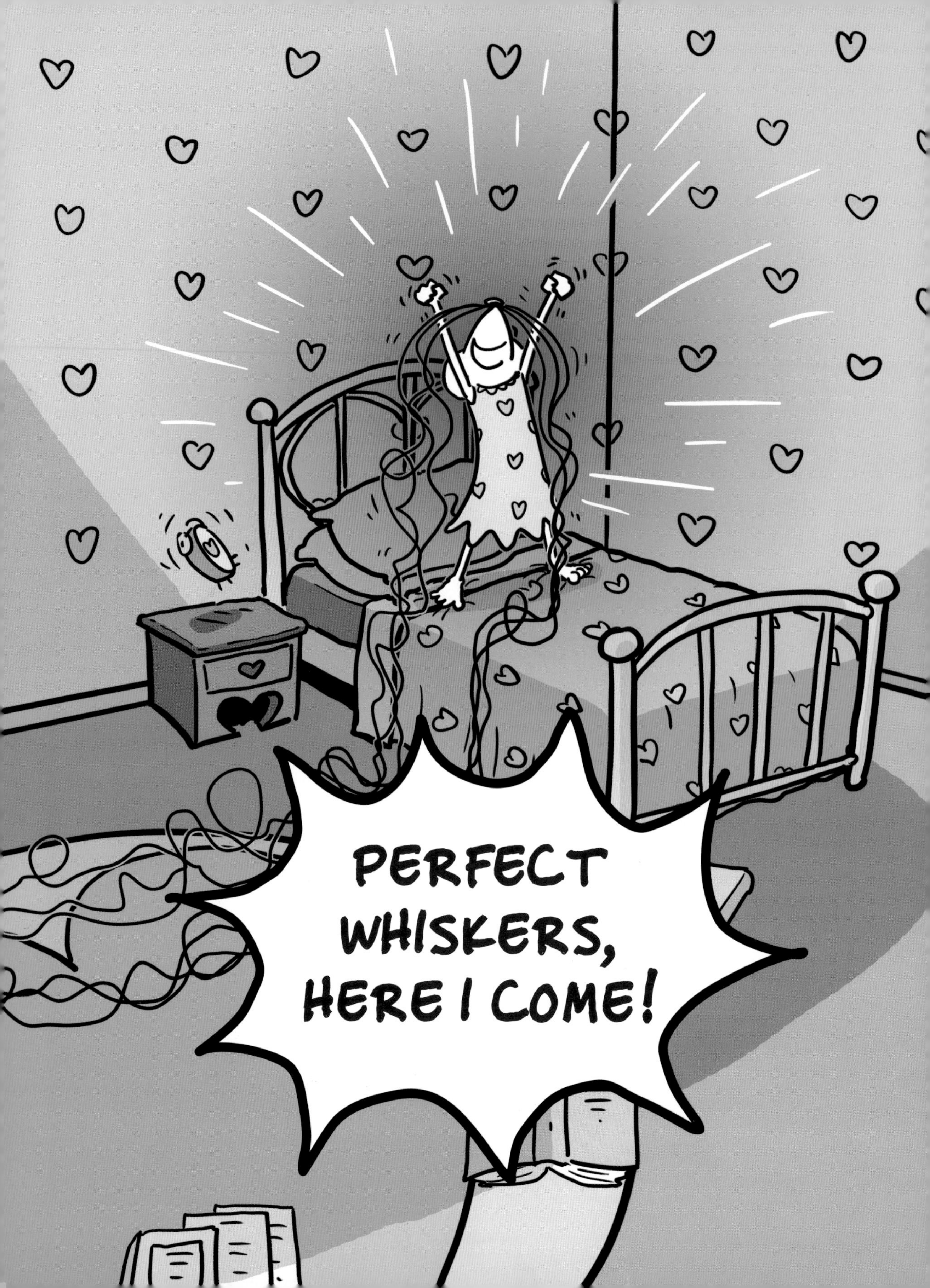
PERFECT WHISKERS, HERE I COME!

PART FOUR

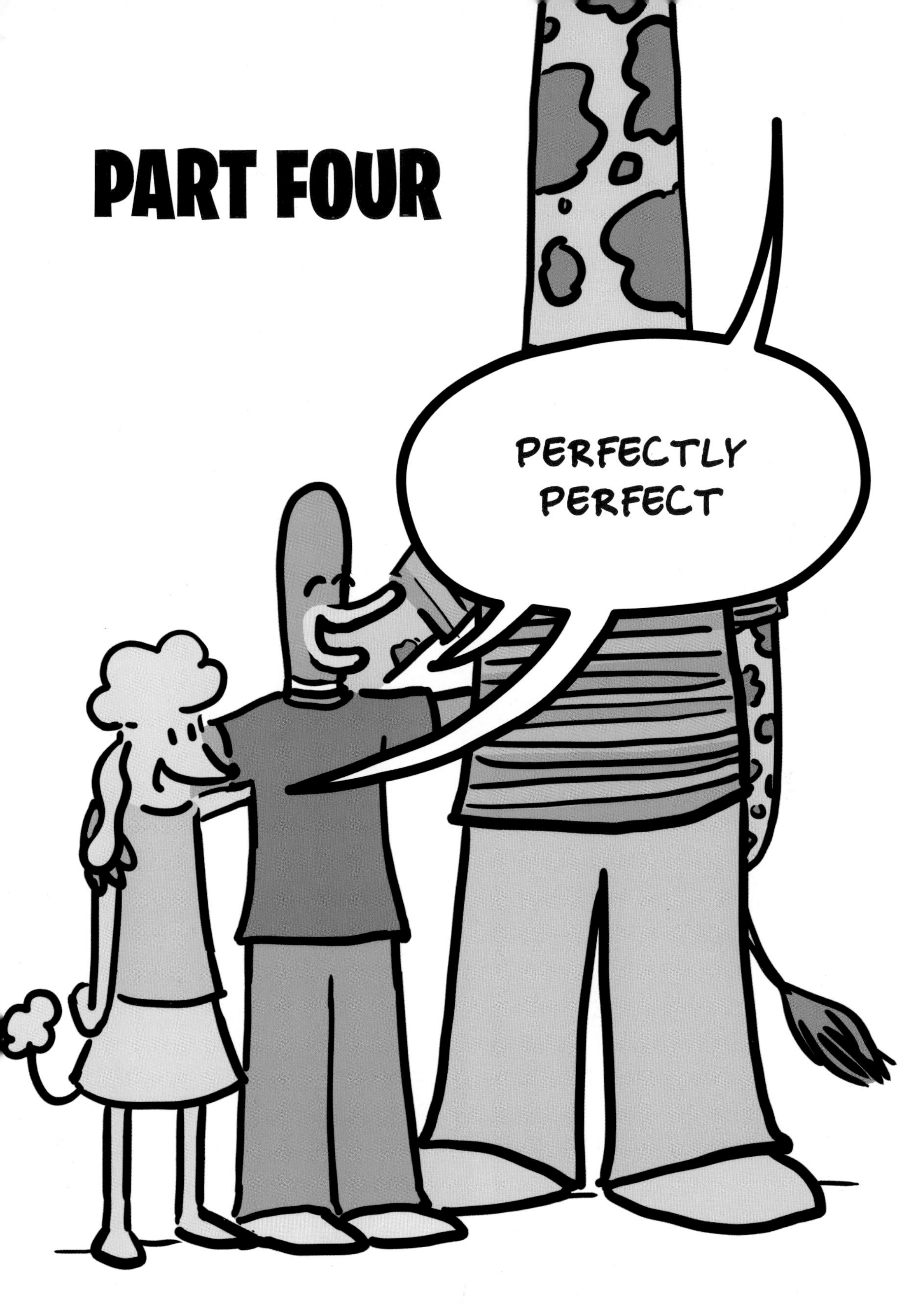
PERFECTLY PERFECT

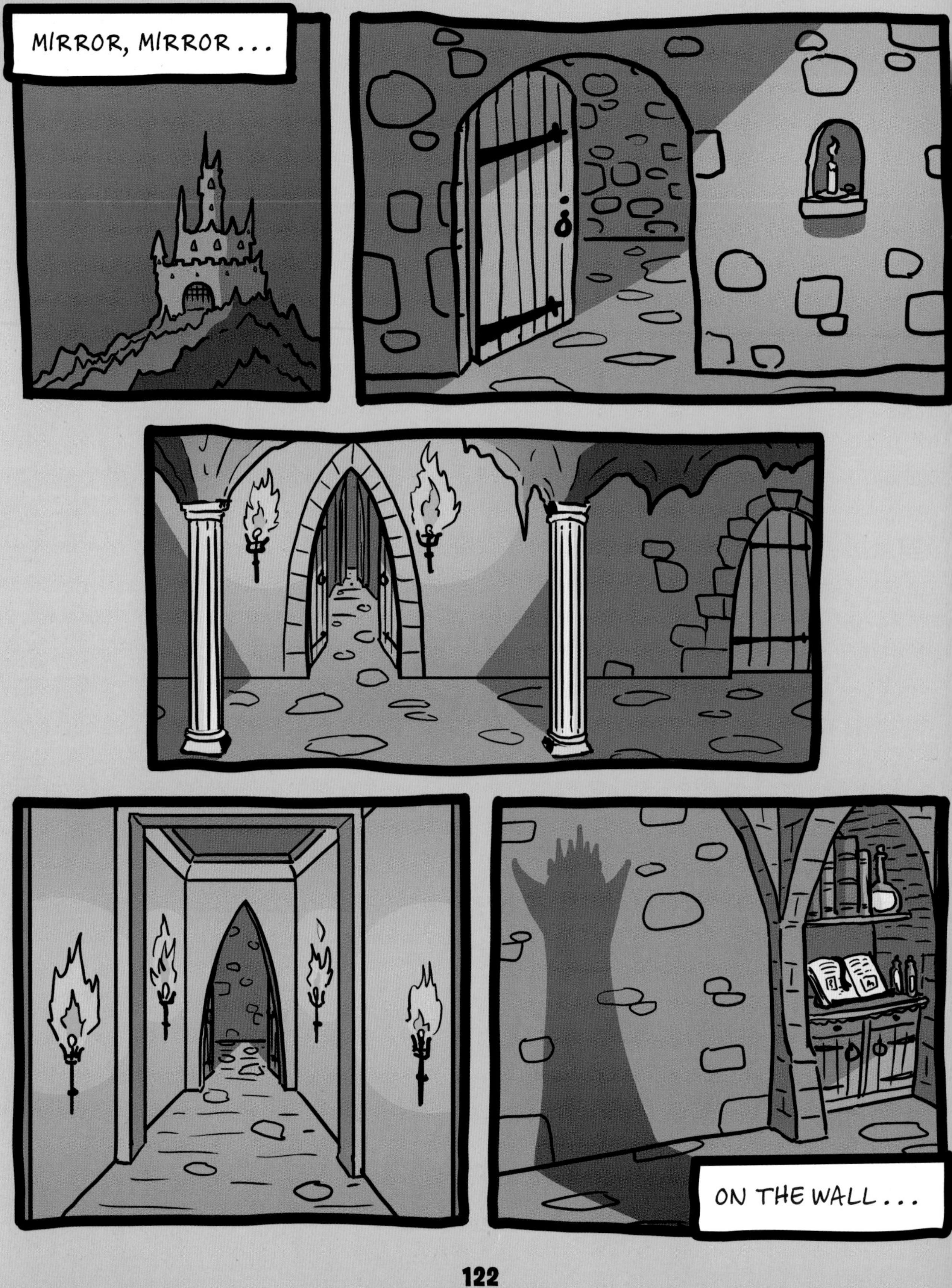
MIRROR, MIRROR . . .
ON THE WALL . . .

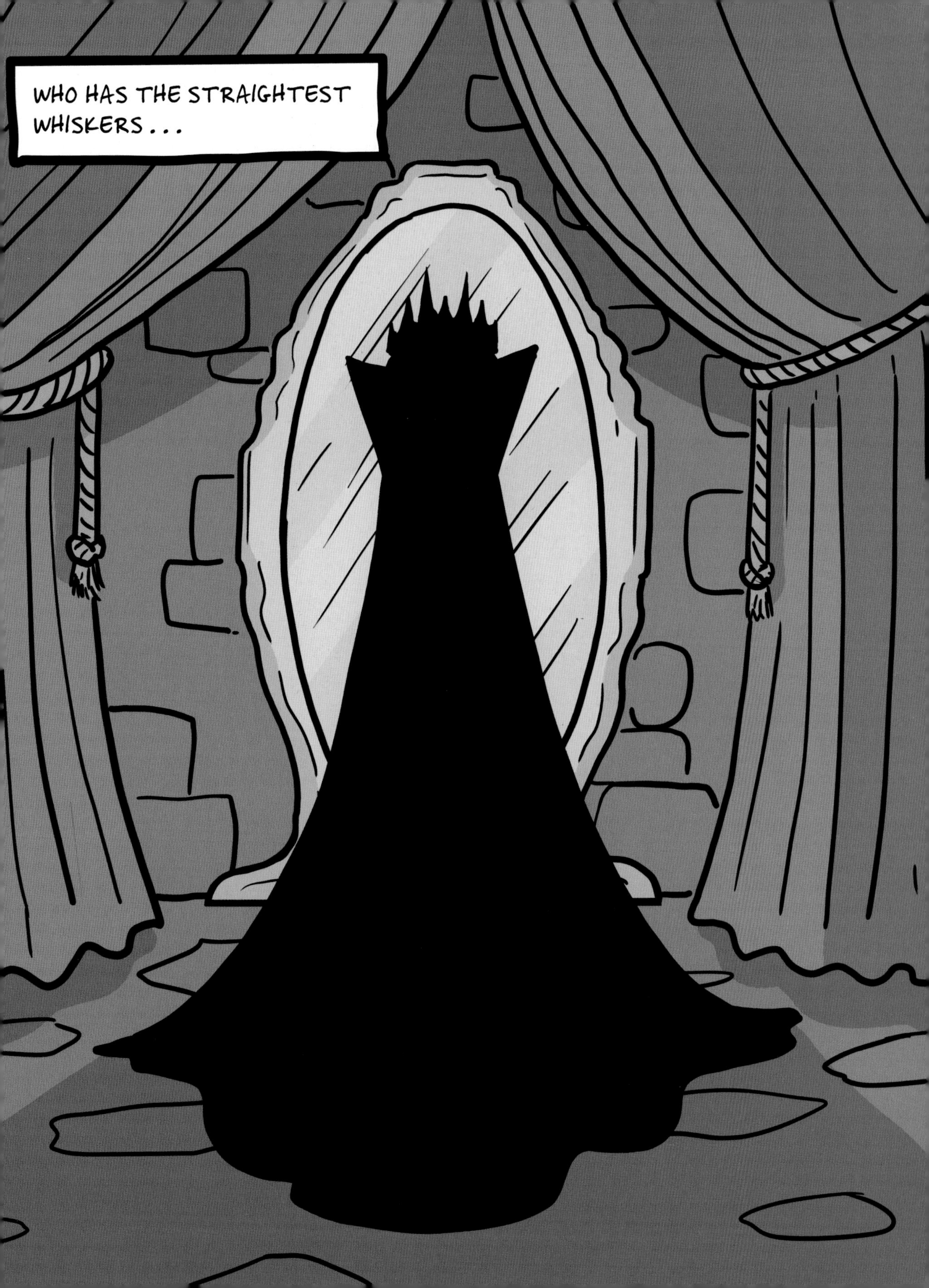
WHO HAS THE STRAIGHTEST WHISKERS . . .

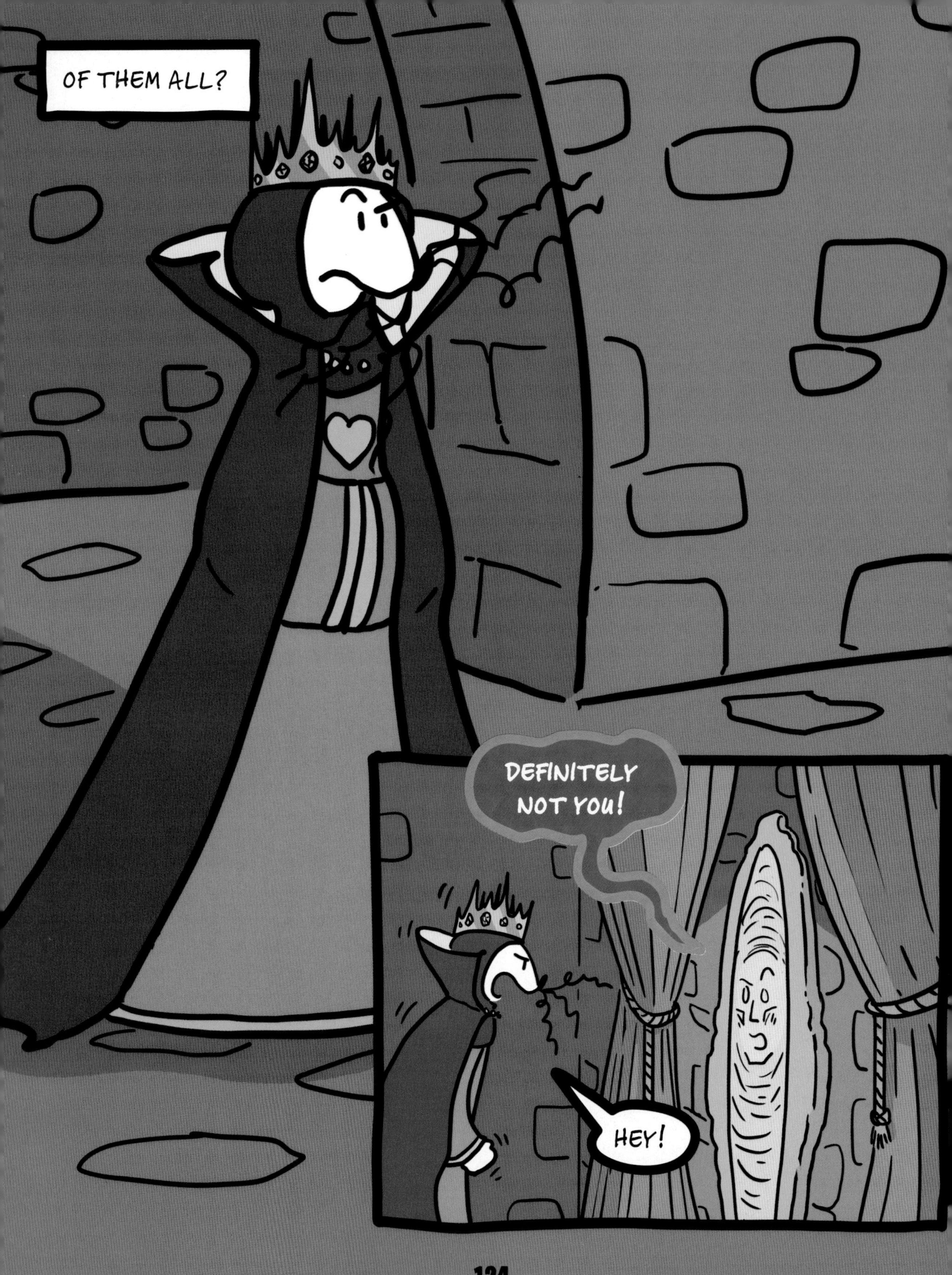
OF THEM ALL?
DEFINITELY NOT YOU!
HEY!

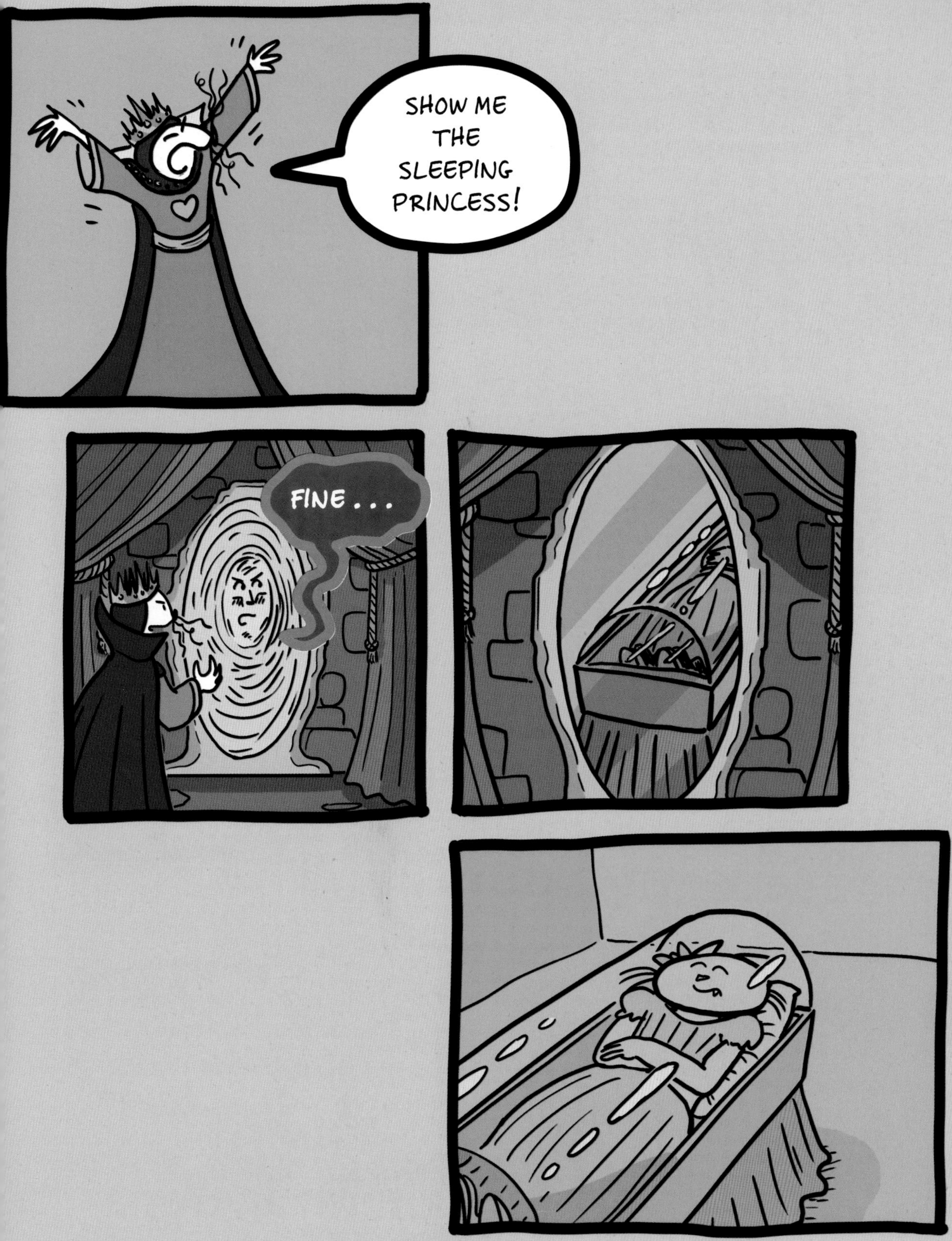
SHOW ME THE SLEEPING PRINCESS!
FINE...

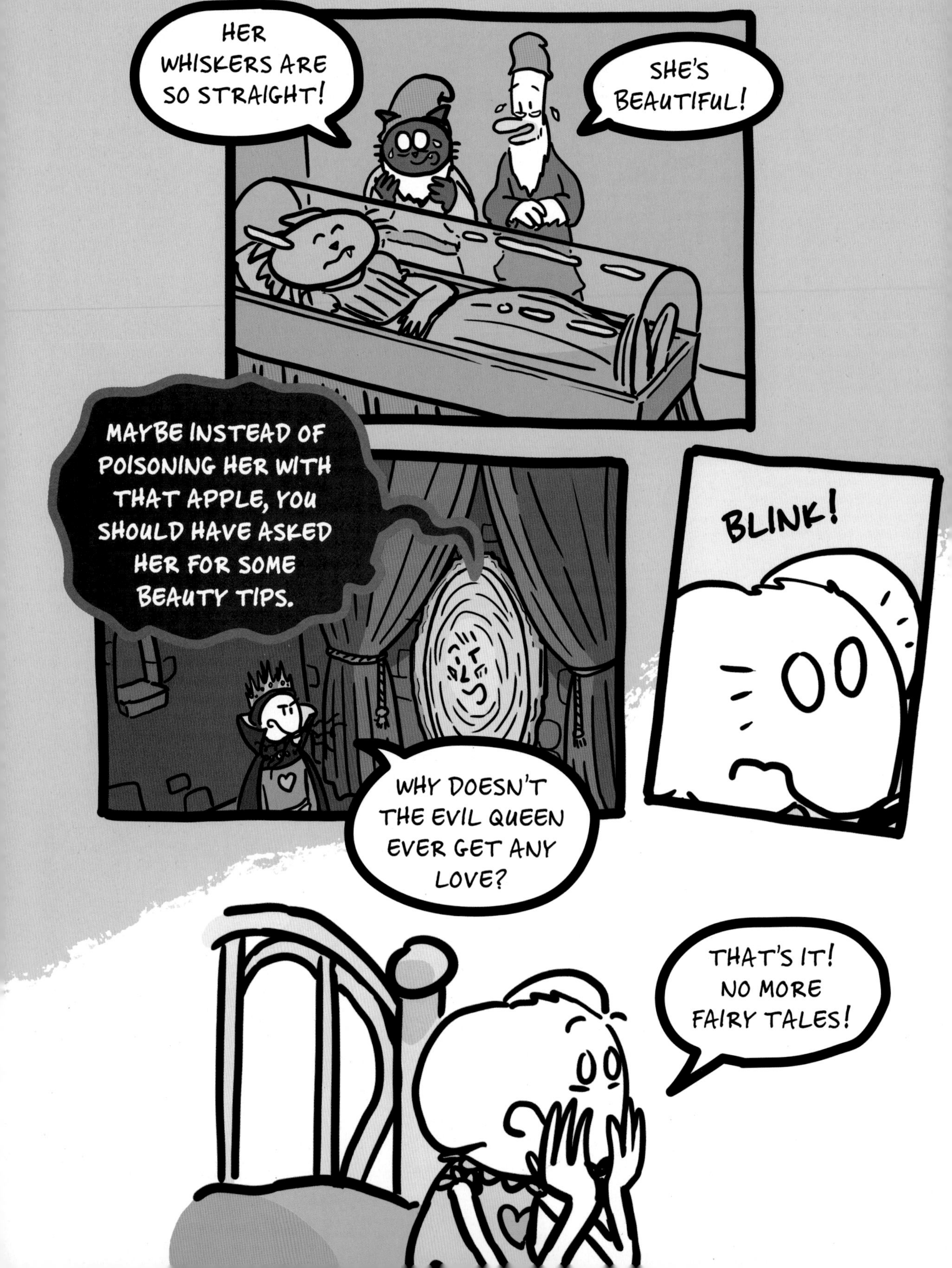

HER WHISKERS ARE SO STRAIGHT!
SHE'S BEAUTIFUL!
MAYBE INSTEAD OF POISONING HER WITH THAT APPLE, YOU SHOULD HAVE ASKED HER FOR SOME BEAUTY TIPS.
WHY DOESN'T THE EVIL QUEEN EVER GET ANY LOVE?
BLINK!
THAT'S IT! NO MORE FAIRY TALES!

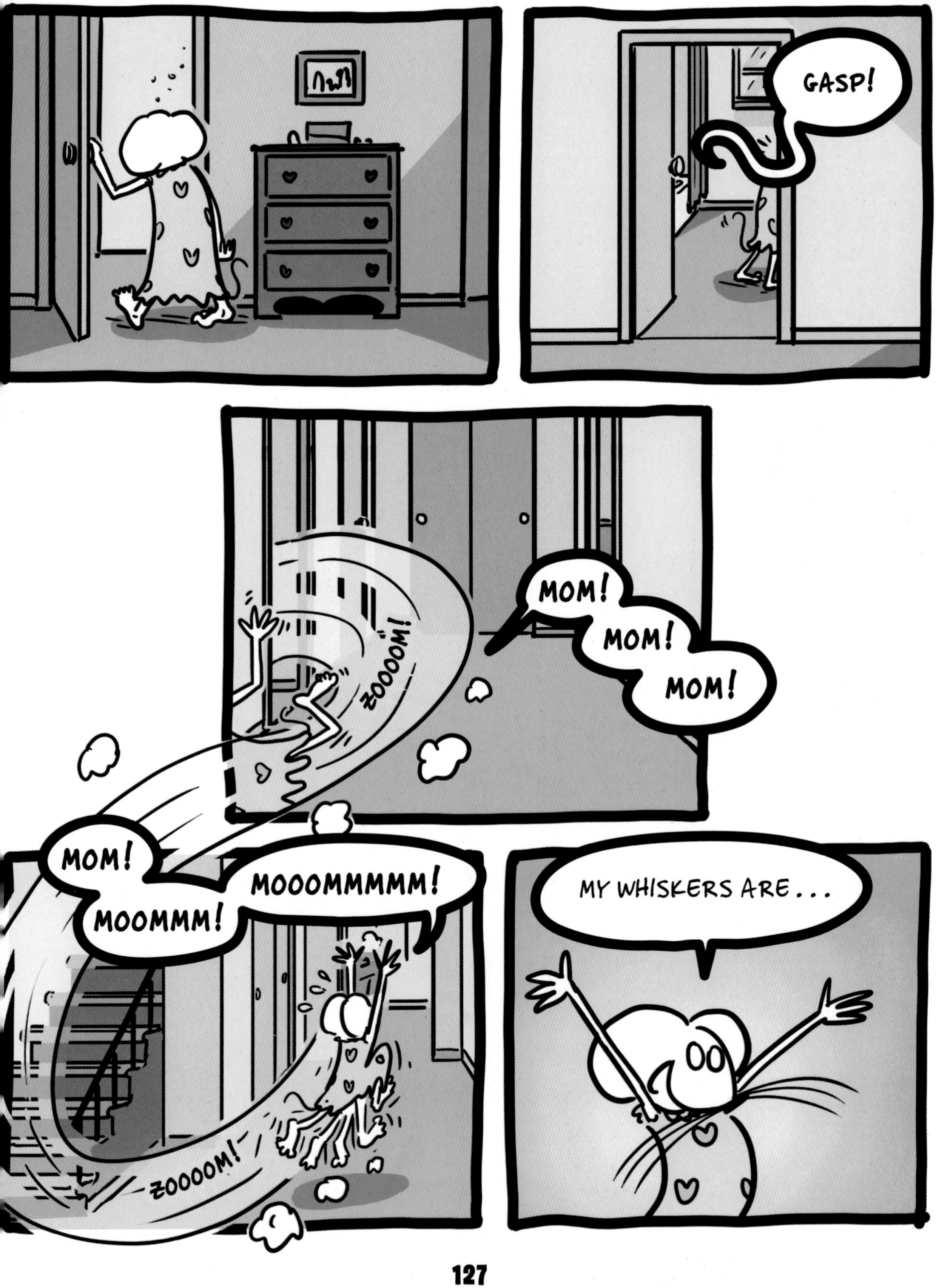
GASP!
MOM!
MOM!
MOM!
ZOOOOM!
MOM!
MOOMMM!
MOOOMMMMM!
ZOOOOM!
MY WHISKERS ARE . . .

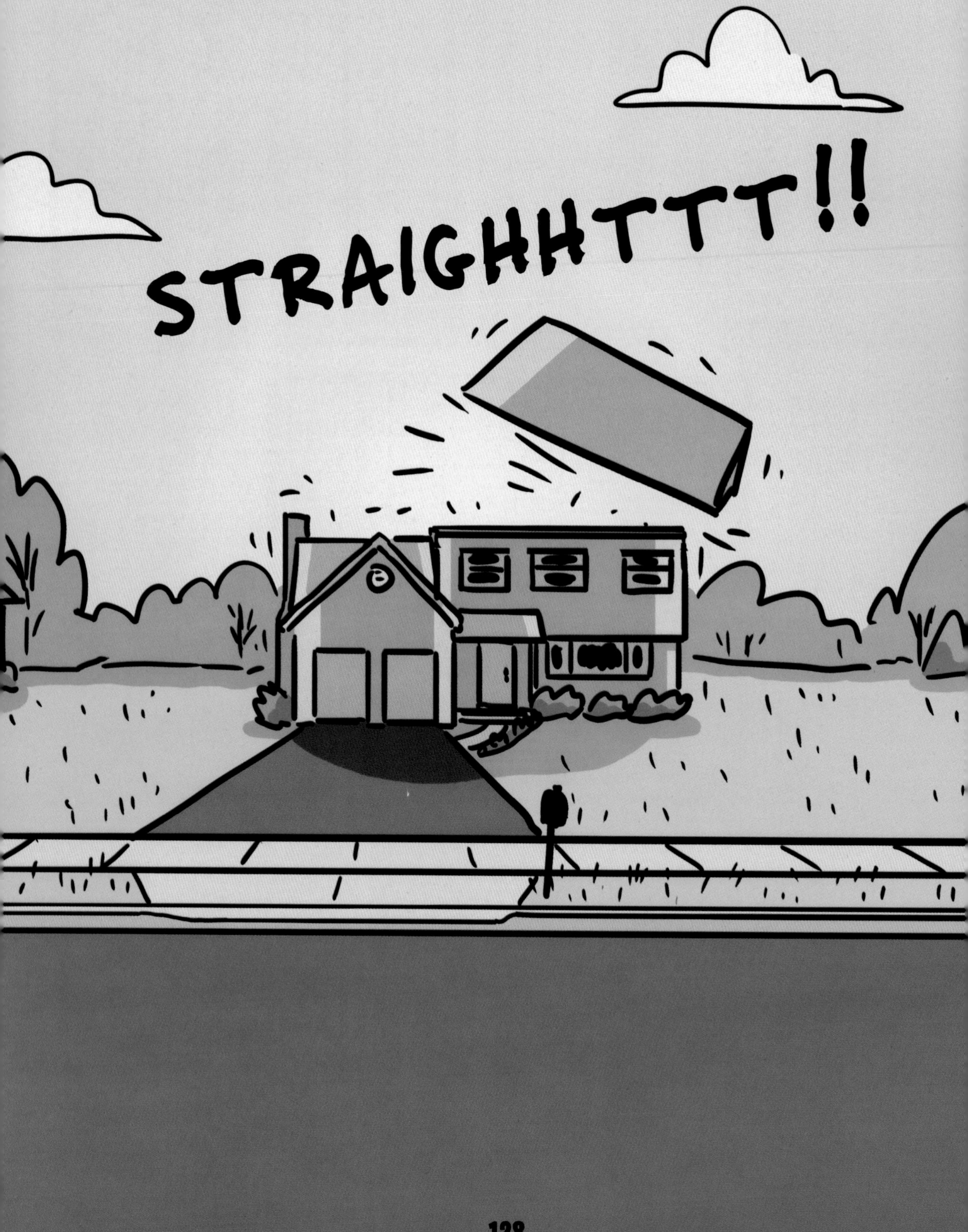
STRAIGHHTTTT!!

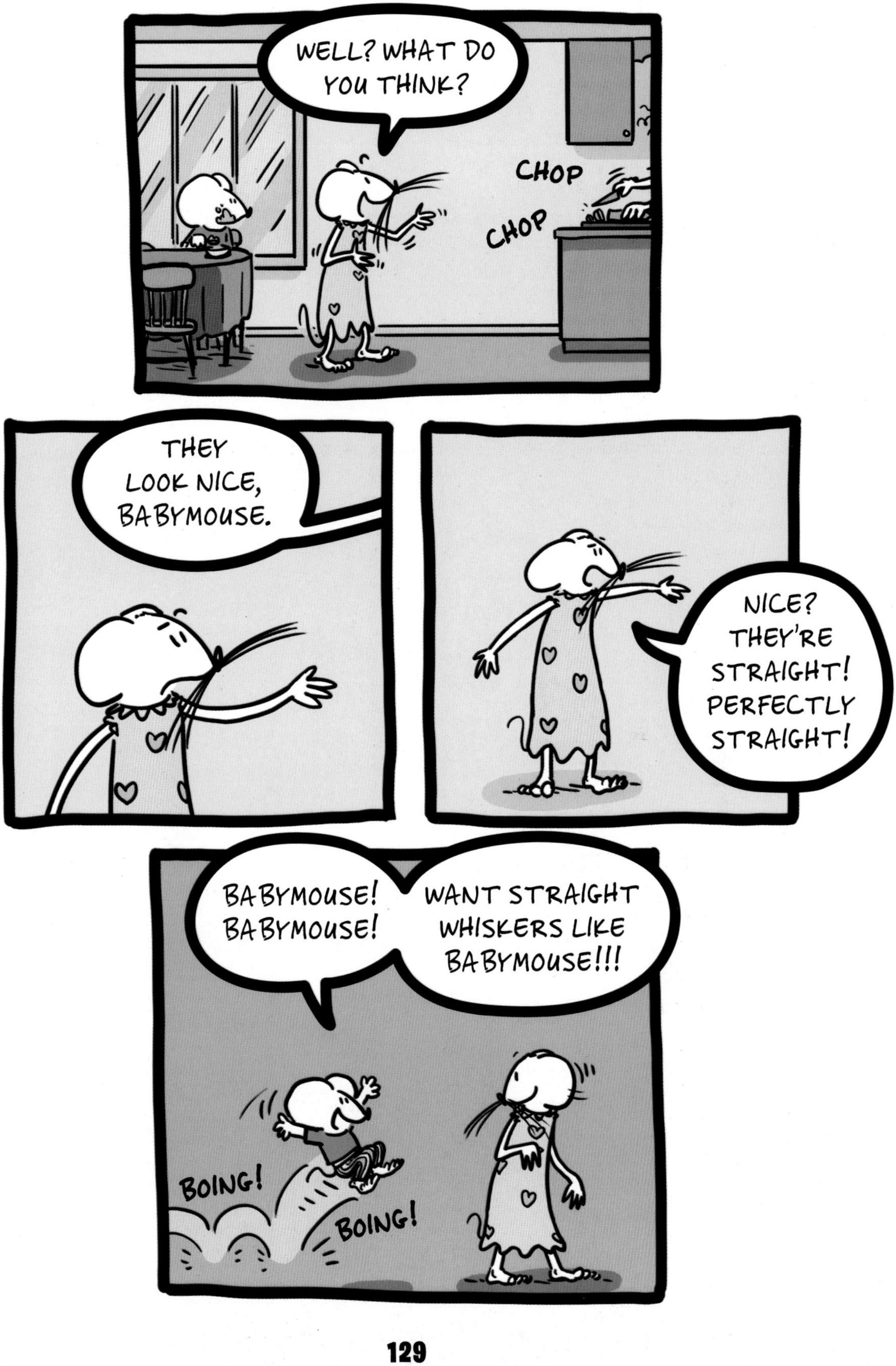
WELL? WHAT DO YOU THINK?
CHOP
CHOP
THEY LOOK NICE, BABYMOUSE.
NICE? THEY'RE STRAIGHT! PERFECTLY STRAIGHT!
BABYMOUSE! BABYMOUSE!
WANT STRAIGHT WHISKERS LIKE BABYMOUSE!!!
BOING!
BOING!

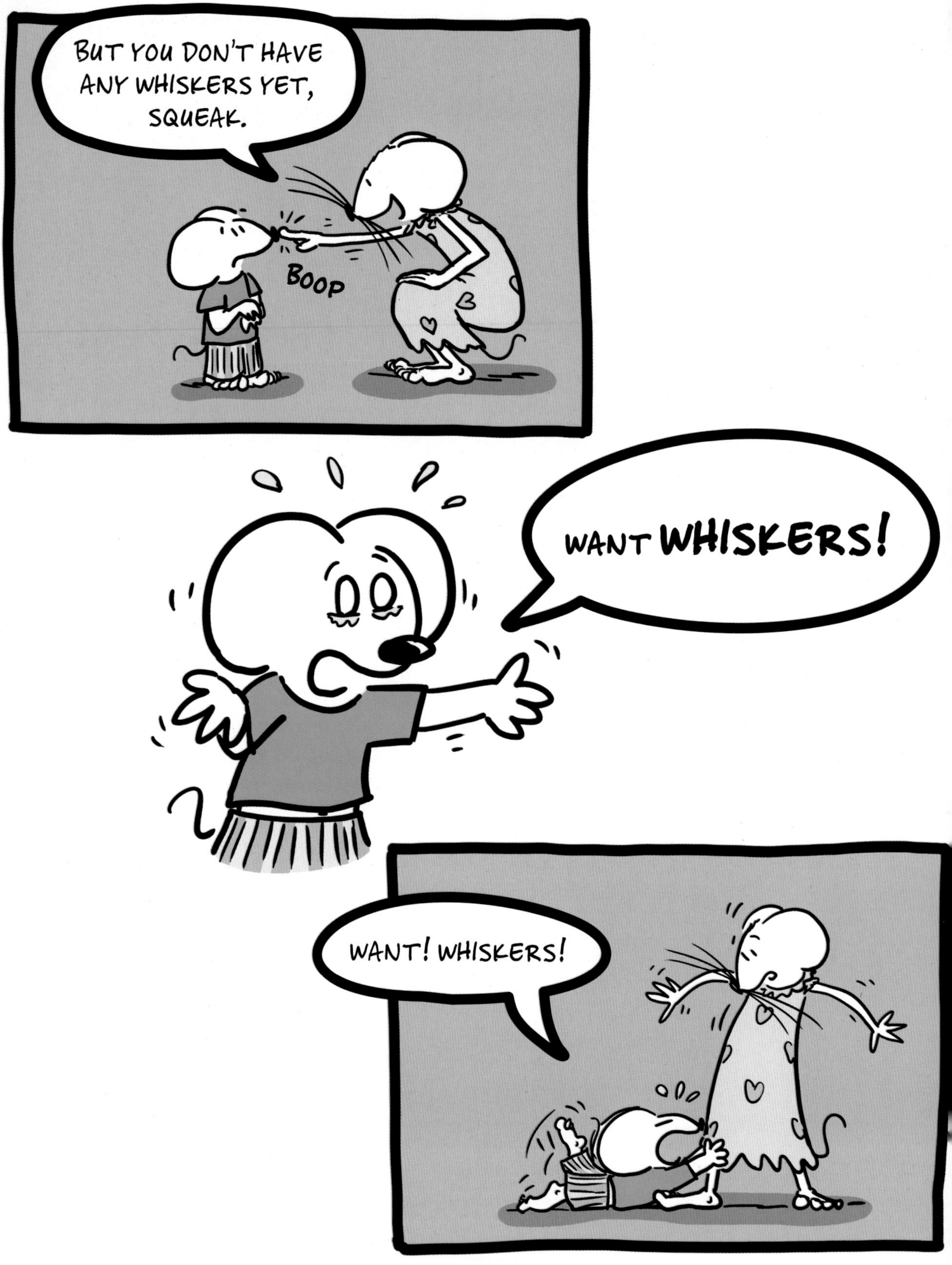
BUT YOU DON'T HAVE ANY WHISKERS YET, SQUEAK.
BOOP
WANT WHISKERS!
WANT! WHISKERS!

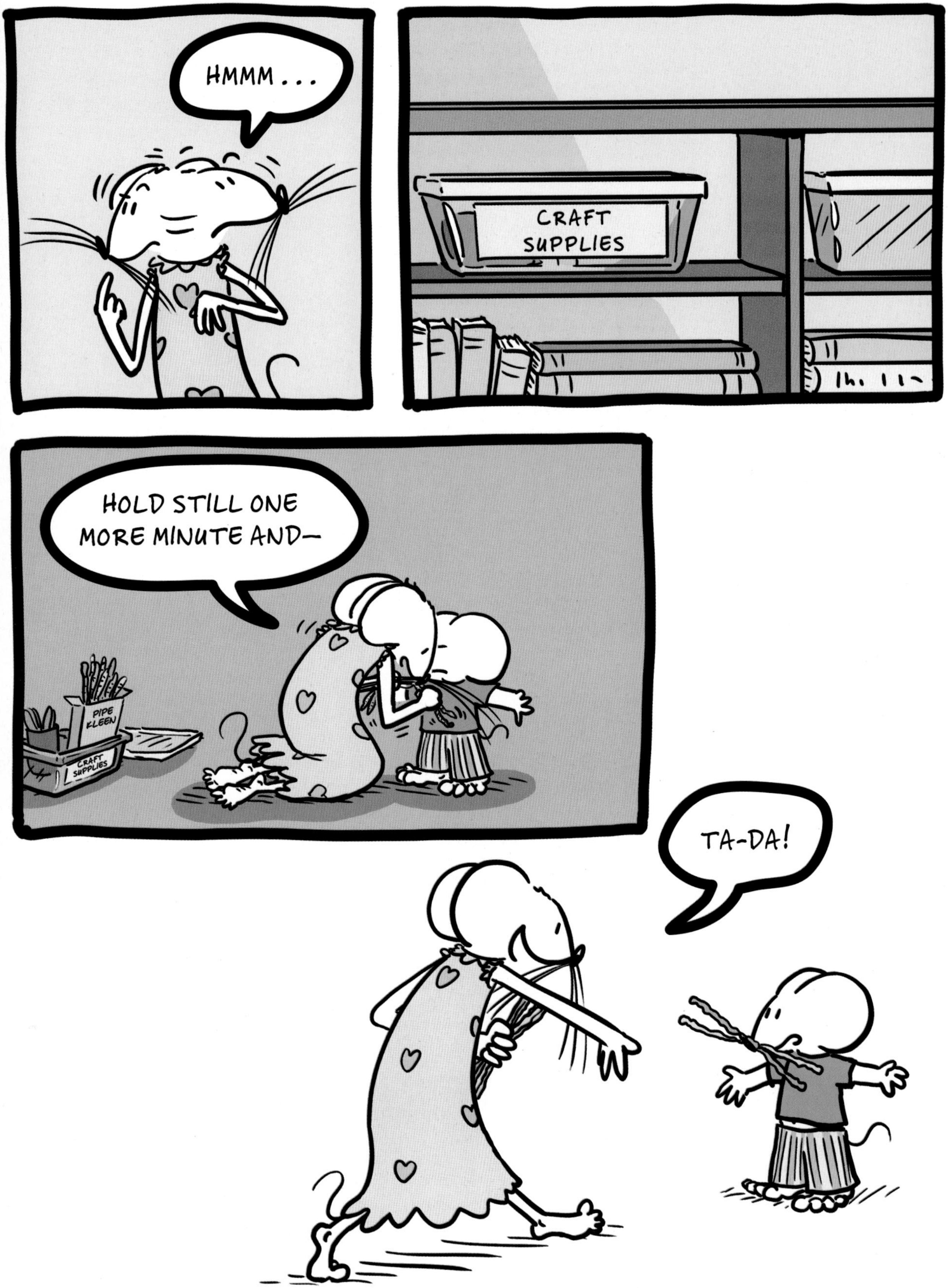
HMMM . . .
CRAFT SUPPLIES
HOLD STILL ONE MORE MINUTE AND—
PIPE KLEEN
CRAFT SUPPLIES
TA-DA!

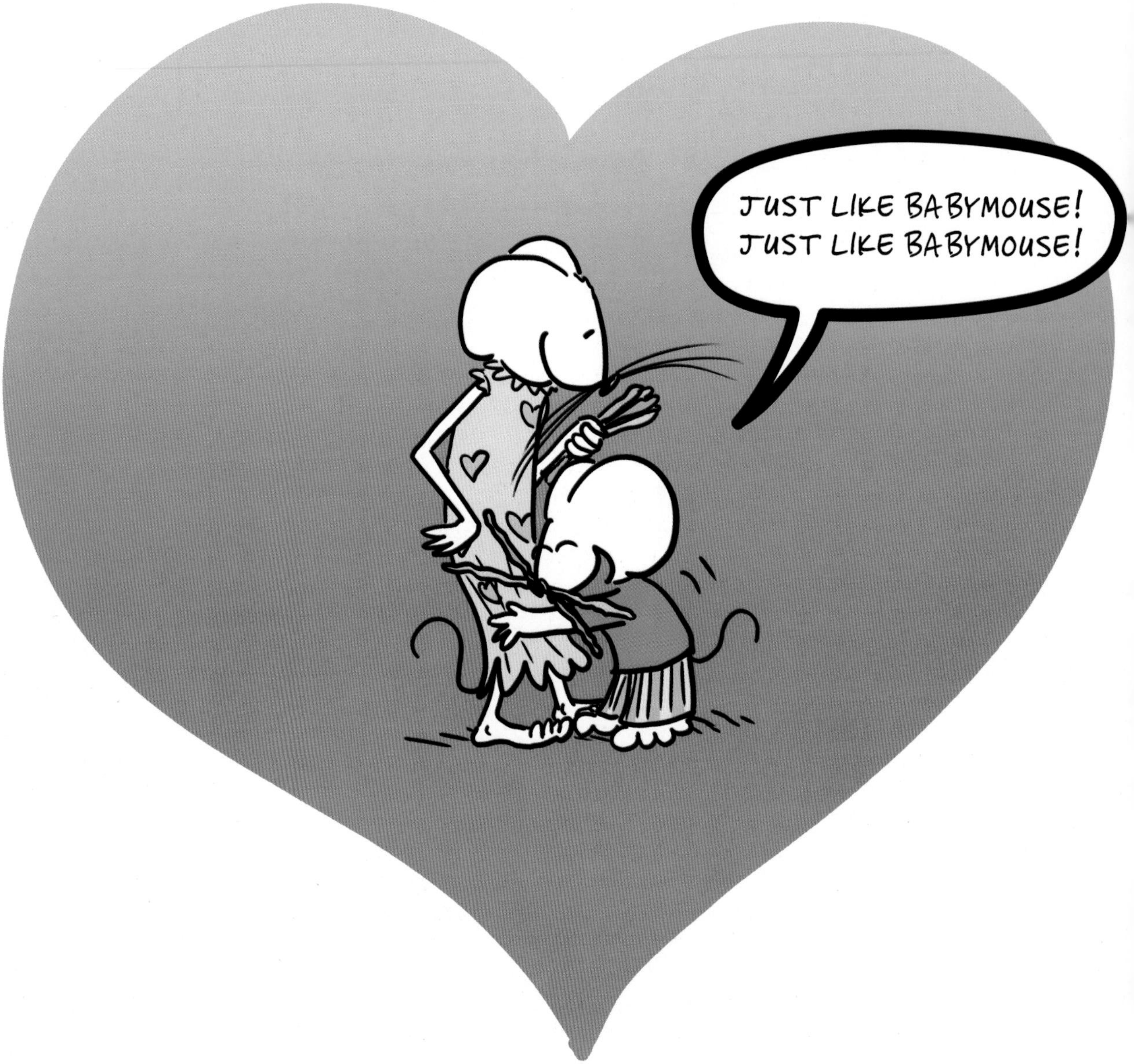
JUST LIKE BABYMOUSE!
JUST LIKE BABYMOUSE!

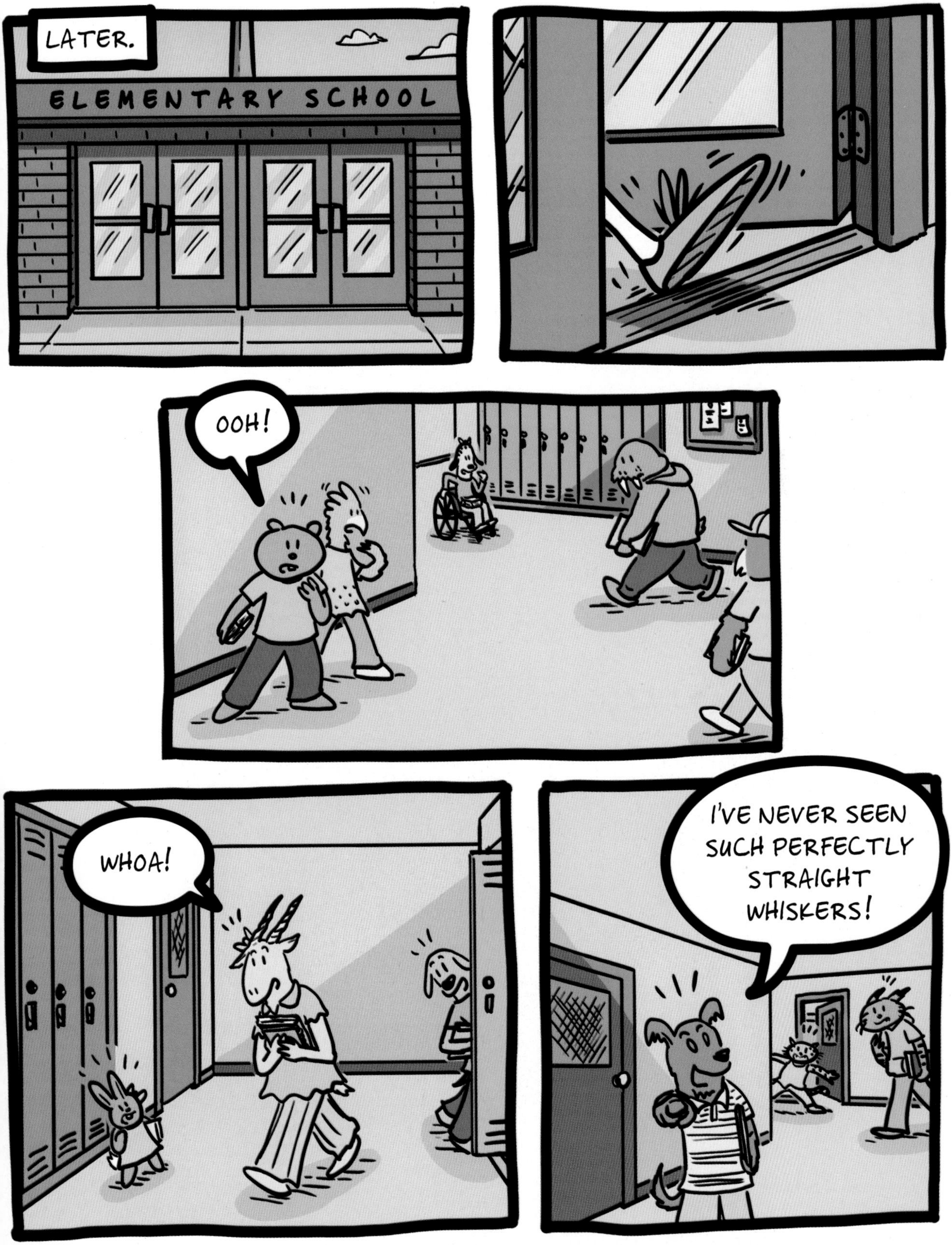
LATER.
ELEMENTARY SCHOOL
OOH!
WHOA!
I'VE NEVER SEEN SUCH PERFECTLY STRAIGHT WHISKERS!

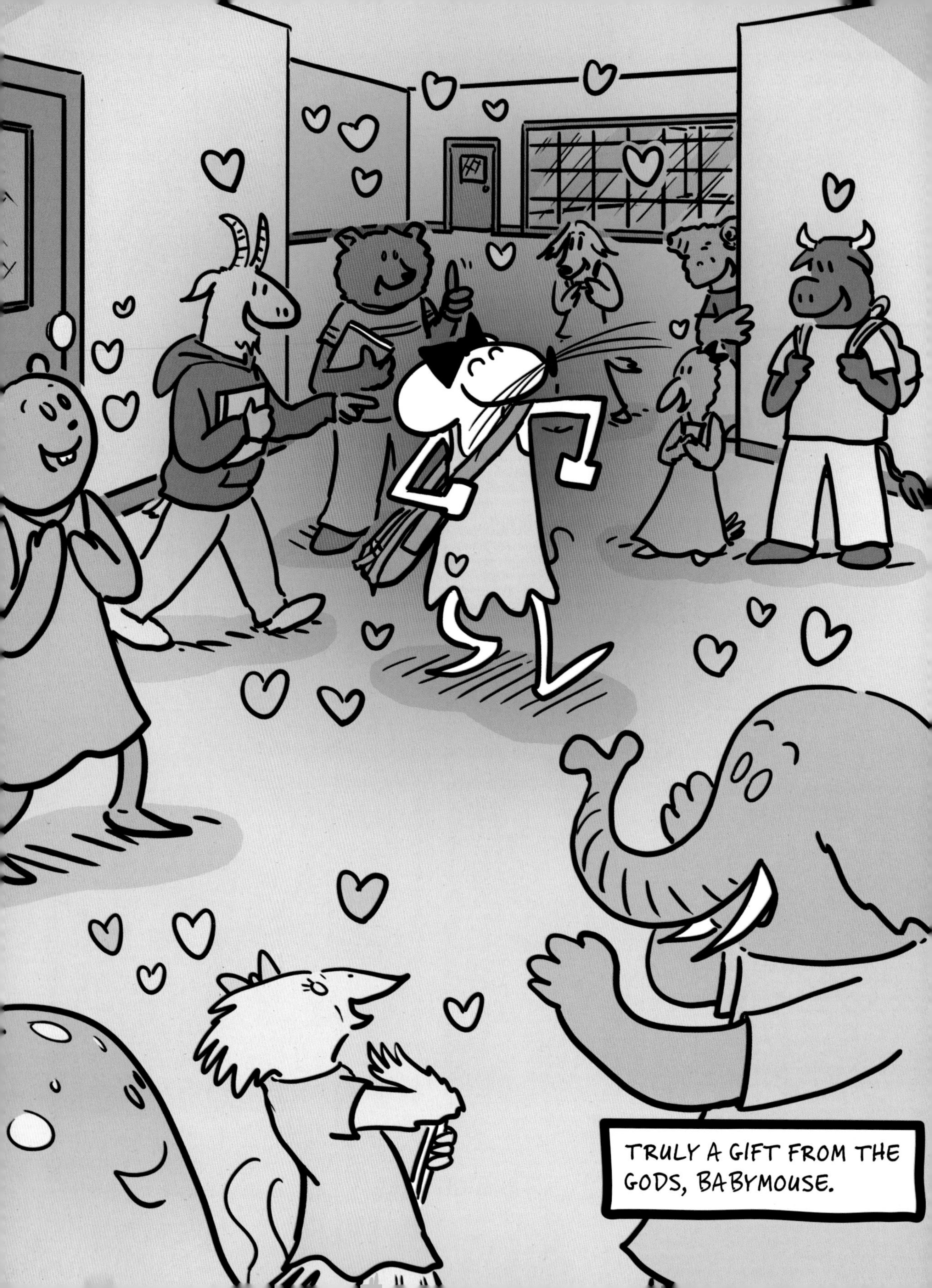
TRULY A GIFT FROM THE GODS, BABYMOUSE.

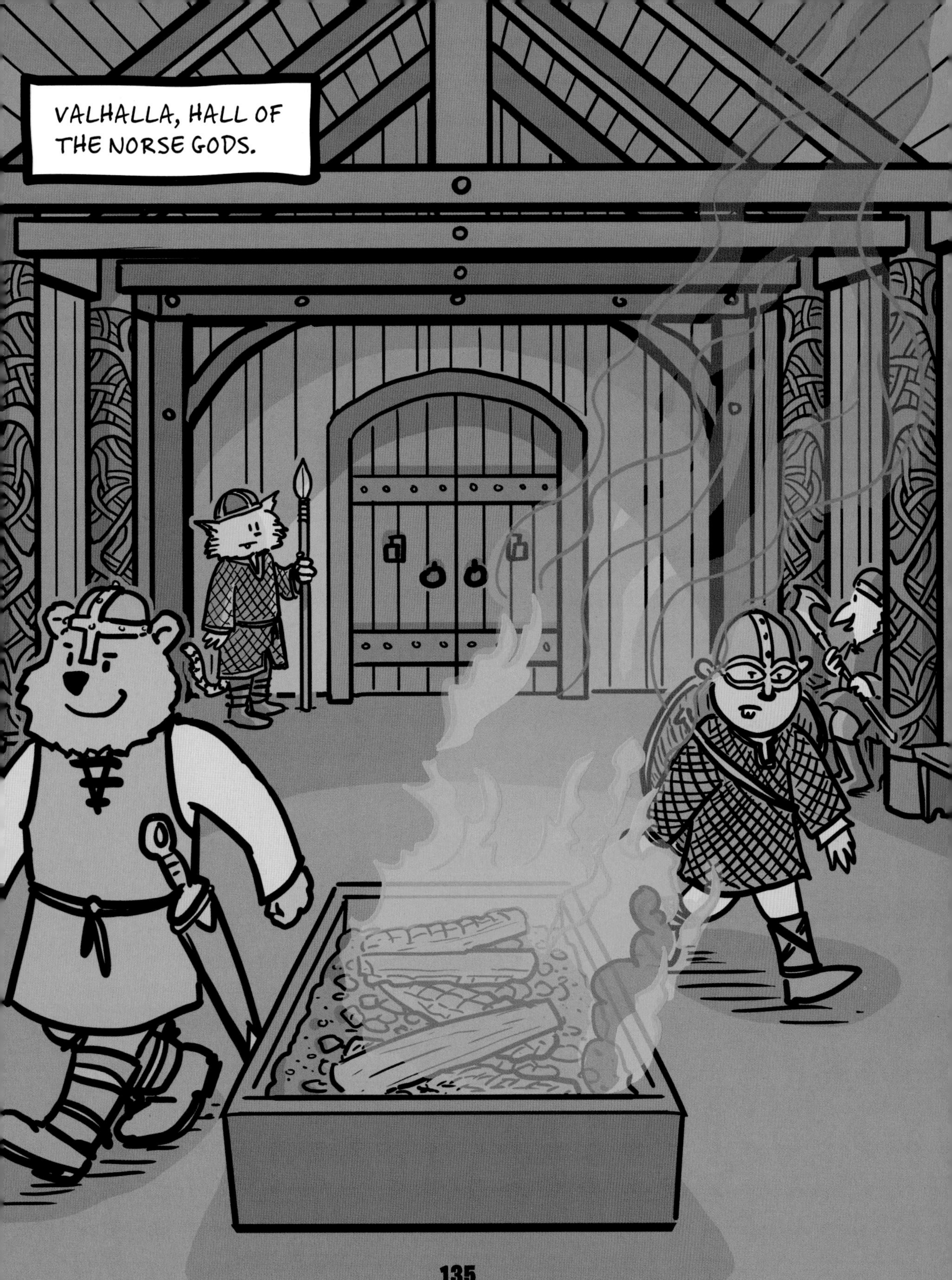
VALHALLA, HALL OF THE NORSE GODS.

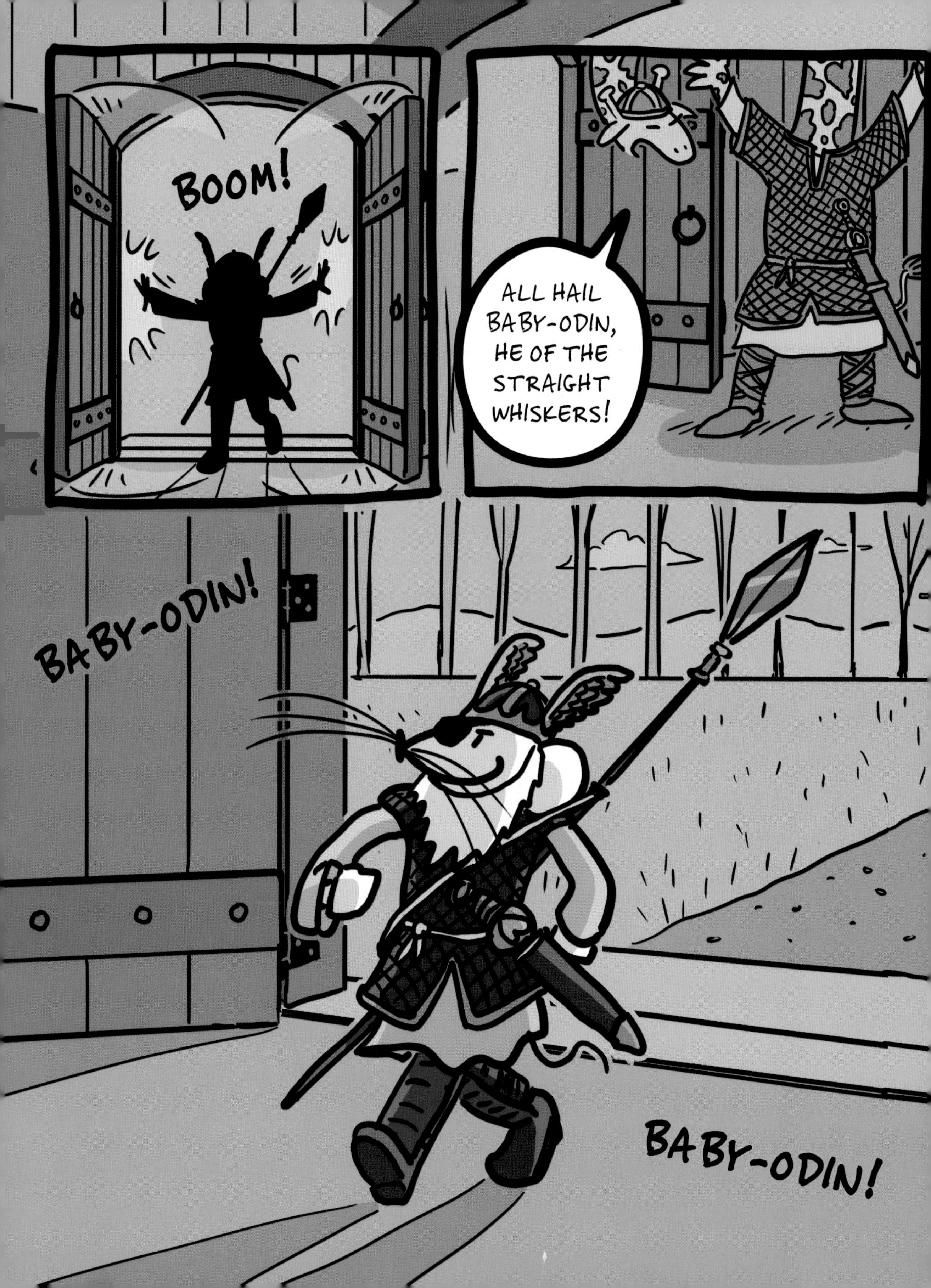
BOOM!
ALL HAIL BABY-ODIN, HE OF THE STRAIGHT WHISKERS!
BABY-ODIN!
BABY-ODIN!

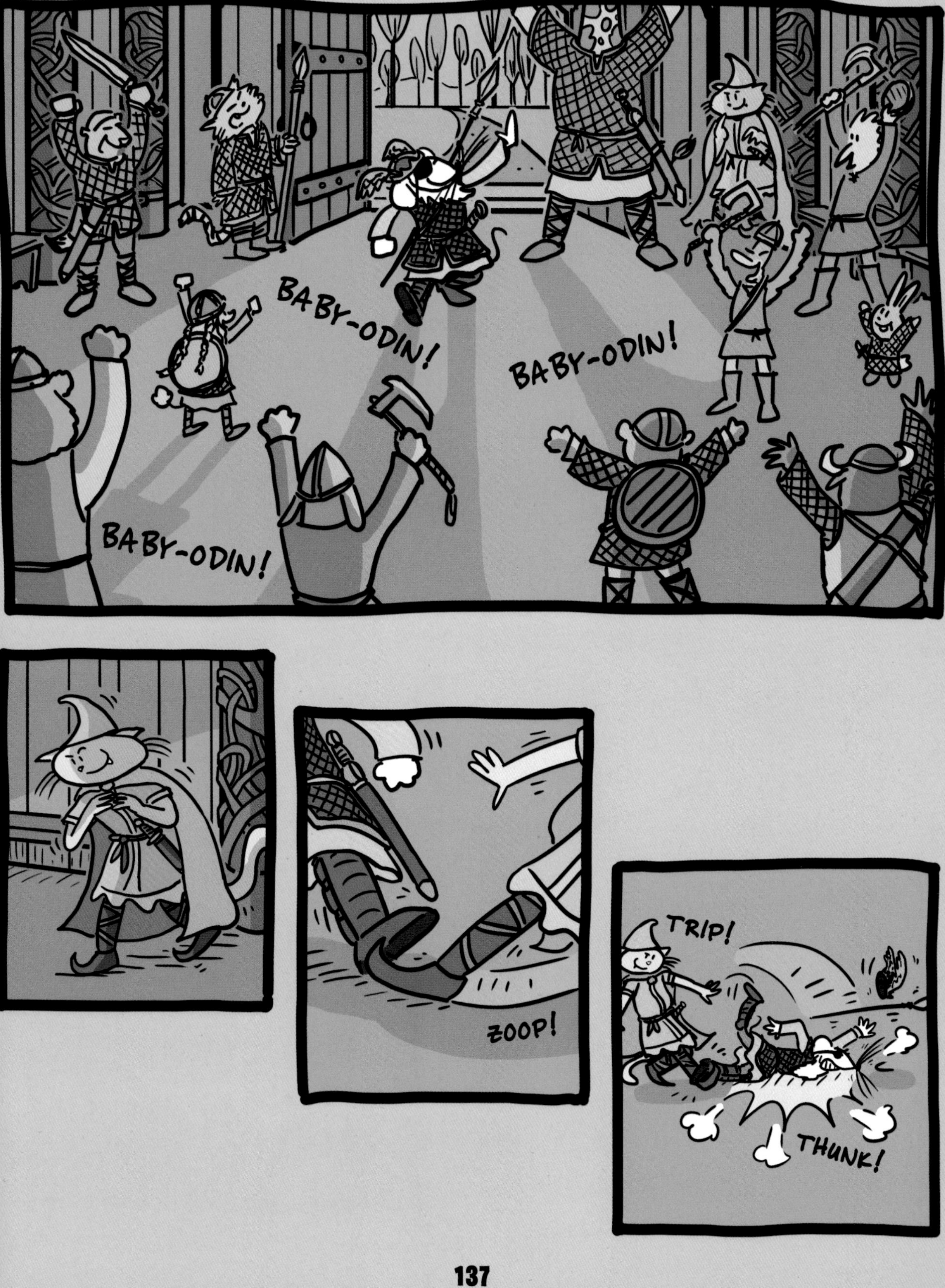
BABY-ODIN!
BABY-ODIN!
BABY-ODIN!
ZOOP!
TRIP!
THUNK!

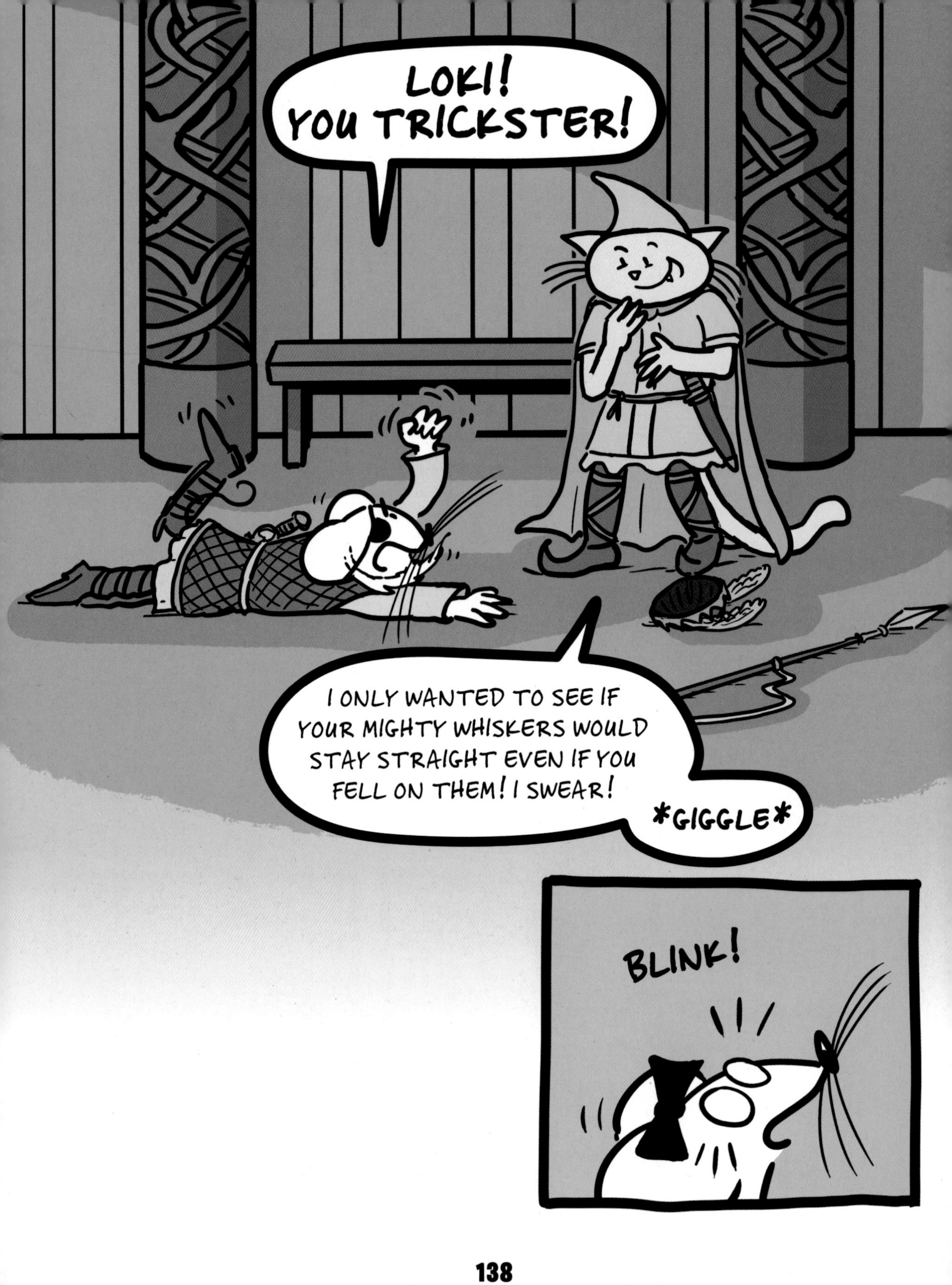
LOKI! YOU TRICKSTER!
I ONLY WANTED TO SEE IF YOUR MIGHTY WHISKERS WOULD STAY STRAIGHT EVEN IF YOU FELL ON THEM! I SWEAR!
GIGGLE
BLINK!

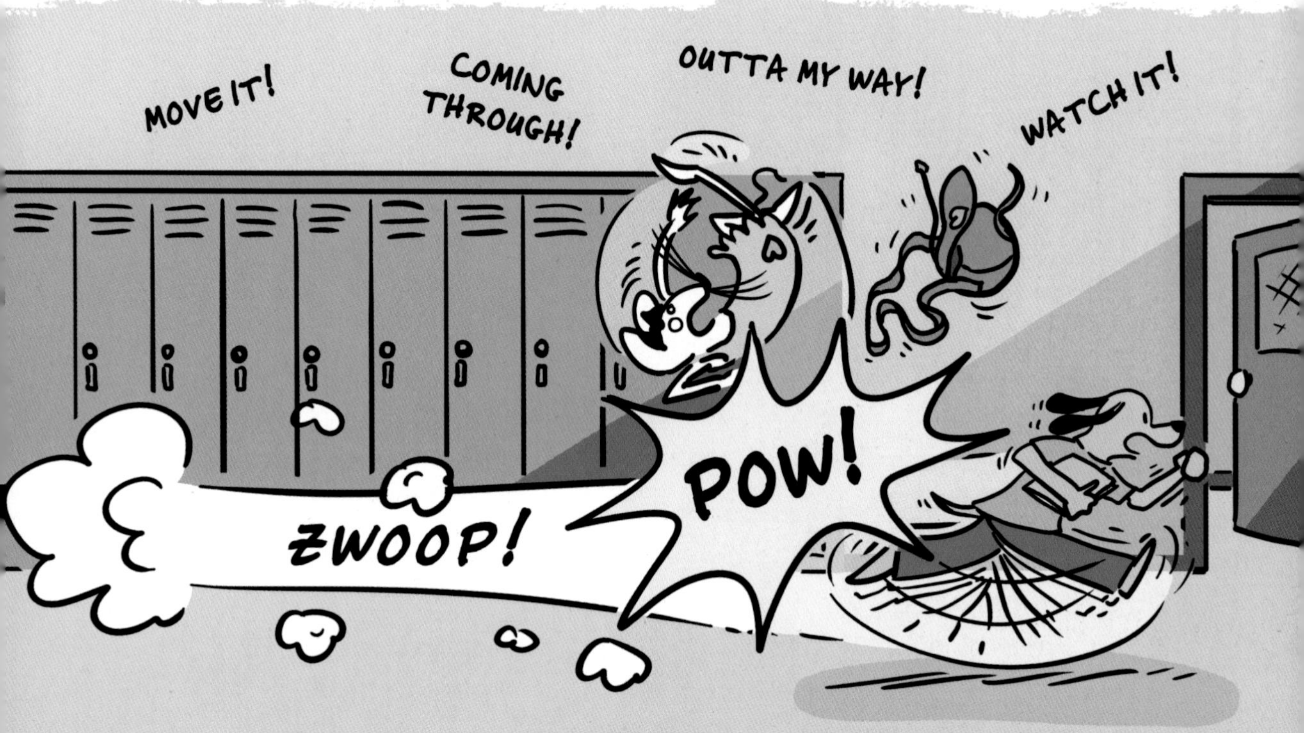
MOVE IT!
COMING THROUGH!
OUTTA MY WAY!
WATCH IT!
ZWOOP!
POW!

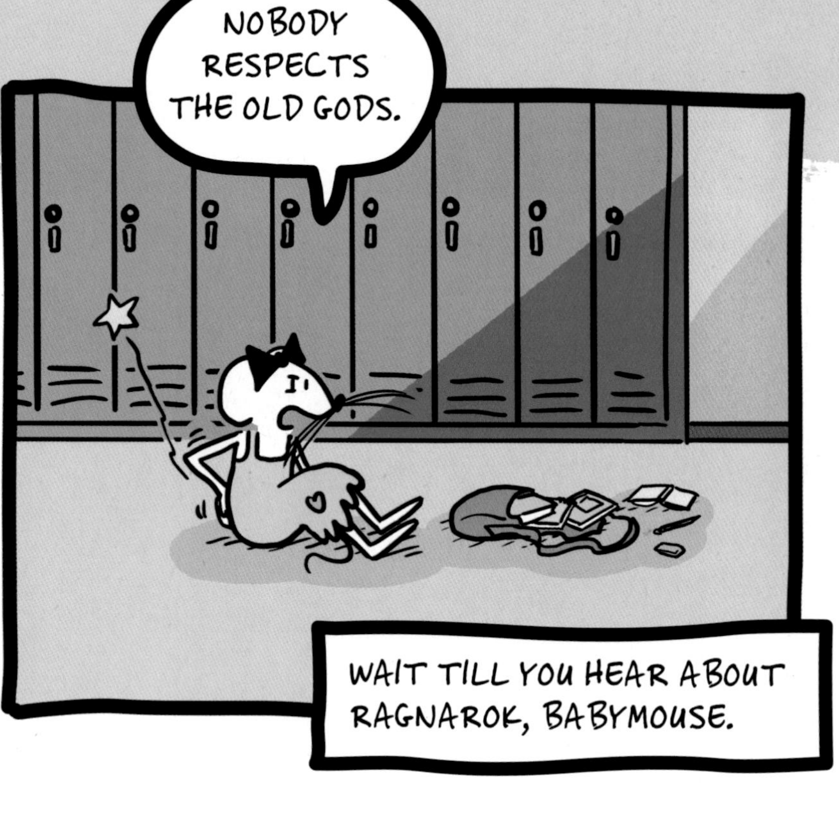
NOBODY RESPECTS THE OLD GODS.
WAIT TILL YOU HEAR ABOUT RAGNAROK, BABYMOUSE.

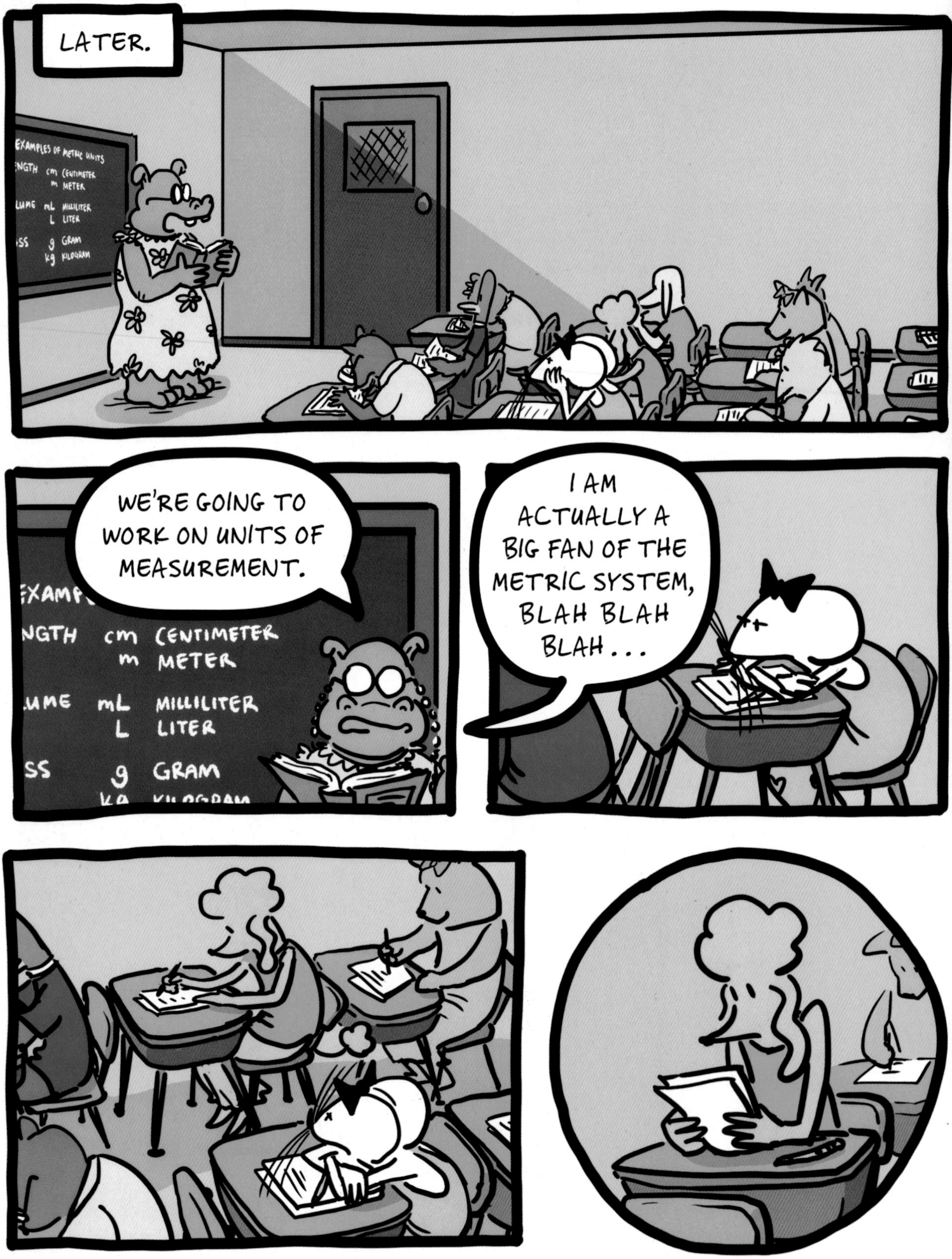
LATER.
WE'RE GOING TO WORK ON UNITS OF MEASUREMENT.
cm CENTIMETER
m METER
mL MILLILITER
L LITER
g GRAM
I AM ACTUALLY A BIG FAN OF THE METRIC SYSTEM, BLAH BLAH BLAH . . .

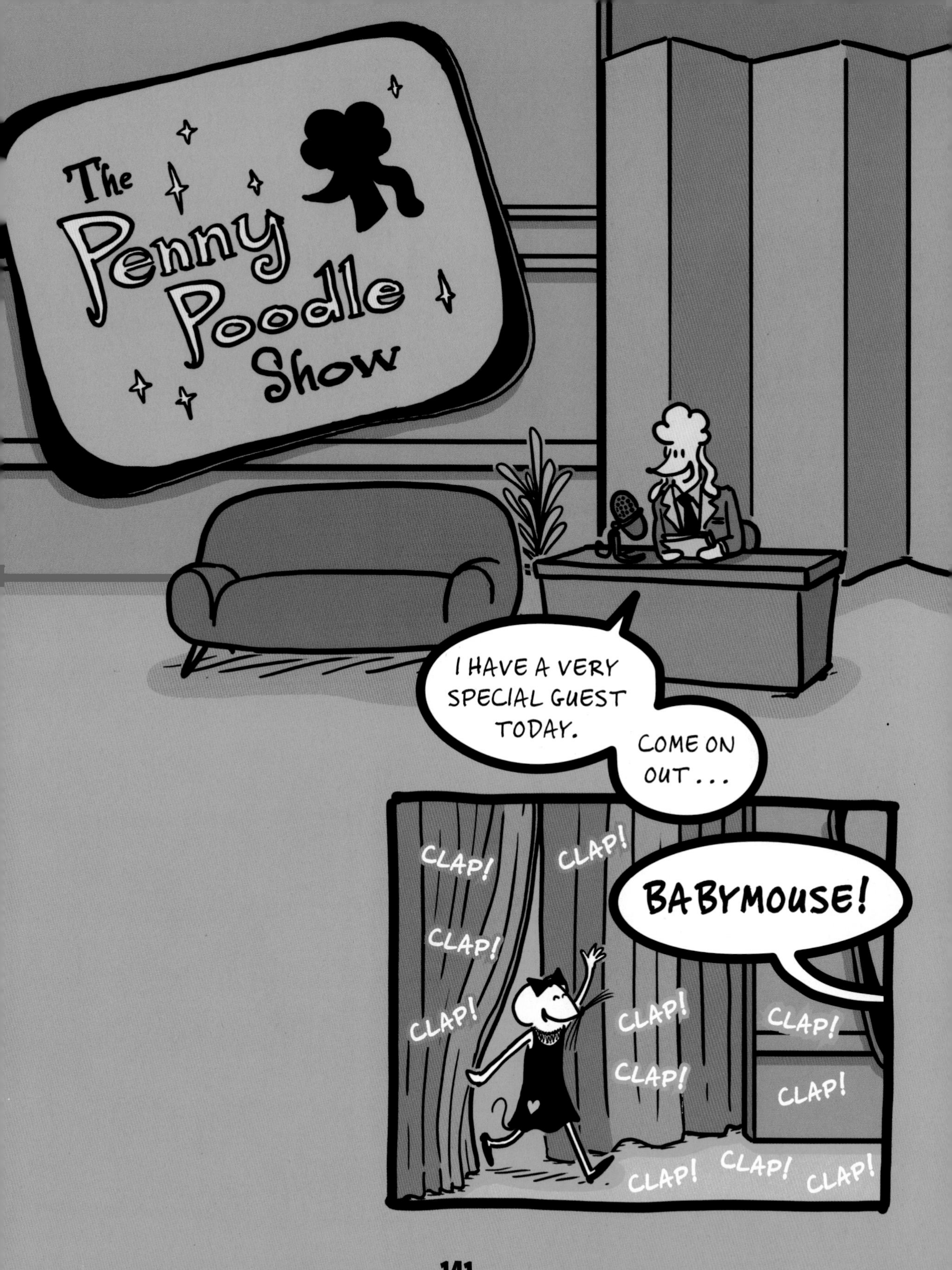
The Penny Poodle Show
I HAVE A VERY SPECIAL GUEST TODAY.
COME ON OUT . . .
CLAP! CLAP!
BABYMOUSE!
CLAP! CLAP! CLAP! CLAP! CLAP! CLAP! CLAP! CLAP! CLAP!

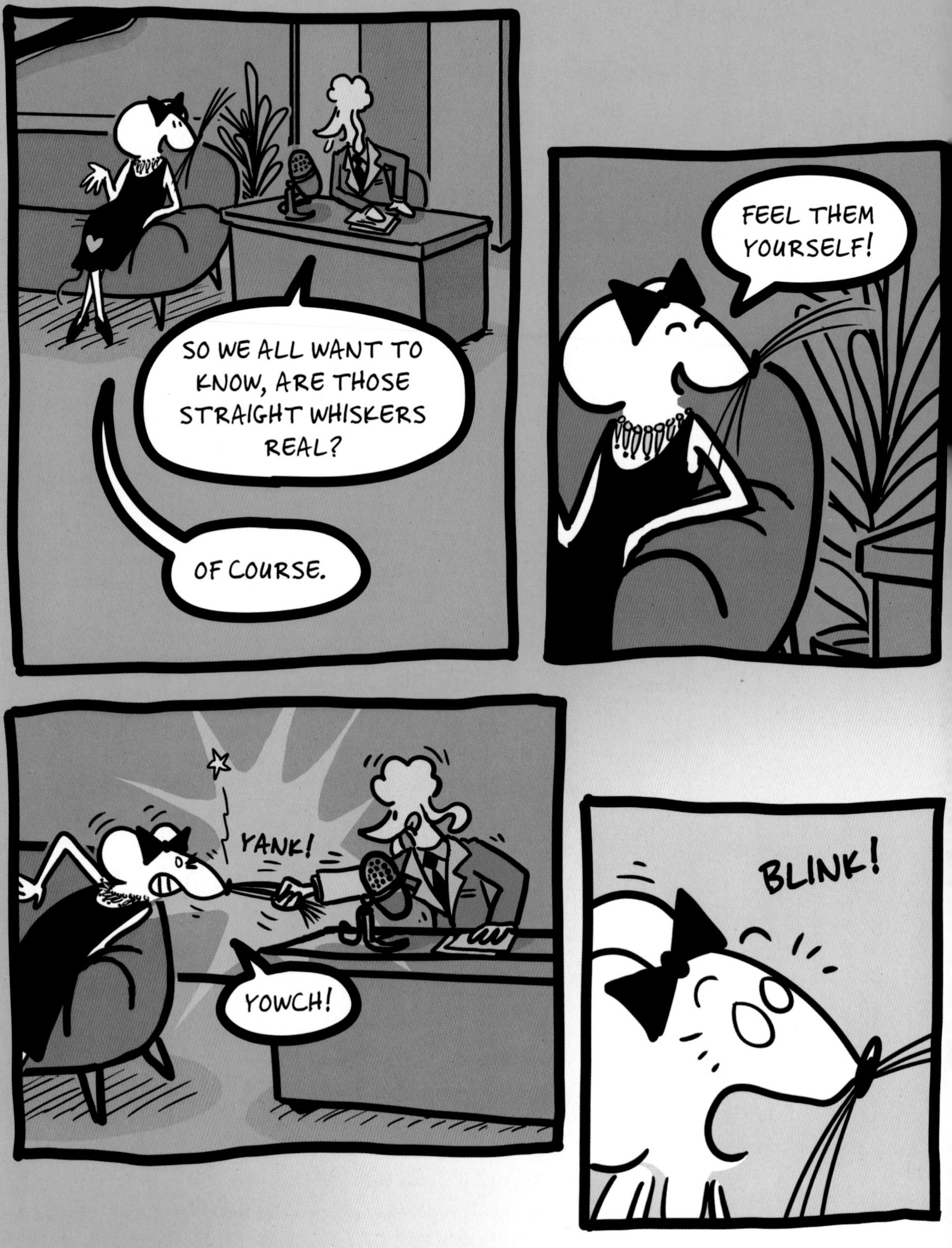
SO WE ALL WANT TO KNOW, ARE THOSE STRAIGHT WHISKERS REAL?
OF COURSE.
FEEL THEM YOURSELF!
YANK!
YOWCH!
BLINK!

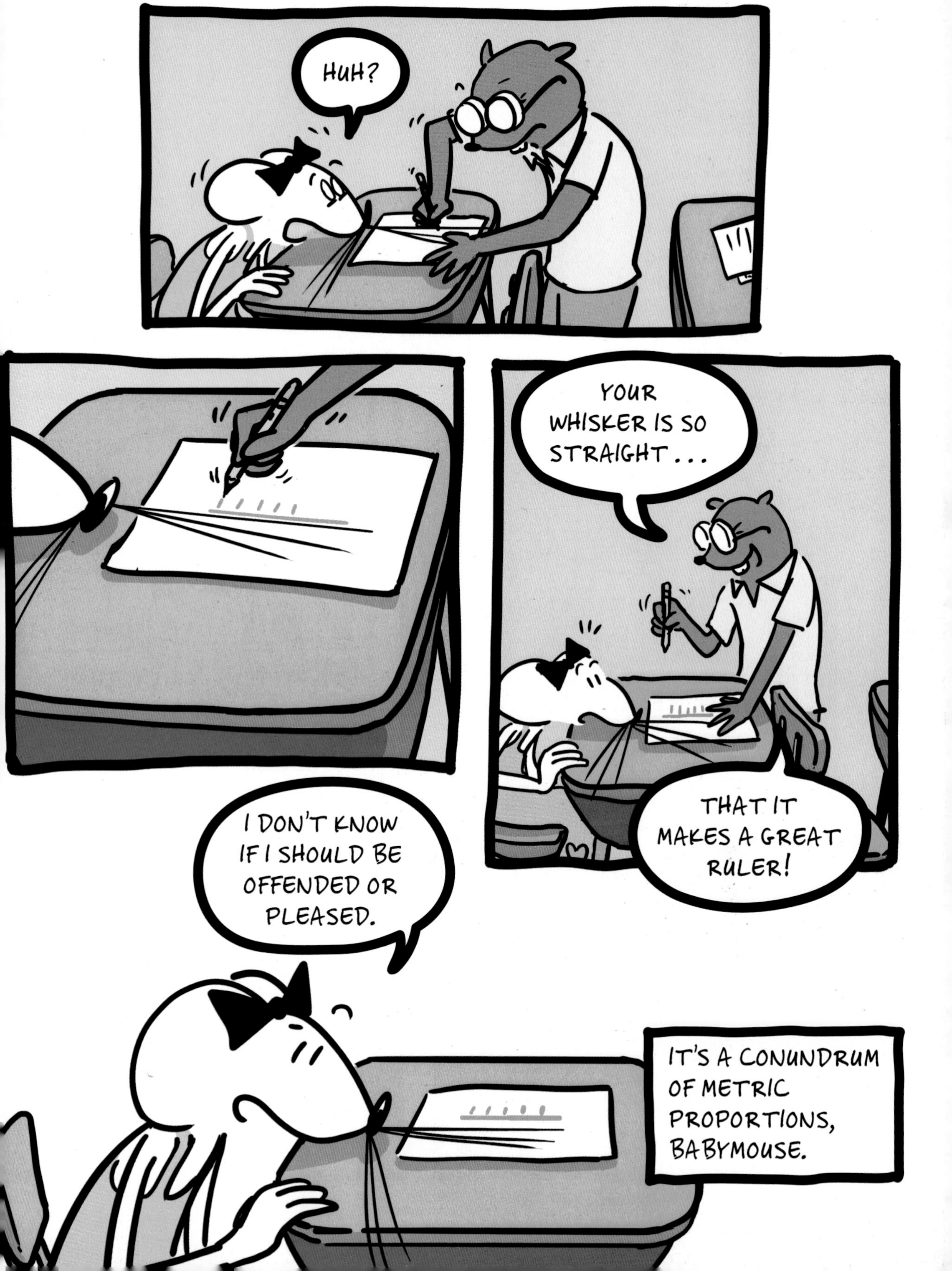
HUH?
YOUR WHISKER IS SO STRAIGHT . . .
THAT IT MAKES A GREAT RULER!
I DON'T KNOW IF I SHOULD BE OFFENDED OR PLEASED.
IT'S A CONUNDRUM OF METRIC PROPORTIONS, BABYMOUSE.

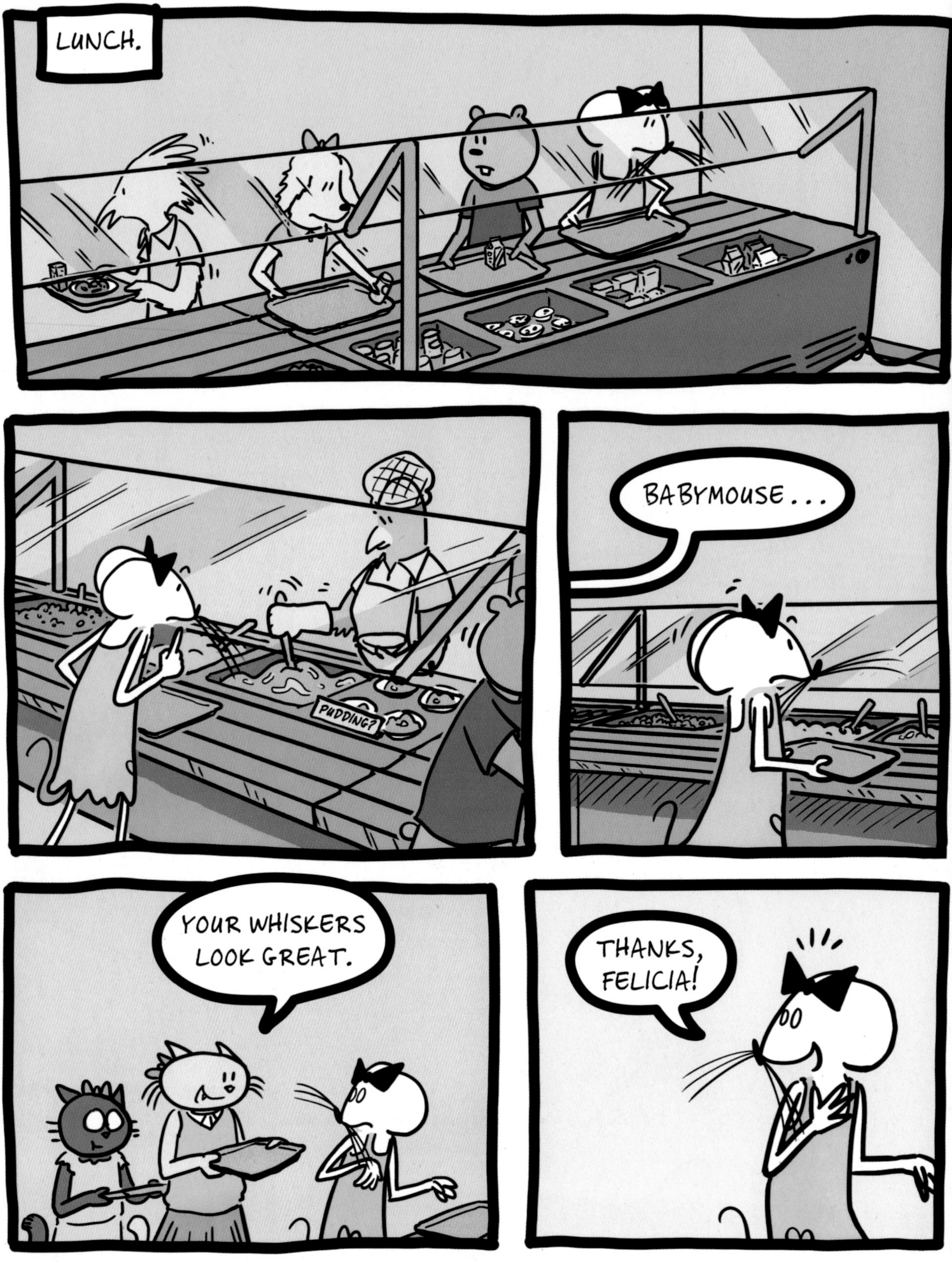
LUNCH.
PUDDING?
BABYMOUSE . . .
YOUR WHISKERS LOOK GREAT.
THANKS, FELICIA!

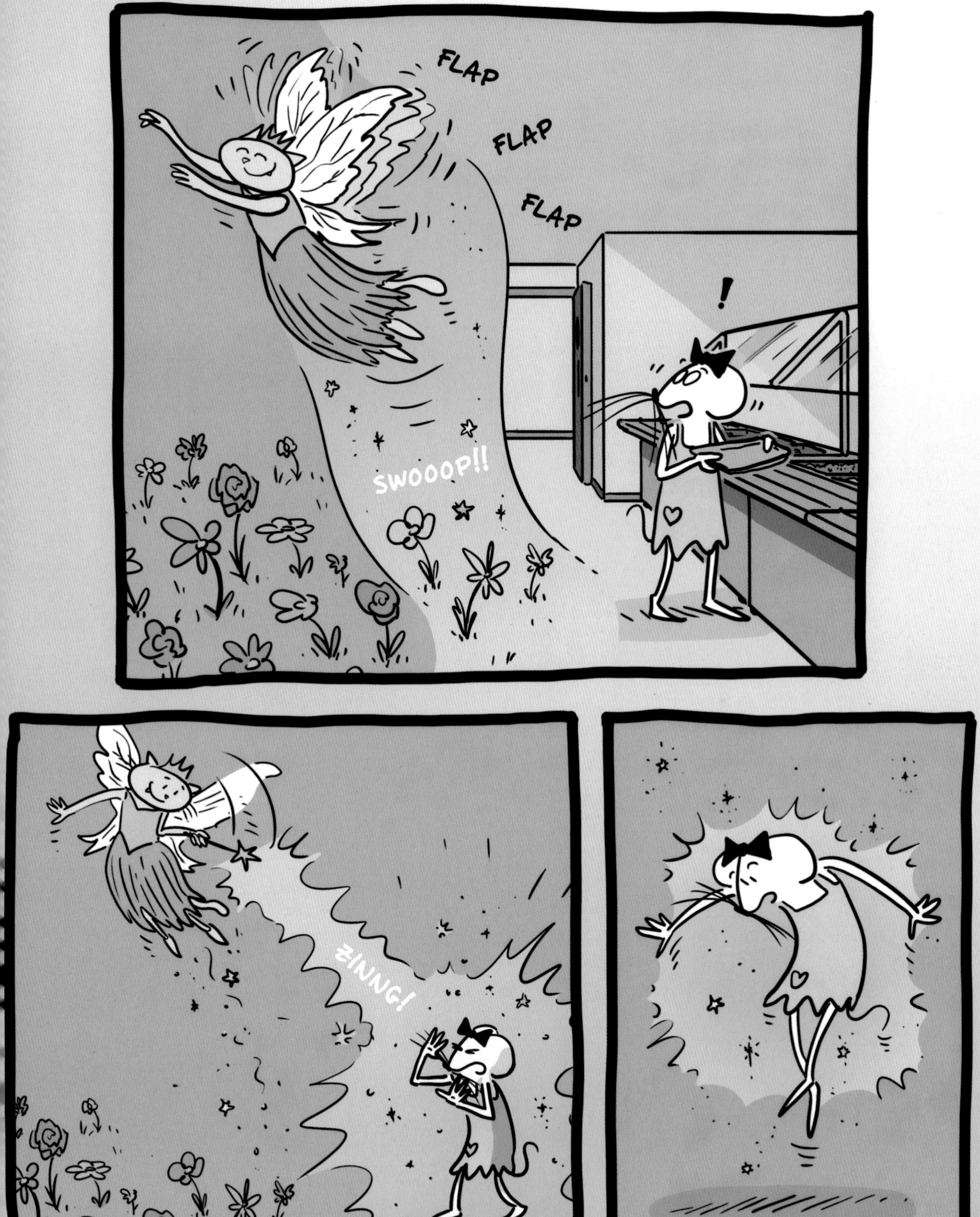
FLAP
FLAP
FLAP
!
SWOOOP!!
ZINNG!

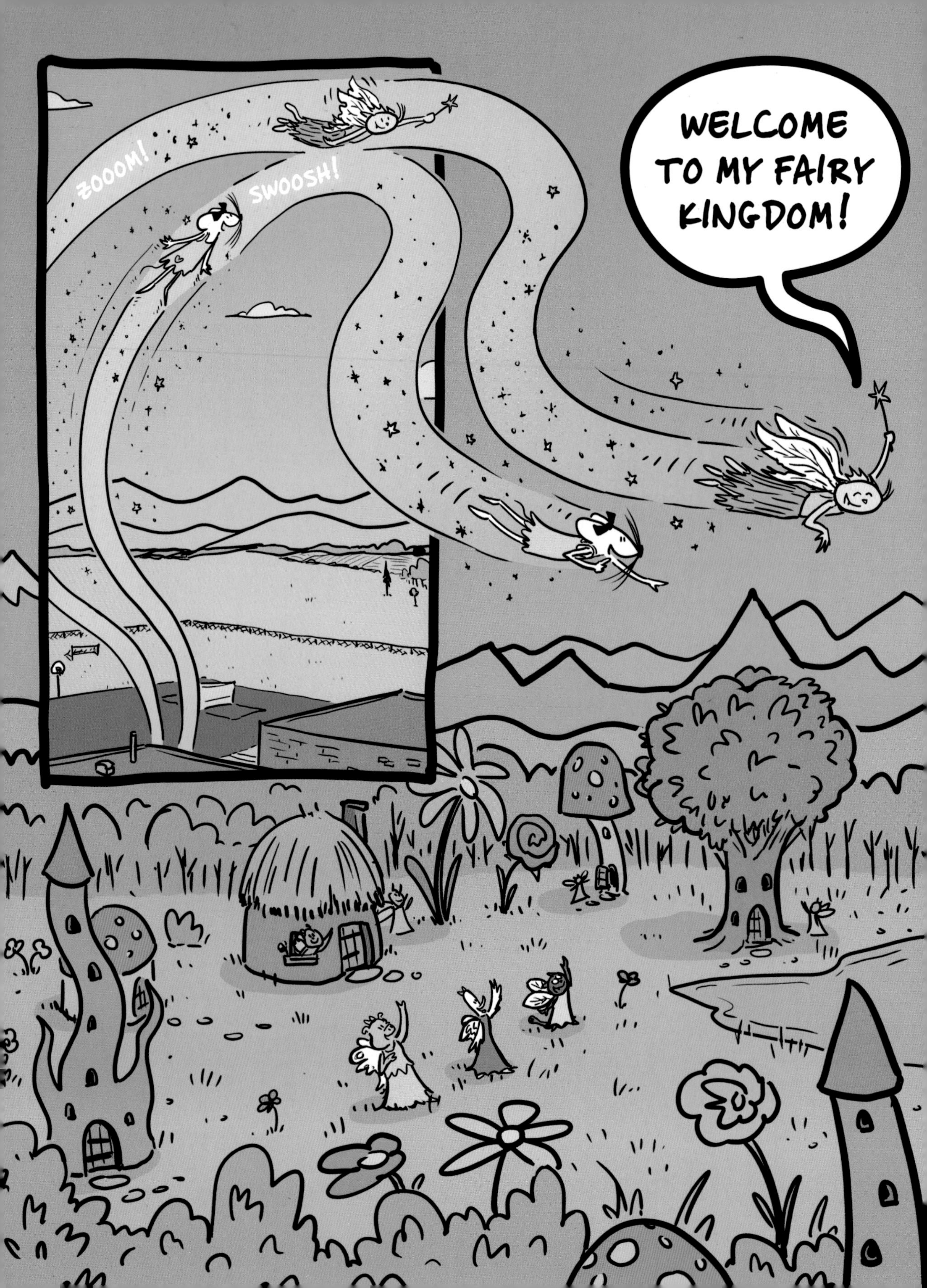
ZOOOM!
SWOOSH!
WELCOME TO MY FAIRY KINGDOM!

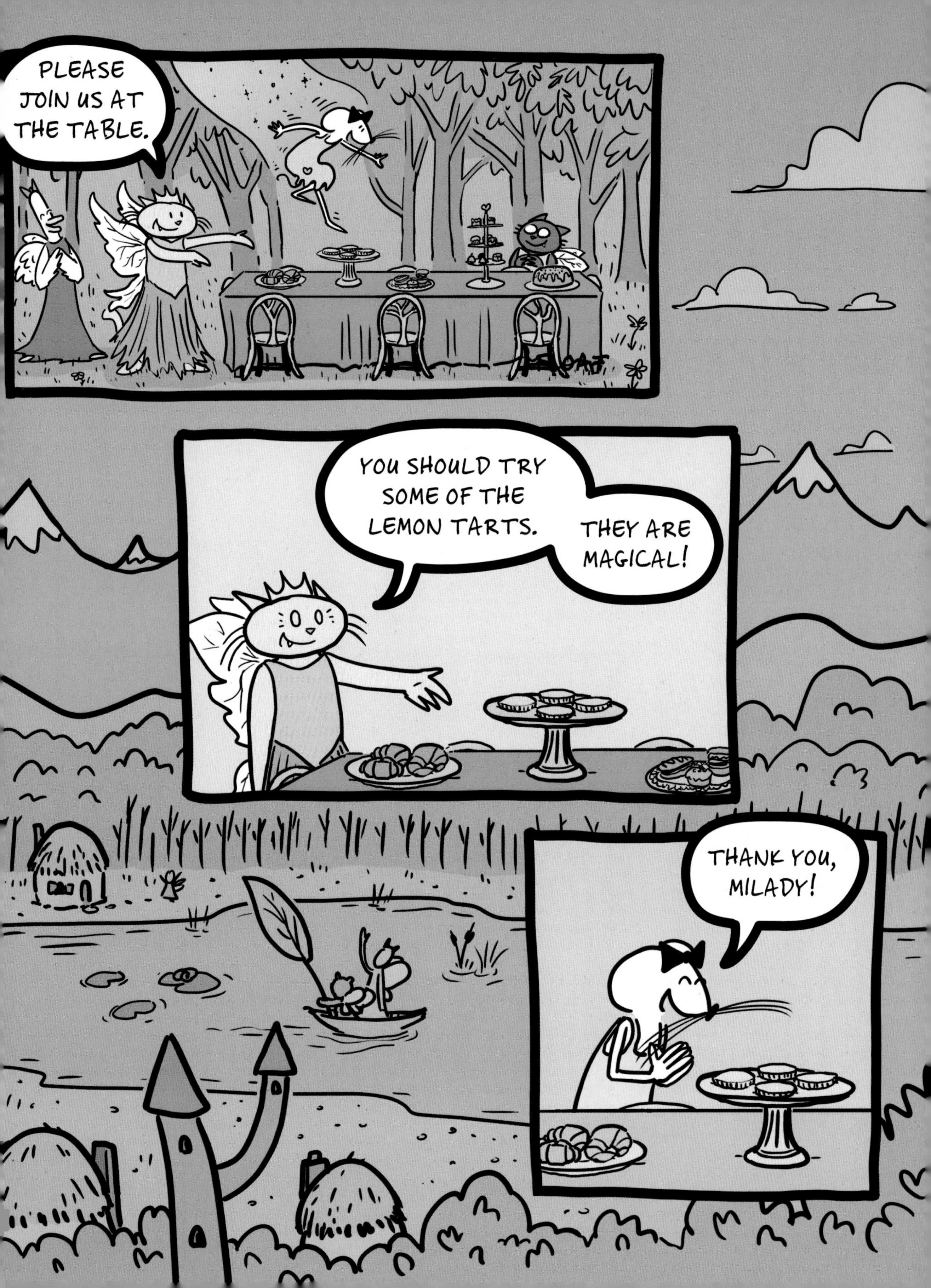
PLEASE JOIN US AT THE TABLE.
YOU SHOULD TRY SOME OF THE LEMON TARTS.
THEY ARE MAGICAL!
THANK YOU, MILADY!

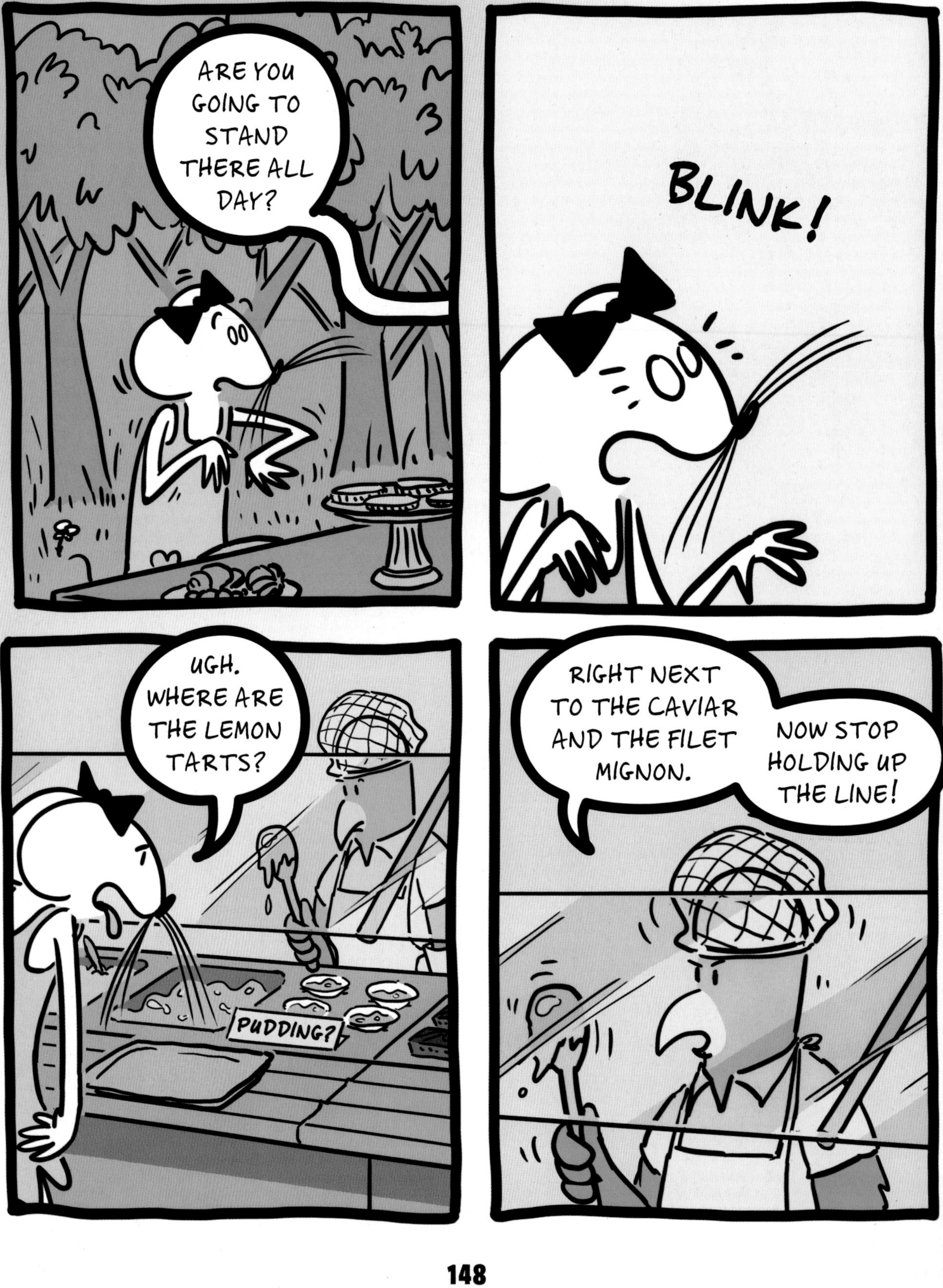
ARE YOU GOING TO STAND THERE ALL DAY?
BLINK!
UGH. WHERE ARE THE LEMON TARTS?
PUDDING?
RIGHT NEXT TO THE CAVIAR AND THE FILET MIGNON.
NOW STOP HOLDING UP THE LINE!

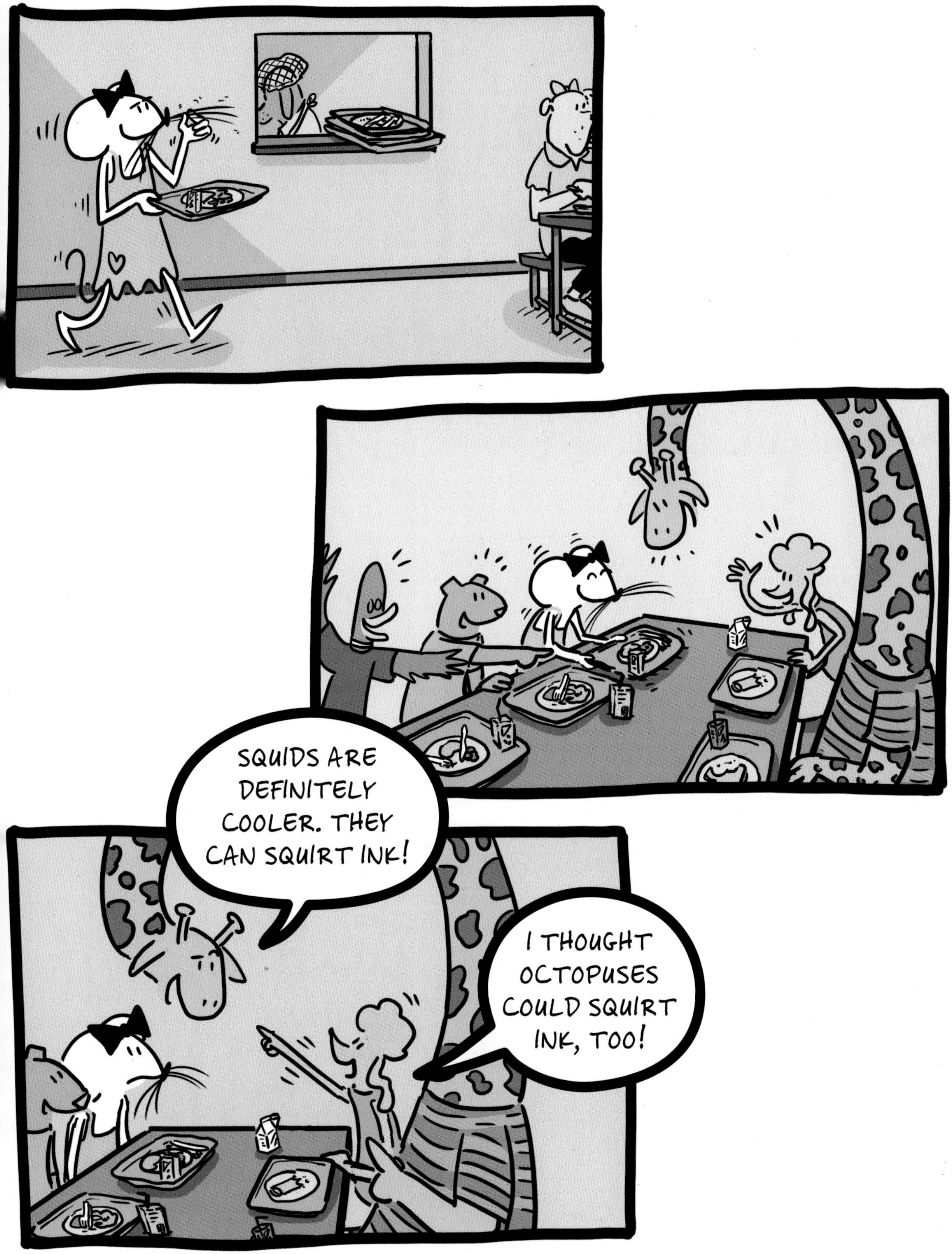
SQUIDS ARE DEFINITELY COOLER. THEY CAN SQUIRT INK!
I THOUGHT OCTOPUSES COULD SQUIRT INK, TOO!

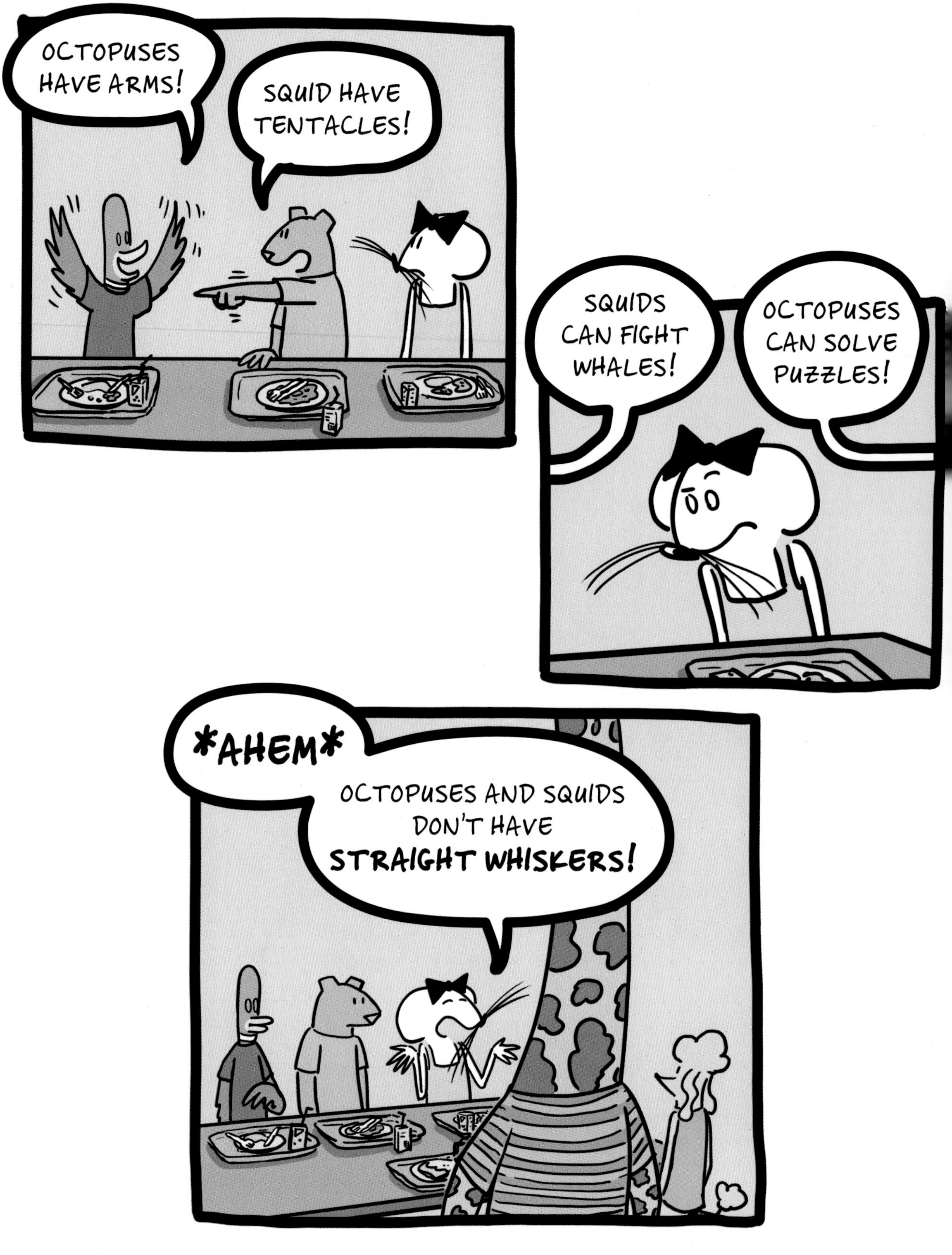
OCTOPUSES HAVE ARMS!
SQUID HAVE TENTACLES!
SQUIDS CAN FIGHT WHALES!
OCTOPUSES CAN SOLVE PUZZLES!
AHEM
OCTOPUSES AND SQUIDS DON'T HAVE **STRAIGHT WHISKERS!**

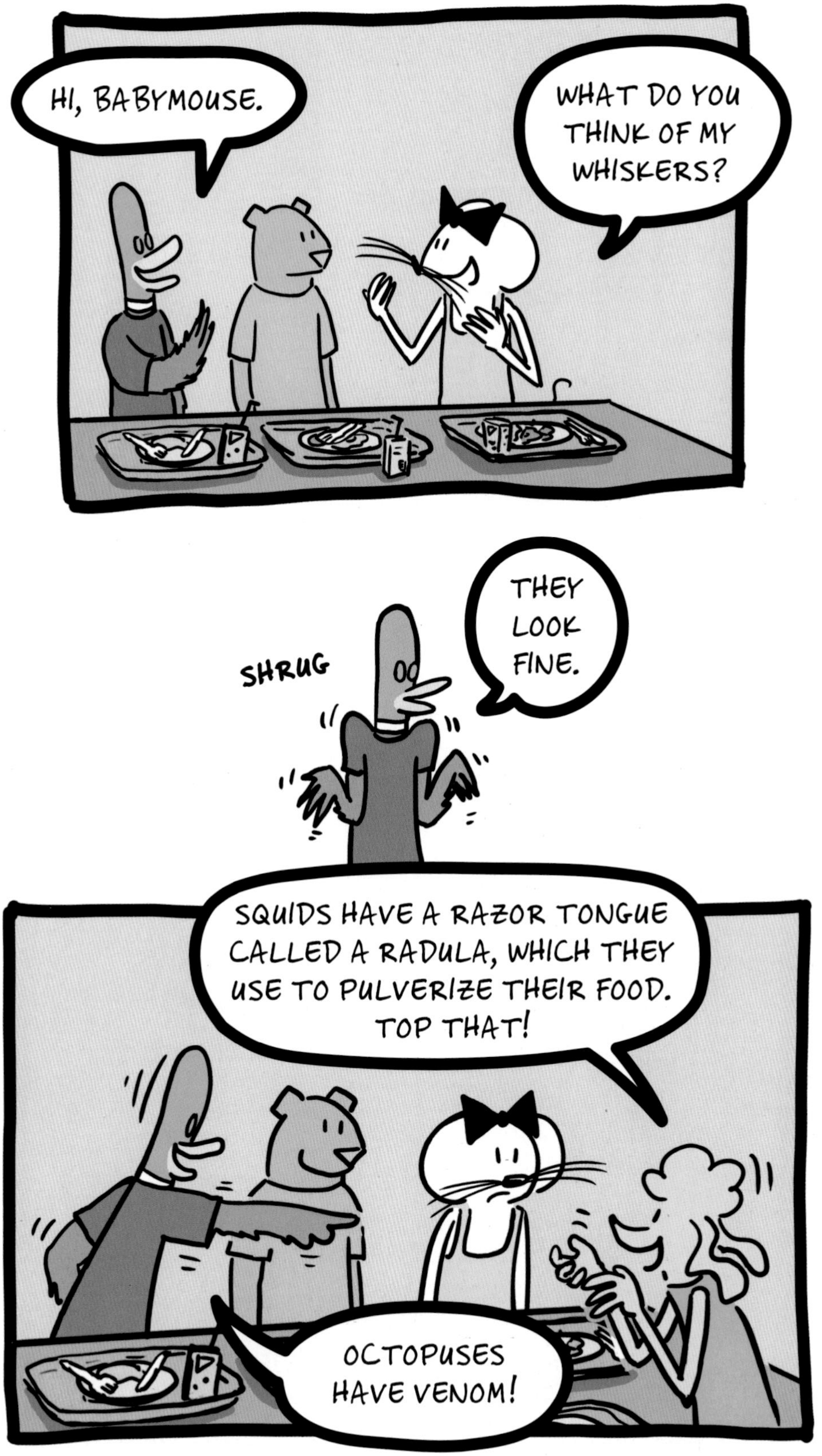
HI, BABYMOUSE.
WHAT DO YOU THINK OF MY WHISKERS?
SHRUG
THEY LOOK FINE.
SQUIDS HAVE A RAZOR TONGUE CALLED A RADULA, WHICH THEY USE TO PULVERIZE THEIR FOOD. TOP THAT!
OCTOPUSES HAVE VENOM!

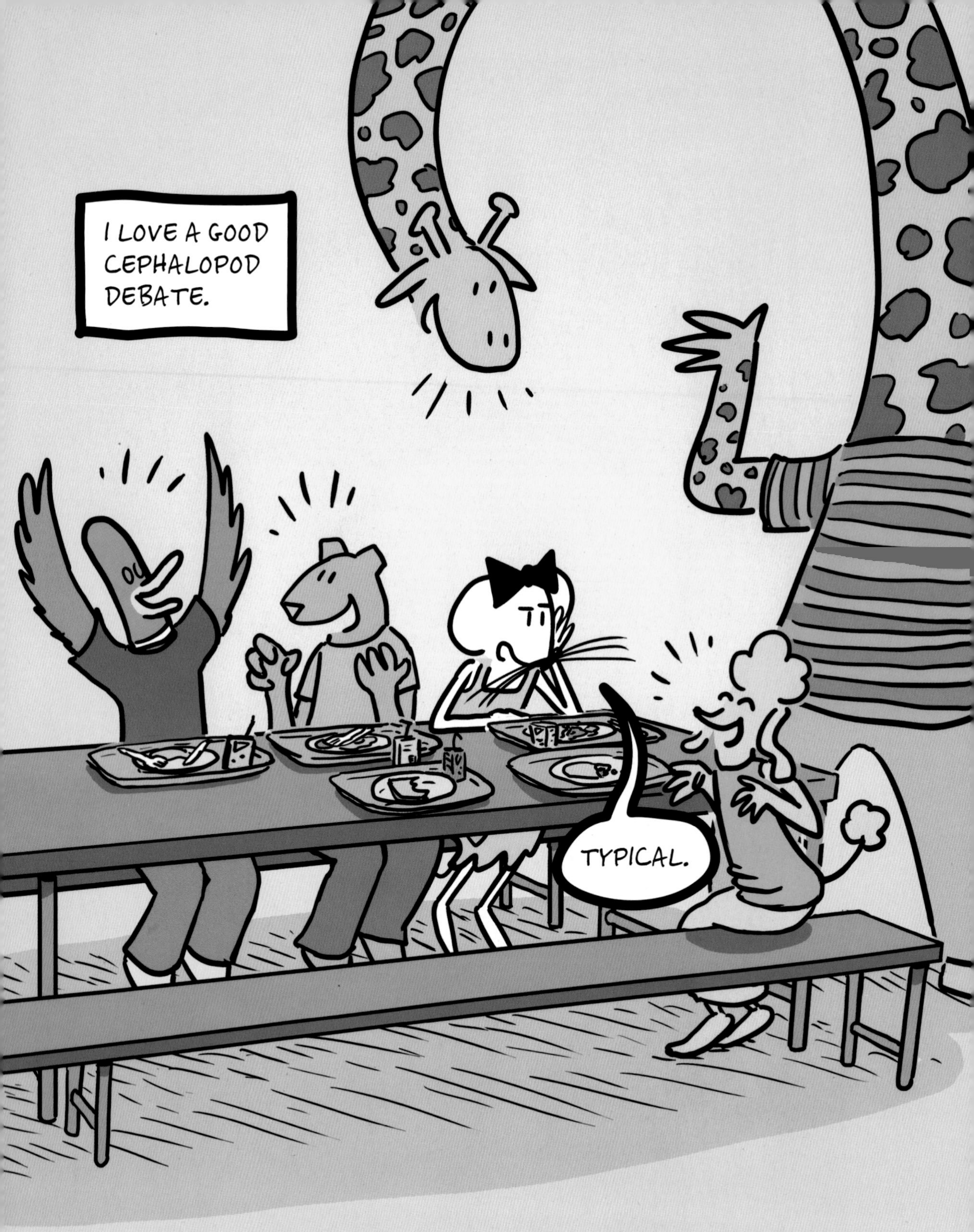
I LOVE A GOOD CEPHALOPOD DEBATE.
TYPICAL.

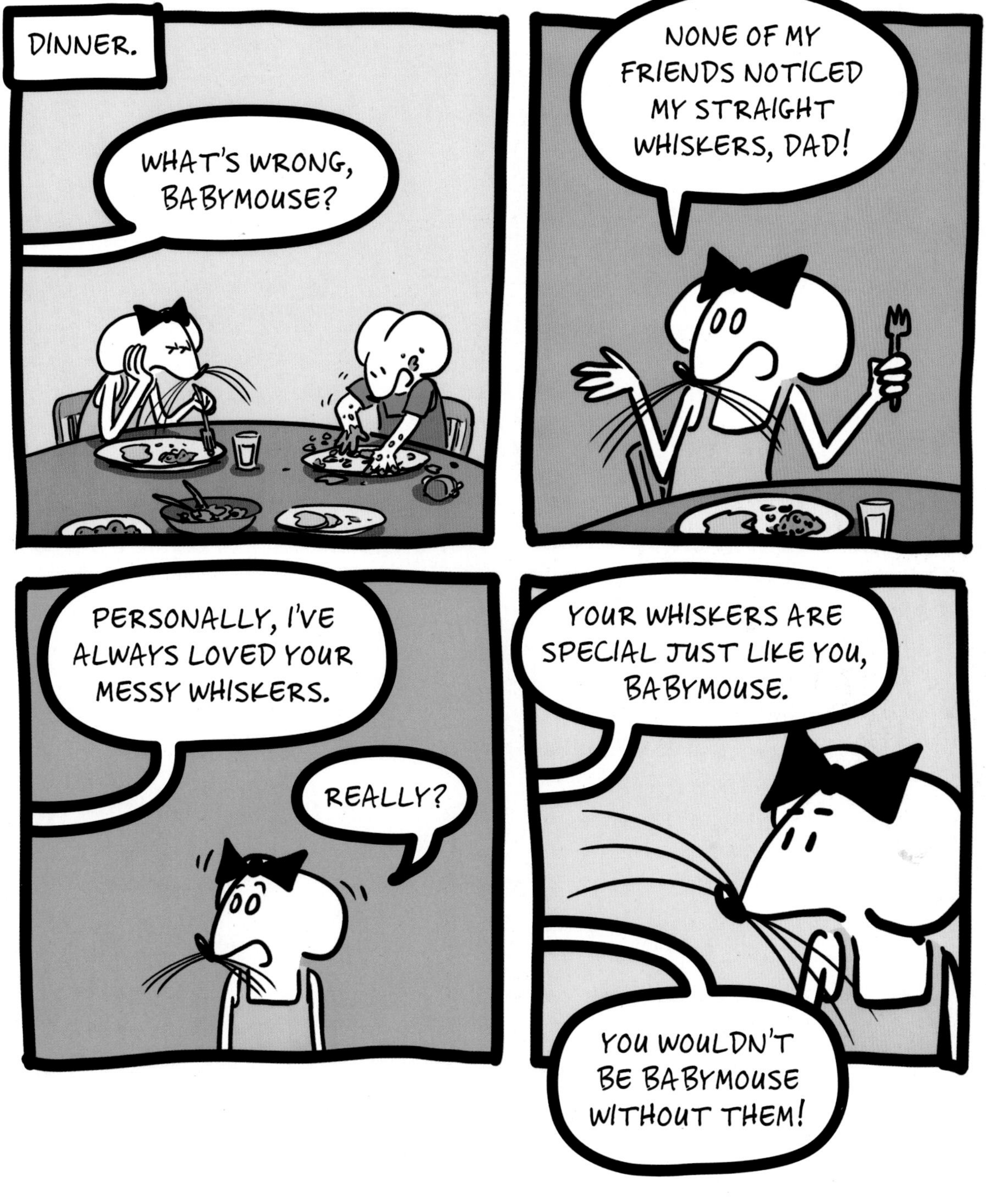
DINNER.
WHAT'S WRONG, BABYMOUSE?
NONE OF MY FRIENDS NOTICED MY STRAIGHT WHISKERS, DAD!
PERSONALLY, I'VE ALWAYS LOVED YOUR MESSY WHISKERS.
REALLY?
YOUR WHISKERS ARE SPECIAL JUST LIKE YOU, BABYMOUSE.
YOU WOULDN'T BE BABYMOUSE WITHOUT THEM!

THAT NIGHT.

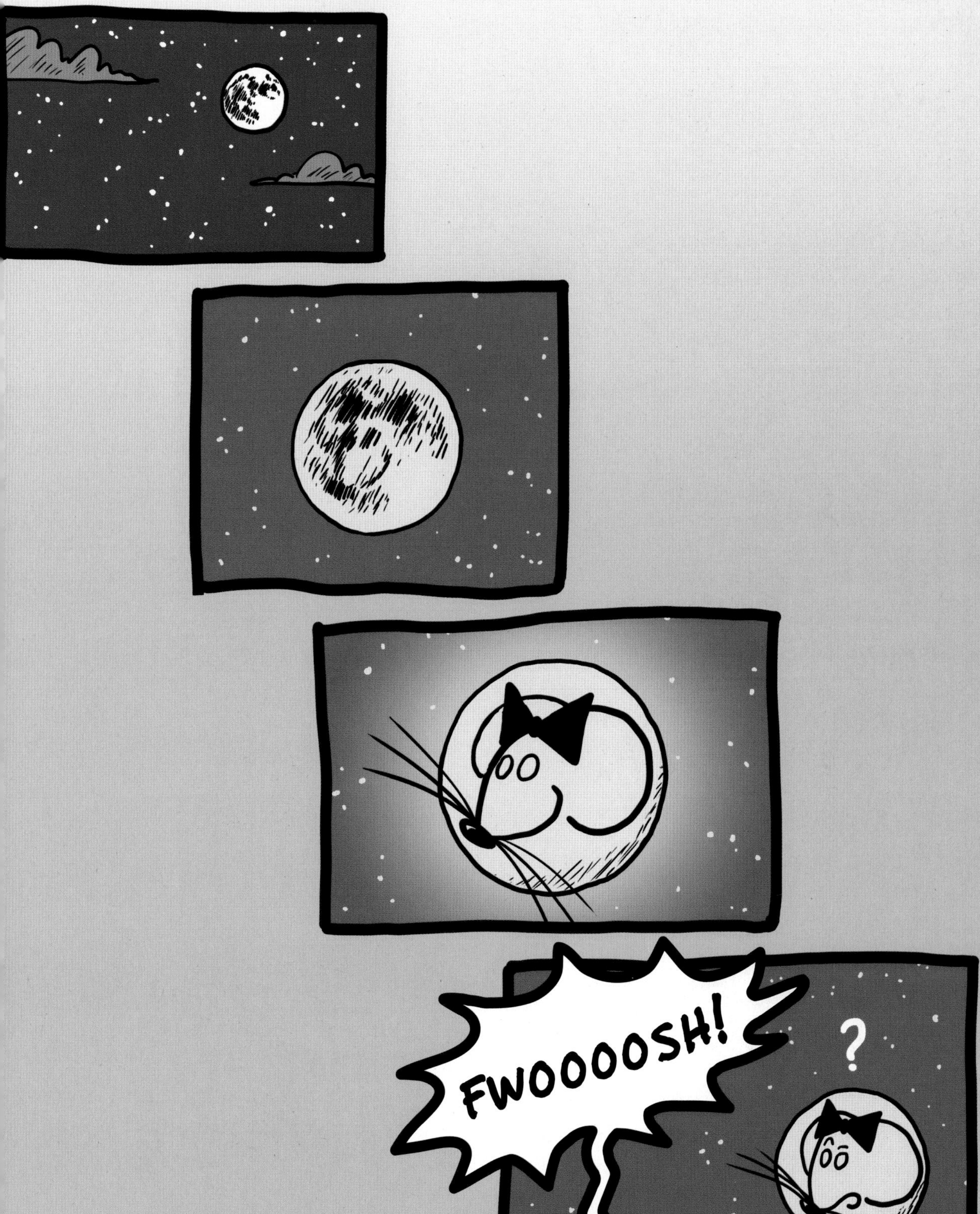
FWOOOOSH!
?

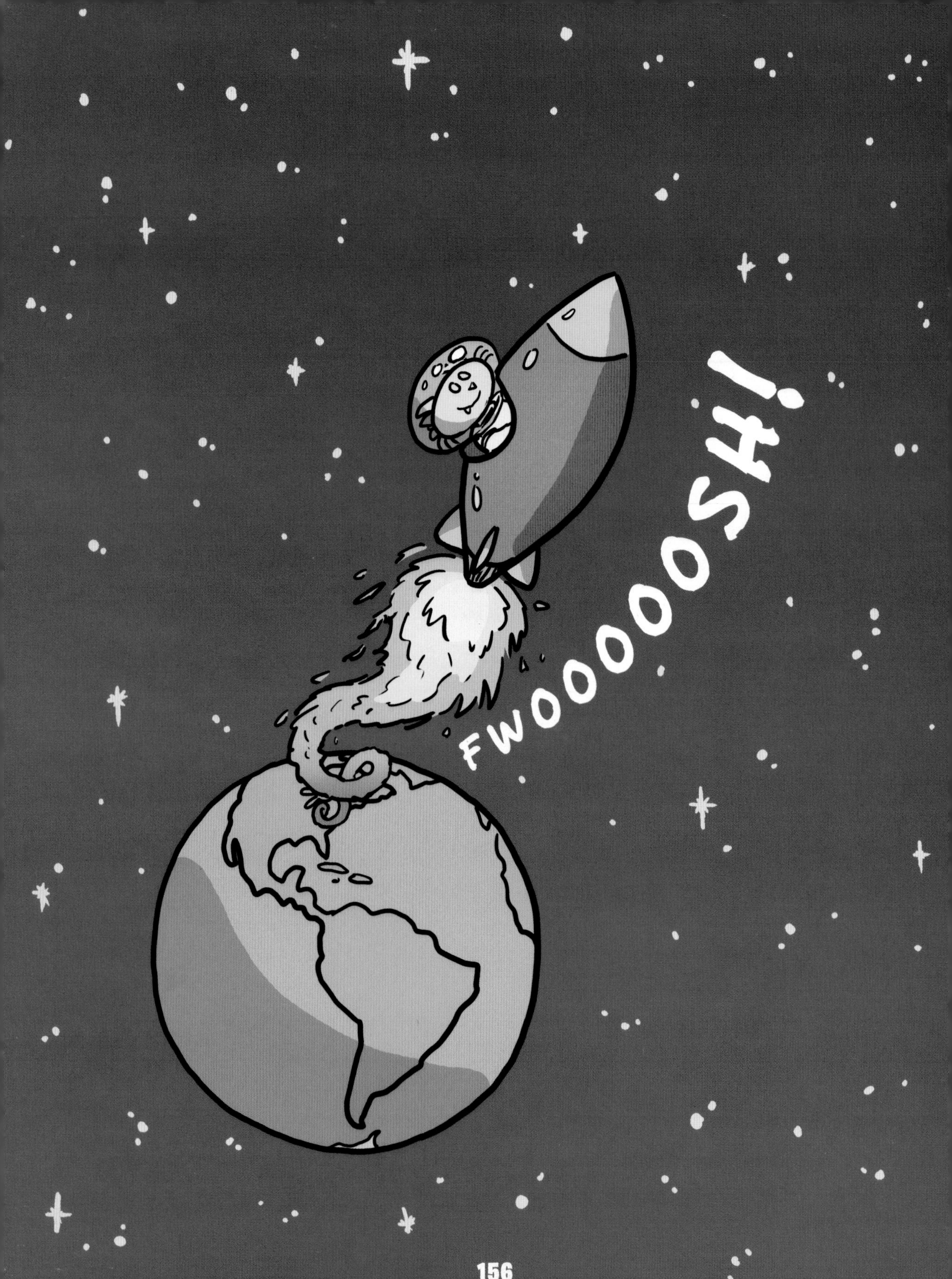
FWOOOOOSH!

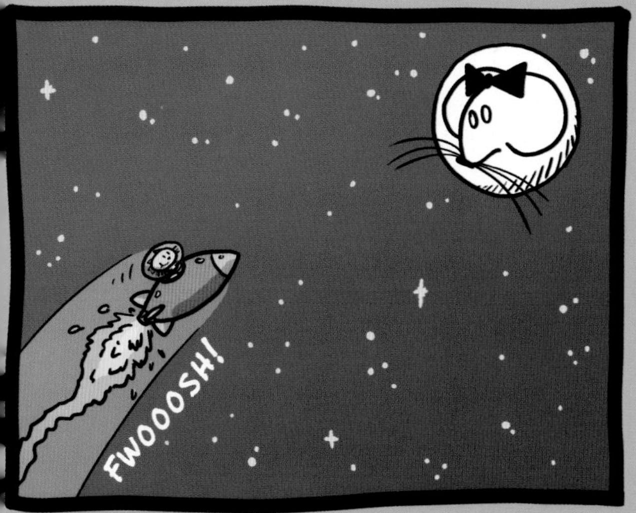
FWOOOSH!

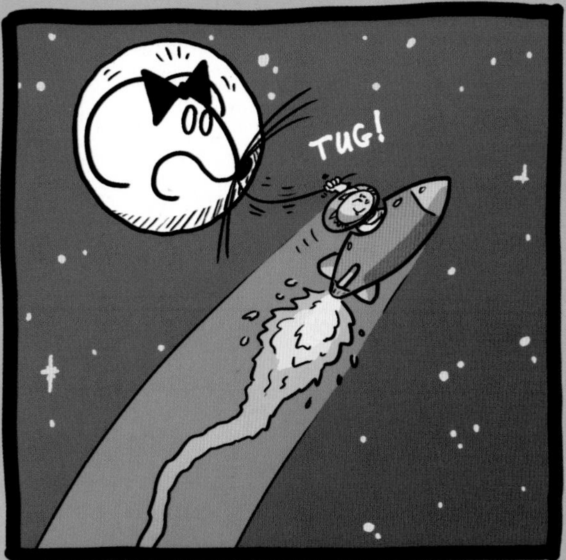
TUG!

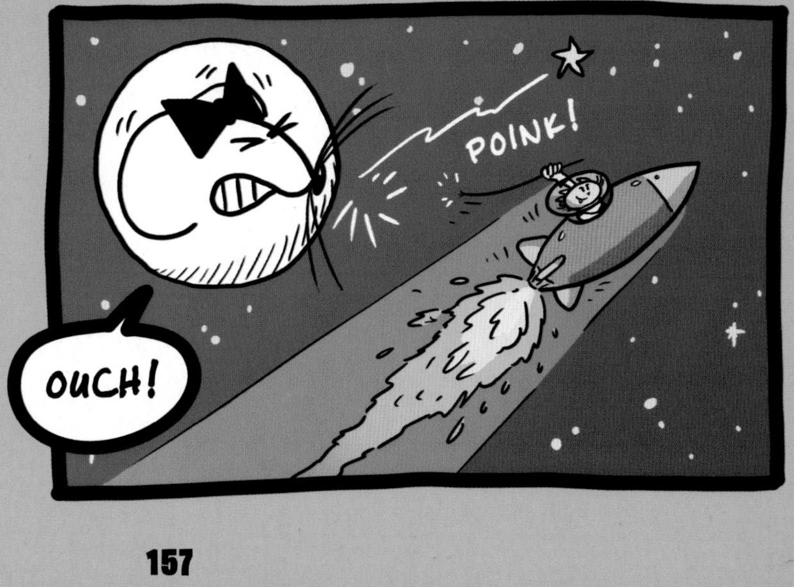
POINK!
OUCH!

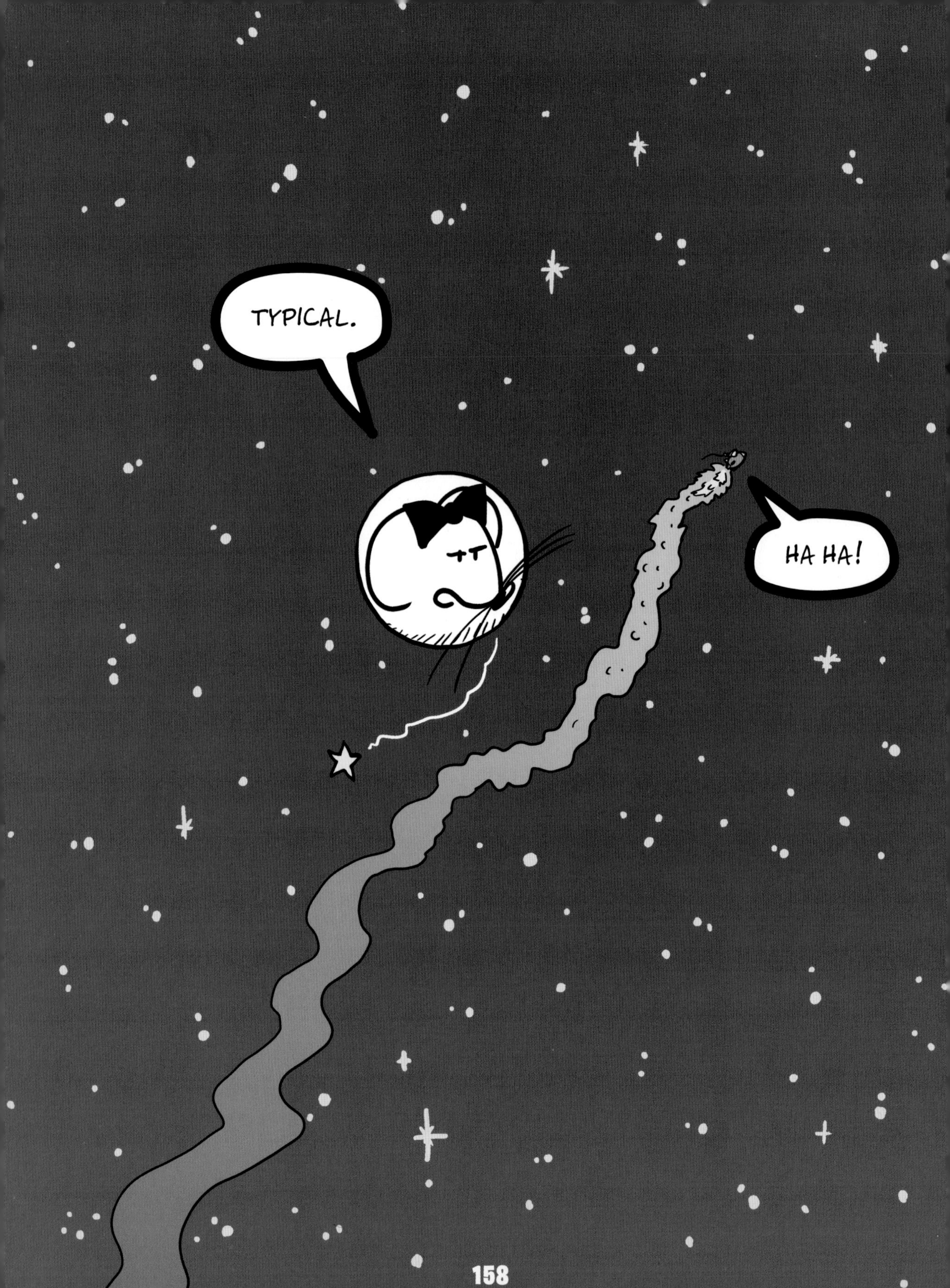
TYPICAL.
HA HA!

PART FIVE

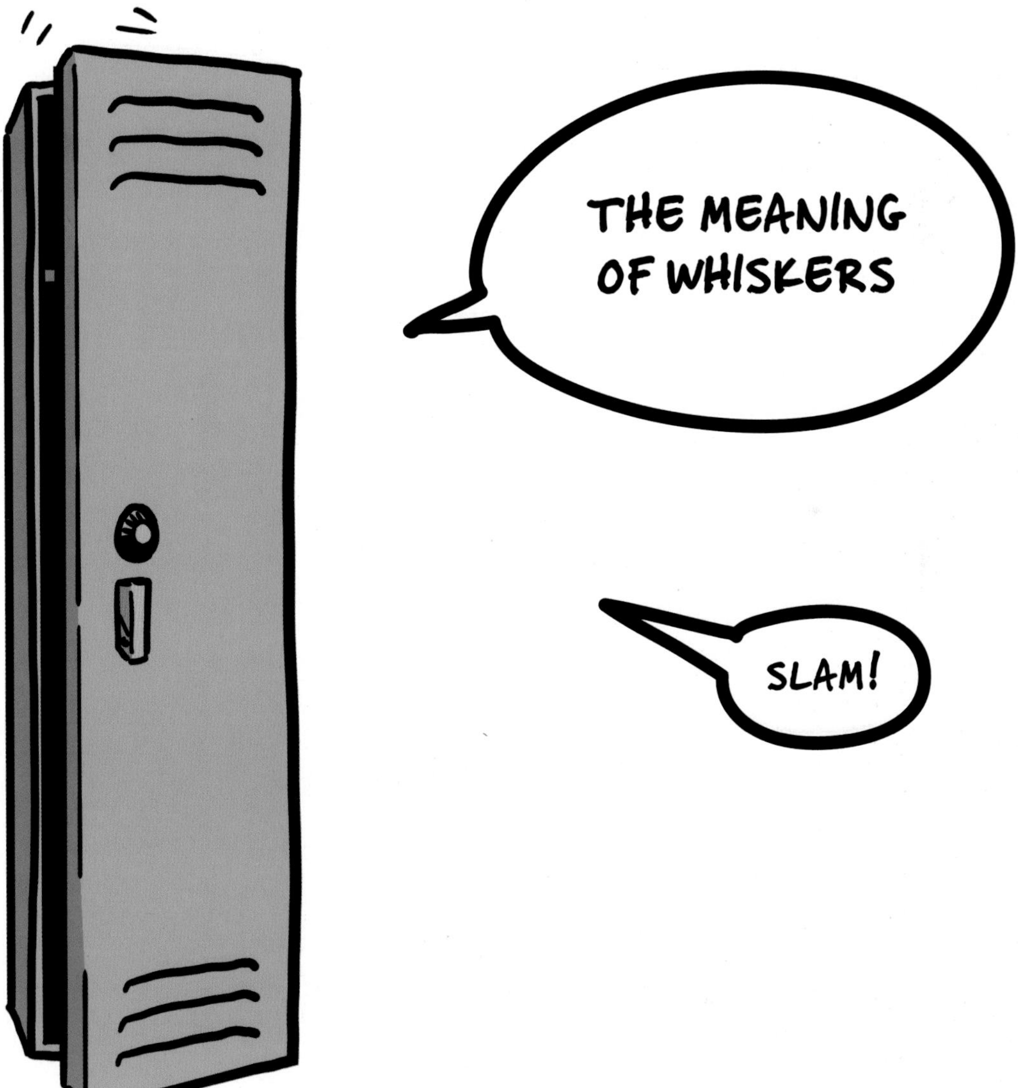
THE MEANING OF WHISKERS
SLAM!

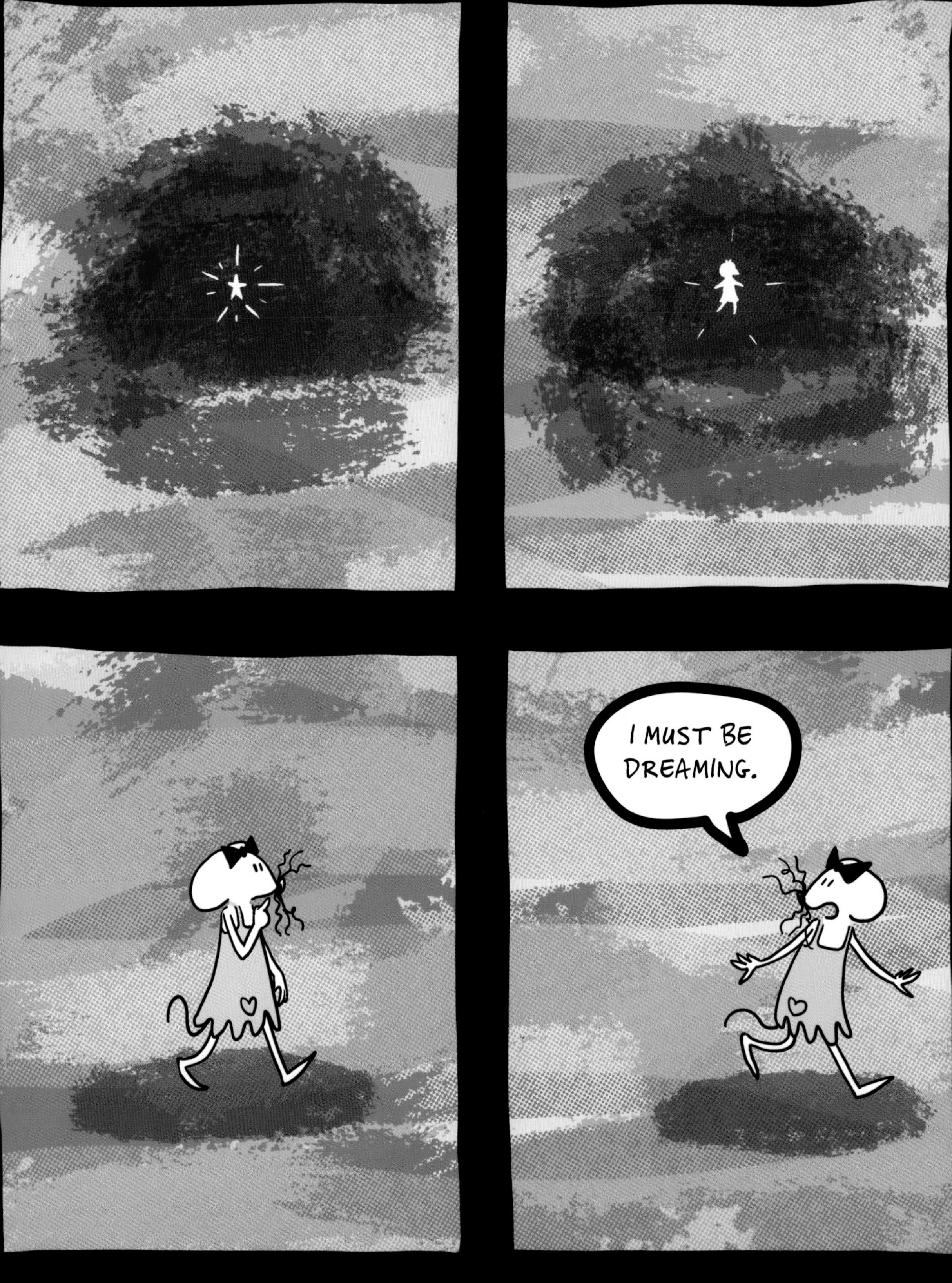
I MUST BE DREAMING.

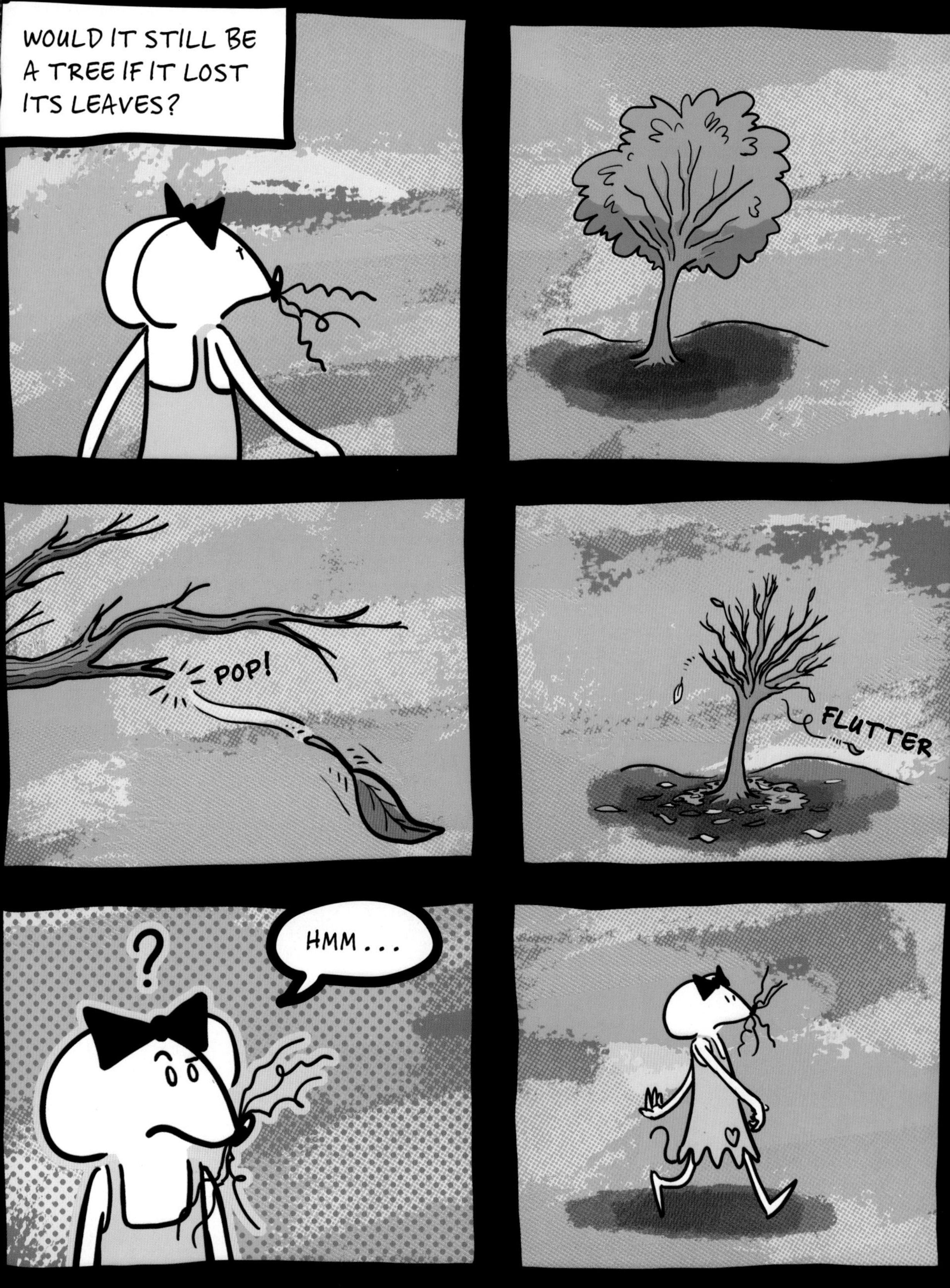
WOULD IT STILL BE A TREE IF IT LOST ITS LEAVES?
POP!
FLUTTER
?
HMM...

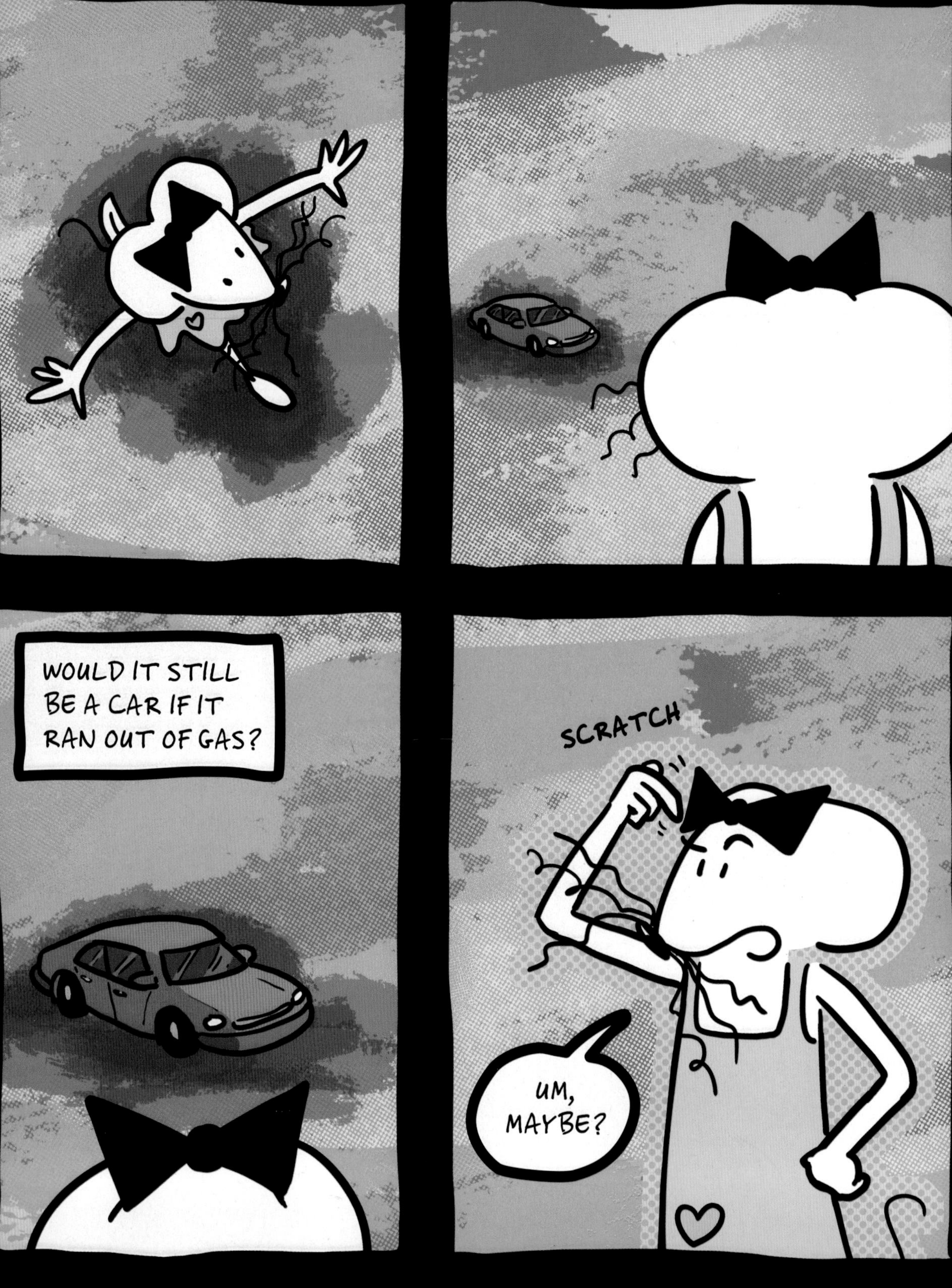
WOULD IT STILL BE A CAR IF IT RAN OUT OF GAS?
SCRATCH
UM, MAYBE?

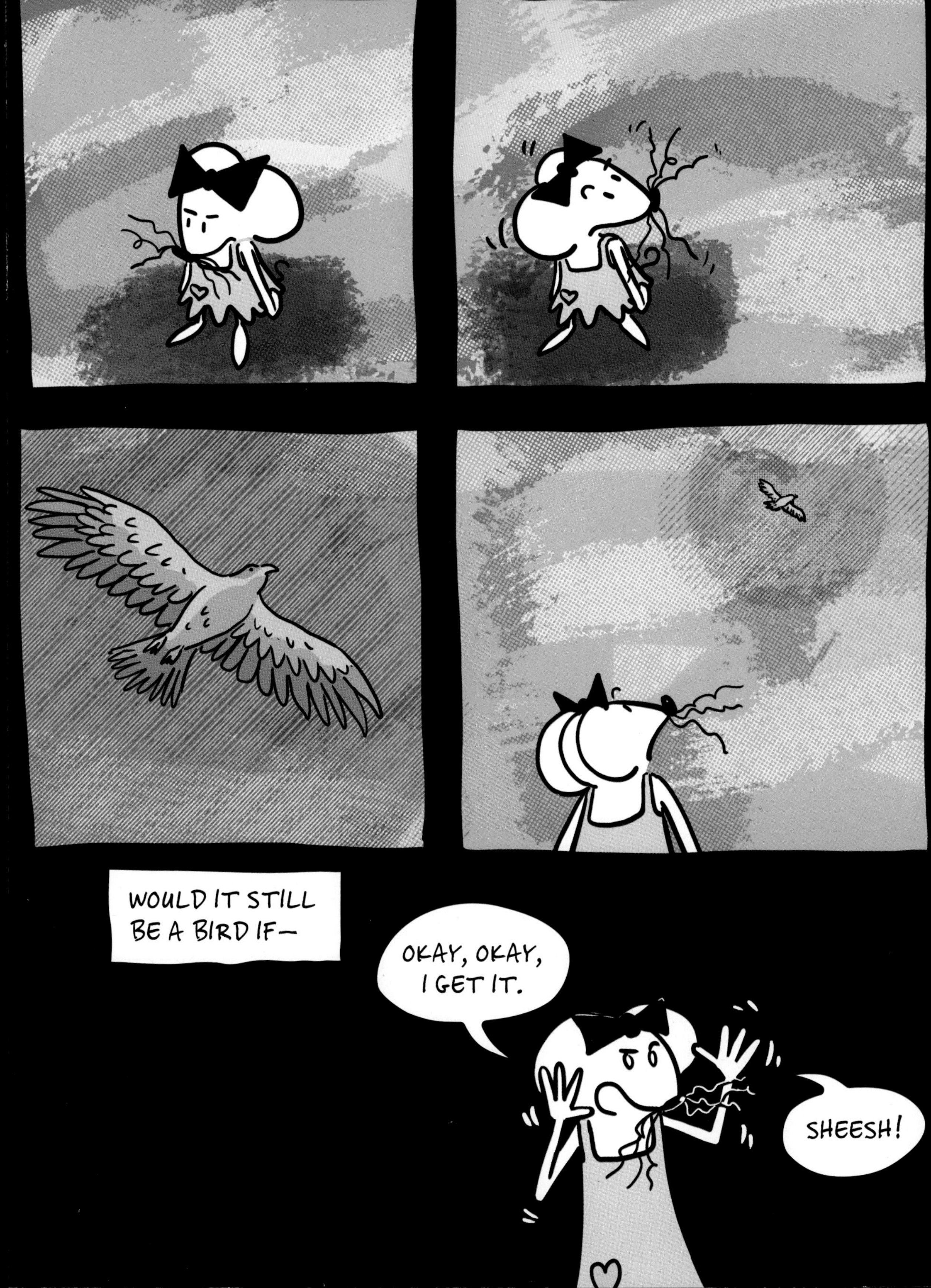
WOULD IT STILL BE A BIRD IF—
OKAY, OKAY, I GET IT.
SHEESH!

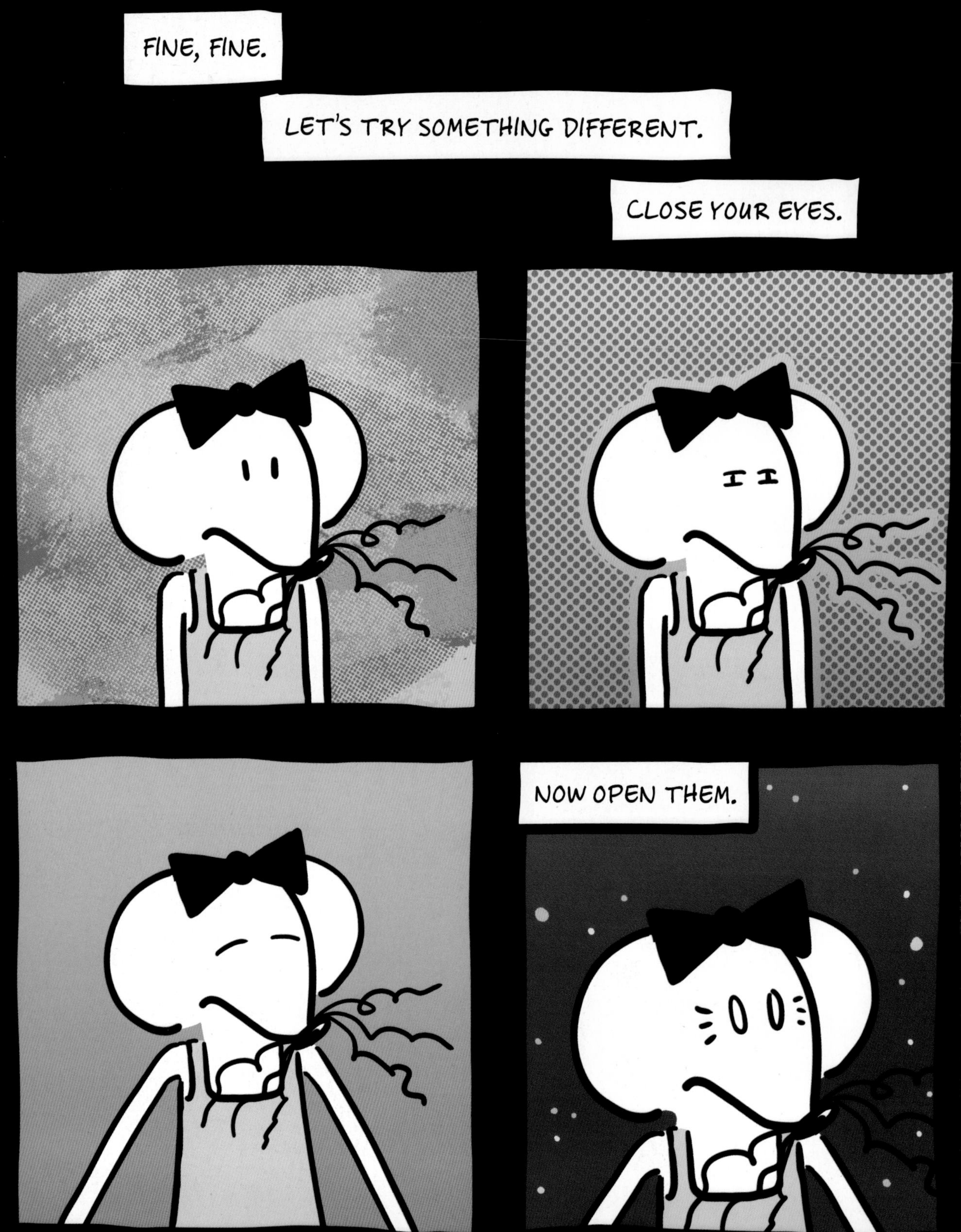
FINE, FINE.
LET'S TRY SOMETHING DIFFERENT.
CLOSE YOUR EYES.
NOW OPEN THEM.

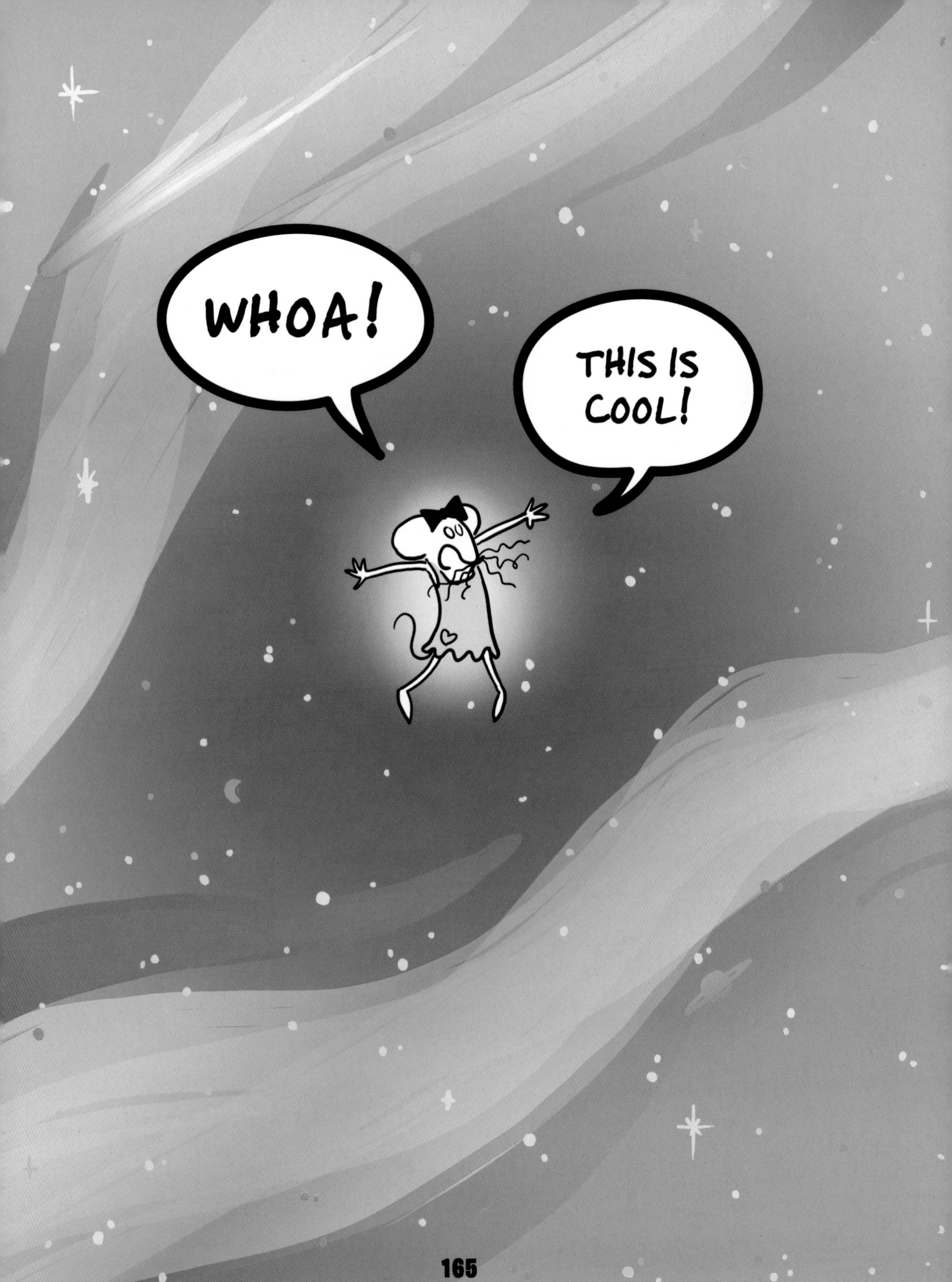
WHOA!
THIS IS COOL!

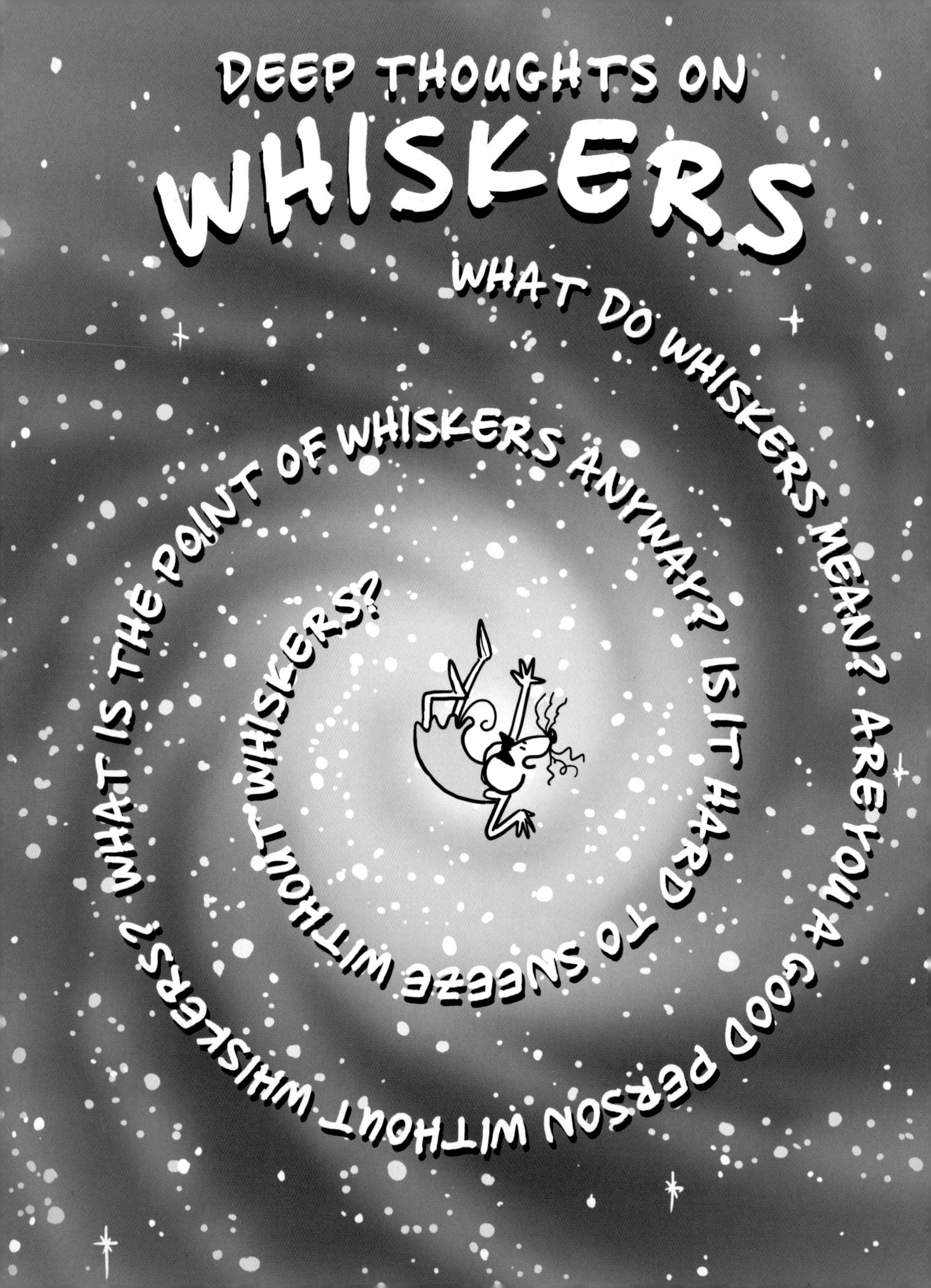
DEEP THOUGHTS ON
WHISKERS
WHAT DO WHISKERS MEAN? ARE YOU A GOOD PERSON WITHOUT WHISKERS? WHAT IS THE POINT OF WHISKERS ANYWAY? IS IT HARD TO SNEEZE WITHOUT WHISKERS?

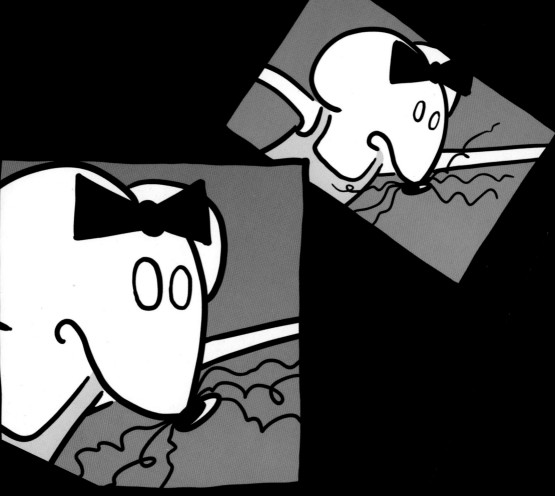

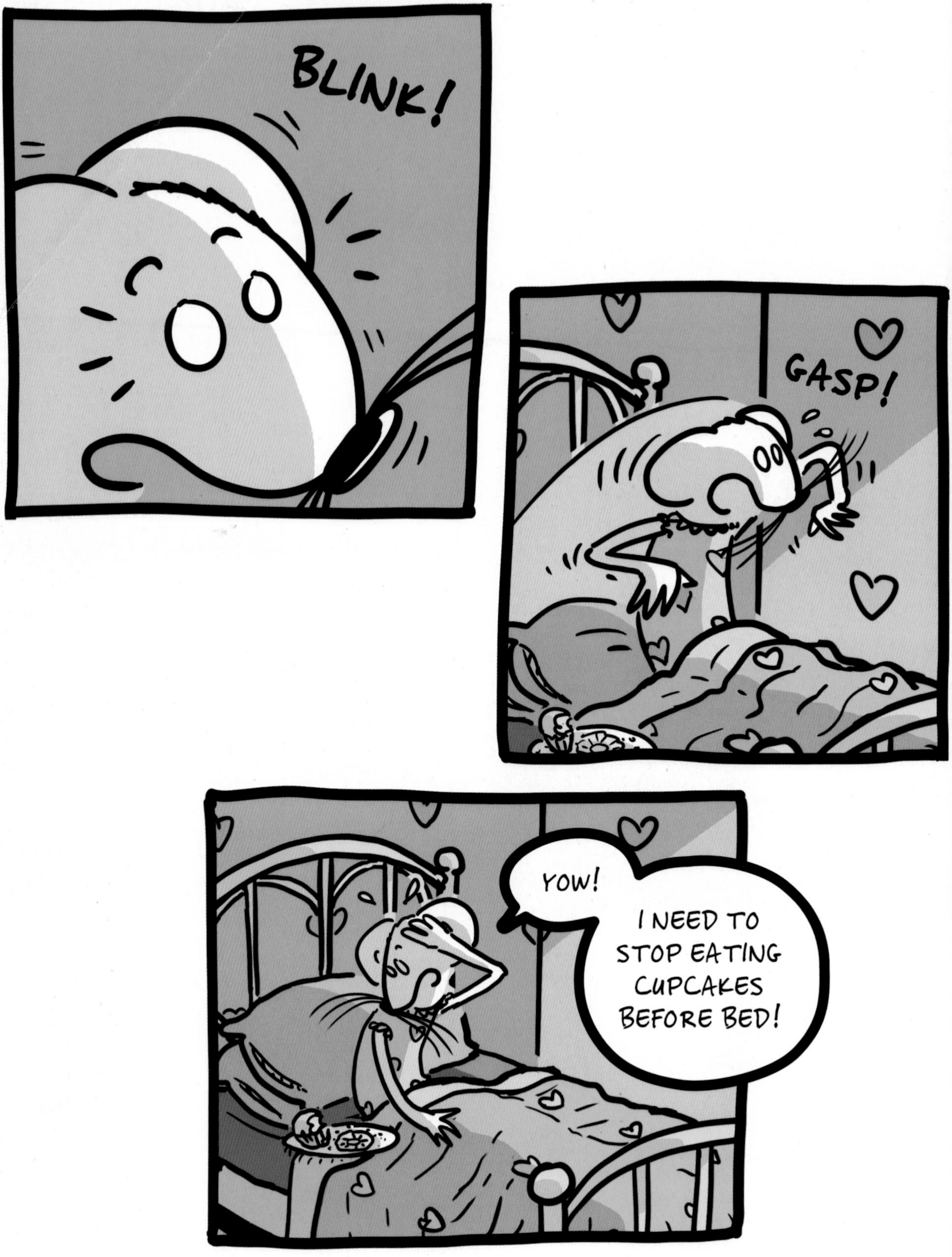
BLINK!
GASP!
YOW!
I NEED TO STOP EATING CUPCAKES BEFORE BED!

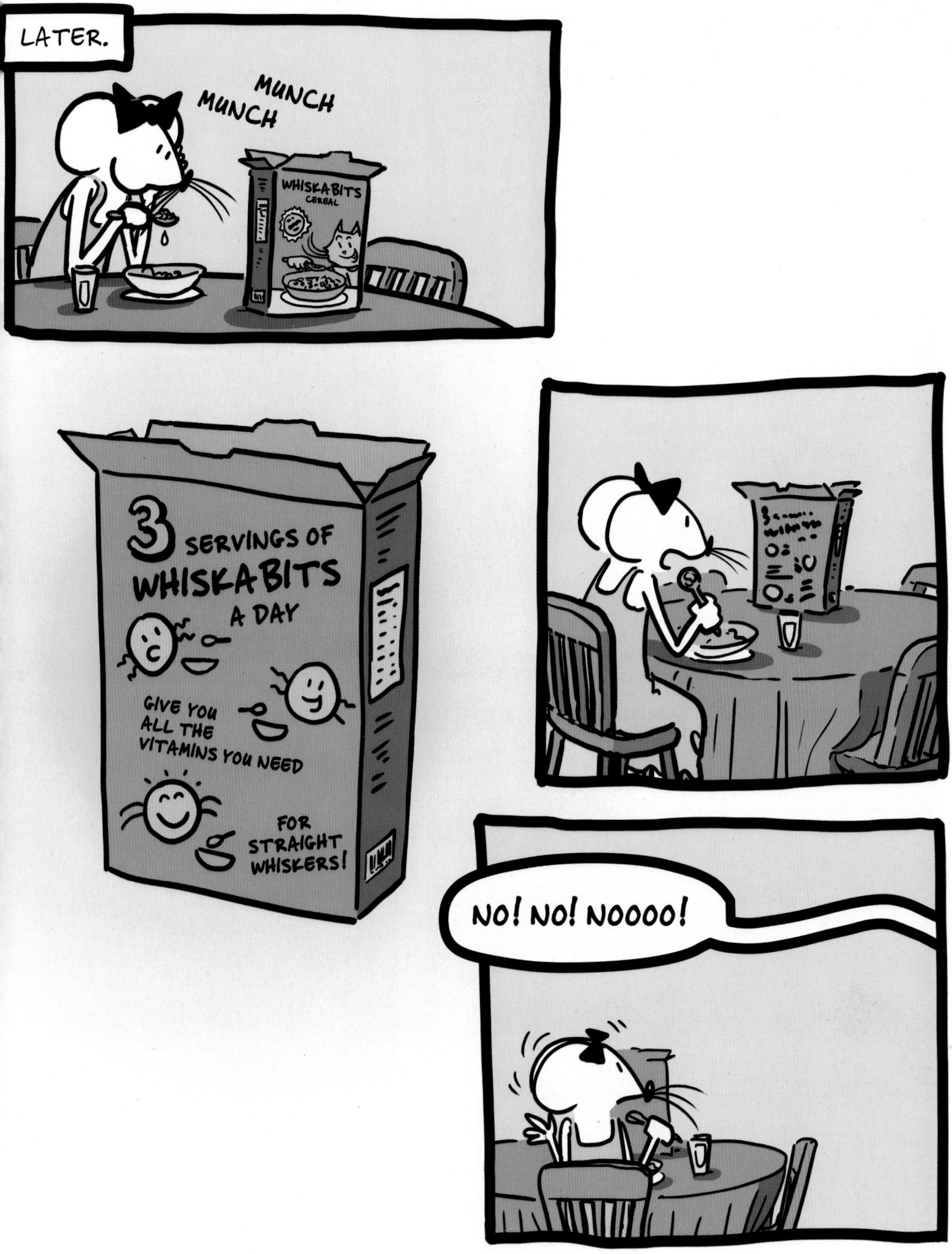
LATER.
MUNCH
MUNCH
WHISKABITS
CEREAL
3 SERVINGS OF
WHISKABITS
A DAY
GIVE YOU
ALL THE
VITAMINS YOU NEED
FOR
STRAIGHT
WHISKERS!
NO! NO! NOOOO!

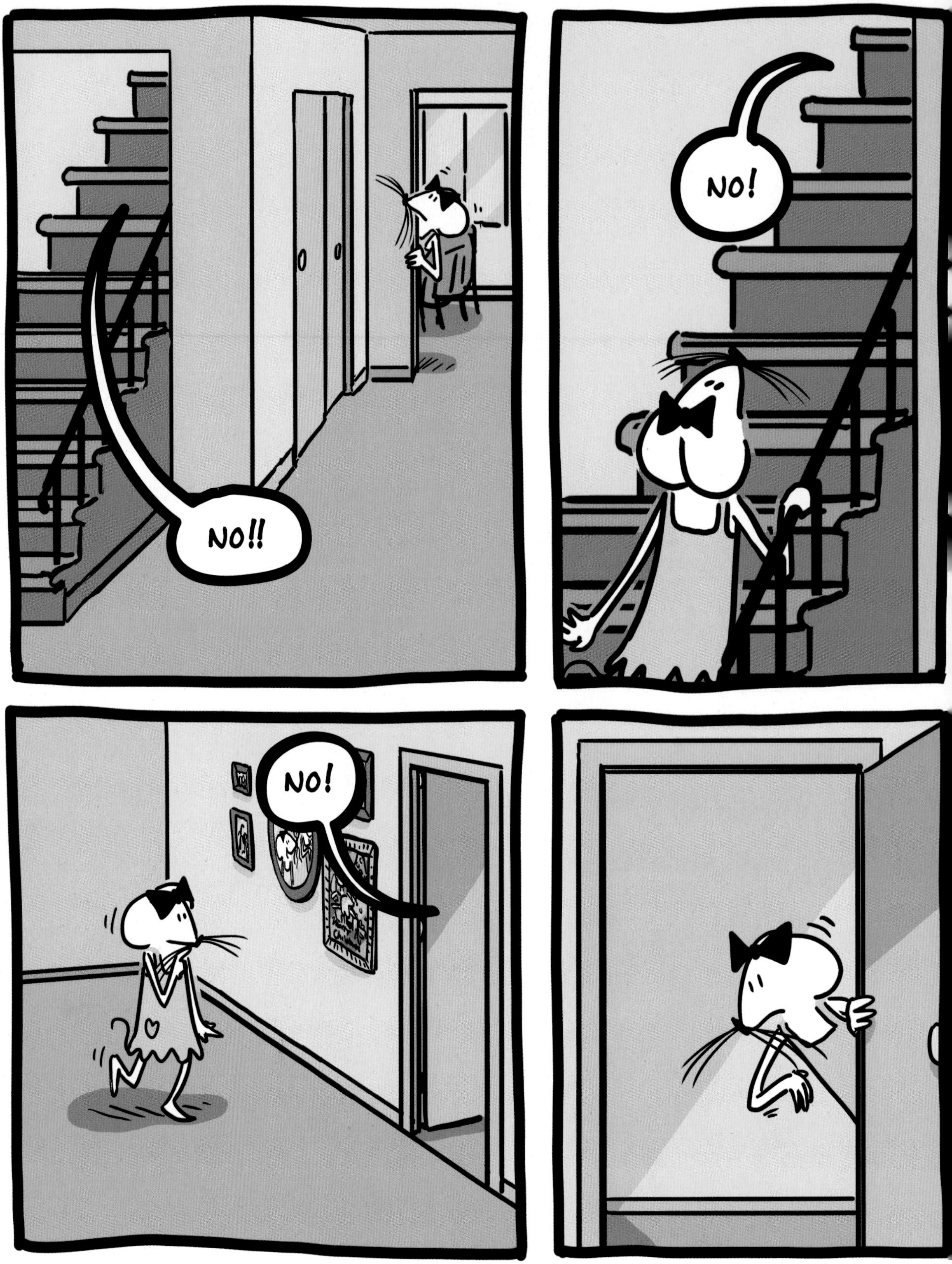
NO!!
NO!
NO!

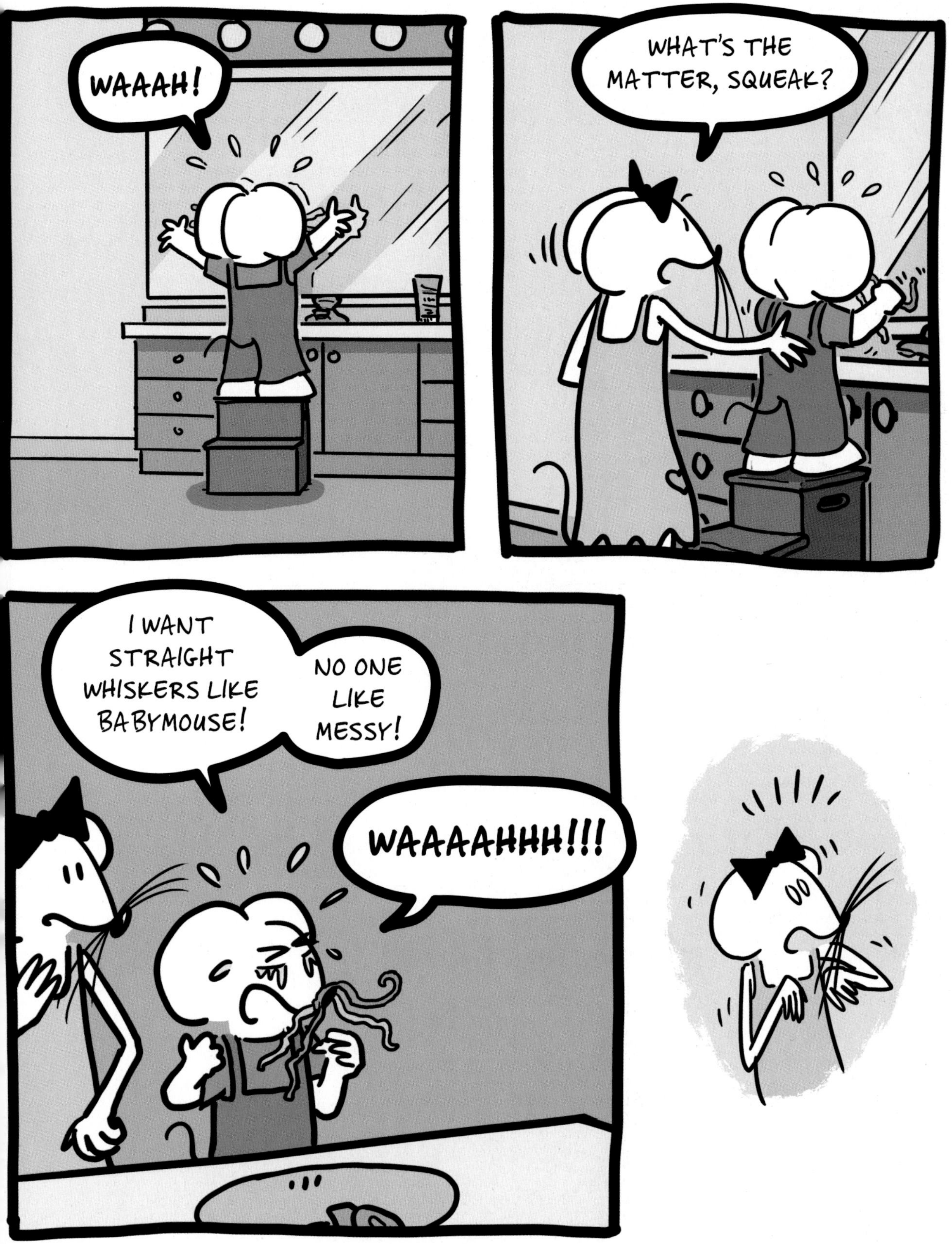
WAAAH!
WHAT'S THE MATTER, SQUEAK?
I WANT STRAIGHT WHISKERS LIKE BABYMOUSE!
NO ONE LIKE MESSY!
WAAAAHHH!!!

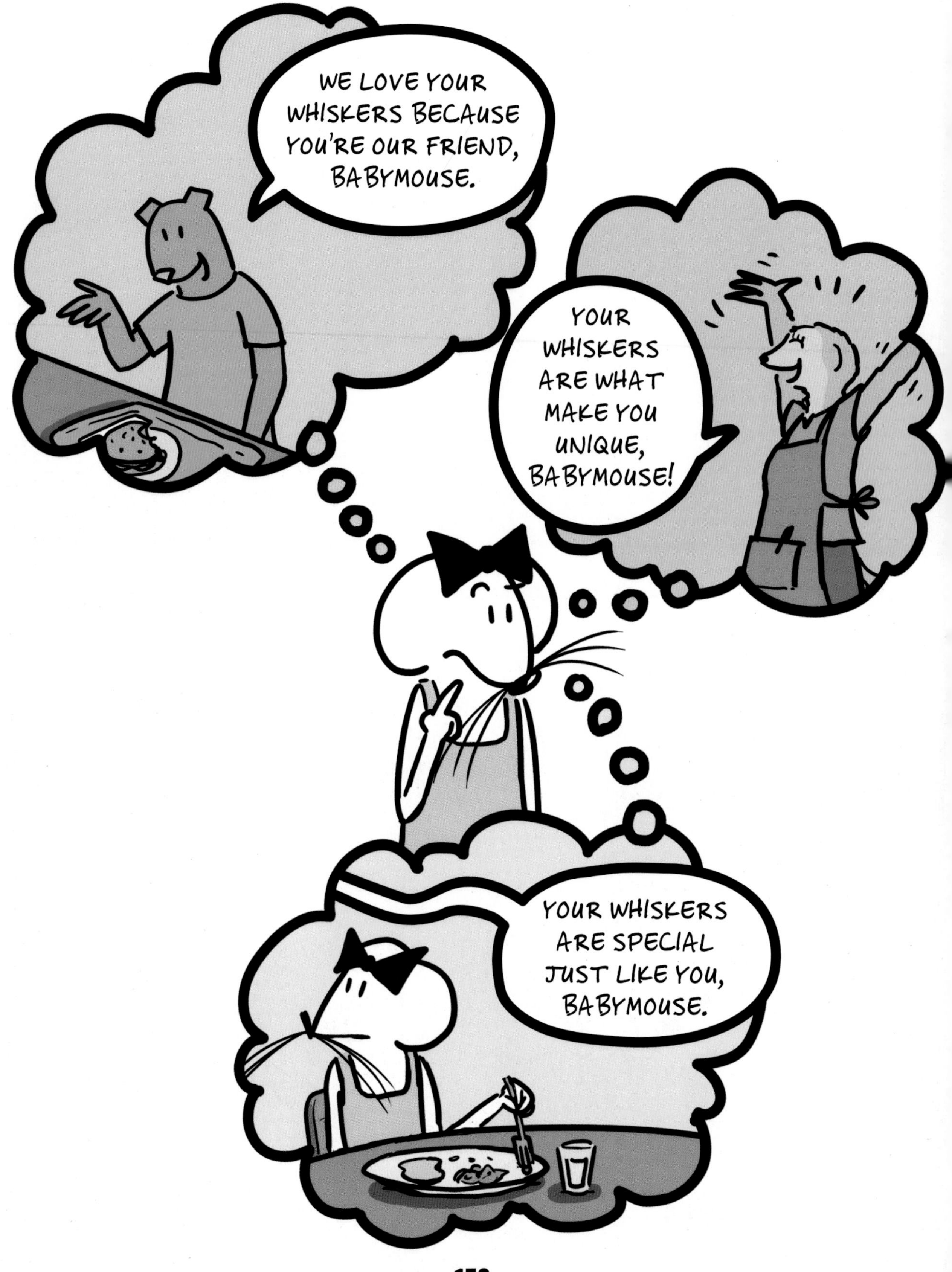
WE LOVE YOUR WHISKERS BECAUSE YOU'RE OUR FRIEND, BABYMOUSE.
YOUR WHISKERS ARE WHAT MAKE YOU UNIQUE, BABYMOUSE!
YOUR WHISKERS ARE SPECIAL JUST LIKE YOU, BABYMOUSE.

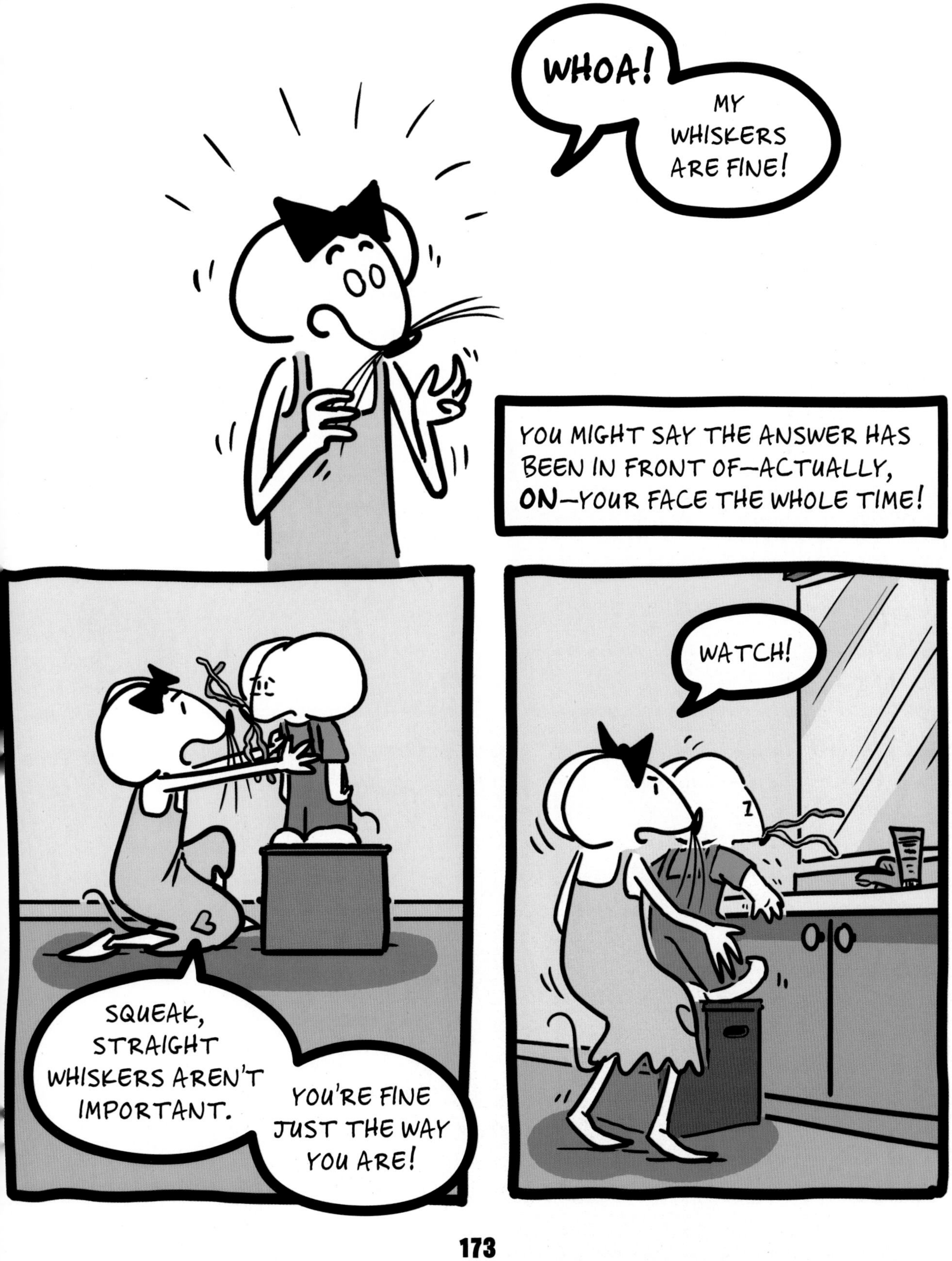
WHOA!
MY WHISKERS ARE FINE!
YOU MIGHT SAY THE ANSWER HAS BEEN IN FRONT OF—ACTUALLY, **ON**—YOUR FACE THE WHOLE TIME!
SQUEAK, STRAIGHT WHISKERS AREN'T IMPORTANT.
YOU'RE FINE JUST THE WAY YOU ARE!
WATCH!

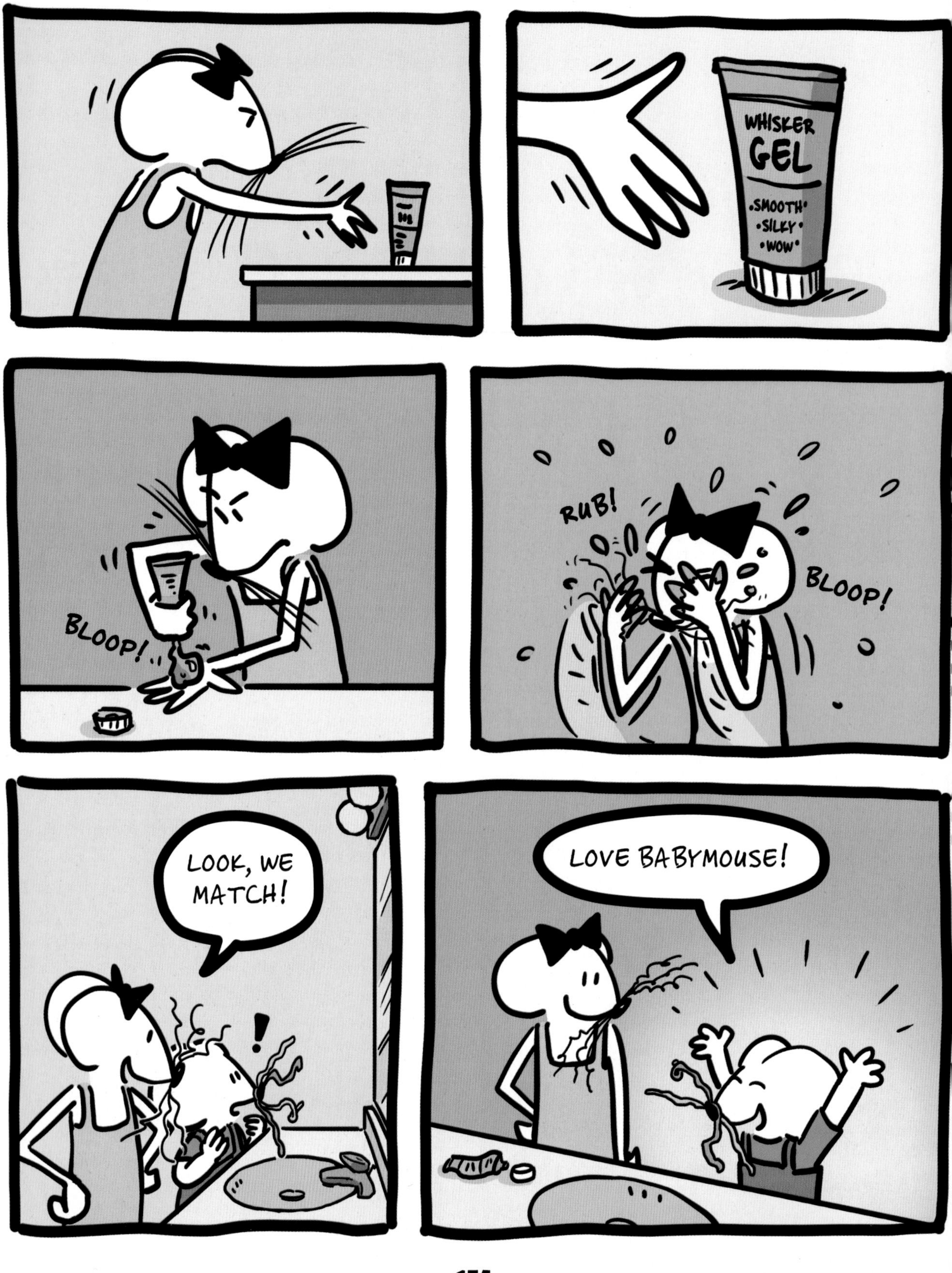
WHISKER
GEL
•SMOOTH•
•SILKY•
•WOW•
BLOOP!
RUB!
BLOOP!
LOOK, WE MATCH!
LOVE BABYMOUSE!

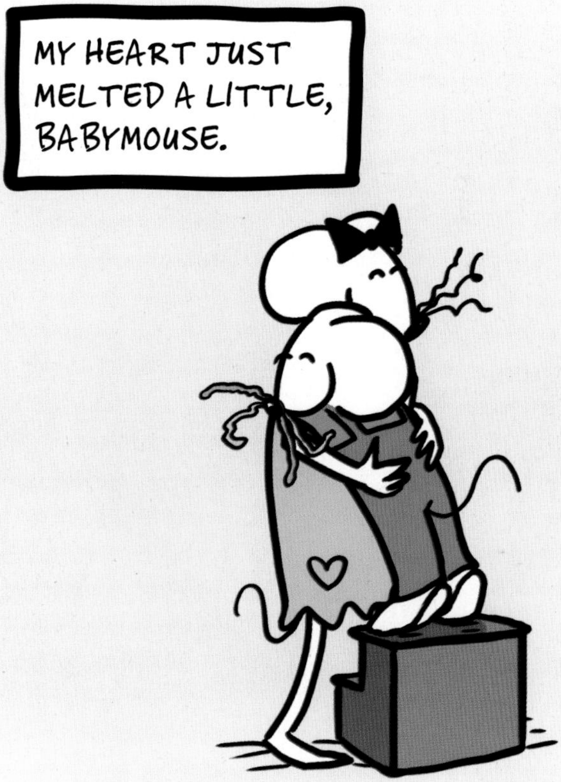
MY HEART JUST MELTED A LITTLE, BABYMOUSE.

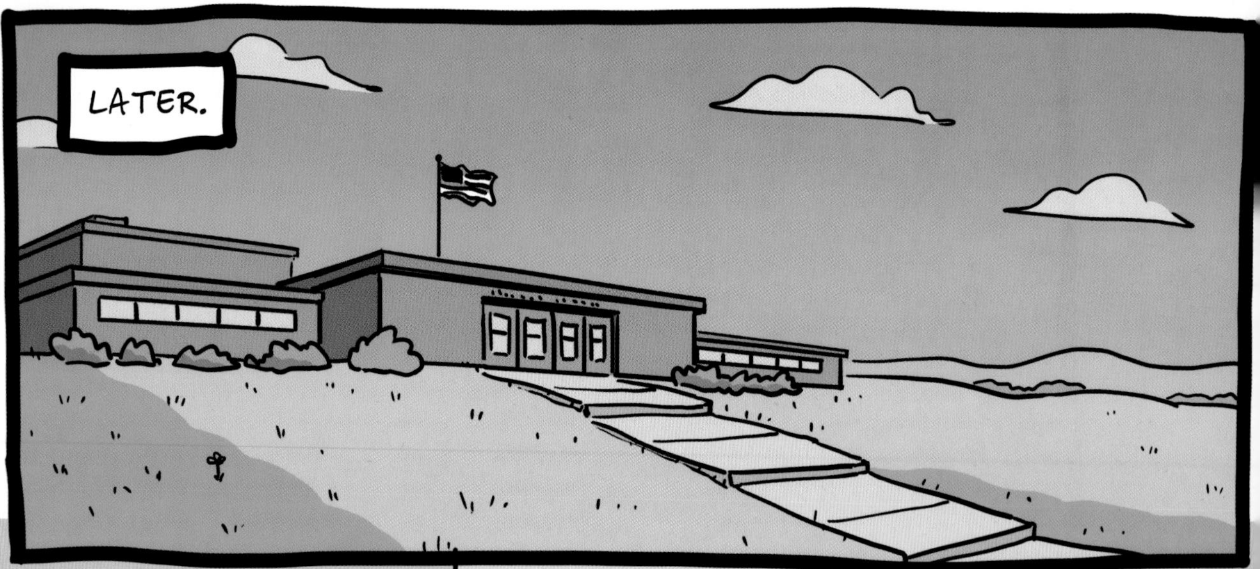
LATER.

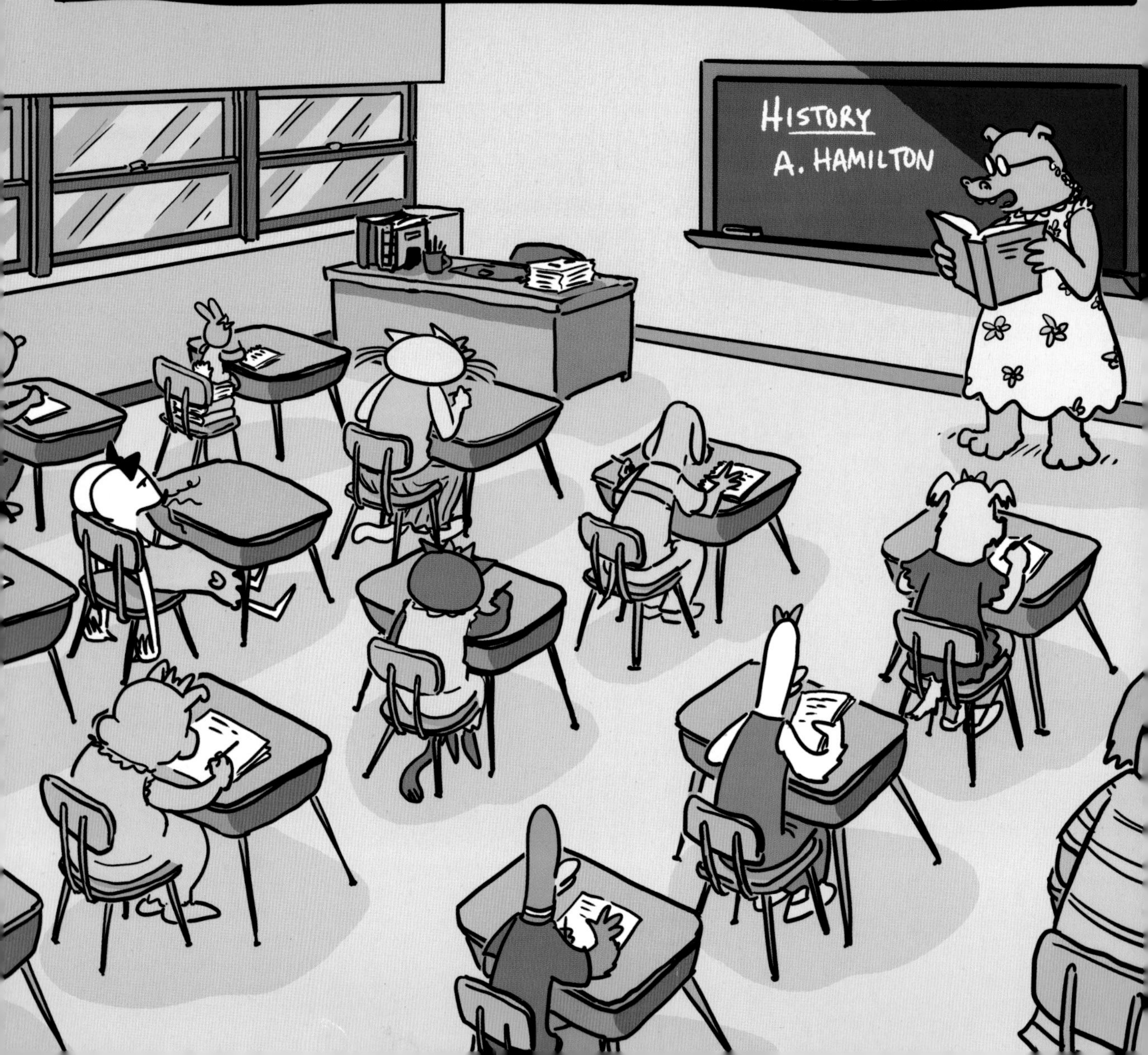
HISTORY
A. HAMILTON

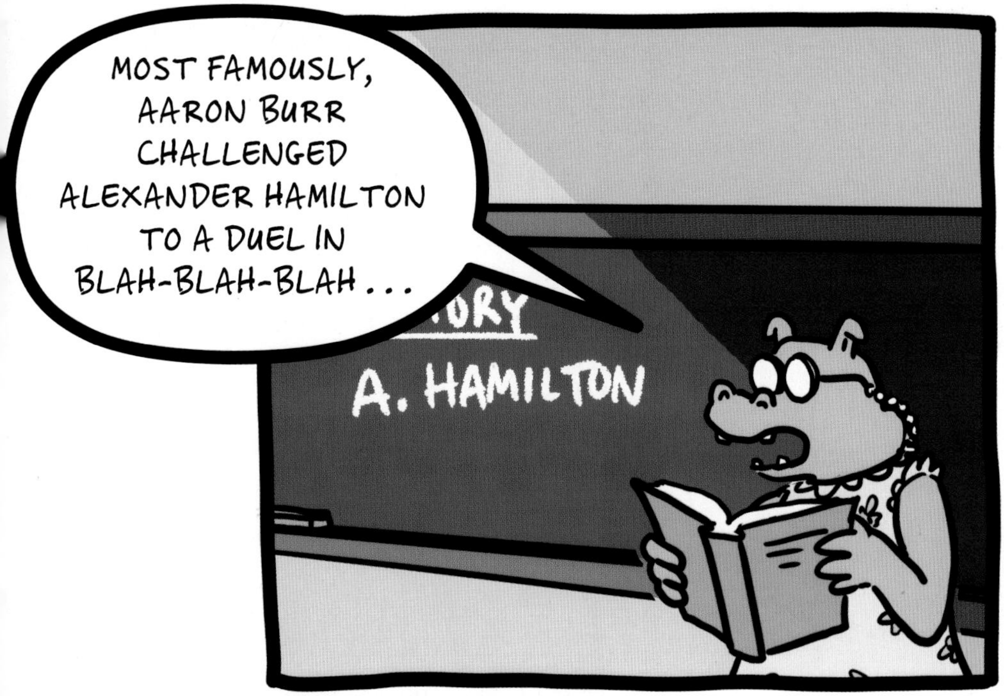
MOST FAMOUSLY, AARON BURR CHALLENGED ALEXANDER HAMILTON TO A DUEL IN BLAH-BLAH-BLAH . . .
TORY
A. HAMILTON

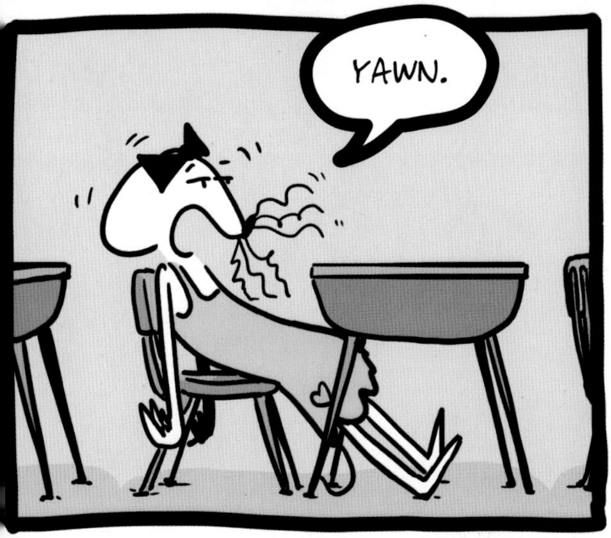
YAWN.

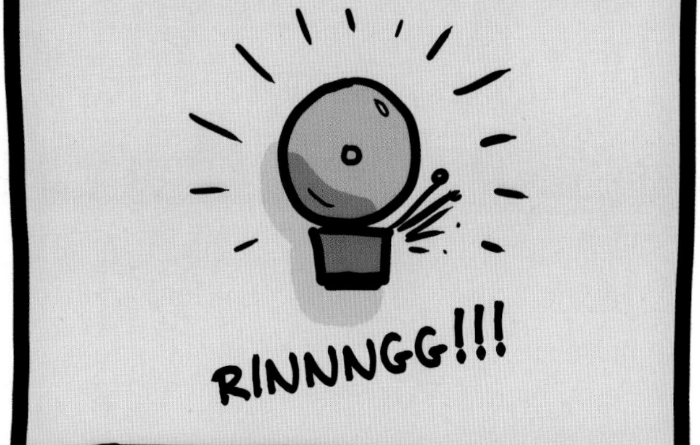
RINNNGG!!!

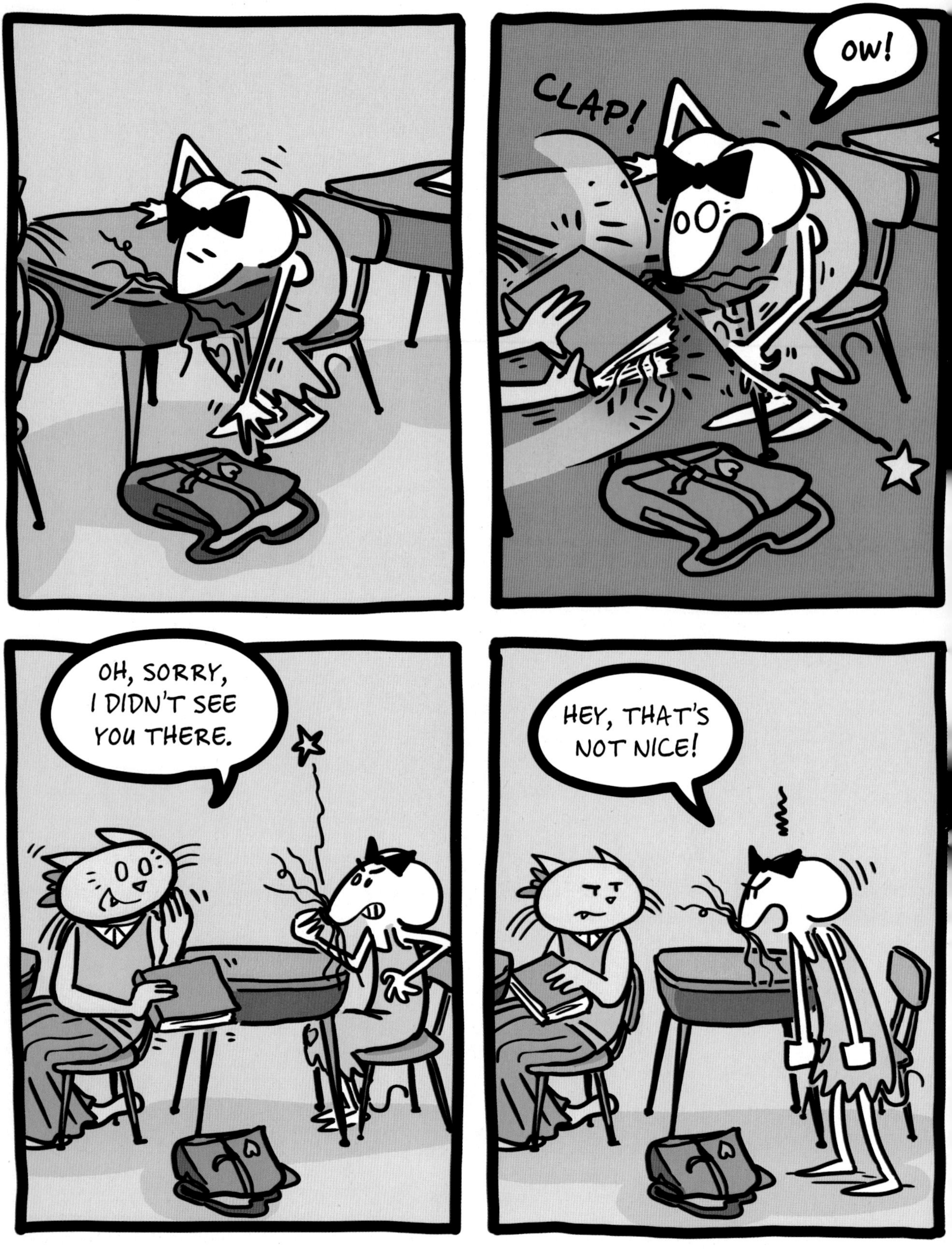
CLAP!
OW!
OH, SORRY, I DIDN'T SEE YOU THERE.
HEY, THAT'S NOT NICE!

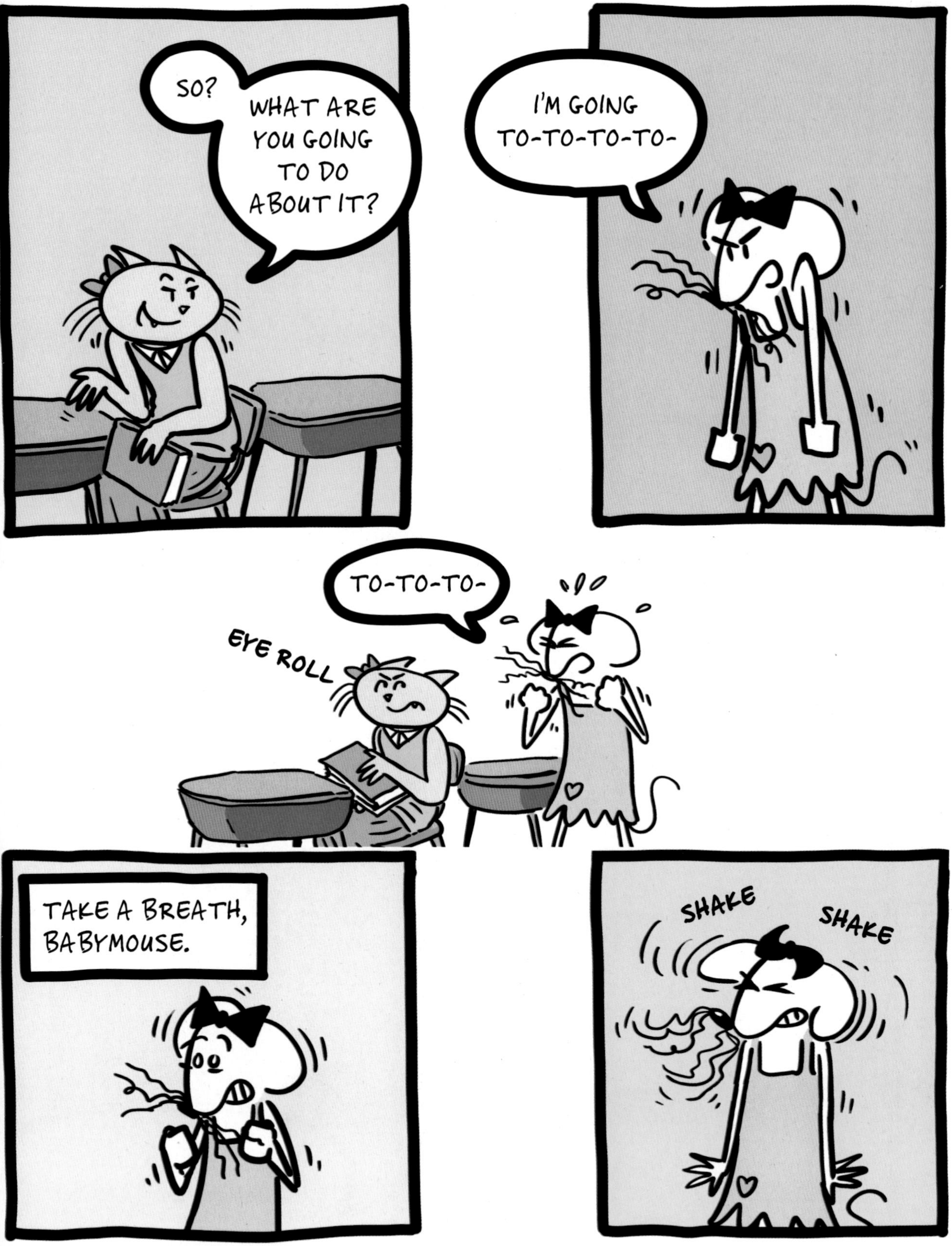
SO?
WHAT ARE YOU GOING TO DO ABOUT IT?
I'M GOING TO-TO-TO-TO-
TO-TO-TO-
EYE ROLL
TAKE A BREATH, BABYMOUSE.
SHAKE
SHAKE

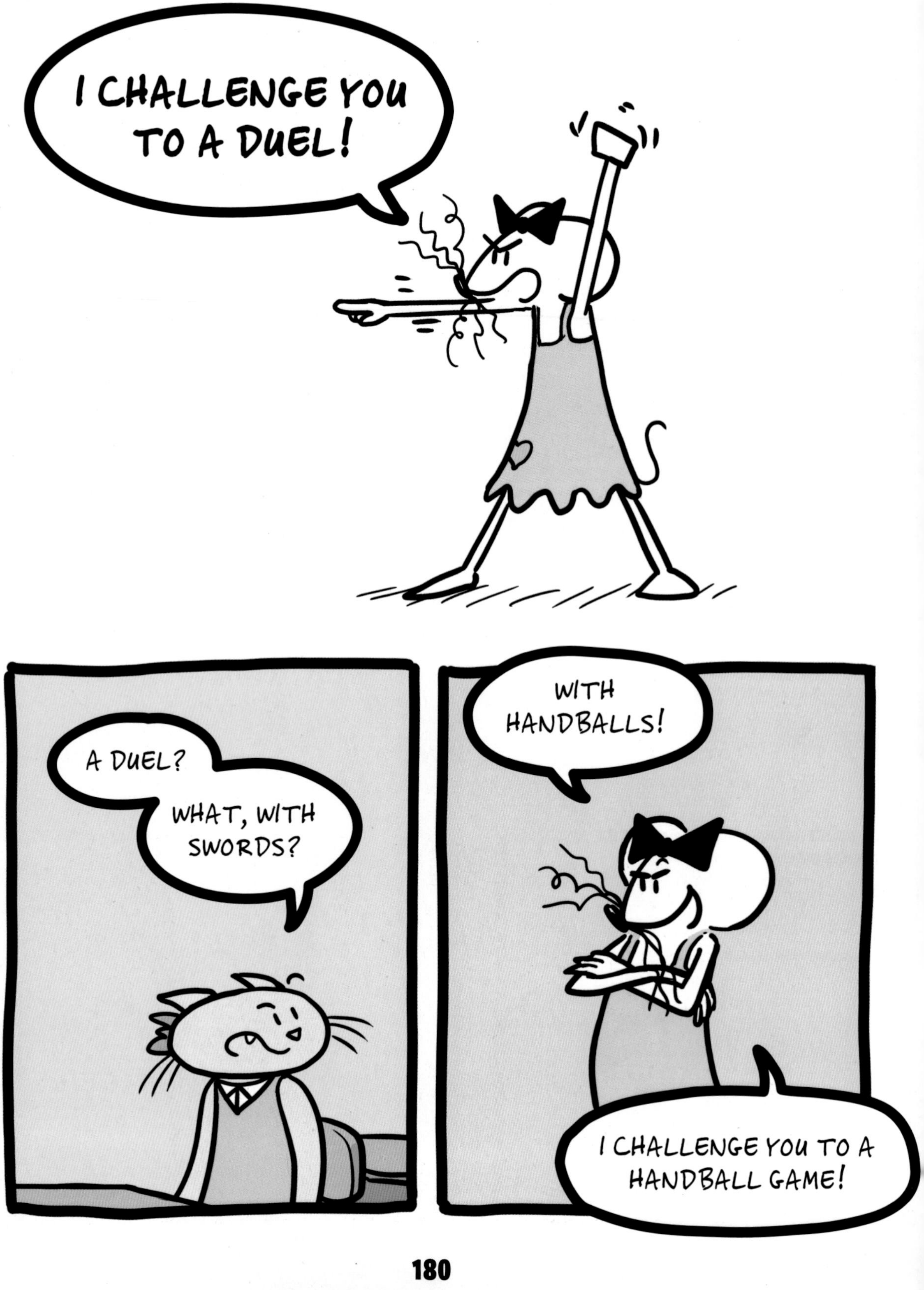
I CHALLENGE YOU TO A DUEL!
A DUEL?
WHAT, WITH SWORDS?
WITH HANDBALLS!
I CHALLENGE YOU TO A HANDBALL GAME!

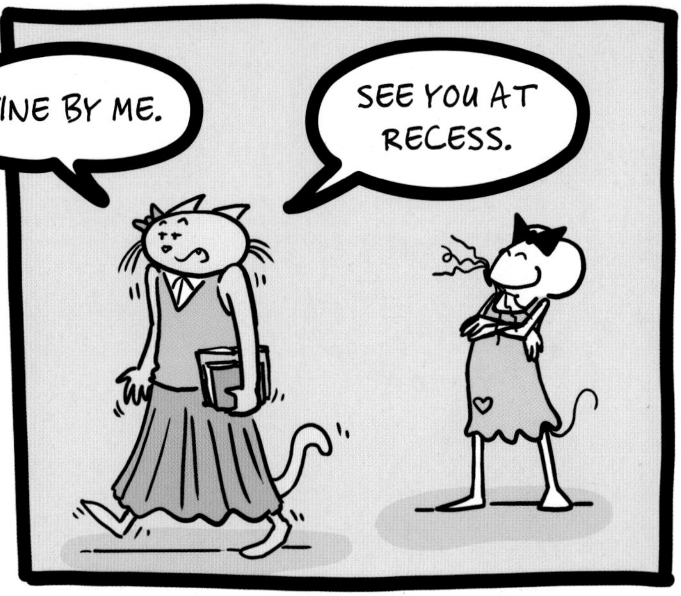
FINE BY ME.
SEE YOU AT RECESS.

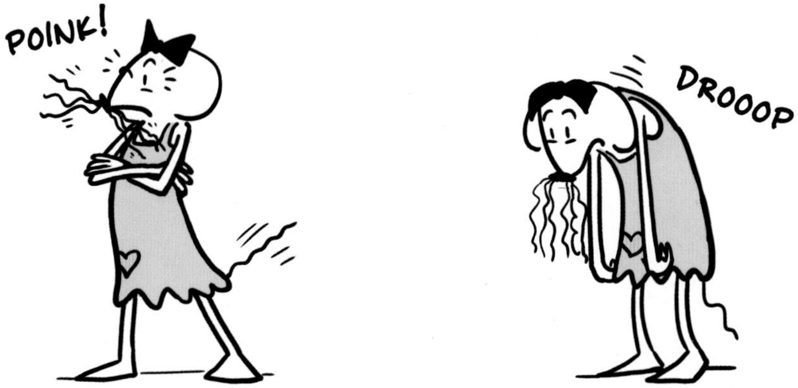
POINK!
DROOOP

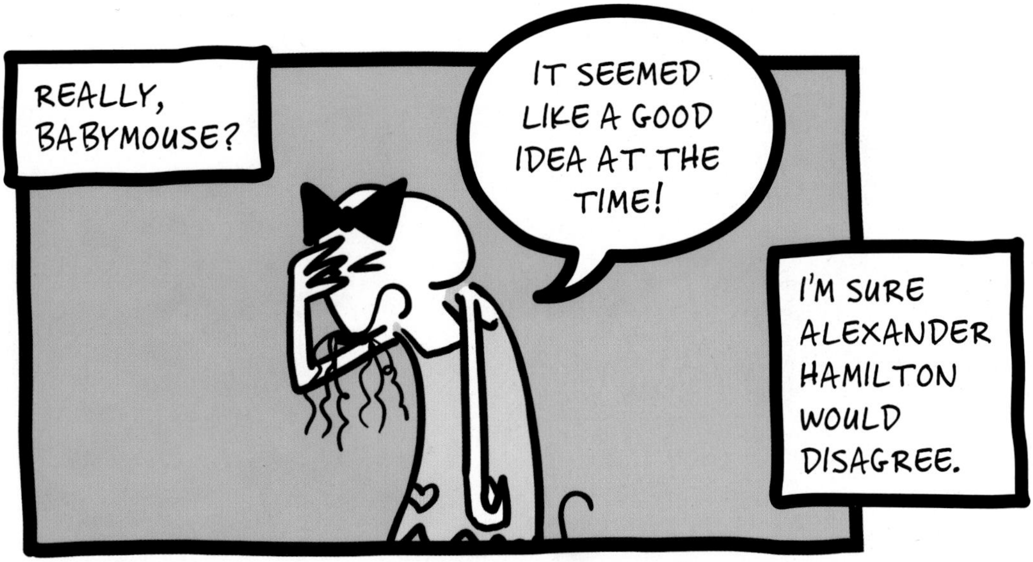
REALLY, BABYMOUSE?
IT SEEMED LIKE A GOOD IDEA AT THE TIME!
I'M SURE ALEXANDER HAMILTON WOULD DISAGREE.

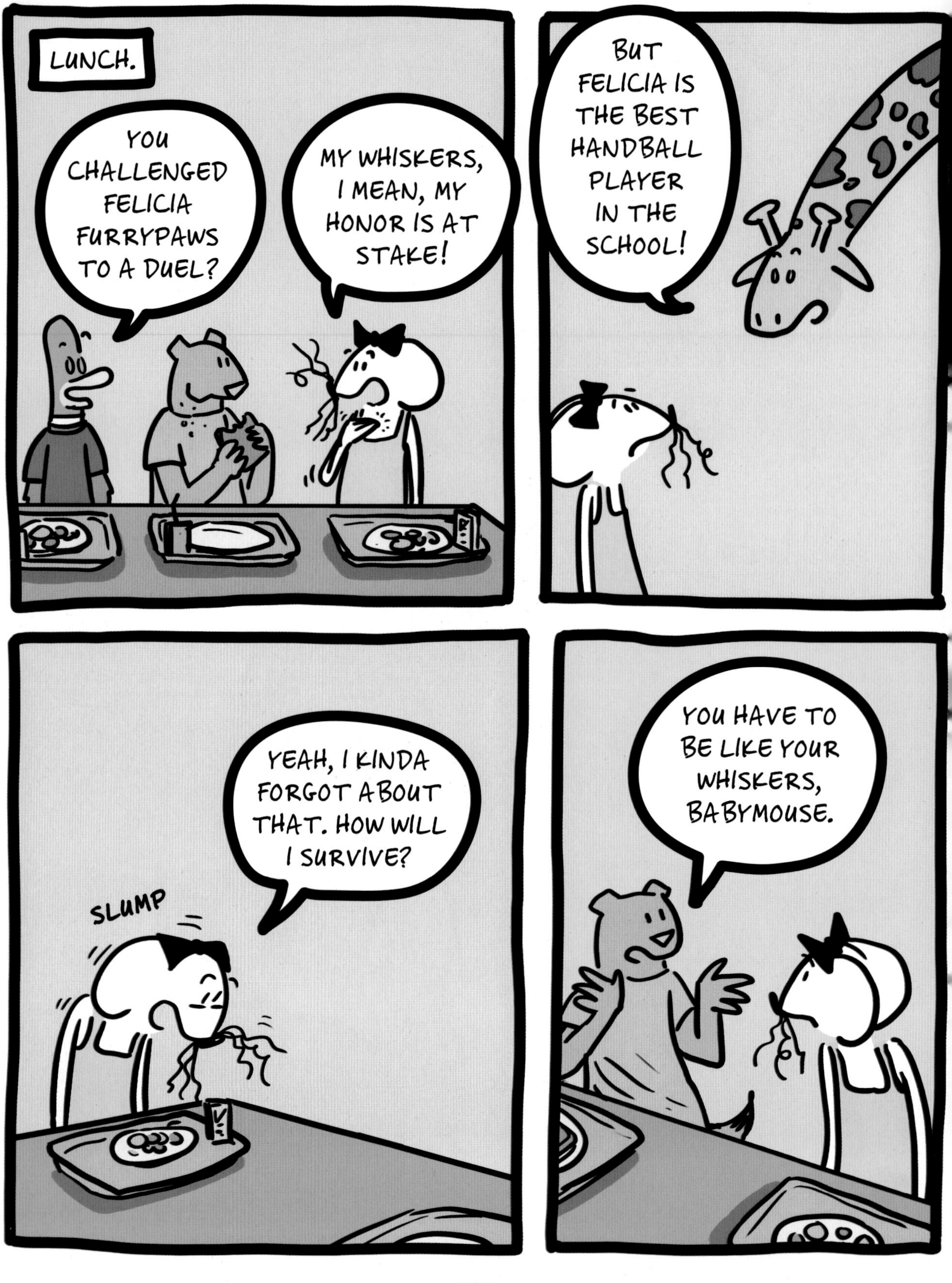
LUNCH.
YOU CHALLENGED FELICIA FURRYPAWS TO A DUEL?
MY WHISKERS, I MEAN, MY HONOR IS AT STAKE!
BUT FELICIA IS THE BEST HANDBALL PLAYER IN THE SCHOOL!
YEAH, I KINDA FORGOT ABOUT THAT. HOW WILL I SURVIVE?
SLUMP
YOU HAVE TO BE LIKE YOUR WHISKERS, BABYMOUSE.

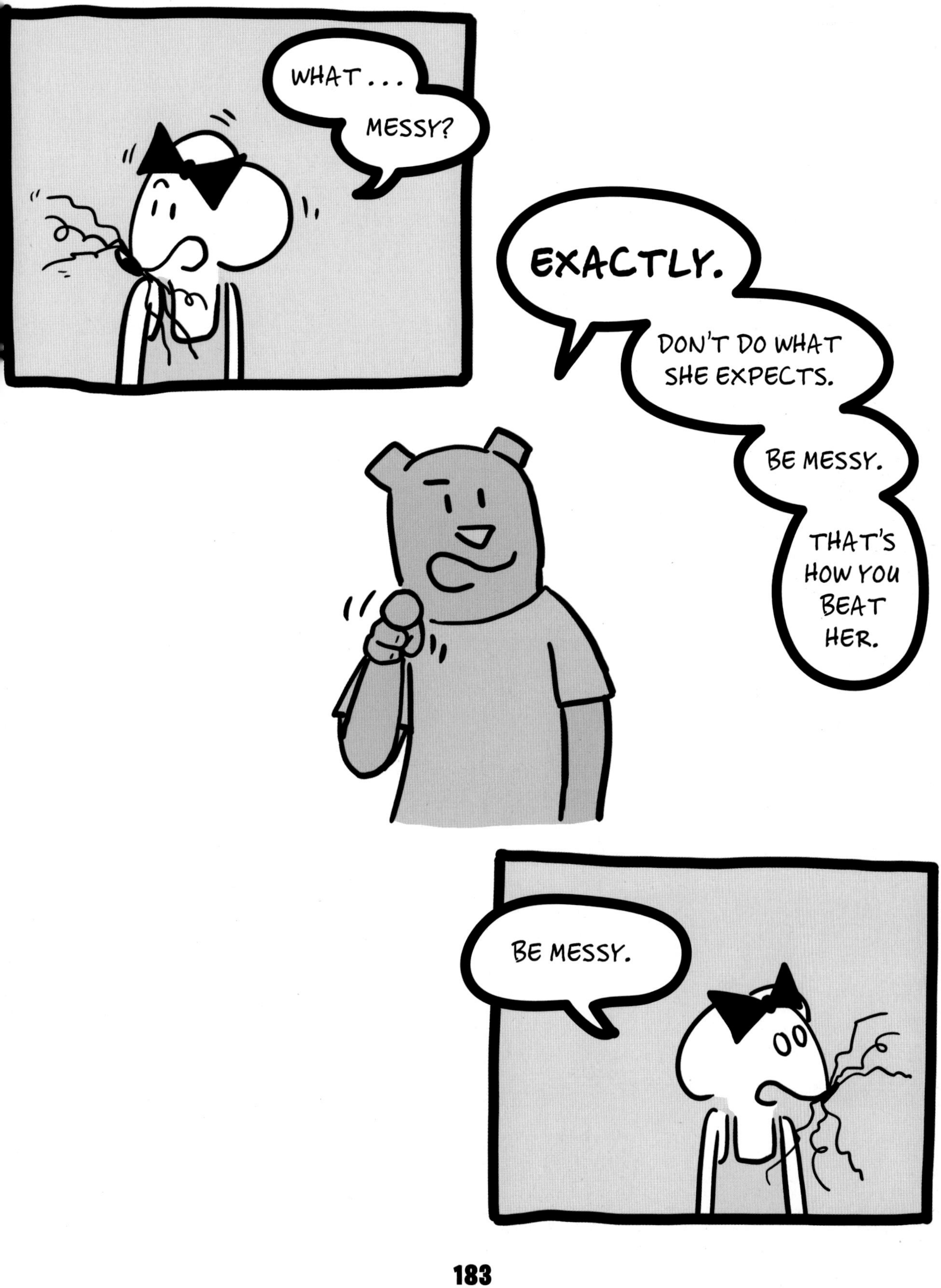
WHAT . . .
MESSY?
EXACTLY.
DON'T DO WHAT SHE EXPECTS.
BE MESSY.
THAT'S HOW YOU BEAT HER.
BE MESSY.

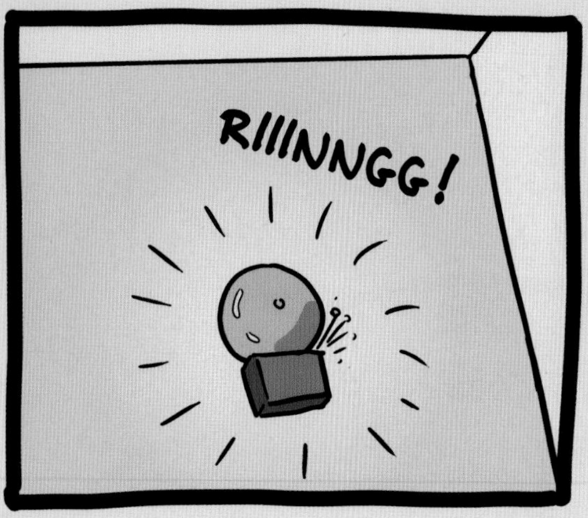
RIIINNGG!

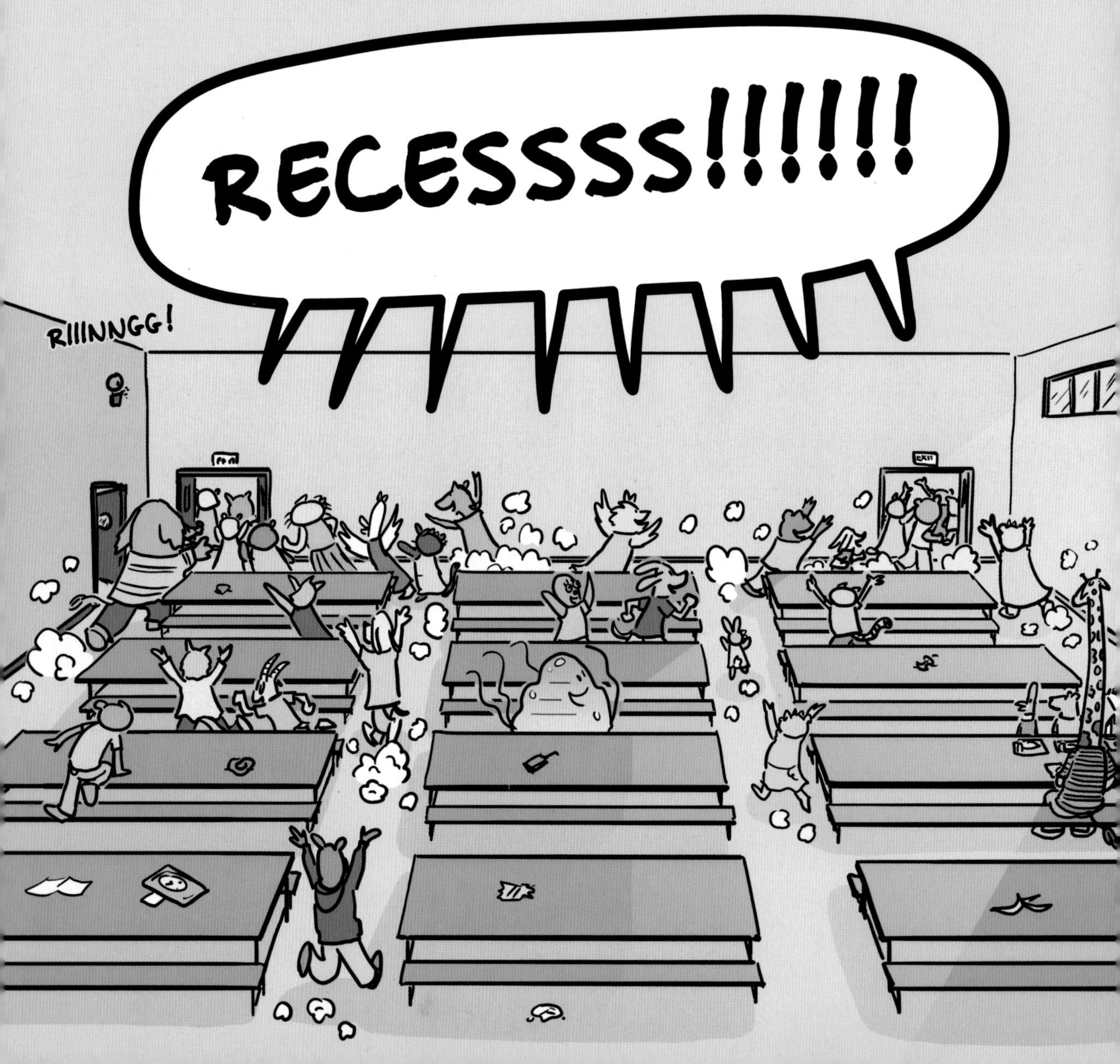
RIIINNGG!
RECESSSS!!!!!!

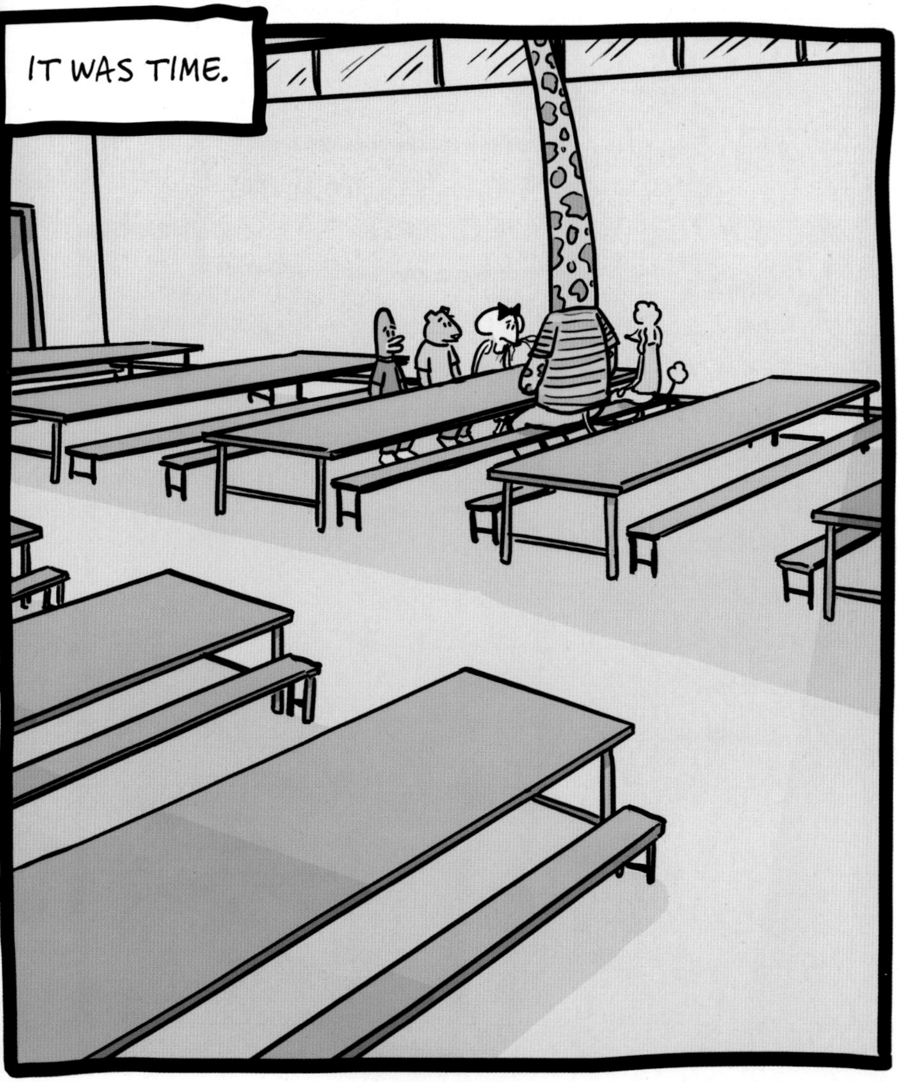
IT WAS TIME.

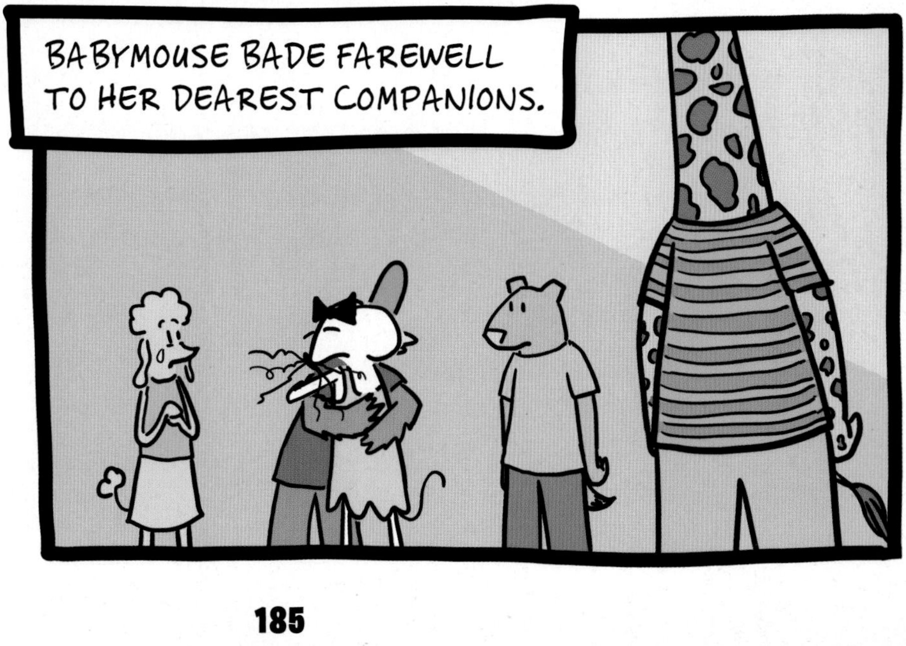
BABYMOUSE BADE FAREWELL
TO HER DEAREST COMPANIONS.

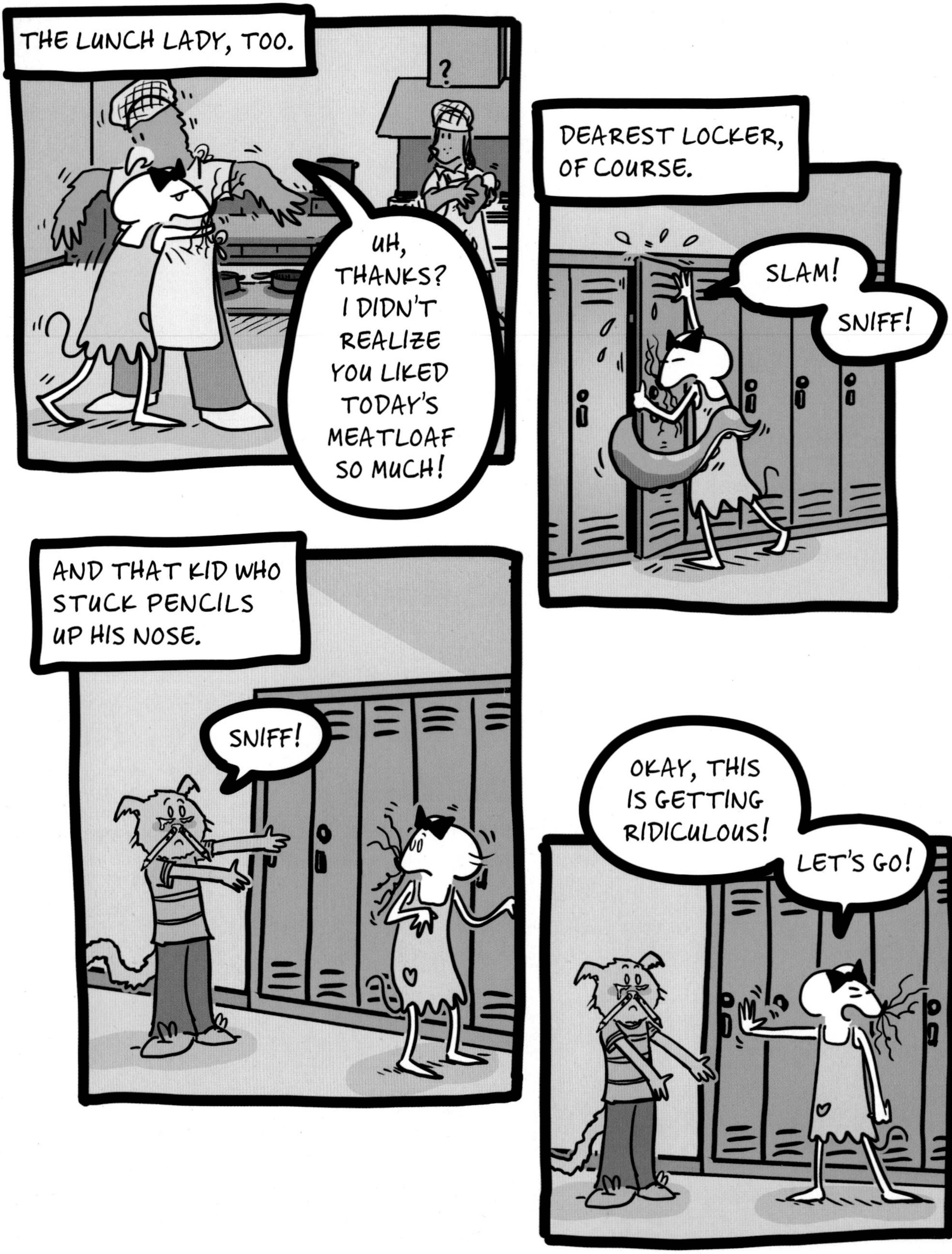
THE LUNCH LADY, TOO.
?
UH, THANKS? I DIDN'T REALIZE YOU LIKED TODAY'S MEATLOAF SO MUCH!
DEAREST LOCKER, OF COURSE.
SLAM!
SNIFF!
AND THAT KID WHO STUCK PENCILS UP HIS NOSE.
SNIFF!
OKAY, THIS IS GETTING RIDICULOUS!
LET'S GO!

GULP!

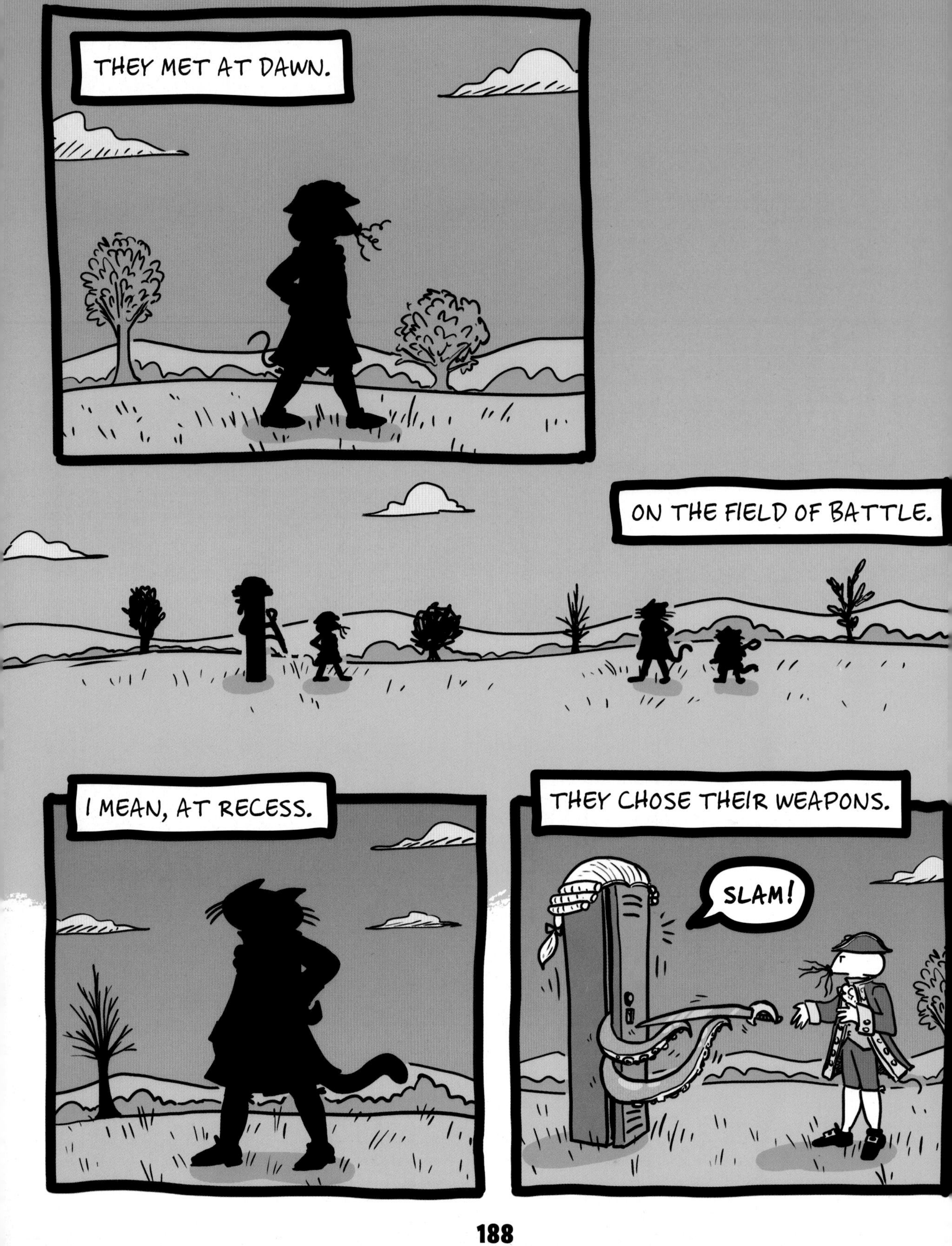
THEY MET AT DAWN.
ON THE FIELD OF BATTLE.
I MEAN, AT RECESS.
THEY CHOSE THEIR WEAPONS.
SLAM!

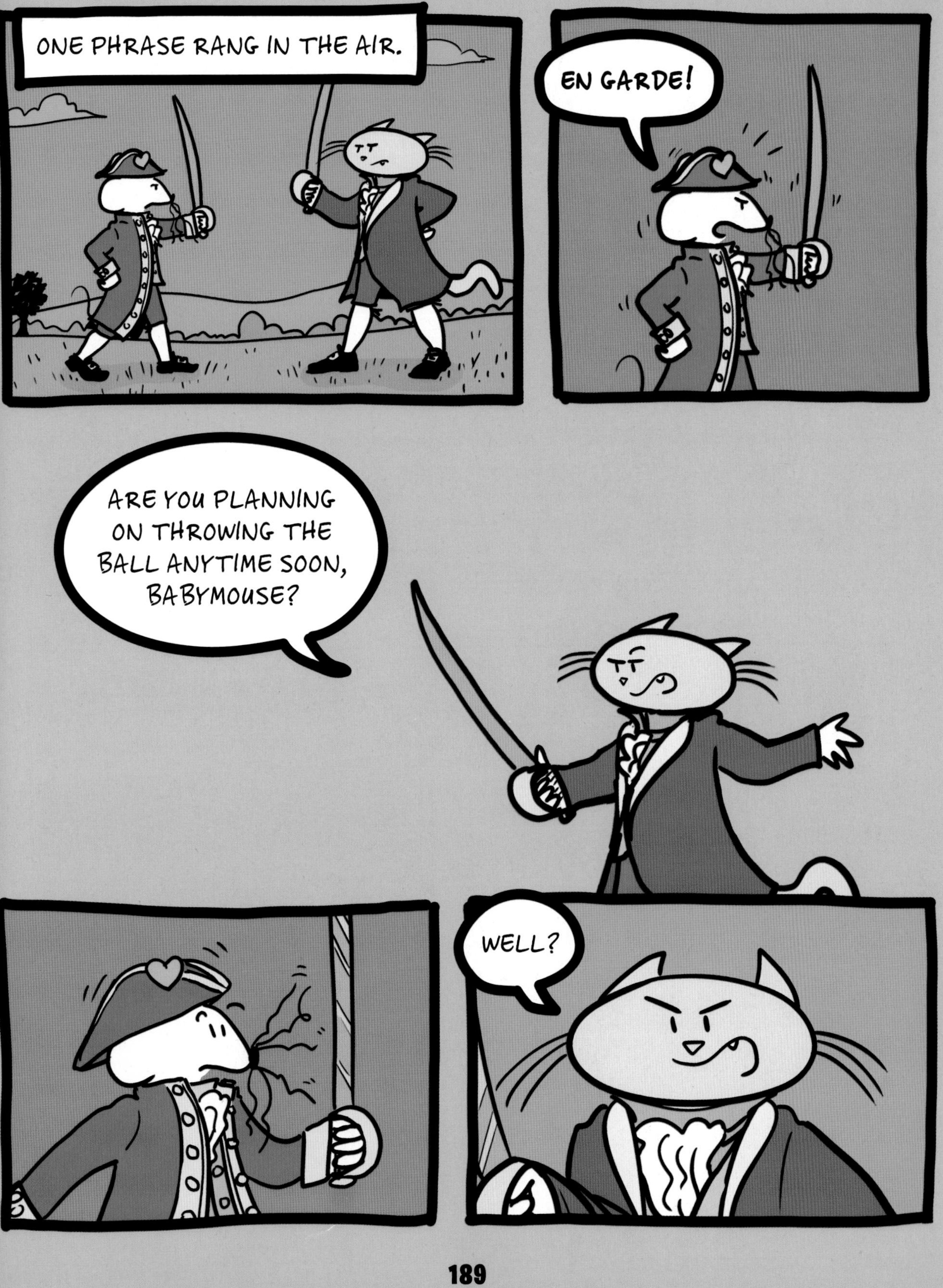
ONE PHRASE RANG IN THE AIR.
EN GARDE!
ARE YOU PLANNING ON THROWING THE BALL ANYTIME SOON, BABYMOUSE?
WELL?

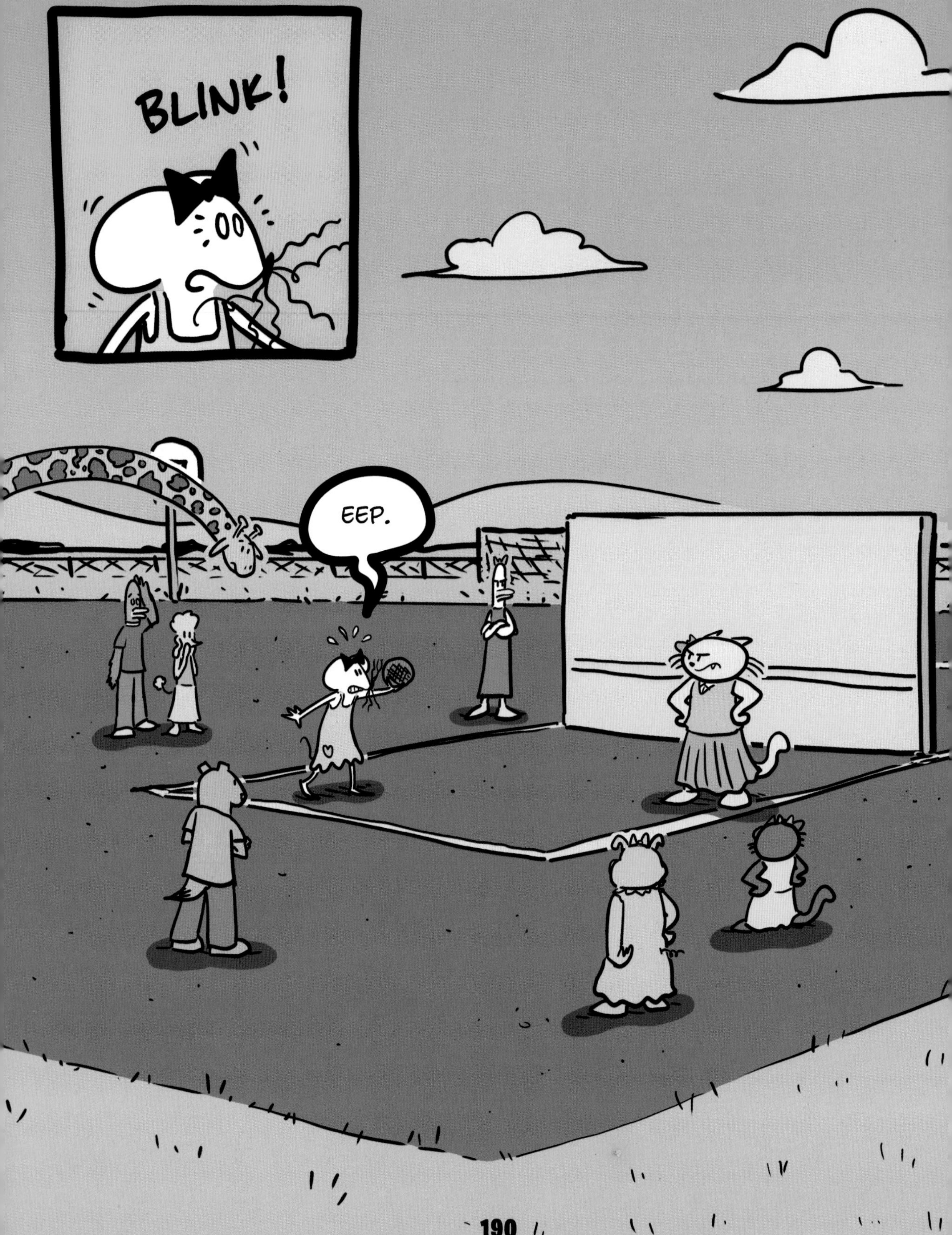
BLINK!
EEP.

NNGH!

SWISH!

ZIP!

BOP

BOING

BOP!

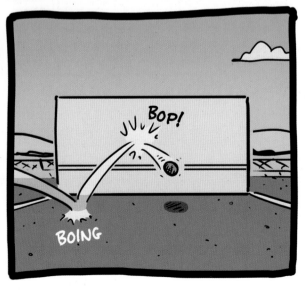

BOP!

BOING

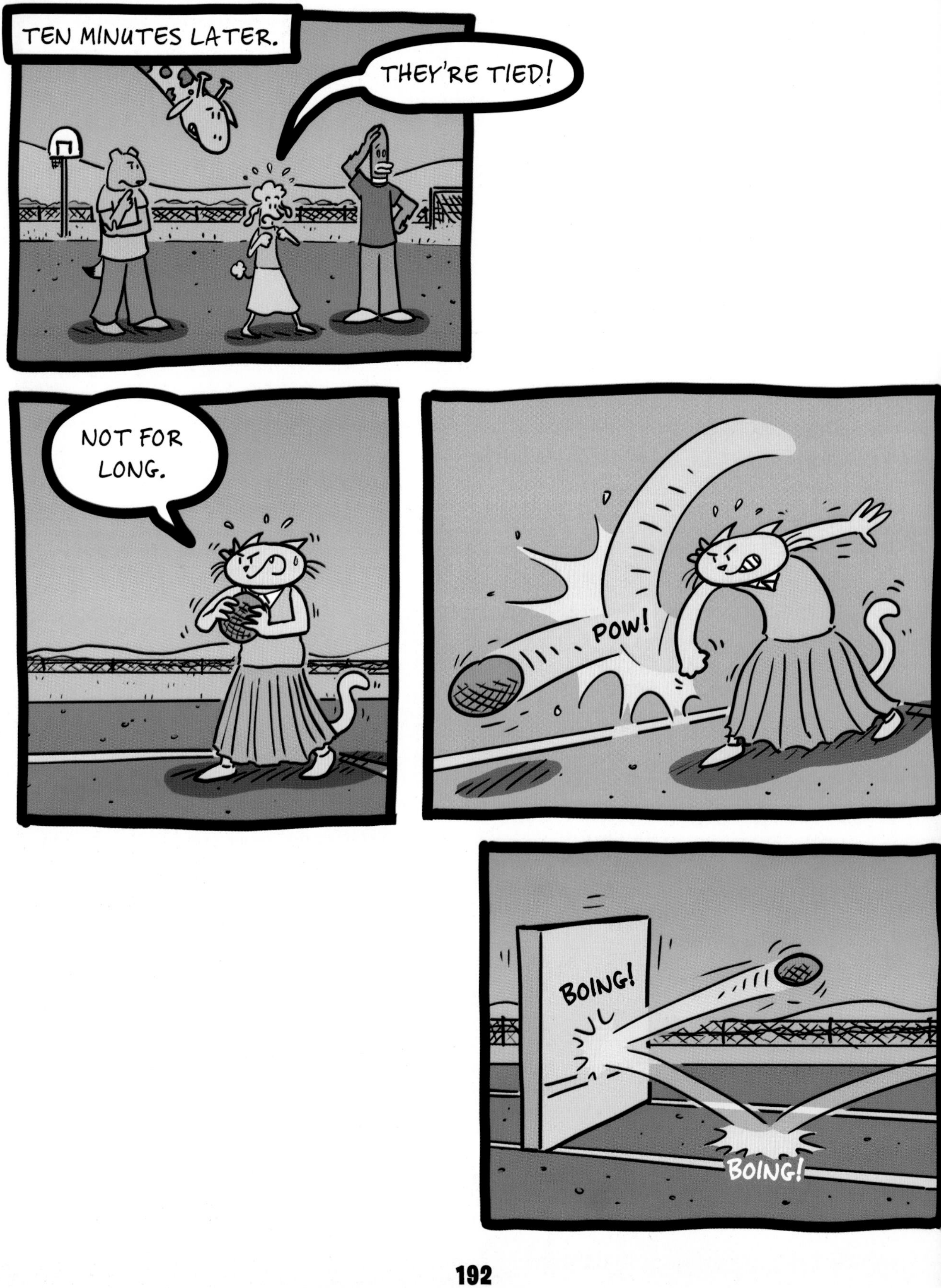
TEN MINUTES LATER.
THEY'RE TIED!
NOT FOR LONG.
POW!
BOING!
BOING!

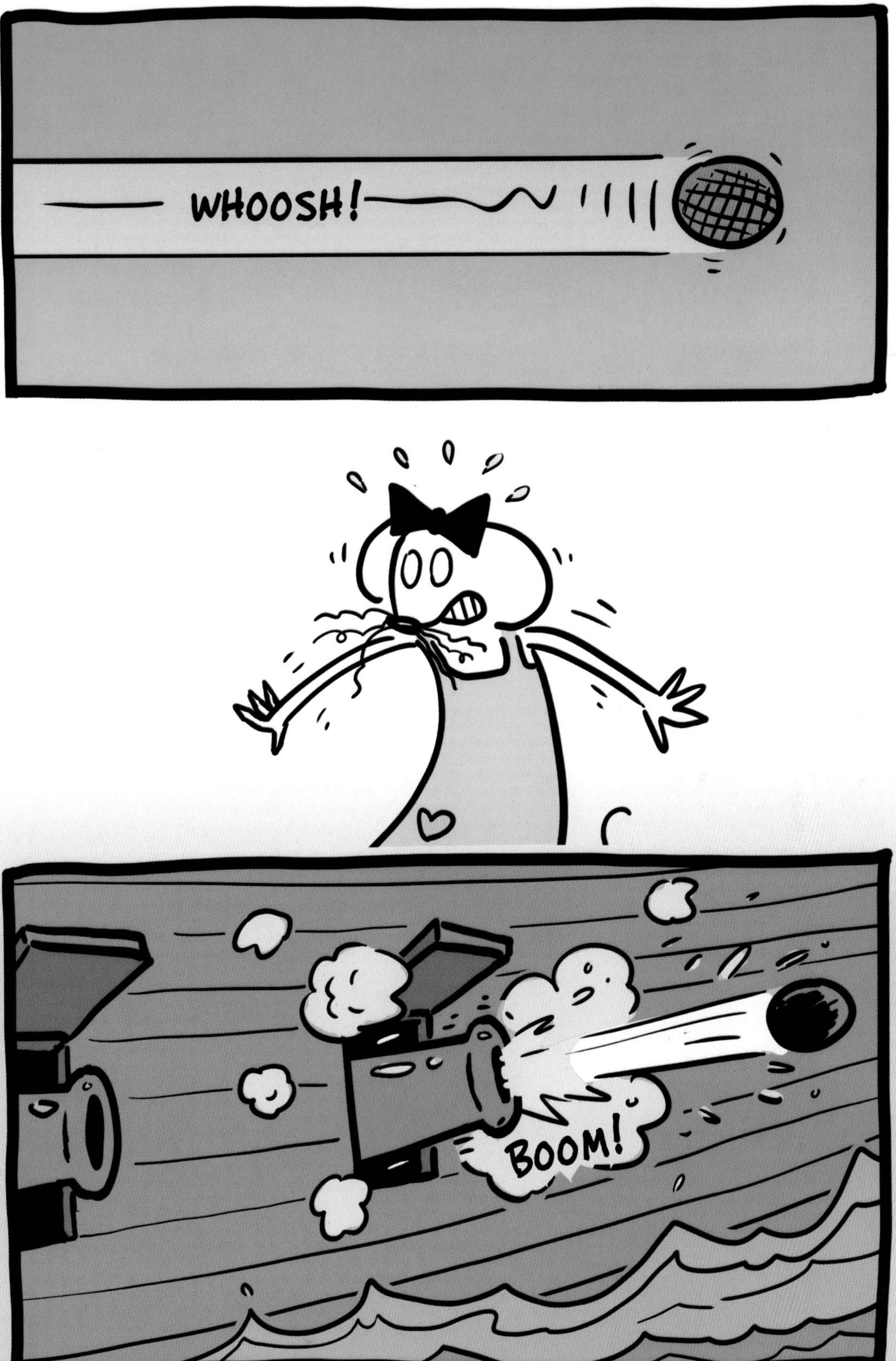
WHOOSH!
BOOM!

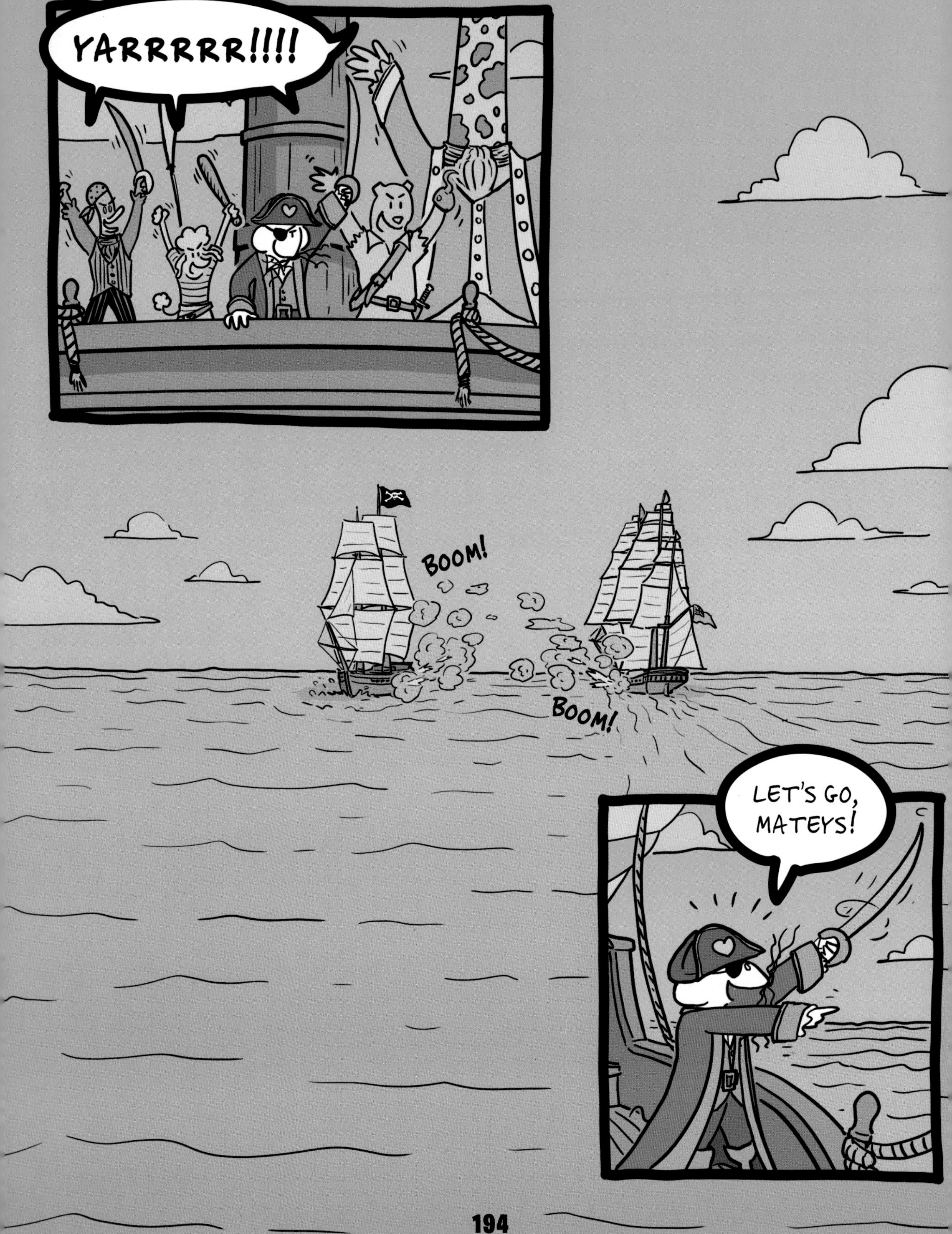
YARRRRRR!!!!
BOOM!
BOOM!
LET'S GO, MATEYS!

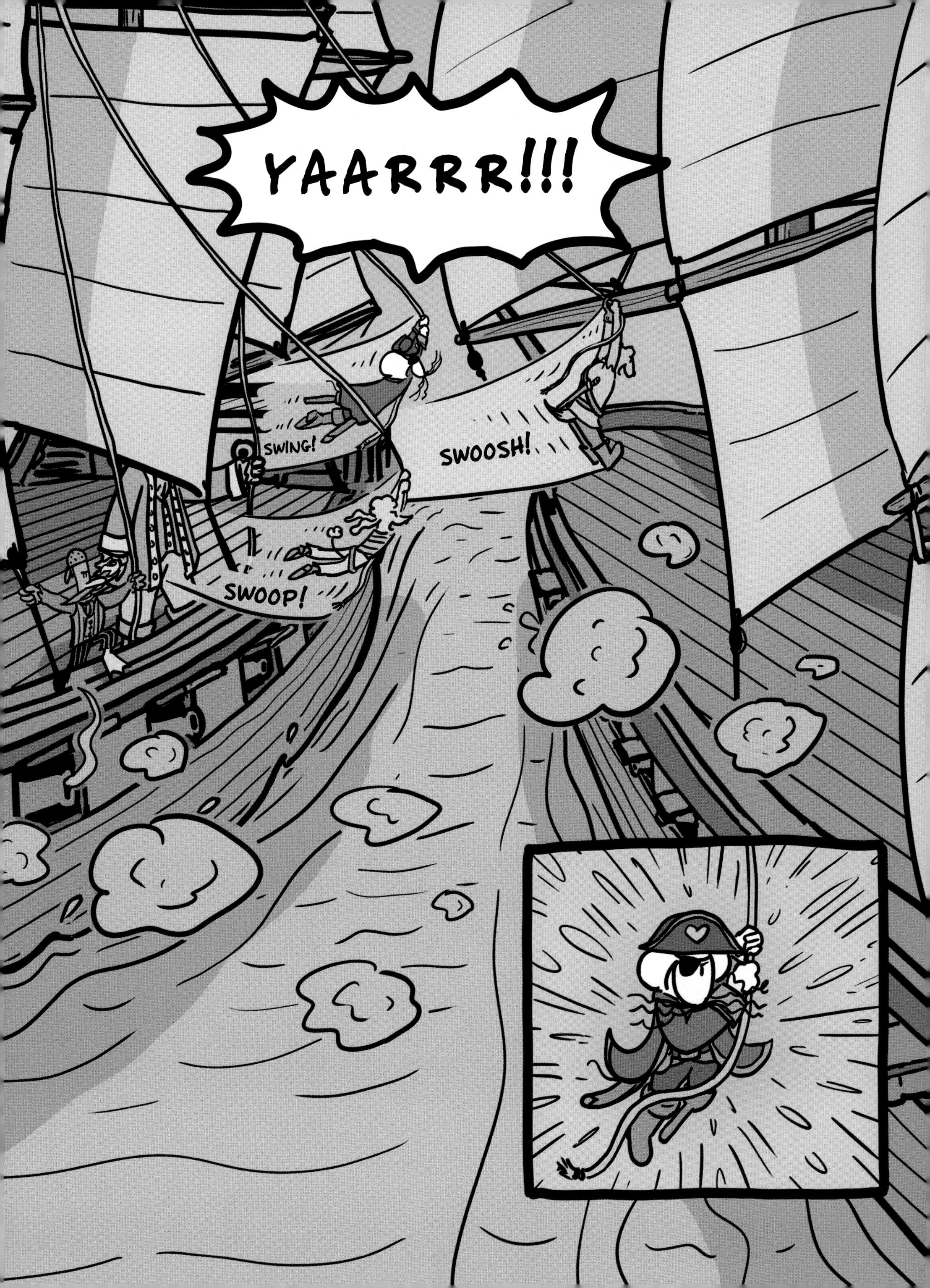
YAARRRR!!!
SWING!
SWOOSH!
SWOOP!

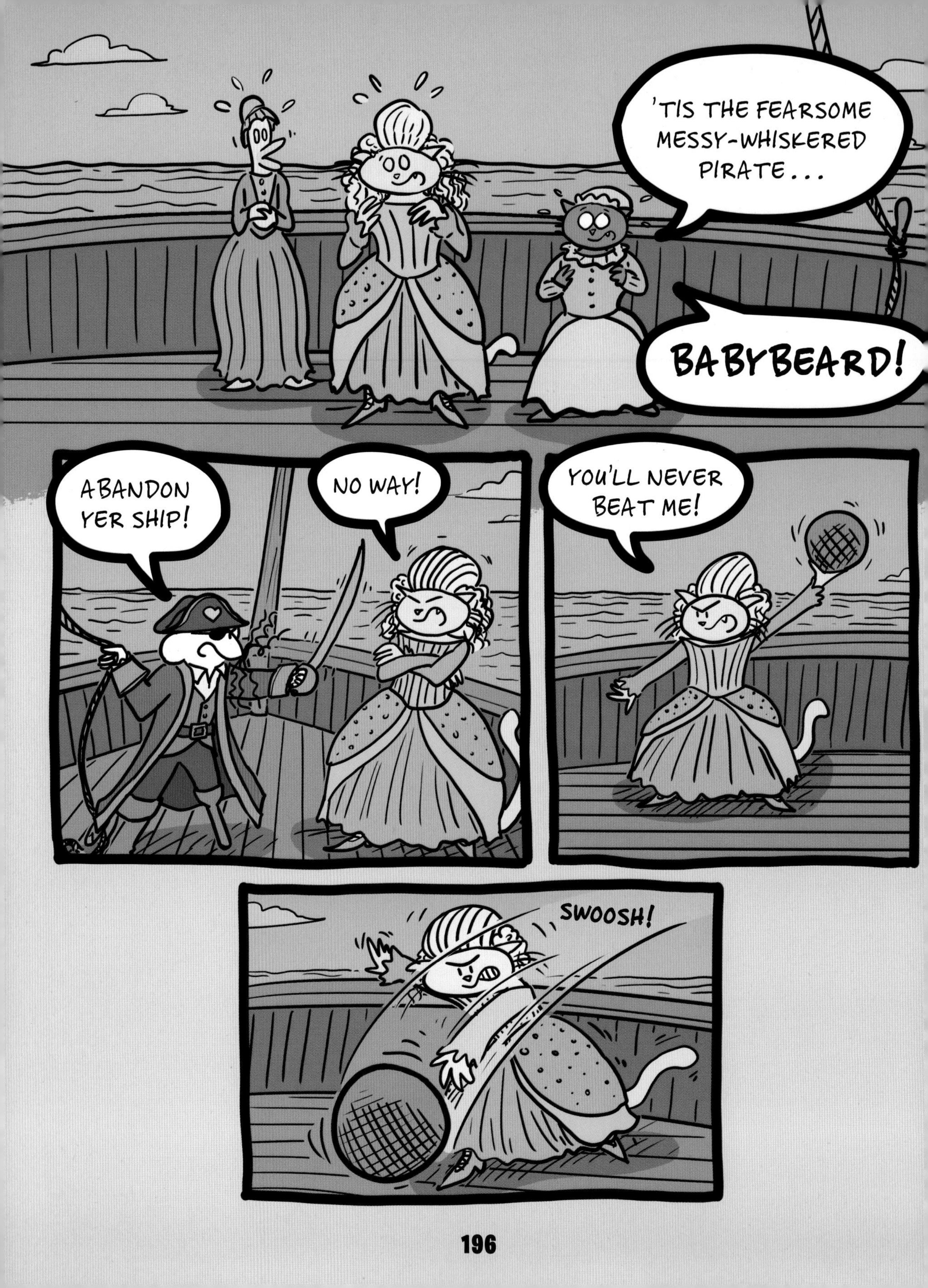
'TIS THE FEARSOME MESSY-WHISKERED PIRATE...
BABYBEARD!
ABANDON YER SHIP!
NO WAY!
YOU'LL NEVER BEAT ME!
SWOOSH!

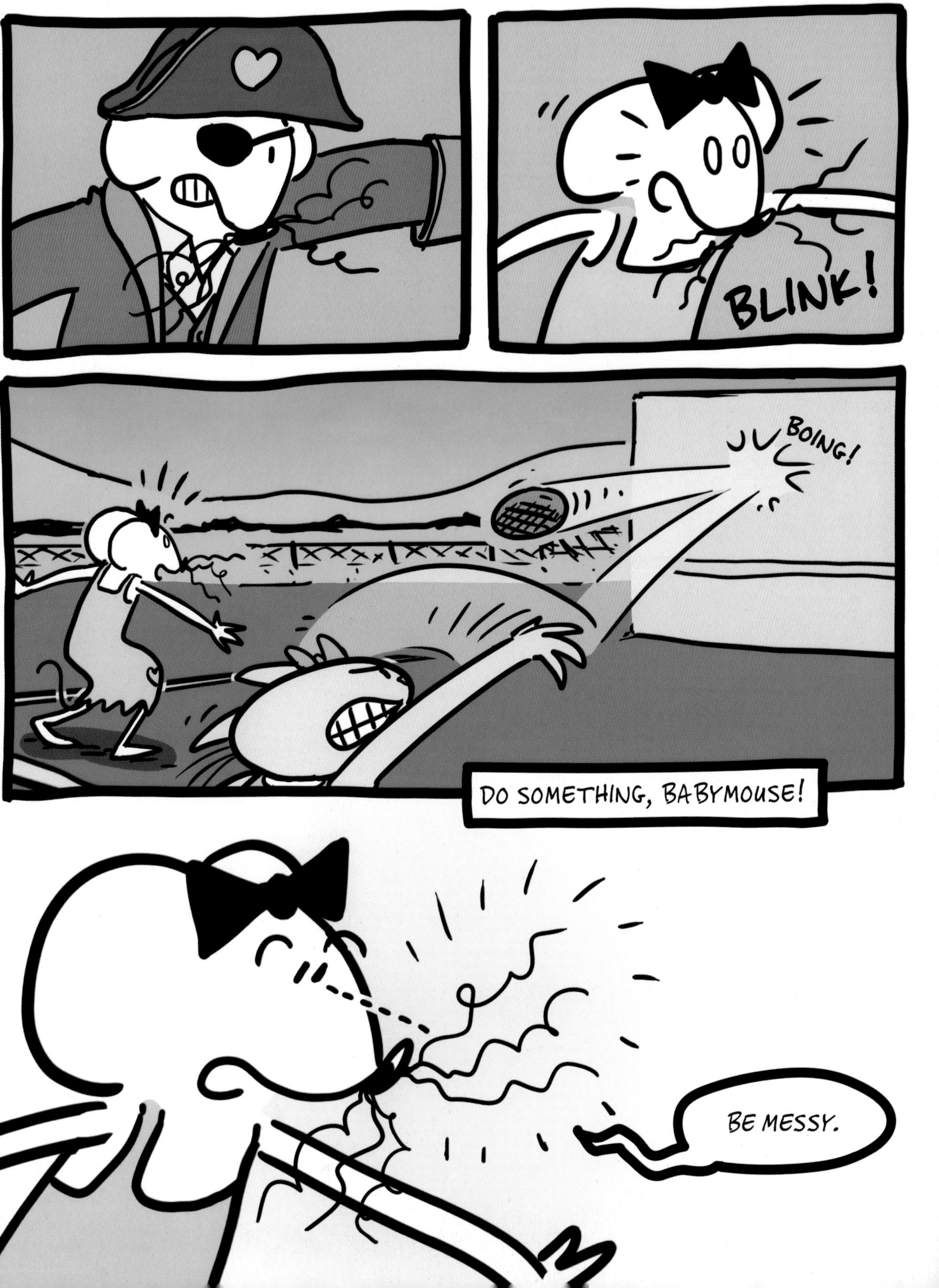
BLINK!
BOING!
DO SOMETHING, BABYMOUSE!
BE MESSY.

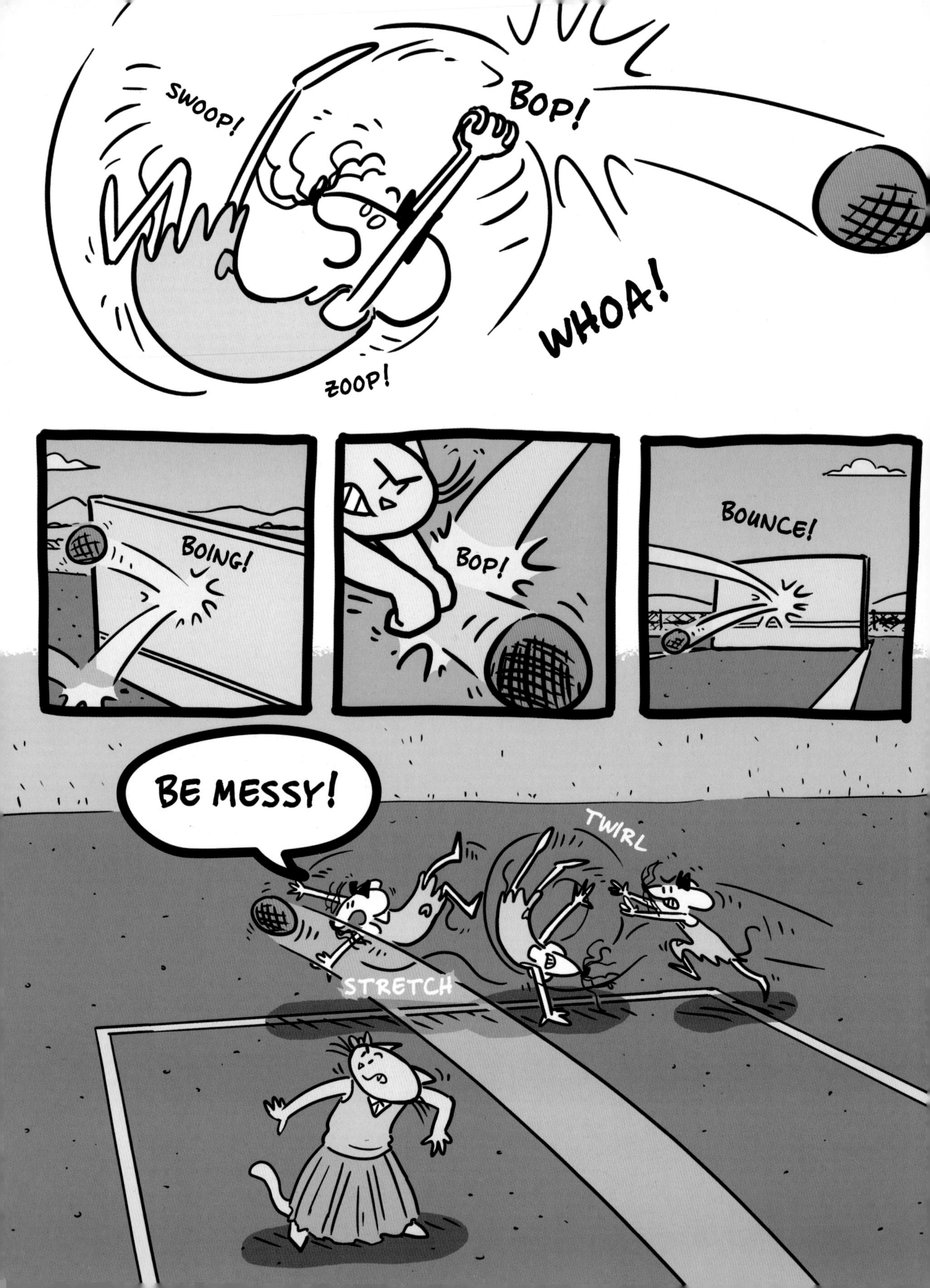
SWOOP!
BOP!
WHOA!
ZOOP!
BOING!
BOP!
BOUNCE!
BE MESSY!
TWIRL
STRETCH

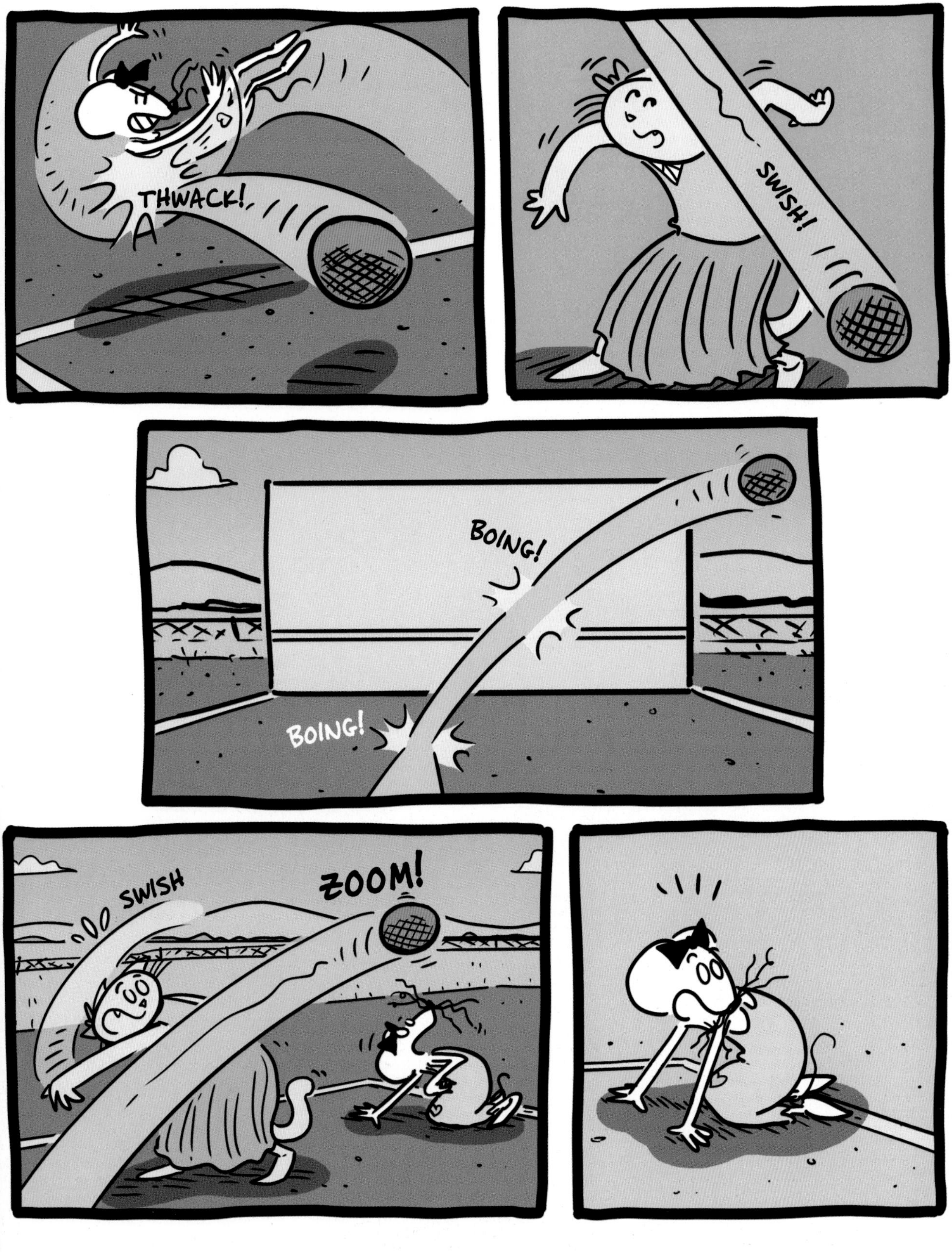
THWACK!
SWISH!
BOING!
BOING!
SWISH
ZOOM!

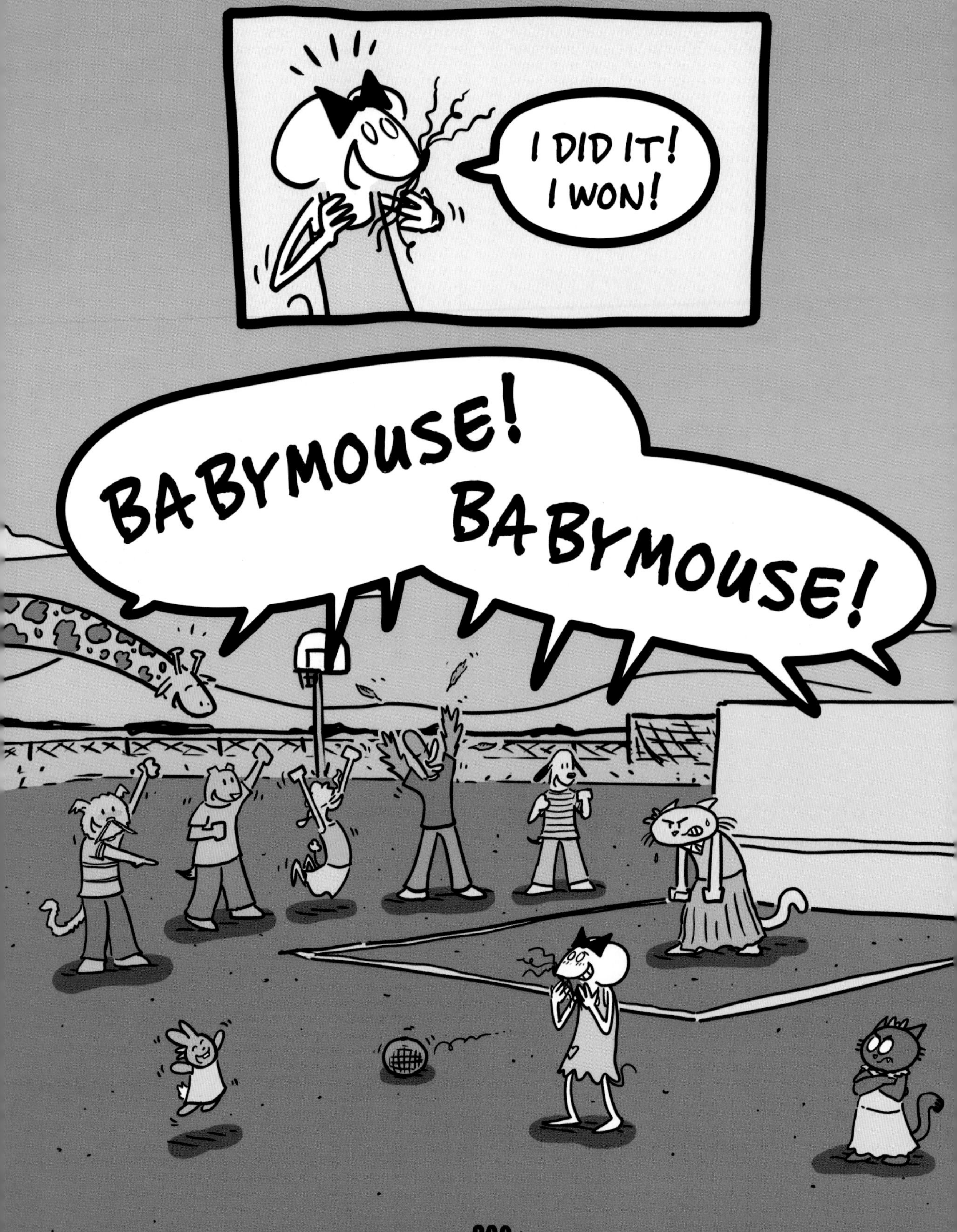
I DID IT! I WON!
BABYMOUSE! BABYMOUSE!

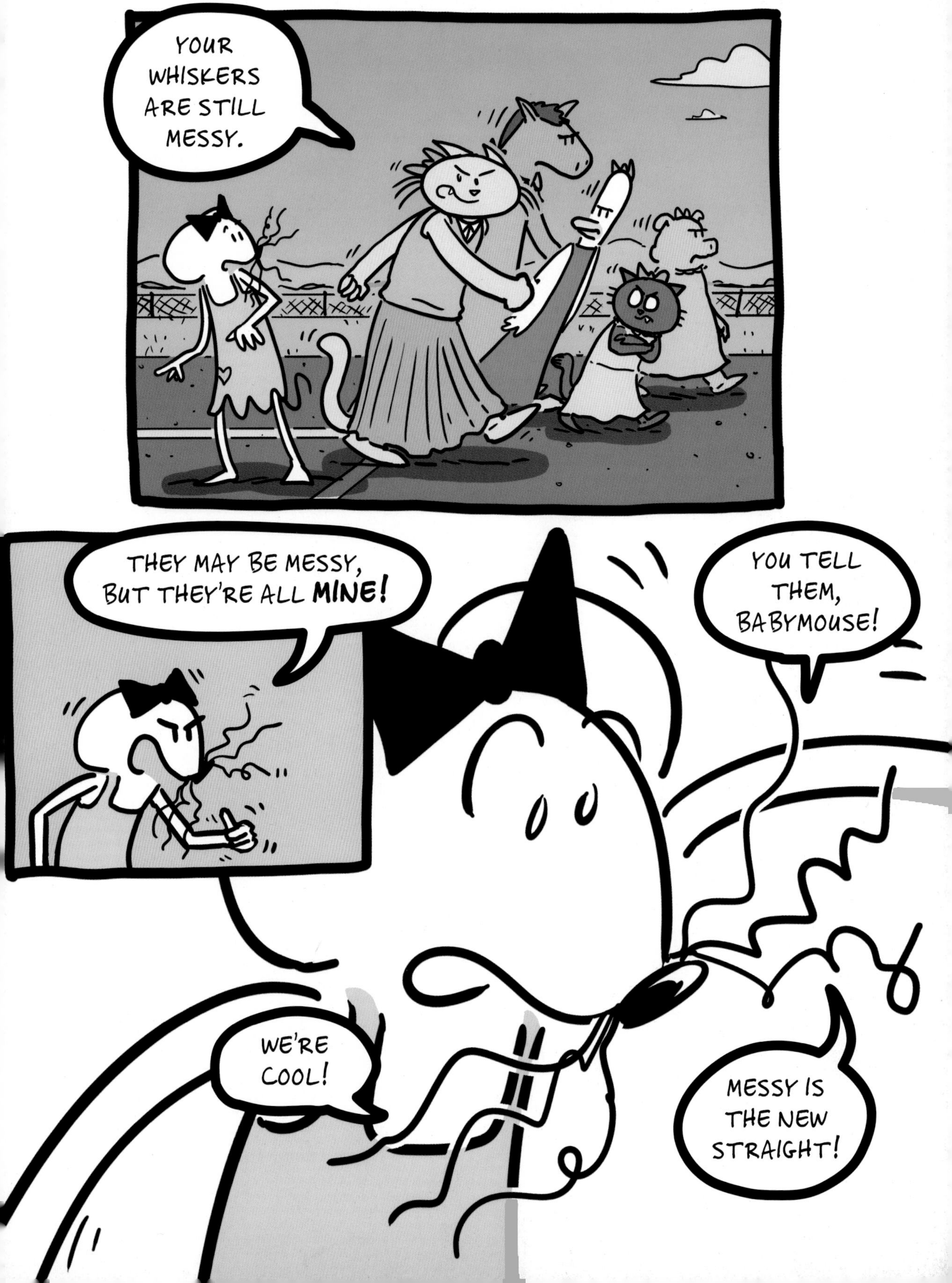
YOUR WHISKERS ARE STILL MESSY.
THEY MAY BE MESSY, BUT THEY'RE ALL **MINE**!
YOU TELL THEM, BABYMOUSE!
WE'RE COOL!
MESSY IS THE NEW STRAIGHT!

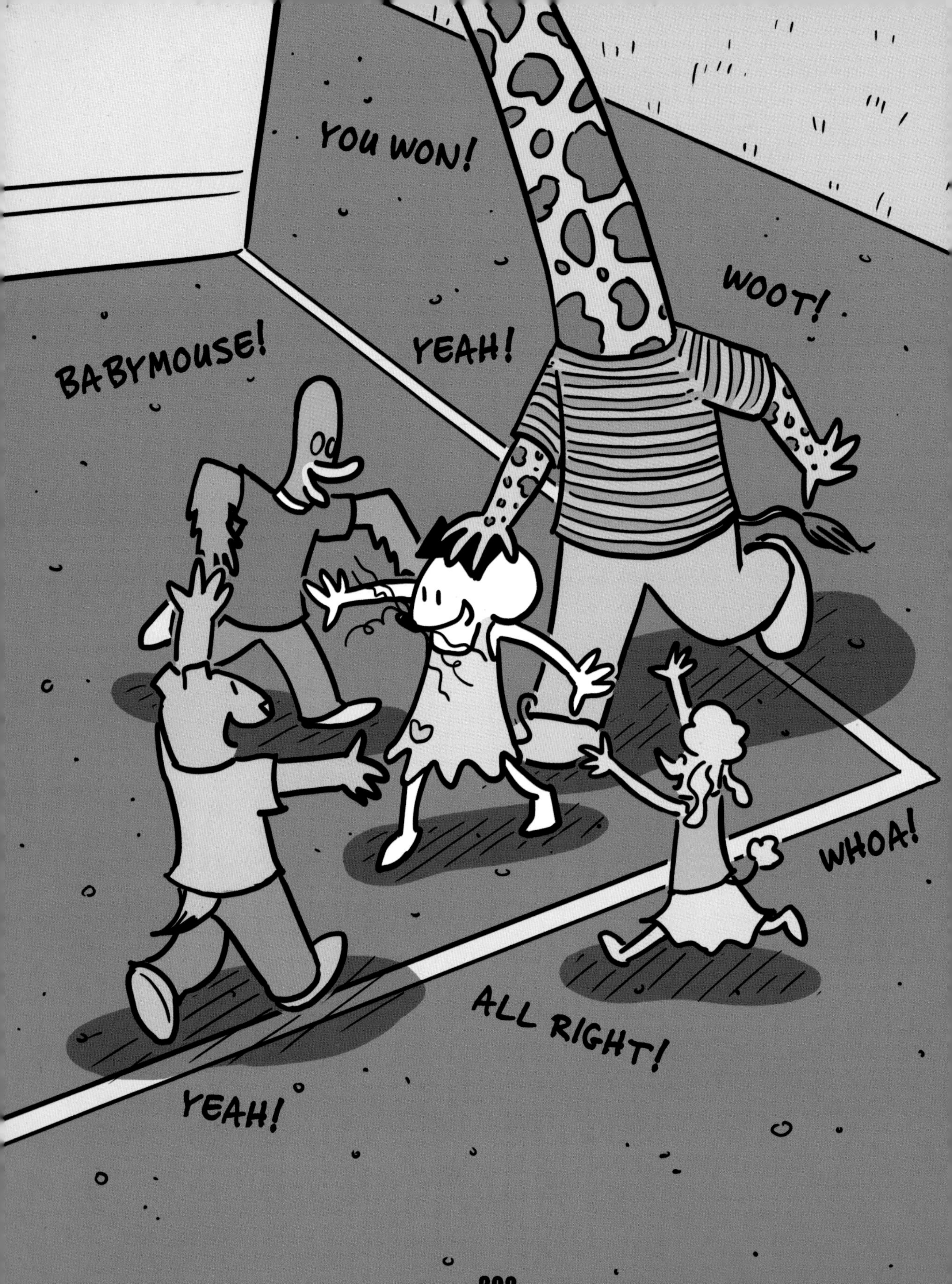
YOU WON!
WOOT!
YEAH!
BABYMOUSE!
WHOA!
ALL RIGHT!
YEAH!

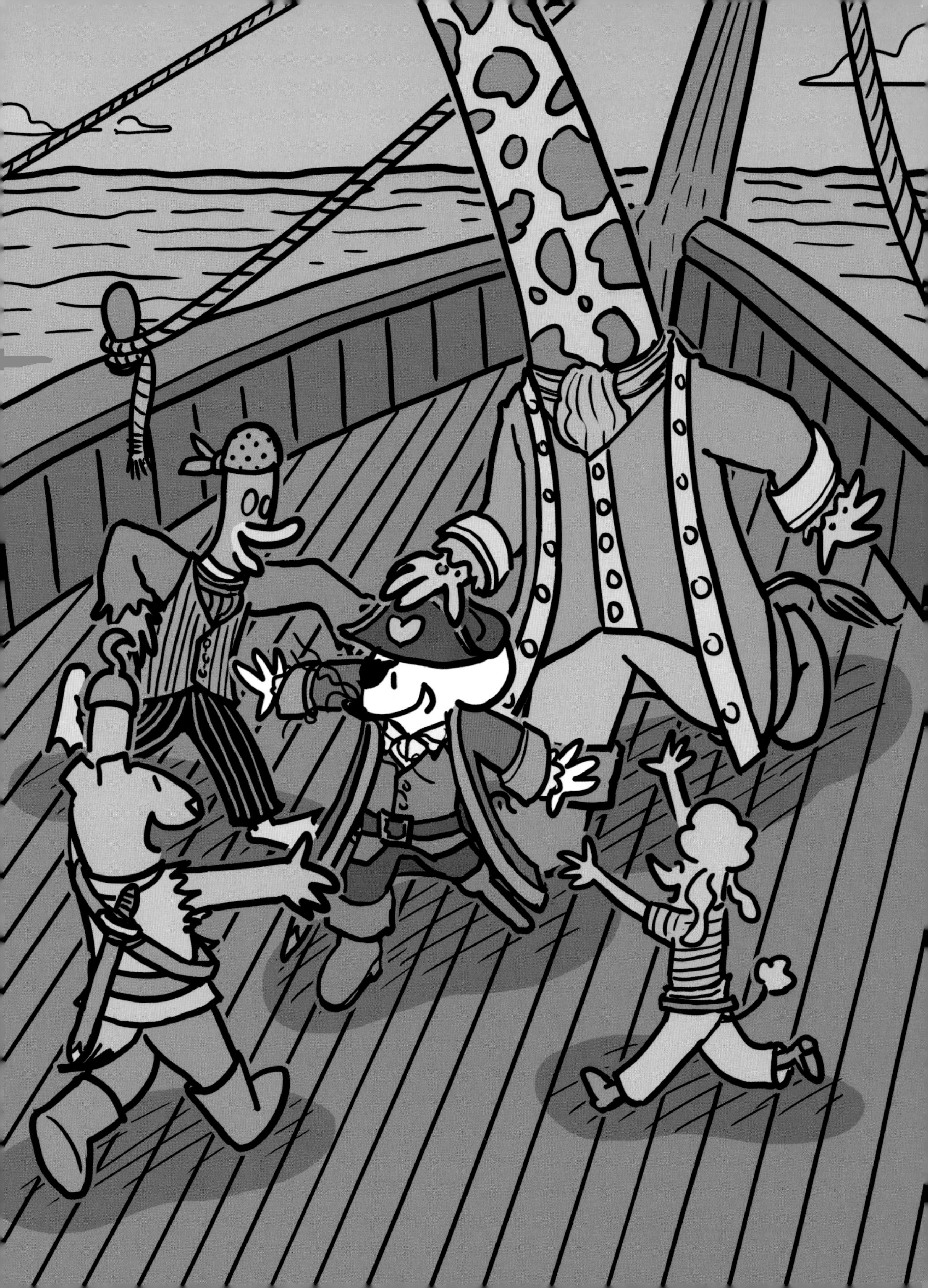

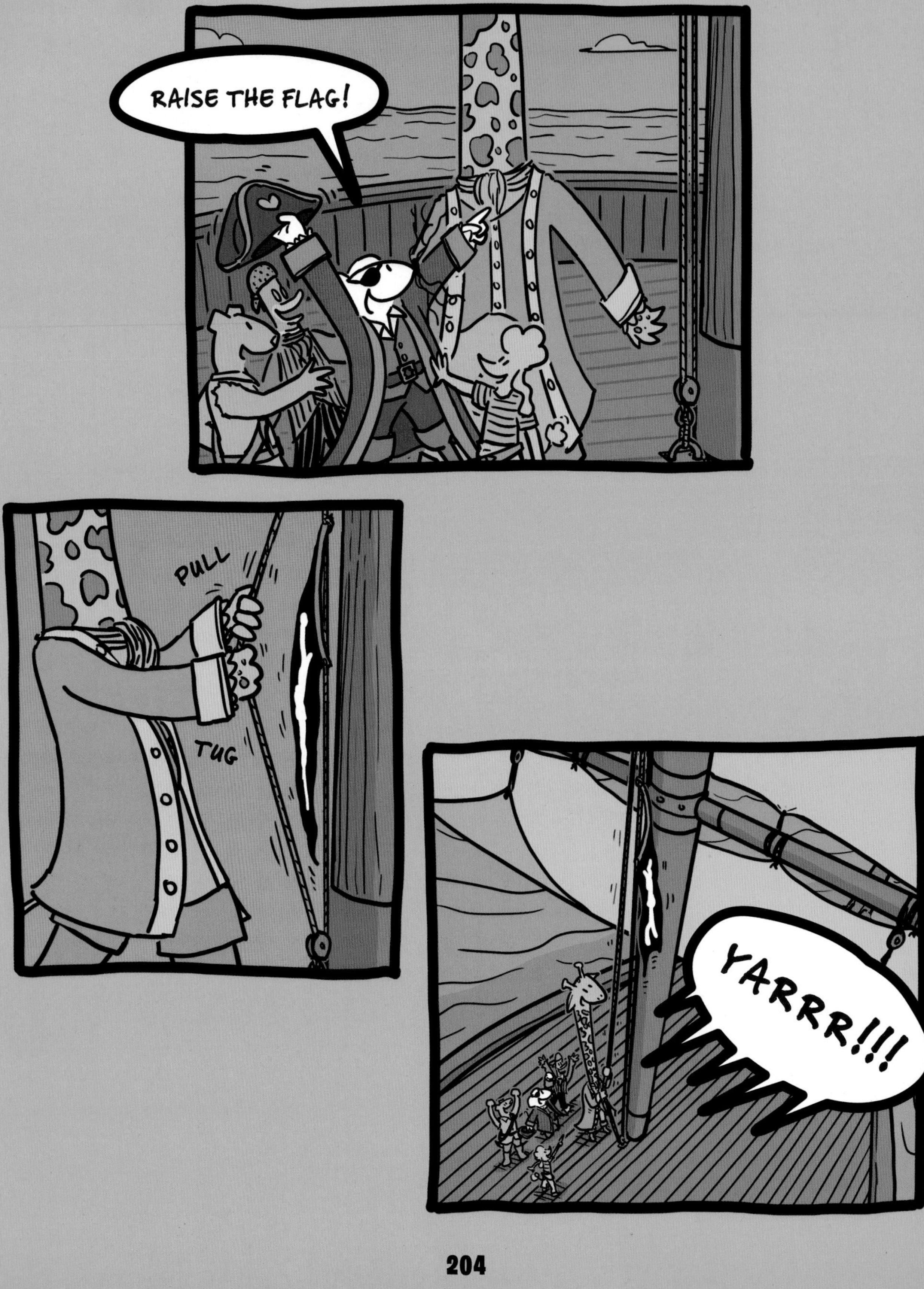
RAISE THE FLAG!
PULL
TUG
YARRR!!!

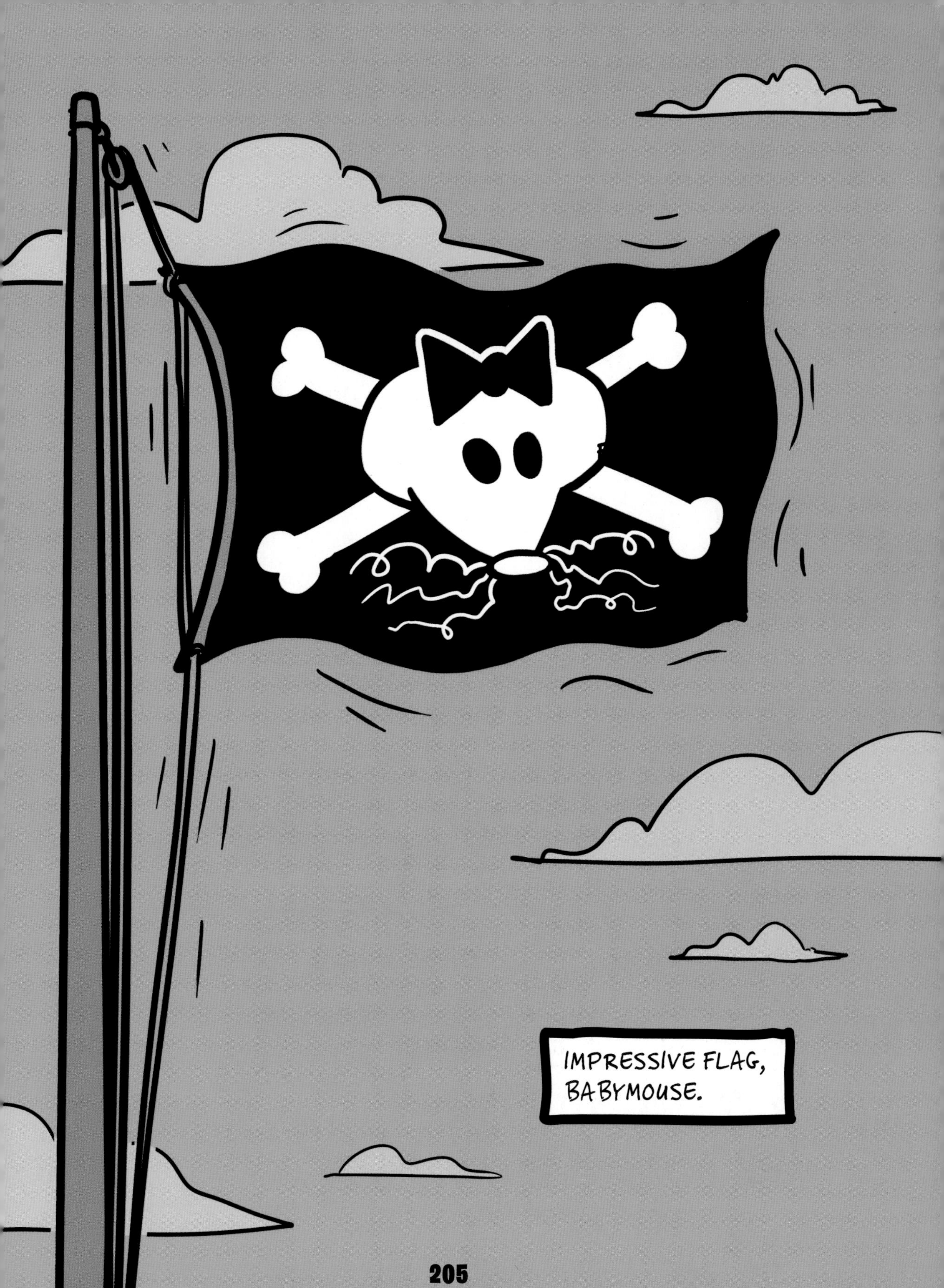
IMPRESSIVE FLAG, BABYMOUSE.

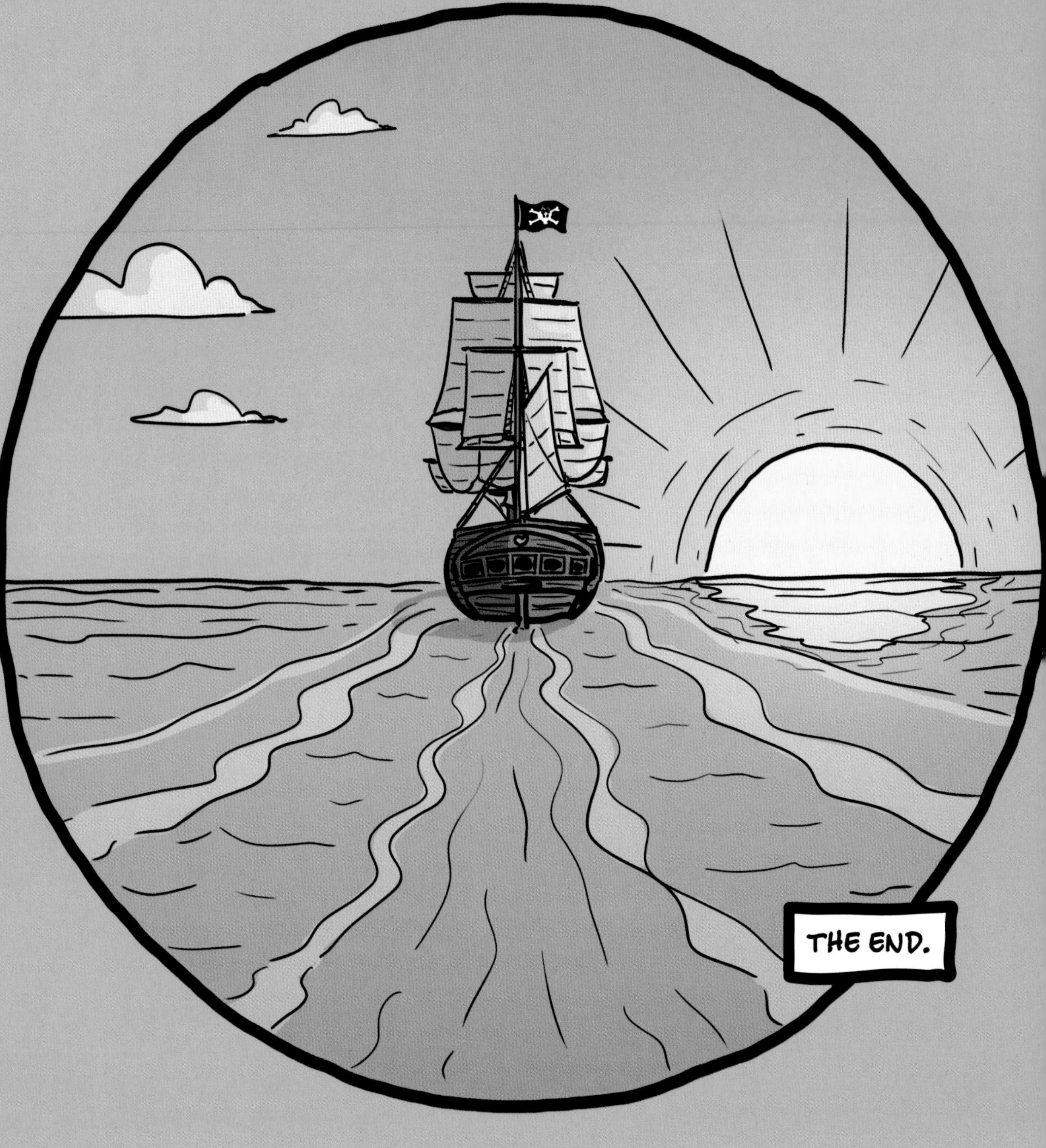
THE END.

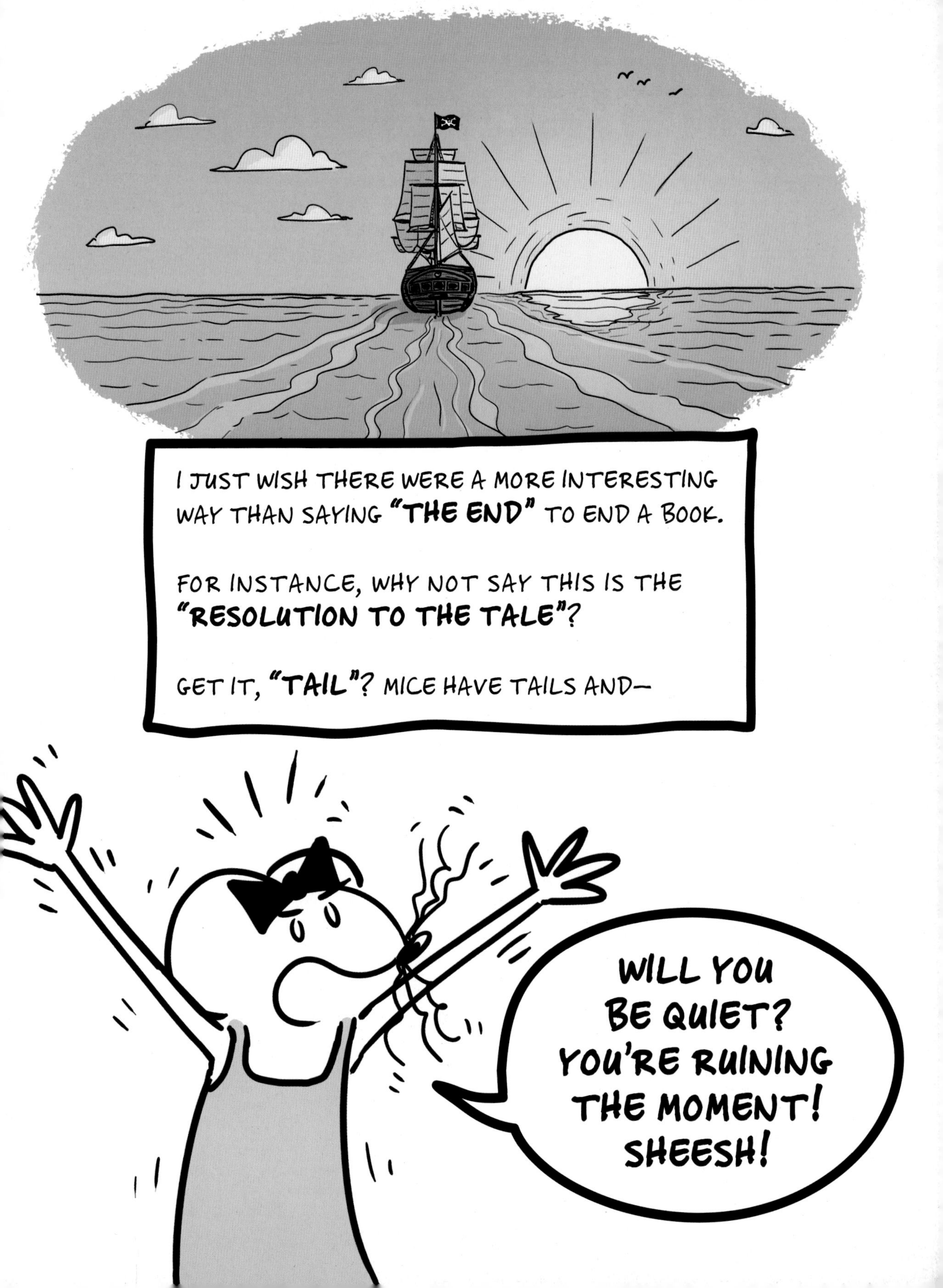
I JUST WISH THERE WERE A MORE INTERESTING WAY THAN SAYING "THE END" TO END A BOOK.
FOR INSTANCE, WHY NOT SAY THIS IS THE "RESOLUTION TO THE TALE"?
GET IT, "TAIL"? MICE HAVE TAILS AND—
WILL YOU BE QUIET? YOU'RE RUINING THE MOMENT! SHEESH!

AND NOW A WORD FROM
BABYMOUSE'S WHISKERS

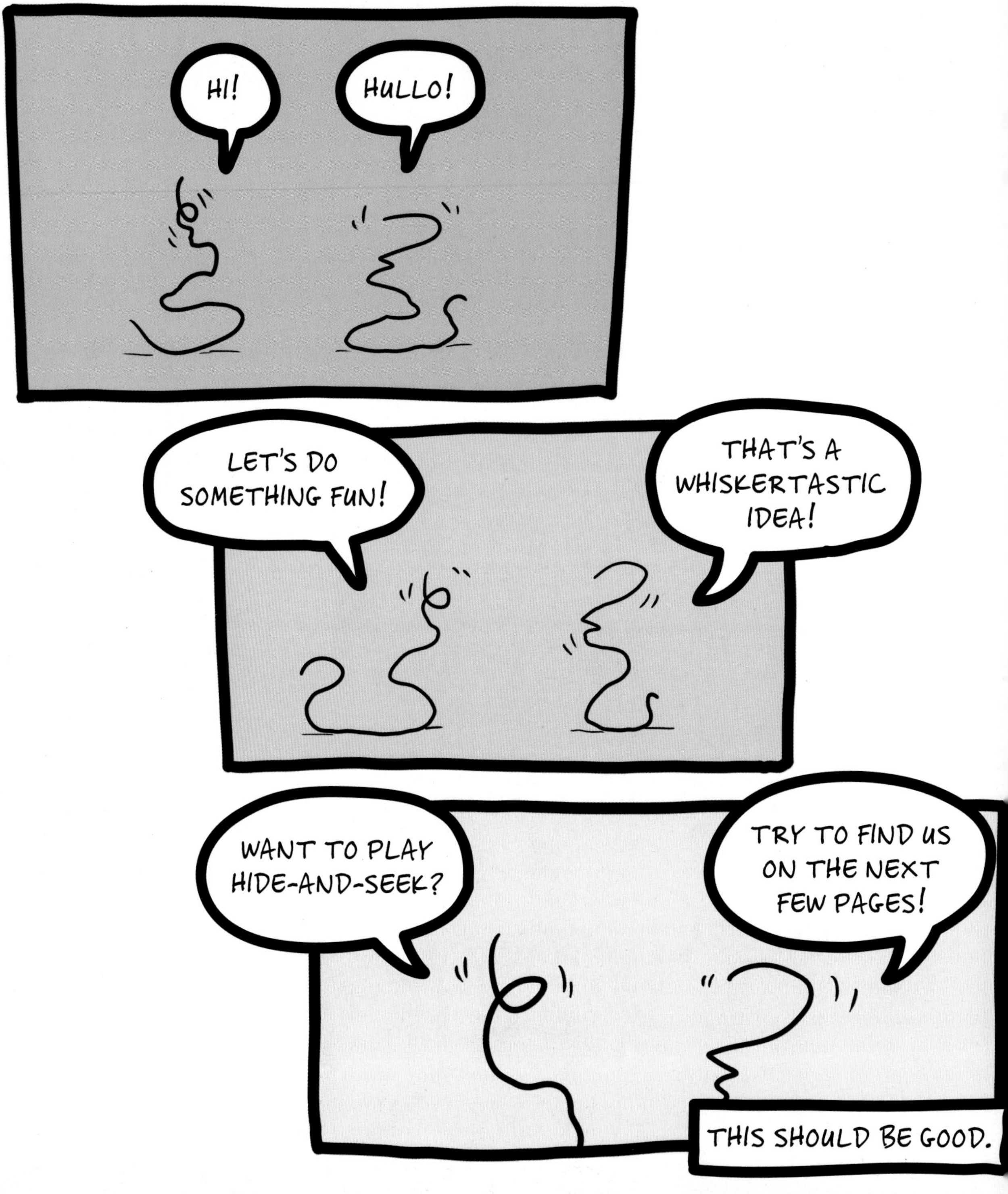
HI!
HULLO!
LET'S DO SOMETHING FUN!
THAT'S A WHISKERTASTIC IDEA!
WANT TO PLAY HIDE-AND-SEEK?
TRY TO FIND US ON THE NEXT FEW PAGES!
THIS SHOULD BE GOOD.

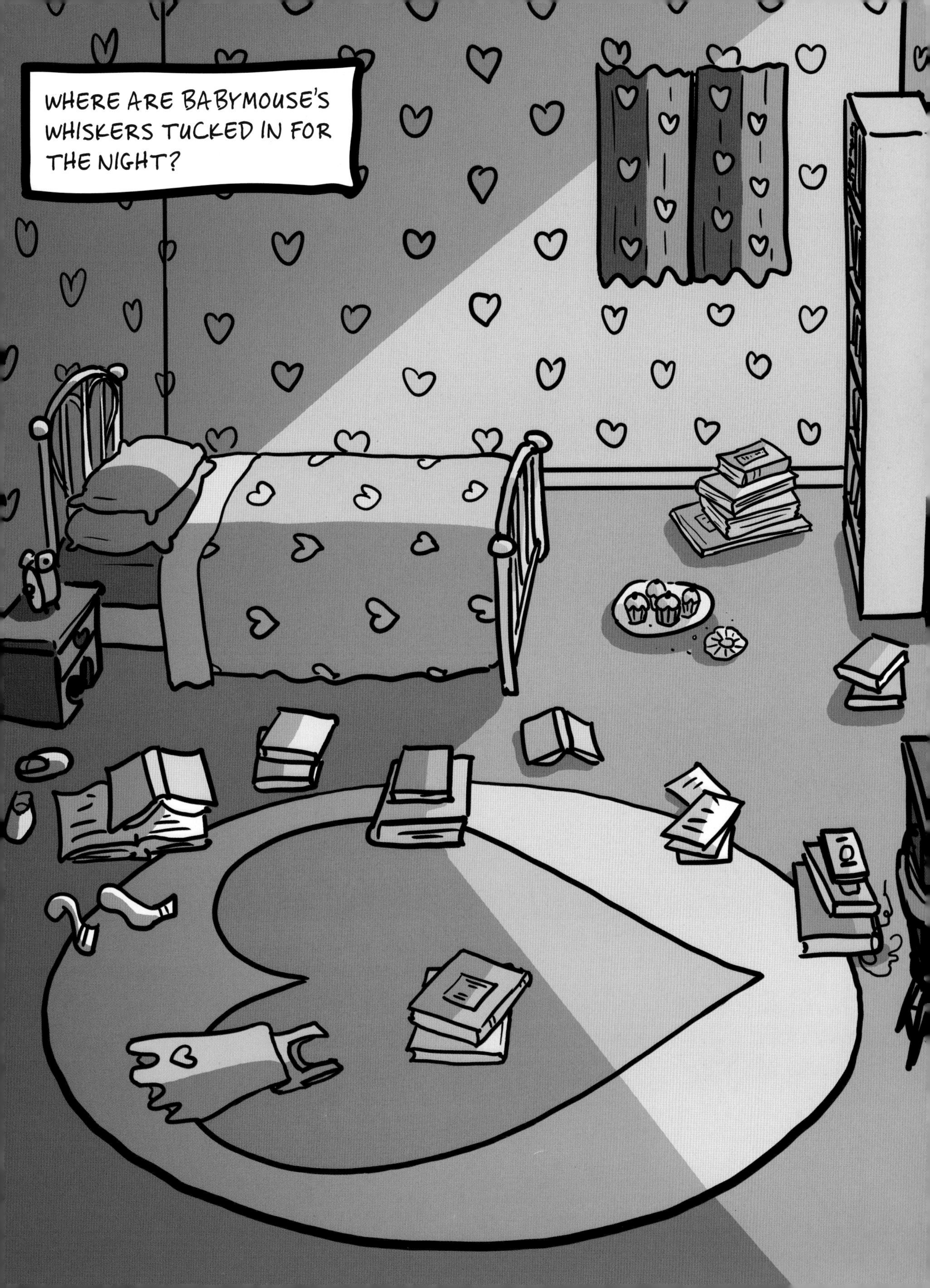
WHERE ARE BABYMOUSE'S WHISKERS TUCKED IN FOR THE NIGHT?

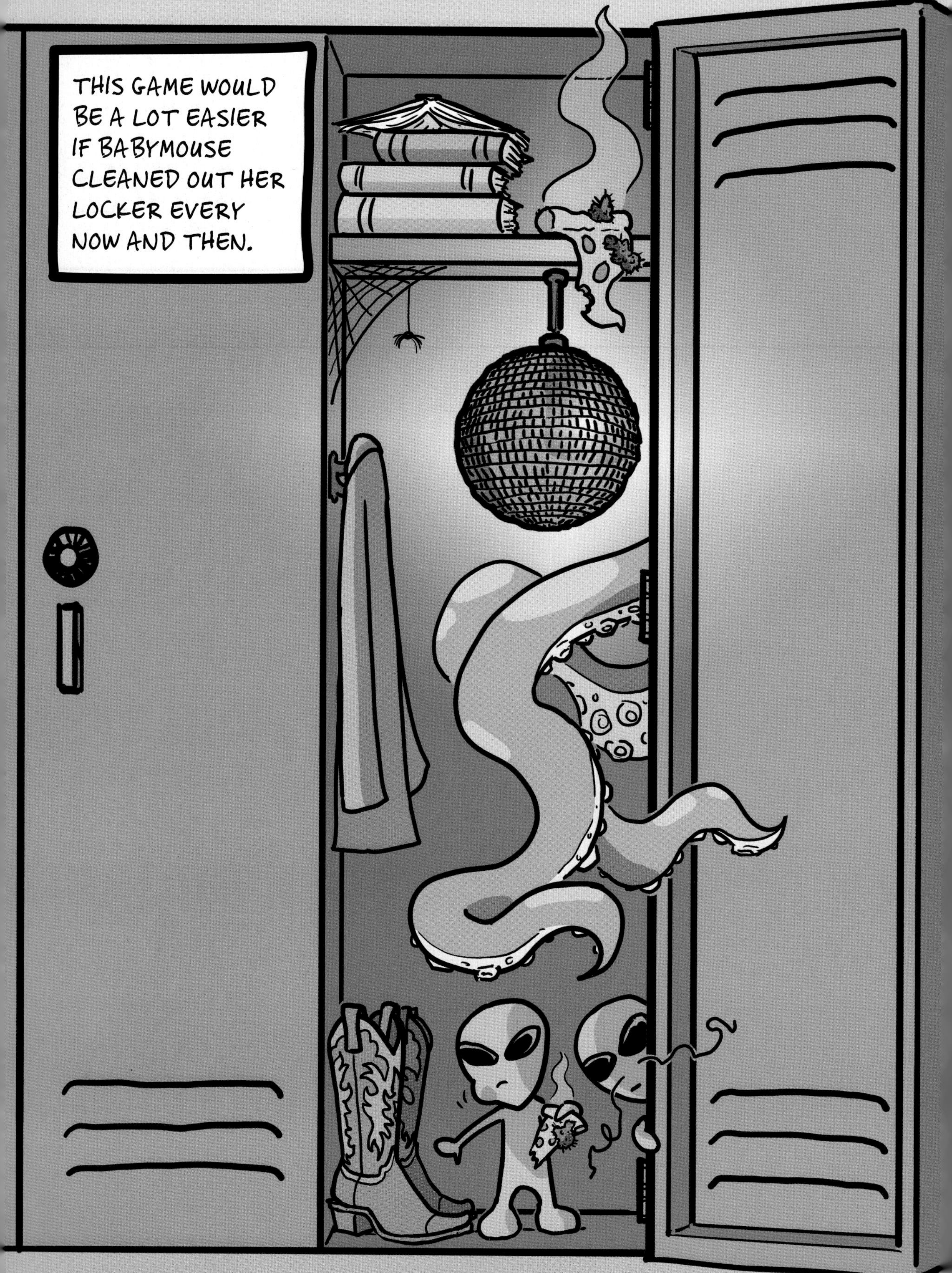
THIS GAME WOULD BE A LOT EASIER IF BABYMOUSE CLEANED OUT HER LOCKER EVERY NOW AND THEN.

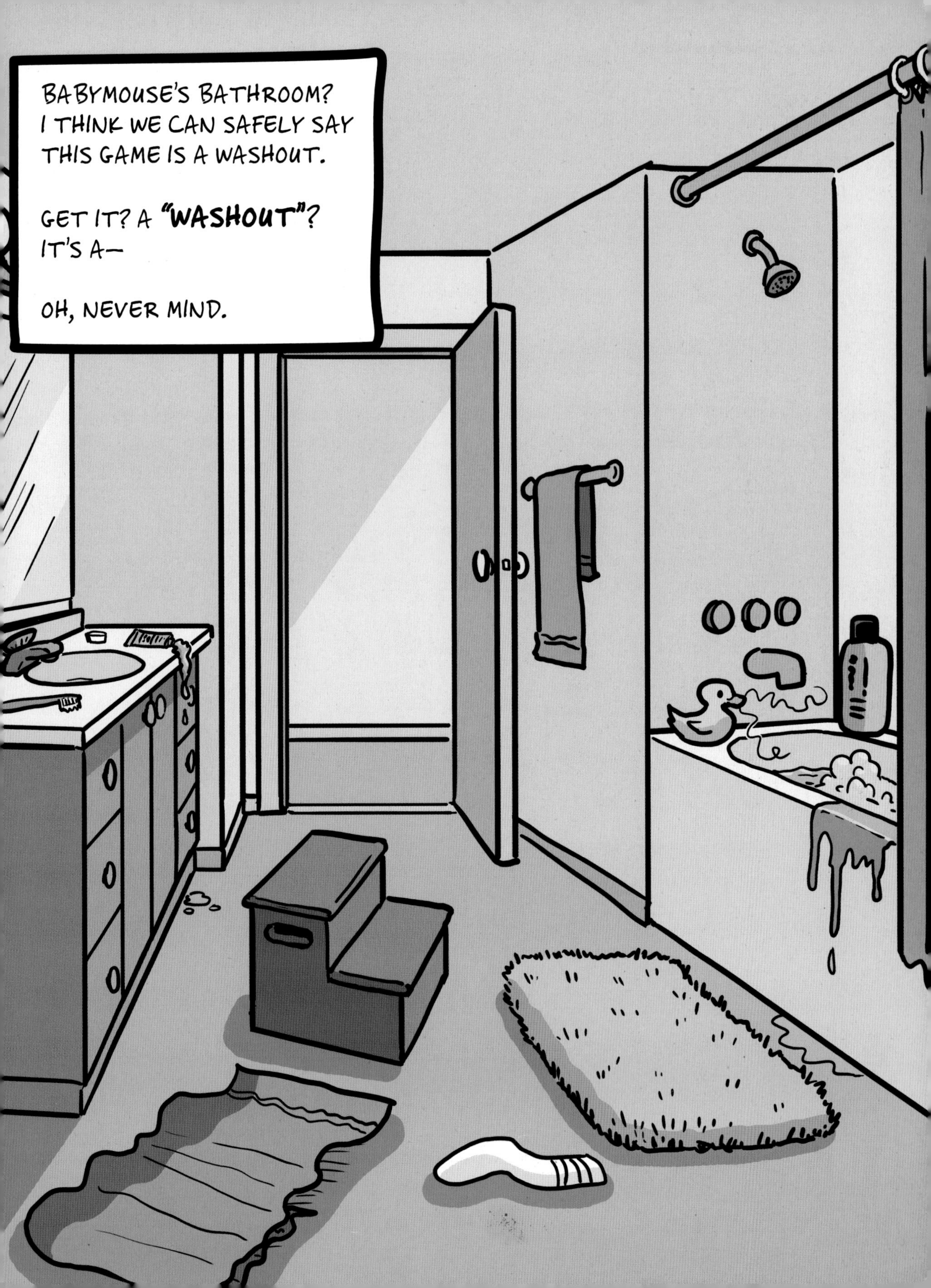
BABYMOUSE'S BATHROOM? I THINK WE CAN SAFELY SAY THIS GAME IS A WASHOUT.
GET IT? A "**WASHOUT**"? IT'S A—
OH, NEVER MIND.

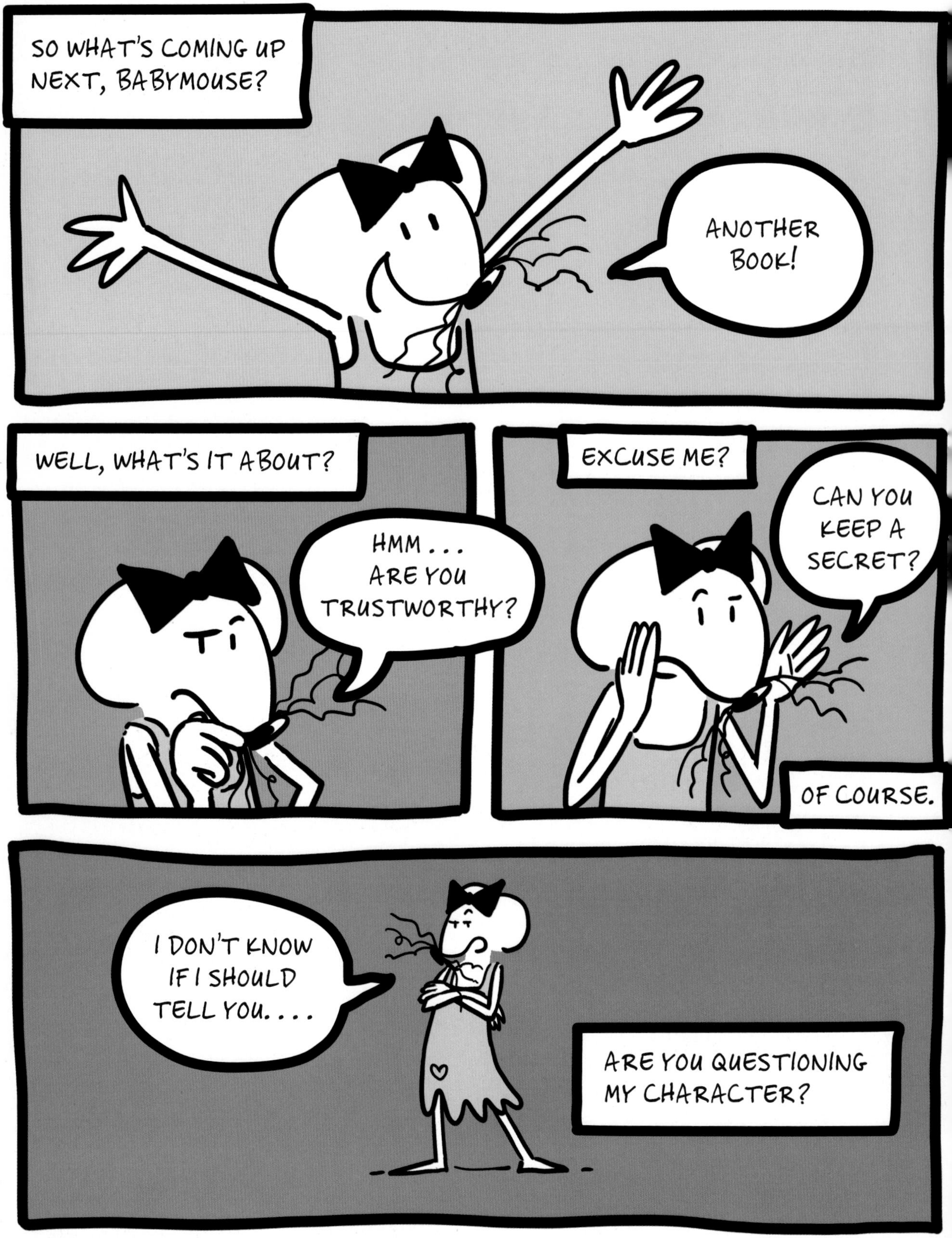
SO WHAT'S COMING UP NEXT, BABYMOUSE?
ANOTHER BOOK!
WELL, WHAT'S IT ABOUT?
HMM . . . ARE YOU TRUSTWORTHY?
EXCUSE ME?
CAN YOU KEEP A SECRET?
OF COURSE.
I DON'T KNOW IF I SHOULD TELL YOU. . . .
ARE YOU QUESTIONING MY CHARACTER?

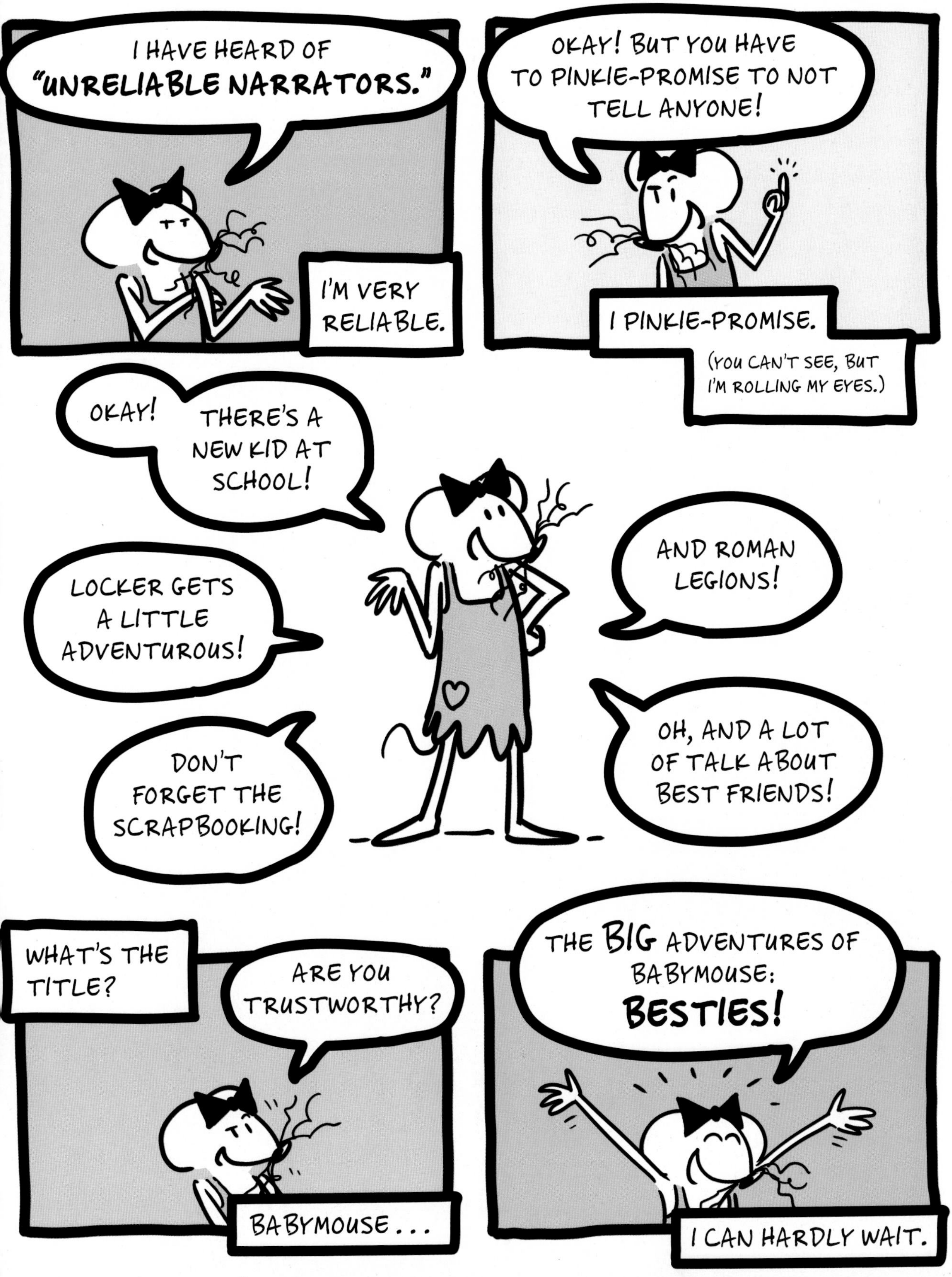
I HAVE HEARD OF "UNRELIABLE NARRATORS."
I'M VERY RELIABLE.
OKAY! BUT YOU HAVE TO PINKIE-PROMISE TO NOT TELL ANYONE!
I PINKIE-PROMISE.
(YOU CAN'T SEE, BUT I'M ROLLING MY EYES.)
OKAY! THERE'S A NEW KID AT SCHOOL!
LOCKER GETS A LITTLE ADVENTUROUS!
DON'T FORGET THE SCRAPBOOKING!
AND ROMAN LEGIONS!
OH, AND A LOT OF TALK ABOUT BEST FRIENDS!
WHAT'S THE TITLE?
ARE YOU TRUSTWORTHY?
BABYMOUSE . . .
THE BIG ADVENTURES OF BABYMOUSE: BESTIES!
I CAN HARDLY WAIT.

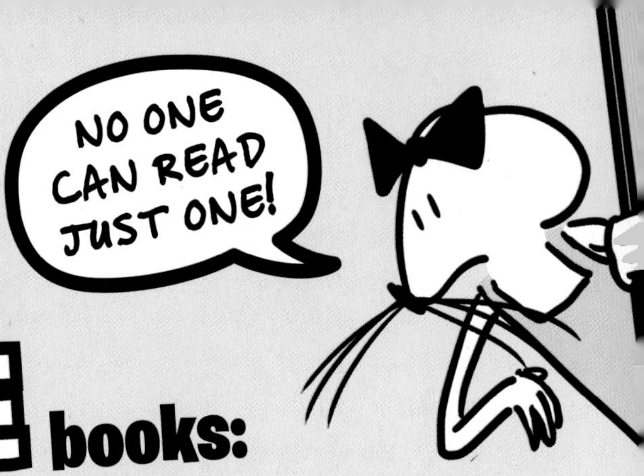
NO ONE CAN READ JUST ONE!

Be sure to read ALL the BABYMOUSE books:

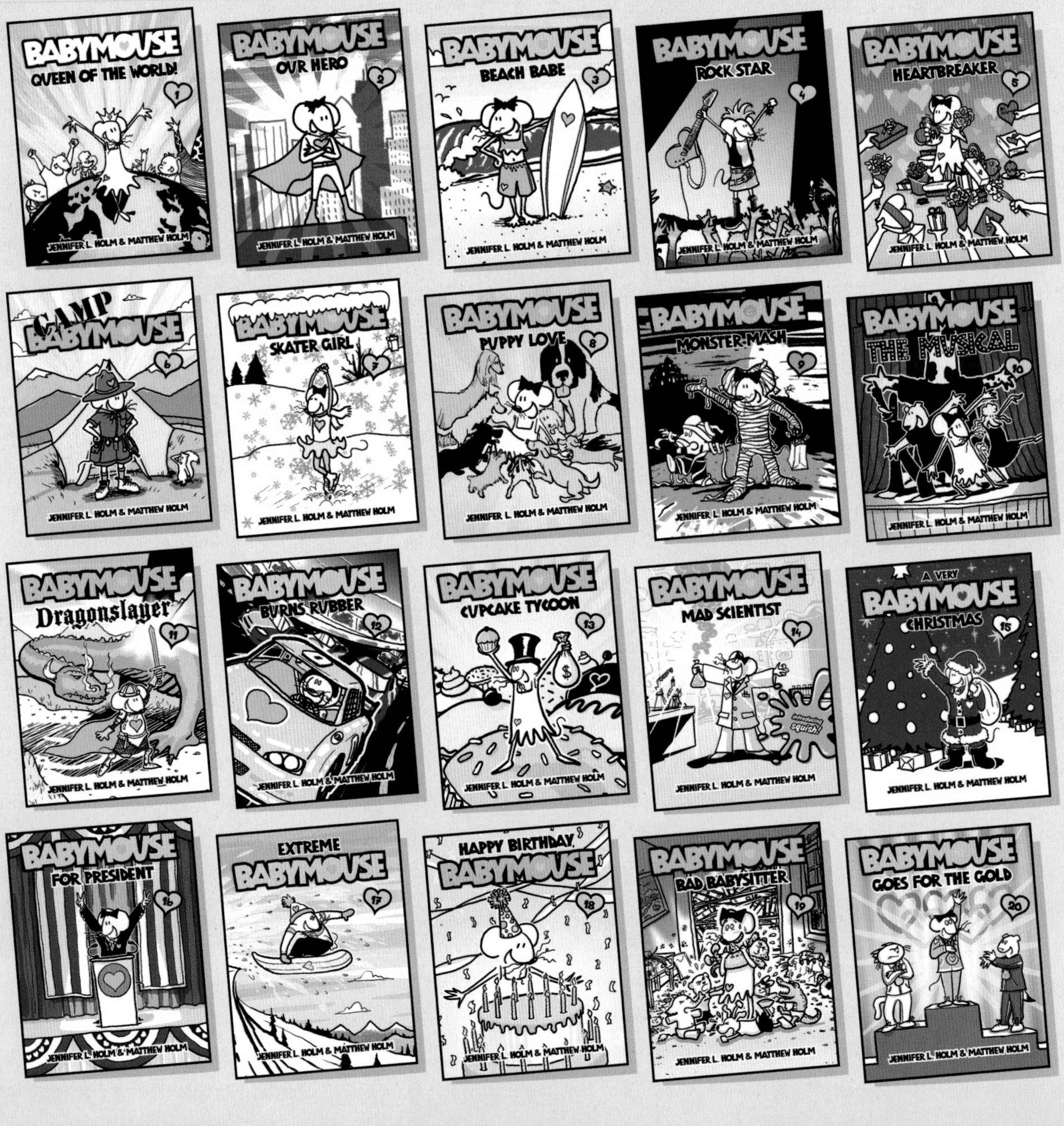
BABYMOUSE QUEEN OF THE WORLD! 1
JENNIFER L. HOLM & MATTHEW HOLM
BABYMOUSE OUR HERO 2
JENNIFER L. HOLM & MATTHEW HOLM
BABYMOUSE BEACH BABE 3
JENNIFER L. HOLM & MATTHEW HOLM
BABYMOUSE ROCK STAR 4
JENNIFER L. HOLM & MATTHEW HOLM
BABYMOUSE HEARTBREAKER 5
JENNIFER L. HOLM & MATTHEW HOLM
CAMP BABYMOUSE 6
JENNIFER L. HOLM & MATTHEW HOLM
BABYMOUSE SKATER GIRL 7
JENNIFER L. HOLM & MATTHEW HOLM
BABYMOUSE PUPPY LOVE 8
JENNIFER L. HOLM & MATTHEW HOLM
BABYMOUSE MONSTER MASH 9
JENNIFER L. HOLM & MATTHEW HOLM
BABYMOUSE THE MUSICAL 10
JENNIFER L. HOLM & MATTHEW HOLM
BABYMOUSE Dragonslayer 11
JENNIFER L. HOLM & MATTHEW HOLM
BABYMOUSE BURNS RUBBER 12
JENNIFER L. HOLM & MATTHEW HOLM
BABYMOUSE CUPCAKE TYCOON 13
JENNIFER L. HOLM & MATTHEW HOLM
BABYMOUSE MAD SCIENTIST 14
introducing squish!
JENNIFER L. HOLM & MATTHEW HOLM
A VERY BABYMOUSE CHRISTMAS 15
JENNIFER L. HOLM & MATTHEW HOLM
BABYMOUSE FOR PRESIDENT 16
JENNIFER L. HOLM & MATTHEW HOLM
EXTREME BABYMOUSE 17
JENNIFER L. HOLM & MATTHEW HOLM
HAPPY BIRTHDAY, BABYMOUSE 18
JENNIFER L. HOLM & MATTHEW HOLM
BABYMOUSE BAD BABYSITTER 19
JENNIFER L. HOLM & MATTHEW HOLM
BABYMOUSE GOES FOR THE GOLD 20
JENNIFER L. HOLM & MATTHEW HOLM

BABYMOUSE
TALES FROM THE LOCKER

Watch out, middle school! Here comes Babymouse.

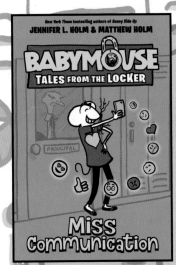

IT'S GREEN....
IT'S BLOBBY....
IT'S GROSS....

IT'S squish!

Do you like comics? Do you like laughing till milk comes out of your nose?

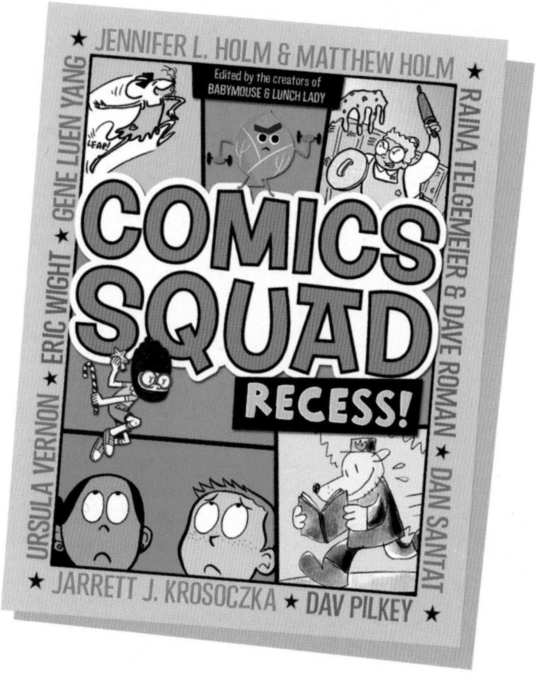

JENNIFER L. HOLM & MATTHEW HOLM
Edited by the creators of BABYMOUSE & LUNCH LADY
COMICS SQUAD
RECESS!
RAINA TELGEMEIER & DAVE ROMAN
DAN SANTAT
DAV PILKEY
JARRETT J. KROSOCZKA
URSULA VERNON
ERIC WIGHT
GENE LUEN YANG

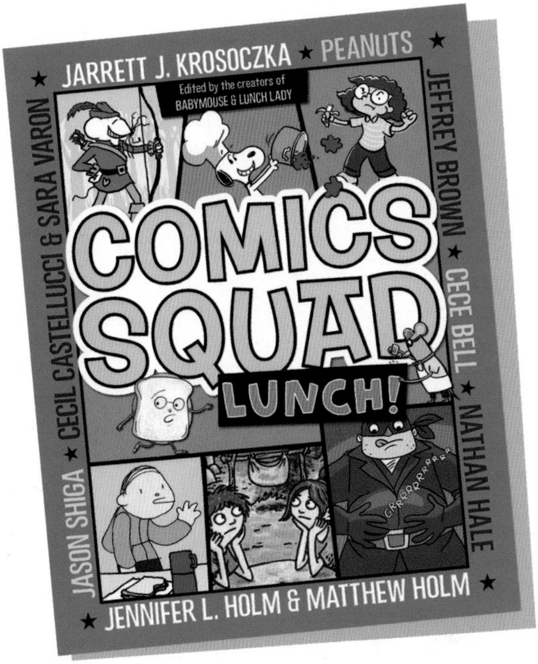

JARRETT J. KROSOCZKA
PEANUTS
Edited by the creators of BABYMOUSE & LUNCH LADY
COMICS SQUAD
LUNCH!
JEFFREY BROWN
CECE BELL
NATHAN HALE
JENNIFER L. HOLM & MATTHEW HOLM
JASON SHIGA
CECIL CASTELLUCCI & SARA VARON

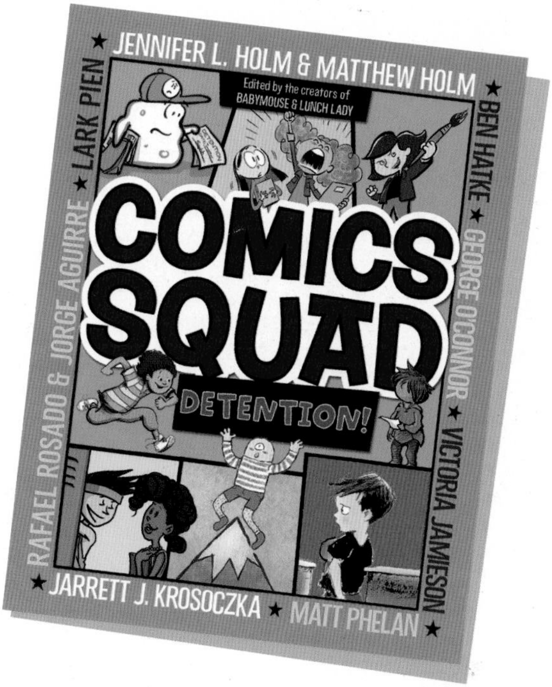

JENNIFER L. HOLM & MATTHEW HOLM
Edited by the creators of BABYMOUSE & LUNCH LADY
COMICS SQUAD
DETENTION!
BEN HATKE
GEORGE O'CONNOR
VICTORIA JAMIESON
MATT PHELAN
JARRETT J. KROSOCZKA
RAFAEL ROSADO & JORGE AGUIRRE
LARK PIEN

JENNIFER L. HOLM & MATTHEW HOLM

are a *New York Times* bestselling sister-and-brother team. They are the creators behind the Babymouse, Squish, and My First Comics series. The Eisner Award-winning Babymouse books have introduced millions of children to graphic novels. Jennifer is also the *New York Times* bestselling author of *The Fourteenth Goldfish* and several other highly acclaimed novels, including three Newbery Honor winners—*Our Only May Amelia, Penny from Heaven,* and *Turtle in Paradise.* Her latest project is *Turtle in Paradise: The Graphic Novel.* Matthew is also the author of *Marvin and the Moths* with Jonathan Follett.